THE MEN IN THE TREES

MARSH MYERS

MCMLXVII

Laughing Boy Fiction
Copyright © 2014 by Marsh Myers
All rights reserved.

ISBN: 0989071529
ISBN-13: 978-0-9890715-2-9

1. Teens - fiction
1. Teens - Science fiction & fantasy - fantasy

First edition
Printed in the United States of America
by Laughing Boy Fiction

DEDICATION

For my mom,
long my best proofreader and loudest cheerleader.

CONTENTS

ACKNOWLEDGMENTS

Writing a first book is a little bit like building a house. No sooner do you get it built than you realize there were a hundred things you would've done differently. So it was with the 2013 publication of my first novel, <u>His Life Abiding</u>. In the year and a half between that book's release and this one, I've learned a great deal about publishing, writing and self-discipline. One of the things I learned early on was to benefit from the opinions of family, friends, readers and editors. I was very fortunate to have a diverse group of people read <u>The Men in the Trees</u> prior to it being finalized. In fact, some of them read multiple drafts and though this didn't necessarily reduce the number of "remodels" the book went through, it did make the end product better. It's only fitting that I acknowledge them here.

Tracy Charles
David Josephs
Jake Kreager
Karen McGarrity
Michaela Martin
Brooke Myers
Dawn Myers
Myles Myers
Dawn O'Leary

With many thanks for all your efforts.

CHAPTER ONE

Rose dreamt all night of ghosts. No, she corrected herself, not ghosts — spirits. Those wispy creatures found in fairy tales who resided in trees or under the loamy earth. She dreamt they had crept around her in the dark, crouched over her and sniffed at her face like a house cat might examine a dead mouse. They had softly touched her hair, whispered about her, watched her sleep. The dreams finally roused her around 4 a.m. and she'd spent the last few hours sitting with her back to the wall, her sleeping bag pulled in tightly around her, waiting for the sun to finally rise.

Rose didn't believe in supernatural beings. She prided herself on being an educated woman with a reasonable mind, so dreaming about fluttering spirits who congregated around her as she slept was both unusual and disconcerting. She immediately began to look for a reasonable explanation behind the images, and to suppress the undeniable emotional reaction she'd had to them. Rose understood the science behind the human mind, how it constantly collected information, filing it away as chemical codes among its furrows and channels. Most of that information would simply sit there, rarely if ever utilized during the normal course of a human life. But at night, during the dream state, the subconscious mind would sometimes find those bits of information, combine them with emotion, and distill out dreams.

So, Rose told herself, creeping spirits weren't really anything paranormal as much as they were symbols for... what? Curiosity? Adventure? Anxiety? She had plenty of all three in her life right now, perhaps more than most people her age who were using their retirement years to take it easy, not uproot their lives completely. And certainly sleeping in an empty house hadn't helped.

By the time the first light of dawn broke through the windows on the other side of the room, Rose had rationalized her dreams to the point where she could wriggle out of the sleeping bag, climb wearily to her feet and stretch. The wind had picked up again and around her the house creaked like a ship at sea. The gusts blew the morning dew off the trees nearby; the drops hitting the living room windows with a hollow *plunk, plunk, plunk*. Immediately Rose noted that it sounded like tapping fingers, then just as quickly felt ashamed for scaring herself again. She shivered and clumsily pulled on several more layers of clothing, although it made little difference. Everything felt damp and no matter how many shirts, sweaters and jackets she cloaked herself in, she always felt cold. It took her several minutes to roll up the sleeping bag and tuck it into one of the weathered cardboard cartons sitting near the front door. One more quick inventory of the boxes seemed compulsory, although it was nearly impossible that Rose would've missed anything. Every shelf, every closet, every dark corner had been inspected and anything of value had been located and carefully packed for transport. And if she had found something more, where would she have put it? Her car was already so jammed full of clutter it took considerable ingenuity and some brute strength to find room for the sleeping bag and the last two boxes.

She paused at the driver's side door and took one last look at the house. In the sunlight, it didn't seem nearly as menacing as it had a few hours before. It still creaked in the wind, but whatever spirits she'd imagined creeping through the place had receded into the shadows and now the place just looked gray, derelict and sad. She swung herself into the seat and started the engine. It rattled noisily, sputtered a little, but to her relief didn't fail.

"Hang in there," she said, patting the dashboard gently. "Still a ways to go yet..."

And with that, she drove away.

CHAPTER TWO

There was a woman standing in the garden.

Meryl was used to people cutting through her yard, as the university students often crossed it as a shortcut to class or because they were too lazy to go around. But no one had ever just stopped, as though frozen in place by some magical spell or entranced by the tomato and bean plants now withering with the onset of Fall. Whoever the woman was, she certainly didn't look like the typical student. She had snow-white hair, although Meryl couldn't really estimate her age from so far away. And her body was strangely attenuated with a waist which seemed too high, a torso which seemed too thick, and bowed legs which seemed too long. It was almost as though she'd been hurriedly sculpted from a lump of wet clay and dressed by a blind man.

"Is something wrong?" the young woman sitting on Meryl's couch called. She impatiently crossed her legs and bounced her right foot up and down.

"There's someone standing in my yard," Meryl answered very matter-of-factly. "Just standing there."

"Oh. Do you have another interview after me?"

"No. I don't know who that is." She paused. Distracted.

"I don't mean to hurry you, but I have to be at work in forty-five minutes," the young woman protested.

"Yeah, sorry. That's got me all discombobulated now," Meryl apologized, forcing herself back into her chair. She sat rigidly and tried to concentrate. The girl's foot continued to bounce, her shoe intricately decorated with birds with interlocked wings flying against a cornflower blue canvas. It was nearly as distracting as the stranger standing in the yard. Meryl smiled weakly and said, "Those are really nice shoes" — she struggled to remember the girl's name — "*Crissy*. They're very unusual."

"Thanks," Crissy replied, more animated now that the conversation had turned away from the tedium of discussing rent and house rules. "They're actually just a cheapy pair of canvas shoes, but then I used fabric paints on them. It's kind of a business I have. Customized, hand-painted canvas shoes." She extended her leg and pointed her toes. "Well, go ahead. You can admire."

Meryl leaned closer, feeling a bit ridiculous, and stared earnestly at the girl's feet. "You must be an artist?"

"I classify myself more as a designer. That's my knack, you know? I can take all these elements out in the universe — shapes, colors, forms, textures, whatever — and combine them into these wild new combinations. You can't learn that, y'know. You have to be born with it. That's what really makes someone an artist."

"A shoe artist?" Meryl asked.

It sounded snarky, but Crissy didn't notice and continued to enthuse: "On shoes for now, but I got plans. I'm going to expand to painting jackets as soon as I have enough capital to get that off the ground. That's why I'm looking for a new living situation. To cut costs so I can invest more back into my business. So if I moved in here, I'd be doing a lot of creating because I just live and breathe to create so I hope that's okay?"

Meryl shrugged. "I don't have anything against creativity," she said, inadvertently turning a little in her chair so she could glance out the window again. The woman standing in the garden was already more interesting than Crissy's artistic contribution to the world of women's footwear. It bothered her that she couldn't see the woman in the garden from where she was seated. She resisted the urge to return to the window and asked absently, "Are they hard to clean?"

"Sorry?"

"Your hand-painted shoes and jackets. How do you clean them?"

The young woman looked perplexed.

"I mean, can you throw them into the washer?"

"Oh, you can't wash them. You can't get them wet. It ruins the paint job."

Meryl smiled and this time, despite her efforts, her sarcasm came oozing out: "You can't get them wet?"

"Nah."

"In Oregon? You can't get these shoes wet... *in Oregon?*"

"Right. They're for being beautiful. For style, right. They're not utilitarian."

"Oh, because I would've thought that all shoes are utilitarian. That's like the main thing shoes have to be, isn't it?"

"Not these," the young woman replied, with a trace of haughtiness. "They're just for being beautiful. That's what fashion is. It makes a statement that transcends the utilitarian world."

Meryl had no idea how to reply without sounding like a complete bitch, so she elected to say nothing. An awkward silence settled over them and this time it was Crissy's attention which wandered. "What's that?" she asked, jutting her chin toward the opposite side of the room.

Meryl turned, half-expecting to see the strange woman from the garden peering in the window at them. But the room beyond was as it had always been with its mismatched furniture, a couple of teetering floor lamps she'd procured from a local thrift shop and a heap of unfolded laundry sitting in a basket by the hallway door. "What's what?" she replied.

"That clacking noise. Do you have a dog or something?"

The sound was so ordinary it had passed over Meryl unnoticed. "That's my son playing with his toys. Sorry, he likes banging them together sometimes."

The young woman's left eyebrow arched. It was a tiny gesture of alarm, expressed through the upward movement of a carefully plucked line of hair. It was so slight most people wouldn't have noticed it, but Meryl noticed and felt immediately deflated. This was her sixth interview after all, and the previous five had ranged in quality from poor to disastrous. When the fourth applicant had hurried out after only five minutes, Meryl wondered if her body language, which had sometimes been described by others as being "unsociable," was scaring everyone off. By the fifth applicant however, she realized her mannerisms had little to do with it. It was much more about the clacking of plastic toys from the bedroom; or the childish singing coming out of the bathroom; or the toddler who wandered in and out of the interviews in his search for fruit juice.

Crissy had taken much longer to brooch the subject, which Meryl interpreted more as stupidity than diplomacy. "You have a baby?" she asked, and the obviousness of the answer further annoyed Meryl.

"Well, he's not so much a baby anymore. He's four. His name's Alexander."

"Oh. Wow. How old are you?"

Meryl shifted uncomfortably and said confidently, "I'll be twenty in December."

"Nineteen," the young woman gulped. "You're nineteen?"

"That's right. Twenty in December, so nineteen now. You got it."

Crissy uncrossed her legs and the bouncing foot landed square against the floor. She scooted to the edge of the couch and rested her delicate chin on the knuckles of her left hand. Her expression now showed an intense curiosity, propelled by some proprietary belief that if she was being interviewed for the role of roommate, she was entitled to every detail of Meryl's personal history up front.

"Wow, that's so wild," she said, her voice dripping with false empathy. "How'd you end up living on your own with a baby at nineteen? Did the father take off or something?"

Despite her increasing irritation, Meryl remained civil. "Things just happen, I guess."

The young woman shook her head. "Oh my god. Were you kicked out by your parents?"

"I moved out. I had my own money so I got this place."

"Wow, that's so cool. I wish I'd been able to do that earlier, but I'm still totally broke at twenty-one. My parents are helping me out, at least until my business takes off and my monetary situation stabilizes — then everything'll be golden. I'm gonna pay them back every cent with interest, I already told them that. Except for my tuition and all my school expenses, 'cause that's on them."

"Well, I don't have anyone helping me. I make my own way." Meryl said this with confidence, but Crissy pursed her lips and knitted her brow as though in condolence. Meryl had never felt her circumstances worthy of sympathy. She felt neither fortunate nor unfortunate, no one to be pitied but admittedly not really worthy of great admiration either. Whatever had happened in the past was a done deal and didn't require any commentary or second-guessing from some ridiculous chick in painted shoes. For Meryl, the interview was now over and all that remained was getting Crissy out of the apartment without punching her in the throat.

Meryl rose and crossed her arms. "Guess we better wrap this up. I know you have work soon so I'll let you go."

"Oh, right, right, right," the girl said, glancing quickly at the time on her phone. "Can I ask where the baby's father is? Does he live here too?"

"No. He's in Portland."

"Really? Did you have to escape from him or something? Did he abuse you?"

"Seriously?" Meryl answered with the curl of her upper lip.

"It happens, y'know," Crissy answered. "Domestic violence is rampant in this country with women being the primary victims."

"Fascinating. You must've learned that in a class, huh?"

"I got a 'B' in Women's Studies last semester."

"Well, that's really super." Meryl opened the front door and stepped onto the landing. Crissy followed, prattling on unabated about how she'd found empowerment as a woman through shoe-based artwork. The thought of ejecting the young woman with some kind of savage flourish seemed inappropriate now that Meryl was being lectured about the pervasiveness of violence in American society. She led the girl up the basement stairs and onto the lawn, then added, "Well, for the record, Alexander's father is actually a nice guy. It just didn't work out, that's all."

Crissy was still enthralled. "Wow. Crazy. Almost nineteen and with a five-year-old and out on your own. You should have your own reality show. Seriously. I'd watch it."

"I'm almost twenty and Alexander's four and I hate reality TV."

Then, almost as an after-thought Crissy added: "Yeah, you know, I don't think I can live here. Sorry, but I didn't know you had a baby..."

"He's a toddler and it clearly said I was the mother of one in my ad," Meryl answered.

"Right, but I didn't know he lived here—"

"Where else would he live?"

"I'm just saying this isn't the kind of home environment I'm looking for. No offense, but I really need a place which will stimulate my creativity 'cause that's what I live and breathe. I hope you understand?"

Not only did Meryl feel relieved by the rejection, she was almost ecstatic. "Oh, no worries. That's why I'm having these interviews, right? I mean, if you're going to live with someone you have to be sure of a good fit," she replied.

"Completely agree."

"Well, good bye then. Good luck finding a place."

"Thanks so much," Crissy smiled sympathetically. "Good luck to you and your son, too. I hope thing's work out with you and your boyfriend."

Meryl waited until the girl and her stupid non-utilitarian painted shoes had disappeared down the sidewalk before allowing herself a sigh of relief. Another bad interview and it wasn't even noon yet. Certainly her mood wasn't going to improve since she still had to confront the unknown person loitering in her vegetable garden. She crept around the edge of the house like a hunter stalking prey, only to find the garden was empty except for a single set of large footprints in the soft earth.

Idiocy surrounds me, she thought as she marched back to her basement apartment and slipped the deadbolt behind her. The dwelling was now quiet. Alexander had stopped beating his toys together and she could hear him speaking in his four-year-old dialect, a combination of mispronounced English and singsong nonsense. She followed the chatter down the hall to the back of the house and the bedroom they shared. This was the only time of day when the basement home received any natural light and the child was standing in a puddle of sunshine beneath the window, teetering on the balls of his feet.

He looked up at her, his dark blue eyes sparkling, and squealed, "Maw-mee! There's a lady."

A shadow passed over Alexander as a face appeared at the window. Meryl let out an involuntary gasp. The woman was down on all-fours, cupping her hands around her eyes as she pressed her face to the glass. She smiled. Then waved. It was such an odd thing considering she was, at present, both trespassing and creeping.

"What the fuck?" Meryl said involuntarily.

"Terribly sorry to disturb," the woman quickly bellowed through the glass. "I can't find the door." She was old, or at least that was Meryl's first impression though it was unlikely she was much over sixty. The short crown of curly white hair contrasted dramatically with her dark skin. Her face was thin, faceted, with prominent cheekbones and slender, beautiful eyes.

"What're you doing in my yard?" Meryl snapped. She didn't even attempt to be polite. Crissy of the Painted Shoes had sapped all her patience and, frankly, it didn't seem like she needed to be civil to a weirdo peering through her bedroom window.

"The front door, you see? I can't find it." the woman replied.

"Why do you need to know where my front door is?"

"My apologies. I misspoke." The woman quickly rummaged through her pockets and pulled out one of the "roommate wanted" posters Meryl had plastered all over the university campus. She pressed it to the glass and tapped it with a long, elegant finger. "I meant the front door to here. To two-one-seven-six-A. Is that you?"

"Yes, that's me."

"I'm here about the room for rent, you see. But I can't find the door. I knocked on the door to the big house but no one was home."

"It's a basement apartment. The door's on the west side of the house."

"Which way is west, if you don't mind?"

"To your right, past the garden. If you reach the street you've gone too far." Meryl gestured. "I'll meet you at the steps."

The woman waved again and vanished. Meryl rushed to reach the basement steps first, but it didn't make any difference, as the visitor had once again paused in the garden, this time to admire the tight twists and dangling blossoms of a wisteria vine stretched along the top of the fence.

"This is an exquisite garden," she said, running her fingers gently over the flowers. There was nothing threatening in either her tone or demeanor. In fact, she seemed strangely relaxed for someone who, just minutes before, was acting more like a Peeping Tom than a potential roommate. "Do you read?"

"Of course I read," Meryl smirked.

"No, I meant to say *are you a reader?* Do you enjoy literature?"

"Sure."

"Have you ever read the works of Walt Whitman?"

"No."

"Oh, you must. He's one of those authors who should be required reading for any thinking human being. He crafted these splendid treatises on nature and our connection to the Earth. Whenever I happen across a garden like this, I think of Whitman."

"Really? I think of bees."

The woman laughed. "Yes, I imagine bees like a garden nearly as much as Whitman. Did you design this place?"

Meryl shook her head. "I couldn't grow a plant if my life depended on it. My landlords designed the yard."

"You're not the homeowner?"

"I'm a tenant. The homeowners live in the house, I live in the basement."

"I see now," the woman said, almost apologetically. She moved closer, but seemed to be keeping a respectful distance, perhaps aware that she'd irritated Meryl. "I'm sorry if I startled you. I assure you it's not my usual practice to lurk in people's yards, but I really couldn't find your door."

"No worries," Meryl replied, forcing her shoulders to relax. "But most people call before dropping by."

"Yes, certainly that would've been the expected protocol," the woman acknowledged, fishing around in the pocket of her oversized sweater and pulling out a crushed piece of silver-colored plastic which had once been a cell phone. She held it out in the palm of her opened hand and supplicated, "But, as you can see, I had a casualty recently.

My dear old friend has made her last call. I just haven't been able to part with her yet."

Meryl couldn't help but smile.

The woman returned the smashed phone to her pocket and gave it a little pat like she was tucking it in for a long sleep. Then she grinned broadly and held her hand straight out. "I'm Rose, by the way," she said brightly. Her fingers were cold but soft and she held Meryl's hand for a long time.

"You like gardens and your name is 'Rose?'" Meryl chuckled.

The older woman shrugged. "My sister, Iris, likes them too."

"You're making that up."

"I swear it's true," Rose insisted, quickly crossing her heart with her fingertips. "My father was a farmer, so I guess that was his little joke on us girls."

"Did he have a plant name too?"

Rose grinned roguishly. "I'm almost afraid to tell you..."

"Seriously? He did?"

"His name was 'Herbert.' Everyone called him 'Herb.'"

Meryl rolled her eyes.

"So is the room still available?" Rose asked. "Or did I put you off me?"

Maybe this was all a performance and maybe it wasn't, but Meryl already found this woman to be a better roommate candidate than anyone she'd interviewed in the past week. She had the benefit of age and obviously some education, too. Additional points were given for not asking about Meryl's personal situation nor predicting that she'd be regularly late with the rent check. If she had basic hygiene skills and nothing contagious, then Meryl would move her to the "front runner" position.

Before the rental could be discussed, however, Rose dropped down into a squat and seemed to address Meryl's ankles: "Oh, now what a beauty you are!"

Alexander's little hand touched the back of Meryl's knee. He had followed her out and had silently climbed to the top step. She instinctively pulled him into her arms and balanced him on her hip.

"Just an absolute angel," Rose said, taking a step closer to them. She glanced at Meryl's face and then back at the child. "He has your lovely hair, doesn't he?"

The child's hair was almost exactly the same dark chestnut color as Meryl's, which she usually wore pulled back into a neat ponytail. They also shared the same round face, large eyes framed by thick lashes and dusky complexion. Although it was too early to tell, Meryl secretly hoped the boy would take after his father when it came to his build, avoiding her family's trait of producing shorter, stouter individuals. If he did, he might be the first Panagos to actually exceed five-foot-seven in height.

"Alexander, you know you're not supposed to go out the front door unless mommy says it's okay," Meryl scolded him gently. He ignored her, too engrossed by the almost impossibly tall woman who smelled like fresh jasmine and had waved to him through the bedroom window.

"Alexander's a powerful name, young man, the name of generals and heroes" — Rose said, inducing a giggle — "and my name is Rose, which is the name of a thorny and quite unattractive shrub."

"Are you really interested in renting?" asked Meryl.

"Absolutely."

There was a moment of difficult silence.

"You can tell me if you were hoping for someone else as a roomie," Rose ventured. "Really, you won't hurt my feelings. I'm probably not what most young college girls are expecting."

Meryl felt a little ashamed. If anything, the last two days had proven her expectations about rooming with a college student may have been misguided from the beginning. At least this mature woman, with her unusual clothes and eloquent speech, hadn't recoiled at the sight of Alexander.

"It's really not that," Meryl said apologetically. "But, as you can guess, most of the applicants have been..."

Rose smiled. "The word you're searching for is 'younger,' darling."

"Actually, I was going to say 'immature.'"

"I can imagine, as a young mother, you're probably on a very different level from your peers. Life has to be a little more serious when you're looking out for a child."

"You sound like you have kids."

"Over five hundred of them."

"Huh?"

Rose laughed loudly. "I taught fourth grade for twenty years, and believe me it was quite like parenting. I realize I may not be what you expected, but I hope we can at least discuss the matter? I really need a good roof over my head after living out of that junk-heap," she gestured to small car parked at the end of the garden path. Its interior was stuffed with boxes and jumbled clothing and a great clutter was piled onto the roof beneath a blue plastic tarp strapped down with dozens of bungee cords.

"You're moving?" Meryl asked.

"Have moved. Now arriving," Rose corrected. "Five straight days from Arizona, sleeping on the side of the road and eating more junk food than I care to admit to. I'm not shy to tell you that I'm somewhat desperate at this point."

Meryl smiled. "Me too."

"Perhaps it was fated to be?" Rose grinned broadly. "May I see the room?"

CHAPTER THREE

"Did I tell you that I finally met your roommate?" David mentioned casually to Meryl as he cut open a box of graphic novels. He slid one of the glossy, colorful books into a plastic sleeve, sealed down the edge and handed it to her.

Instead of reacting eagerly, she asked as nonchalantly as possible, "So? What do you think?"

David shrugged. "She wasn't what I was expecting."

"She wasn't what I was expecting either." She neatly pressed an adhesive price tag onto the front of the plastic sleeve and handed it back to David. Their eyes met briefly and she said, "She's nice, right?"

"Oh, yes. She's very nice. Odd though."

"You mean the clothes?"

He looked surprised. "Actually, I wasn't thinking about that. When you live in Corvallis you come to expect some unusual fashion statements. And when you're that tall and a woman, clothes shopping must get a little challenging anyway. No, I'm talking more about her disposition."

"Her *disposition*?" Meryl snorted.

"It's a perfectly good word."

"No one uses that word, David."

"Have it your way. Do you prefer the word *personality*, instead?"

"That's better. So what's your problem with her?"

"I'm kind of imagining her as having been in college for a trillion years with six Master's degrees but with no real life experience because she's spent all her time reading books and doting on her cats."

Meryl chortled. "Not even close, smart guy. She's a retired elementary school teacher. Only one Master's degree."

"And what about the life experience and the cats?"

"She's about twenty years older than you, David, so I assume she's done a few things in that time. She mentioned she was married once, and I'm pretty sure it was to a human, not a cat. I guess that counts as 'experience.'"

David paused, carefully choosing his next words. "Does it concern you that she's so very different from you?" This is where David tried to slip quietly out of his "employer" hat and into his "father-figure" hat and hoped Meryl wouldn't notice. She always noticed, but usually didn't mind. After all, she owed David a lot, perhaps even more than her own parents. She was living in his basement and working in his store. He'd provided occasional loans of money and baby-sat Alexander regularly. And David and her father had been best friends until the latter died a few years earlier, so there was that, too. Really, it seemed like the man had earned the right to offer some unsolicited advice, but Meryl enjoyed making him work for it.

"Is this a black thing?" she asked sharply.

"Oh, c'mon," he moaned.

"It's the twenty-first century, David. An older black woman and an absolutely gorgeous young woman of eastern Mediterranean descent with the silkiest head of hair you'll ever find should be able to cohabitate without being the source of ridicule, you know."

"Don't be daft," he answered tersely.

"*Daft?*" she pressed. "Really? You're going with that?"

"Also a good word," he sniffed, banging another stack of graphic novels down on the countertop as though to punctuate his displeasure with her. "I was just thinking that a young lady like you might better enjoy the company of other young ladies, not someone who's old enough to be your grandmother. It just seemed like an unusual choice to me."

Meryl priced another book and held it out to him. David reached for it and she quickly drew it away. She grinned widely. "Are you worried about me?"

"I know better than that," he replied. "But you know, there's nothing worse in the world than being stuck with a terrible roommate."

"I can think of worse things. But it's not the case anyway. She's quiet, she's neat, she pays for everything in cash and on time — and she doesn't treat Alexander like he's a mangy dog."

"Well, that's good. I just figured maybe you'd want a roommate closer to your own age, who's interested in the same things as you?"

Meryl guffawed. "Good luck finding a person like that. You know, most of the girls who interviewed for the room left thinking I was a giant slut."

"They said that to you?"

"They didn't need to. I could just tell by how they squirmed in their seats or suddenly remembered they promised someone else they were going to room with her anytime I mentioned Alexander. I think most of them decided I was some ignorant whore who got knocked up and ruined my life."

"I hate to tell you this kiddo, but that's human nature. Even in this day and age, people are going to look at you and Alexander and leap to all kinds of conclusions and not give a damn about the truth of it."

"Exactly why I chose Rose," Meryl replied. " Plus, I'm pretty sure she's not going to have guys sleeping over or will be throwing keggers in the yard."

She noticed David smile slightly as he pushed his reading glasses back into his graying hair and examined a book cover closely. For a moment, with his receding hairline and slender face covered in deep creases, he looked more like a scholar studying an ancient manuscript than a middle-aged man who had never outgrown his childhood fascination with superheroes. "Does this look water damaged to you?" he asked absently.   He was trying to change the subject, but Meryl wanted to convince him.

"You know she reads to Alexander at night?" Meryl said.

"Really? What does she read him?"

"Last night it was *Make Way for Ducklings.*"

"I'm not familiar with that title, I'm afraid. What's it about?"

"Ducklings. And making way for them."

He ignored her sarcasm, turned the book over and meticulously inspected the cover for stains or warpage.

Meryl continued: "It's about ducklings crossing a road. She sat in a chair and he sat on the floor and she held the book open so he could see the pictures while she read. Just like a school teacher would do. And she did all the sound effects too."

"Such as?"

"You know, the traffic noises, the ducks quacking. She had Alexander marching around the living room going *buck, buck, buck, buck, buck, buck, buck!*"

This time David didn't repress his smile and it made Meryl feel better. She knew she didn't need his approval, but she did want it.

The front door of the store banged opened and Cameron walked in, swinging his backpack. "Big boss, mini boss," he greeted them. "What're you two grinning about?"

"Meryl's telling me about her new roommate," David answered.

"Some super-fly hottie?" Cameron asked.

"Yes. Tall, dark, exotic looking. Unique sense of style. Enjoys great literature about ducks."

"What does that mean? A brainy chick?"

"Very brainy."

Cameron wrinkled his nose. "Forget it then. I don't want any girl who's smarter than me."

"That severely limits the field for you, doesn't it?" Meryl asked sharply.

Cameron waggled his finger at her. "See, I caught that insult. Sometimes I don't catch them 'cause you're an uber-brainy chick, but *that* one I caught."

"I've been lowering the quality on my insults so you can catch more of them," Meryl responded. "It's been bothering me that you only understand about fifteen percent of my mockery."

He snorted and dropped his backpack behind the register counter, then held his hands up to the universe in supplication. "See, oh great sky gods, this is why brainy chicks are t-r-o-u-b-l-e."

Meryl affixed another price tag, then cupped her chin in the palms of her hands and stared at him wistfully. "Cam, since I'm so much smarter than you, does this mean we'll never be... uh... David, what's a really classy word for 'lovers' but not 'lovers?'"

"Paramours?" David replied.

"Paramours," repeated Meryl.

"I wouldn't rule it out completely," shrugged Cameron. "I could always spare a few minutes to wreck you out in the alley."

"Gross."

Their ritualistic greeting of shared insults now complete, Cameron pinned on his name badge, walked over to where Meryl and David were working and thumbed through their neatly stacked piles of plastic-ensconced comic books. "Anything particularly badass come in?" he asked.

"We've already put all the badass stuff in the 'New Arrivals' section," Meryl said. "Can you dust the collectibles cases? They're looking really tacky."

"Sure thing, boss lady. But I want to hear about the roommate. Despite all her brains, is there anything redeemable about her?"

Meryl smiled and regarded Cameron quickly as he gamboled over to the large glass cases at the front of the store. A Corvallis native, he'd spent the better part of his childhood in David's shop, training, as he said, for his future role as the world's most informed and irresponsible fanboy. He'd done a good job of it. Meryl imagined that his mother and father, the latter of whom was a professor at Oregon State University, spent innumerable nights wishing he would take an interest in something other than the skate park and the combined movies of George Lucas. It probably would never happen. Now approaching his twenty-fourth birthday, Cameron had carved out a unique niche for himself in the tiny community as the guy who knew almost everything about stuff that really wasn't that important. He could recite movie dialogue precisely, providing accents when needed, and had an amazing ability to mentally catalogue every comic, graphic novel, T-shirt, collectible toy and poster in the store. His reputation had reached almost legendary status among the OSU students who frequented the shop, often just to seek Cameron's frivolous counsel without spending a dime in return.

When David had first introduced Meryl to the world of comics and movie memorabilia nearly a year earlier, she felt like an interloper, an upstart. By that time, Cameron had worked in the shop for over six years, and David had bypassed him entirely to make Meryl his assistant manager despite her appalling lack of knowledge or interest in the subject. She was certain Cameron would lead a mutiny. He didn't, and it took a while for Meryl to realize he had no ambition to manage David's comic book store, or any other establishment on Earth. In fact, he considered that level of responsibility contrary to his life's goal of getting through a day with as little bother as possible. Instead, Cameron had surprised Meryl, quietly declaring himself to be her personal majordomo, stepping in quickly to answer those merchandise-related questions she didn't understand, running interference when some of the college boys got too fresh, always covering her shifts when Alexander was sick or throwing an extended tantrum.

"So let's hear it," he called from across the store as he carefully removed and cleaned a cabinet filled with tiny spaceships and superhero effigies. "I want to know about the hottie roommate."

"Hoping to curry some favors, young man?" David asked.

"Holy shit," laughed Cameron, "are you trotting out every twenty-dollar word you know, today?"

"Yup," Meryl replied. "So far you've missed 'disposition' and 'daft.' Plus a bunch more from this morning."

"You know, children," offered David, "your own vocabularies could benefit from my example."

"Oh, and they will!" Meryl assured him with feigned enthusiasm. "Tonight, somehow, I'm going to work the word 'daft' into a conversation with my toddler."

"Yo!" bellowed Cameron. "Pay attention to me! Tell me about the roommate."

Meryl scowled. "She's not right for you, Cam. She's an older woman."

"Older women are cool," Cameron replied. "How much older? Are we talking like a cougar, here?"

"She's sixty-two."

"Sixty-two?"

"Yup."

"Six-period-two-period?"

"Right."

"What the fuck you thinking, girl?"

"Oh, don't start. She's really nice. An older, more mature person is perfect for my situation right now."

Cameron sneered. "She's gonna completely cramp your style, babe. You're gonna meet some rocking college dude with long dreadlocks and soulful eyes who wants to write poems about you, and he's gonna take one look at the granny panties hanging off your shower rod and take off."

"Well, in case you haven't noticed, there's no guy in my life like that right now. Except you, babe."

"That's what I mean," Cameron groaned, ignoring her disingenuous flirting as he waved a polyurethane model of a blue-colored mutant at her. "No big stud for Meryl when Grandma's in the house. You might as well give up now. You're gonna be alone forever."

"Do you believe this?" Meryl snickered to David.

The older man looked up briefly from the stack of graphic novels. "He's got a point," he replied.

"Ha! Thank you!" Cameron cried victoriously.

"You guys, she's a roommate, not my best friend. She's there to help pay the rent so I can finally save some money and start classes at the U."

"If you're worried about money for school, you can easily get scholarships or grants," David said. "You got good grades in high school, right? That alone should qualify you for a tuition waiver."

"Yeah, but waivers, scholarships and grants don't pay for all the day care I'm going to have to find for Alexander. And at this point, I want my degree much more than I want a smokin' hot boyfriend with dreadlocks."

"And soulful eyes," Cameron added.

"Yeah, those too. Preferably two of them. Both equally soulful."

"And he writes poetry about you."

"Hopefully not limericks."

David patted Meryl gently on the hand. "It's totally your decision," he said. "I told you that when we first discussed you getting a roommate, and I'm not saying any of this as your employer or your landlord. I'm saying it as your friend."

"And I'm saying it as someone who thinks granny panties are nasty," Cameron offered.

Meryl ignored Cameron and smiled at David. "Don't worry," she assured him. "I know what I'm doing."

David let Meryl end her shift a little early. The daycare where Alexander spent most of his time during the week was heartless when it came to their pick up policy. If Meryl arrived after 5:30 p.m., they would charge her a dollar per minute until she retrieved Alexander. She'd made that mistake once and was now downright paranoid about her punctuality. Every day she started panicking around 4:45, hoping the shop's night crew would actually show up on time for their shifts. They seldom did, except for Cameron.

The comic book store lay in Corvallis's quaint downtown shopping district, just a short walk to the sprawling OSU campus and an even shorter walk to the loamy banks and green waters of the Willamette River. It occupied the northwest corner of a historic red brick building, nestled between an upscale furniture store and a bakery which specialized in rustic breads and elaborate coffee-based drinks. As Meryl pulled on her jacket and stepped out into the cool, breezy evening, the shop's electric sign clicked on overhead. It depicted a rather oafish-looking android with bulbous flashing eyeballs clutching handfuls of comic books. Above its neon head large letters flickered in fiery red and neon blue: ATTACK OF THE 50-FOOT ROBOT! David had once told Meryl that his dream was to eventually have a 50-foot sign to go with the shop's towering name. However, the City of Corvallis had told him he'd have to settle for what the municipal sign code allowed. Still, it was nice to dream.

Before moving to Corvallis, Meryl couldn't recall a single occasion where she had stepped foot in a comic book or memorabilia store. If the culture shock of moving from Portland, Oregon's largest city, to the comparatively tiny Corvallis hadn't been enough, Meryl suddenly had to contend with understanding an entire subculture devoted to superheroes, arch villains, rampaging orcs and alien invaders. And this devotion wasn't confined merely to young fanboys.

She was surprised to see packs of teenage girls in the store, buying up the latest Manga imports from Japan or commemorative pins and patches to adorn their denim jackets and oversized shoulder bags. On her first day as assistant manager, a stately-looking man of at least seventy had wandered into the store, spent an hour perusing the stacks, and then dropped close to fifty dollars on a dozen different titles. Meryl had awkwardly expressed her surprise at seeing a man of his years taking an interest in comic books.

He smiled kindly, taking no offense at her bewilderment. "You're never too old to enjoy a good story told in small, intricately illustrated boxes," he said.

After that, Meryl tried not to judge anyone who crossed the store's threshold. Everyone needed a little adventure, a touch of fantasy, a bit of excitement. Something, she told herself, her own life was severely lacking.

She walked west along the edge of the campus. Most classes had ended for the day, and the students were flooding the coffee shops, bars and restaurants, forming small tittering groups on the sidewalks or noisy roving mobs celebrating nothing more than the onset of evening. She wandered through them unnoticed, yet felt so conspicuous. Most of these students were only a year or two older than her, but she felt as removed from their world as a bird in the sky must from a fish in the ocean. From the outside looking in, their lives seemed wonderfully — even ridiculously — carefree.

Certainly no one else was rushing to pick up a child so as to avoid late fees that bordered on thievery, she told herself.

Her thoughts were becoming increasingly maudlin but she had trained herself to resist self-pity and increased her pace. The route was always the same — the routine was strangely comforting — down Monroe street then right at the noodle shop. From there, north, where the streets became almost sleepy as she left behind the sound and frolic of the students. For the next ten minutes she didn't encounter anyone except the occasional bicyclist and an old woman out walking her identical Bichon Frisés. She turned twice more and ended up a long, tree-lined avenue with a small daycare center located at the end of the block. She checked the time on her cell phone and sighed. It was only 5:20.

Alexander held her hand as they walked back to the large house with its beautiful garden and her dreary basement apartment. The light over their doorway was burning and inside Meryl could hear classical music playing.

When they entered, it became clear that Rose had been very busy. Prior to Meryl moving in, David had rented the basement to a variety of OSU students and their presence was still evident in the patched over walls and inconsistent paint scheme. The tiny kitchen had taken the worst of it with its scratched cabinets, warped countertops and chipped porcelain sink. But Rose had thoroughly cleaned it and over the previous hour had fixed a pot of something which sat bubbling on the stove and smelled of sweet ham. The rickety card table they ate off was now decorated with vinyl place-mats and a vase filled with flowers Rose had clearly stolen from David and Rachel's garden. Even the grayish-brown carpet, which had always seemed irredeemably ugly, had actually benefited from a thorough vacuuming.

"Wow," Meryl said. "The place looks amazing."

Rose appeared around the corner of the kitchen, with a beach towel tied around her waist like an apron. "You know how you get up some mornings just bursting with energy?" she said cheerfully. "Well, today was one of those days."

"I guess. Did you get everything unpacked?"

"Every single thing. Go take a look."

For nearly a week, the only thing in Rose's bedroom aside from the old sleeping bag spread out in one corner was a lopsided pyramid of piled moving boxes and suitcases. She'd arrived in Oregon without a stick of furniture and Meryl had nothing to loan her since she and

Alexander were still sleeping on mattresses on the floor themselves. Yet somehow, during the course of the day, Rose had transformed the room entirely. Against the far wall was an inexpensive bed and mattress covered in a thick comforter and colorful pillows trimmed with fringe and tassels. On either side of the bed were tall bookshelves she'd arranged with a large number of books, photographs from her teaching days and strange nicknacks including an oversized champagne glass engraved with the words: I'M ALWAYS A WINNER AT THE DESERT WINDS HOTEL & CASINO, LAUGHLIN, NEVADA. Next to the door was a small, second-hand desk with a matching chair, both of which a previous owner had painted a revolting shade of yellow. The right side of the desk was arranged with neat piles of papers which appeared to be photocopies of various historical documents although Meryl couldn't tell exactly of what. Nearby was a large Oregon atlas which had been opened to a section showing the Willamette Valley and parts of the surrounding forest with some parts highlighted in hot pink. A small book, obviously an antique judging by its worn green cover, sat next to the atlas, its pages crammed with small adhesive notes. On the left side of the desk was an antiquated but clearly functional laptop computer, its screen glowing softly with images of tropical islands. Meryl's heart leapt a little at the sight of it. The disconnection she felt from others her age came in many forms. But part of it came from being the only person her age in Corvallis without a computer. Or at least that's how it felt. There'd been no money for those types of conveniences and Meryl had reluctantly survived as a refugee from the Digital Age.

Alexander moved toward the bed, enticed by the pile of pillows. "No, sweetie," Meryl whispered. "This is Rose's room. You can't go in unless you have permission."

"Oh, it's fine," Rose said, as she came down the hall to join them. "You can go in you want, little bug."

The child hurled himself into the pillows and squealed loudly.

27

"I didn't know you had a computer," Meryl said nonchalantly. "I haven't been able to afford one since I moved down here."

"Well, it's as old as the dirt itself but it still works. We even have internet."

Meryl frowned. "We do? How?"

Rose chuckled. "I'm piggybacking on someone's WIFI signal. It must be one of your neighbors. Someone called 'wordmagician?'"

Meryl had to think for a moment, but then exclaimed, "Oh, that's David's wife, Rachel. She's a writer and that's what she calls herself — the 'wordmagician.'"

"Really? What does she write?"

"I'm not really sure what you'd call it. Poetry, I guess. It's very, well, experimental. And then there's the novel she's been working on for years that no one's ever seen." She tried not to sound too disparaging of her friend's wife, but the truth was she and Rachel had never clicked. As modest and generous as David was, Rachel was the epitome of pretentiousness. Quick to criticize but loath to accept any in return. That's probably why she never published anything, Meryl thought.

Rose seemed to pick up on her annoyance and asked with just a hint of sarcasm, "And she does this for a living?"

"David makes the living owning the comic book store. Like I said, Rachel's an artist."

"I see. Well, the artist is lending us some internet."

"That's not going to cost them anything, is it?"

Rose shook her head. "'Wordmagician' won't even notice, I promise. But come, I have another surprise for you."

She led them down the hall to the master bedroom they shared and snapped on the overhead light. Both mattresses were now set on bedsteads and dressed with brand new linens. Meryl's was covered in a satiny blue duvet and Alexander's a shaggy cloak of artificial fur complete with leopard spots. The child squealed in delight and began to roll on the bed like a dog playing in fresh cut grass. Meryl was almost speechless.

She stammered, "Rose, you really shouldn't —"

"Let's not have another word about it," Rose interrupted. "Truly, I can afford it. I just sold my house before moving here and made a few shekels from it and the rent I'm paying here is a third of what my mortgage was. Plus, I bought everything on sale. So please, please don't tell me how my gift makes you feel bad because it was intended to make you feel good."

"It's just that I can't repay you," Meryl replied, sheepishly.

"And it's not expected. I did it because I wanted to, not because I expect anything in return."

Although she tried to resist, a sense of inadequacy began to creep through Meryl, starting in her belly and moving steadily toward her heart. With the exception of David's kindnesses — and he was family for all intents and purposes — she'd been happy to make her way without accepting handouts from others. She'd come up with the idea of taking in a roommate to cut costs after all, but it had never occurred to her that the roommate would buy her anything.

"Mah-mee, I like muh nube bed," Alexander announced, having rolled himself up in the fur mantle so only his small feet were hanging out.

She hesitated, only to have Rose quickly chime in: "At least give it a test drive before you make up your mind." And with that, she gently took Meryl by the shoulders and lowered her onto the bed. She sunk a good six inches into the cool fabric. It was like floating on water, and Meryl was almost inclined to close her eyes and sleep right then but Rose clearly had more on the evening's agenda.

"I hope you don't mind that I cooked," Rose bellowed as she headed back down the hallway to the kitchen. They followed obediently as the older woman crossed to the large pot bubbling on the stovetop and gave it a quick stir with a wooden spoon. "It was just so easy to throw a bunch of stuff together and let it simmer on a low flame. And it's always nice to come home to a hot meal. Come now, you two. Let's eat."

Meryl and Alexander obediently scooted into their seats as Rose placed a large pan of freshly-baked cornbread on the table.

"Now, in my family, we don't stand on ceremony," she told them. "We help ourselves, we eat 'til we're full, but we don't waste food." She ladled out a bowl of steaming soup and set it before Meryl. It smelled rich and salty, a colorful conglomeration of beans, vegetables and neatly diced chunks of ham.

"This smells wonderful," Meryl said. "What is it?"

"Ten bean and ham soup. Something my mama used to make. We ate simple meals at home, but they were always nutritious. I got most of the ingredients at that farmer's market I found downtown. Do you shop there?"

"No," Meryl replied. "I always forget about it."

"Oh, you should go, sweetie. It's one of the perks of living in an area surrounded by farms." She looked over at Alexander who had scooted to the edge of his seat and was looking anxiously at Meryl's steaming bowl. "Now for you," she said to the child, "I made something special."

She returned to the stove and quickly arranged a plate of macaroni and cheese and cut green beans for Alexander. The boy beamed and made some awkward attempts to use his spoon, gripping it like one would a baseball bat. A dollop of noodles landed on the floor.

"You didn't need to fix something different for him," Meryl protested gently.

"Honey, I worked with small children long enough to know that boys his age aren't interested in ten bean soup. It's much too exotic. It was no bother to make him something he'd actually eat."

Rose seated herself and the three of them ate in silence. Alexander finished first, a quarter of his meal having ended up on the floor, and squirmed anxiously until Meryl sent him off to watch cartoons. For a very long while, the two women sat across from each other, silently preoccupied with their individual bowls of soup and steaming slabs of buttered cornbread. For the last week, they had engaged each other as strangers thrust into a common space — with deliberate and often exaggerated courtesy. But tonight it was suddenly different — nice and uncomfortable at the same time. Meryl felt like she needed to make a gesture.

"I guess maybe we should tell each other a little about ourselves?" she said tentatively, almost rhetorically.

Rose smiled. "What a super idea," she replied. "I guess, with all the hubbub of the move, we really haven't had any time to get to know each other."

"Not that it's required," Meryl began to babble. "I mean, your business is your business... It's not an interrogation. You don't have to do it. I've never had a roommate before."

Rose chortled and rested her chin on her wrist, gazing at Meryl pensively. "Would you believe neither have I?"

"Really?"

"Not a single one. When I was in college I lived at home. Then I lived with my ex for thirteen very long years, but he was more like a small child than a roommate, so I don't think he counts, does he?"

Meryl shook her head. "I don't think so. Anymore than parents do."

"I have a suggestion," Rose said excitedly, "so this doesn't feel like an inquisition. You ask me three questions — the top three things you want to know about me — and I will ask you three things about you."

"Okay. Umm. Anything?"

"Sure."

"What happened to your husband?"

"We divorced about thirty years ago. We married young and were together for what seemed like an eternity. He was a very nice man, but he had a problem with being too nice to other ladies. He wasn't willing to stop being nice to other ladies, so I gave him his freedom so he could be nice to whoever he wanted whenever he wanted. He lives in Phoenix now. He's remarried a couple of times. He has a bunch of kids too."

Meryl suddenly felt a little sorry for Rose, but she was laughing and clearly the memory didn't bother her. There was a resiliency there Meryl admired. She thought for a moment and then asked: "Why did you move to Oregon?"

"What an outstanding question. After I retired from teaching, I found myself trapped in Kingman, Arizona, which is a most unremarkable town. I guess I didn't notice how unremarkable the place was while I was working because I had something to occupy my days, you know? But when you retire, you go through this period where you wake up in the morning and realize you don't have anything to do."

"Yeah, like the first week after summer vacation begins?" Meryl offered. "You can't quite believe that you don't need to be up at 6 a.m. to get to school."

"Exactly. When that happens, you find ways to fill your time. I finally decided I was spending too much of my day doing really silly stuff just to kill the hours. So, I decided I needed a new place with new scenery. I sold off my house, loaded up the car and drove to Corvallis."

"Okay, but I'm not sure you answered my question," Meryl laughed. "That's why you left Arizona. I want to know why you came to Oregon."

Rose bit her lip. Her next words were carefully chosen. "I came to Oregon to seek my fortune."

Meryl waited for more, but it didn't come. She decided to press it. "What kind of fortune?"

Rose looked surprised. "Why, the only kind that matters my friend — the kind that'll buy you a big beautiful house filled with gorgeous things and a fancy car in the driveway."

"How? Are you gonna start a business or play the stock market or something?"

"Uh, I think that's a fourth question."

"Okay, I take it back."

Rose shrugged. "It's okay. Let's just say that there are different ways to get rich and not all of them are about playing the stock market or being a captain of industry."

"Oh, you're very mysterious," Meryl grinned.

"Okay, my turn!" Rose exclaimed. "First question: where do you want to be in your development as a human being in the next year?"

"That's easy. I want to be attending classes at OSU in marine biology. Then I want to move with Alexander to Hawaii and study whales."

"What marvelous goals. Good for you. Second question: Do you like your job?"

"To be honest," she said, "not really. I mean, I've come to appreciate comic book art in a big way over the last few months, but I don't think I'll become a collector or anything. David and Rachel arranged the job for me like they arranged this apartment — because they felt bad for me."

She waited for the last question, certain she knew what it would be. But instead, Rose asked, "How do you like Corvallis?"

"Okay, you're cheating," Meryl insisted.

"Cheating? How do you cheat at asking questions?"

"Because I don't think you're asking questions you really care about."

"How do you mean?"

Meryl turned and looked at Alexander, who was rocking on his heels in front of the television and singing softly in his broken toddler-speak.

Rose arched an eyebrow. "My dear," she laughed, "that's what we called the 'eight-hundred pound gorilla in the room.'"

"Huh?"

"'The eight-hundred pound gorilla' is that thing that everyone in the room notices but no one wants to talk about for fear of upsetting it. I confess I wasn't going to bring up Alexander. It seemed too personal when we've only known each other for a week."

"You may be the first person I've met here who hasn't bothered to ask," Meryl sighed. "That subject's pretty much why I couldn't find a roommate my own age."

"Well, sweetie, that's because they just don't know, do they? How could most nineteen-year-olds ever imagine the responsibility you have when they're still living on their parents' good graces? My goodness, it must be so completely strange to them."

"Plus, they're kinda idiots," Meryl added impulsively.

Rose laughed loudly. "Yes, I suspect they are. Okay, since you have rejected my third question, let me chose a new one: Do you want me to ask you about Alexander?"

Meryl couldn't remember a time when she'd been given that choice. She'd spent most of the last few years either explaining or defending the boy. Now, suddenly, someone was asking her if she even wanted to talk about it at all. After thinking about it for a long moment, she said almost apologetically, "No."

"Okay," Rose nodded. She didn't seem offended or even surprised.

"It's just that... well... I get tired of talking about it..."

Rose held up her hand and Meryl fell silent. "As you correctly said," the older woman answered, "your business is your business and this is not an interrogation. Simple-Simon. You tell me when you want to tell me, and only if you want to. Deal?"

Meryl felt a warm sensation crawl along her back, over her shoulders and up her neck. To her delight, she realized that it wasn't just the heat from the ten bean soup. "Deal," she answered.

Rose cut her another lump of cornbread and they talked for the next hour about the town, the farmer's market, the Willamette River and all sorts of interesting facts about whales.

CHAPTER FOUR

Meryl's cell phone chirped exactly six minutes before her alarm was set to chime. Almost instinctively she found the device in the dark and quickly set it to "vibrate" before it could rouse Alexander. She pulled the covers up over her head and activated the tiny blue screen. It read:

TESS: U UP?

Hearing from Tess always produced mixed feelings — and only partly because she insisted on texting so damn early. They'd been best friends in high school and Tess had been loyal enough to stay in touch even though they hadn't seen each other in over a year. Meryl was certain her old friend was laboring under the belief that one day they'd be reunited in Portland and could resume the cloistered comfort of their high school lives. She'd never been able to convince Tess there was no going back, that the child sleeping across the room and the realities of her present situation made her high school years seem like a distant and troubled dream.

The phone trembled as a second text arrived. TESS: U THERE????

Meryl's thumbs were slow to function, but she managed to type back: YA WATS UP?

TESS: HAVE SOMETHING TO TELL U

Meryl fumed. Nothing could be so important as to rob her of six minutes sleep and Tess was notorious for finding great importance in the most trivial things. What was it this time? One of the

36

cheerleaders who'd been mean to them in the tenth grade had put on twenty pounds? The Homecoming King was now selling shoes at Foot Locker? Tess had received *another* speeding ticket?

Reluctantly, Meryl tapped back: AND?????

TESS: TOM CAME INTO MY WORK LAST NITE

Meryl shifted under the covers like she suddenly had ants crawling up her legs. She pushed the pillows into a lump and propped herself against them, keeping the covers over her like a tent so Alexander wouldn't notice she was awake.

Tap-tap-tap.

MERYL: WHY?

TESS: WHY U THINK??? WASNT TO SEE ME FO SHO

MERYL: WAT U TELL HIM???

TESS: NADA. HE JUST HUNG OUT LIKE A LOST PUPPY SAID HE SAW UR MOM RECENTLY.

MERYL: FUCK. HE AND MOM HAVIN CONVOS NOW??

TESS: IDK. HAS SHE CALLED U?

MERYL: NOT IN MONTHS!! SENT ALEX A CARD FOR HIS BDAY BUT THATS ALL. WAT HE SAY?

TESS: TOTALLY FISHING FOR INFO PRETTY LAME

MERYL: YA?

TESS: ASKED HOW U WERE. SAID UR TOTALLY AWESOME MAKING HUGE BANK AND GETTING READY FOR COLLEGE.

MERYL: NICE!!!! Her thumbs paused on the tiny keyboard and she bit her lower lip. There was a huge part of her that knew she shouldn't ask the next question. A larger part compelled her thumbs to act. HE WITH ANYONE?

TESS: U CARE?????

MERYL: NO. JUST ASKIN.

TESS: ALONE

MERYL: HE SAY ANYTHING ABOUT ALEXANDER?

TESS: ASKED ABOUT HIM YA. WANTED TO KNOW HOW HE DOIN IN SCHOOL

MERYL: OMFG WAT AN ASSHOLE. DOESNT EVEN KNOW ALEXANDER'S CORRECT AGE??

TESS: HUN, TOM = DIMWIT. ;)

MERYL: LOL TRUE THAT

The tiny device went still for a long moment, the blue screen staring blankly up at Meryl. Then *tap-tap-tap*. WAT ELSE?

TESS: HMMM HE LOOKS GOOD

MERYL: HE ALWAYS DID

TESS: SERIOUS THO. NOT SO MANY ZITS. CLEARLY HITTING THE GYM. HES HUGE!!

MERYL: STEROIDS!!!!!!!!!!????

TESS: CUD B! THEY MAKE U STUPID RIGHT?

MERYL: AND MAKE UR DICK SMALL AND STERILE

TESS: EXCELLENT WE DONT NEED THAT BOY SPREADING HIS GENES ANYMORE

Ouch. Meryl was certain the last text was probably unintentional, and it was quickly followed by another.

TESS: SRY HUN. IM AN ASS. DIDNT MEAN IT THAT WAY

MERYL: I KNOW NO WORRIES BITCH :)

TESS: LOL

MERYL: PRETTY SURE HIS STUPID GENE SKIPS A GENERATION ANYWAY SO ALEX SAFE LMAO

The soft clicking of their conversation finally roused Alexander who slid out of the shaggy cocoon he'd made out of his new bedding and staggered into the bathroom across the hallway. Meryl heard the toilet seat bang against the tank and the broken sound of water hitting water, then the bathroom tile, then water again.

MERYL: GOTTA GO ALEXANDERS UP PEEING ON THE BATHROOM FLOOR AGIN

TESS: HAHA TEACH THAT BOY TO AIM!!!!
MERYL: WORKIN ON IT. HMU LATER
TESS: KK LOVE U
MERYL: LOVE U TOO BITCH

She'd no sooner snapped the phone shut when Alexander scampered back into the room and threw himself headlong into her covers, head-butting her on the left hip.

Meryl groaned and pulled the blankets off her head. "Baby, I told you, no Ultimate Fighting moves on mommy."

"Mah-mee weed me," he replied, shoving the corner of a small green book into Meryl's sternum.

"Oh, sweetie, it's too early for stories," Meryl said. "Mommy doesn't even have her contacts in yet."

Alexander sat up on his haunches, blinked at her with wide, dark brown eyes, and extended the book again. "Weed me now? Pees."

She reluctantly took the book and turned it over in her hands. It was small, thick, and heavy. The edges of the green cover were tattered and the pages inside were dog-eared with multi-colored sticky notes poking out at different angles. The title was almost indecipherable, having been scuffed away by what must've been years of use: *The American Boy's Adventure Reader.*

"Alexander," she said. "Whose book is this?"

"Rodes," he replied.

It was only then that Meryl recognized it as the book she'd seen sitting on Rose's desk the previous night. There was an immediate flush of embarrassment, though it was unlikely her roommate was even aware of the book's disappearance. She cocked her head to one side and listened for sounds of movement in the rest of the apartment. Nothing. Rose must be gone, she quickly concluded. The older woman was usually out of the house by 7 a.m. and would often stay away until late afternoon. Since Rose didn't work, Meryl couldn't figure out what occupied so much of her time but felt it was probably impolite to ask.

"Alexander, remember how mommy said that you can't go into Rose's room without asking?" she asked him.

The child looked alarmed and immediately launched into a long description of how he'd found the book on the living room floor and, concerned with its safety, he decided to promptly give it to his mother. To the four-year-old mind, this was a completely credible explanation.

Meryl handed it back to him. "You need to put the book back where you found it, please."

Alexander's mouth stretched into a long, thin line and Meryl waited to see which of the standard toddler reactions he'd go with this morning. He chose defiance. "Noooo," he moaned, in a tone which was a combination of incipient anger and building guilt.

"You know it's wrong to steal and lie about it, Alexander."

"I dinna!"

"Yes. You. Did."

The boy held up a forefinger, his way of punctuating a point and admonishing her at the same time. "Mah-mee, I mad at you!" he stated, his face now flush with emotion. Meryl choked back a laugh. Her natural response was to go with sarcasm, but he didn't understand the concept and it usually just elicited a tantrum. She held out the book again and said nothing.

"No!" he snapped, immediately leaping off the bed. "I'll weed myself." He pulled several books from his pile of belongings on the far side of the room and, without giving Meryl a second glance, stamped noisily down the hallway. A few seconds later, Meryl heard the television switch on. It wasn't a perfect solution, but at least he wasn't on the floor screaming. Give him fifteen minutes of cartoons and his outrage would be forgotten, she mused.

Meryl lifted the book back to her nose and inhaled deeply. It smelled bitter, like old linen and dust. Almost idly she flipped open the cover to the title page and squinted to read it:

THE AMERICAN BOY'S ADVENTURE READER,
State of Oregon, United States of America, Published 1915.

A one-hundred-year old school book. Certainly it seemed like something a retired teacher might own, if only as a curiosity. The tome was divided into several sections, each containing stories related to the history and the natural wonders of Oregon. There was a tale about pirate ships wrecking on the rocky ocean reefs and another about a vicious grizzly bear that devoured livestock and seemed impervious to bullets. Some expounded on the bravery of white settlers who battled both unpredictable weather and "uncivilized heathens" — which Meryl construed to mean anyone who wasn't a white settler. But what intrigued her most were all the notations and careless doodles which had clearly been left in the margins by a young man who'd undoubtedly left this world before Meryl had even been born. Whoever the commentator had been, he seemed particularly interested in a story entitled "The Cursed Gold Mine," having circled various passages, drawn arrows from words to his own comments, and sketched tiny maps of mountains and rivers. 'Crick, 3-4 days' was written in one area. 'Valley to mountains' noted in another. On top of these original notes, Rose had added her own squares of adhesive note paper. One was pasted right over the first page of the story and contained two lines of numbers written in heavy black marker. Strange symbols broke the numbers into shorter segments, so this clearly wasn't anything as ordinary as a phone number or a zip code. Meryl examined it for a long moment. Maybe it was a bank account number? Or a line of computer code? Why such things would be associated with an early twentieth century children's book made no sense to her.

Intrigued, she lifted up the note and began to read the page below: "In the deep forest primeval of central Oregon, there lies a gold mine forgotten by Time. None will venture there and even the

41

Red Man refuses to approach its crumbling portal. Some say the mine is cursed..."

On the other side of the apartment, the front door banged open and Rose called, "Hey guys, are you up?" Alexander squealed a delighted response and immediately began to describe a powerful hunger which could only be sated by pancakes.

Meryl snapped the book shut and shoved it under her pillow. She felt ashamed. It's not like she was caught rifling through Rose's purse or anything, but her curiosity had kept her from returning the book immediately and it was impossible to do so as long as Rose was in the living room.

"Where's your mommy, sweetie-pie?" Rose asked Alexander.

"Seeping," the child grumbled, apparently still coaxing a small grudge.

"Sleeping? Maybe we need to roust her out of bed with some pancakes?"

Meryl sank deeper into her covers and closed her eyes. She counted the steps it took for Rose to arrive at her bedroom door, holding her breath the entire time. Fortunately, she walked right passed her own bedroom without stopping.

"Hey," Rose whispered gently doorway, "you awake?"

Meryl made the pretense of blinking and stretching. "Yeah."

"Sorry if I'm disturbing you..."

"You're not. I'm just being lazy. If I get up, it means I have to do something productive and I'm just not feeling it right now. You were out early this morning."

Rose's face brightened. "I went to the farmer's market and picked up fresh blueberries. Your young man tells me he is desirous of pancakes, so I figure blueberry pancakes will be that much better. Shall I make you some?"

"I can cook this morning if you like?" Meryl said.

"No, no. You relax. I'm on it. I'll holler when they're ready."

42

Rose vanished and a few moments later Meryl could hear the stove's gas burners crackling and the banging of metal skillets. She pulled the book out from underneath the pillow and felt a strange compulsion to crack it open again, but resisted long enough to creep down the hall and slip it back onto Rose's desk.

Just shortly before 5 p.m., Meryl pulled on her coat and prepared for her walk to THE ATTACK OF THE 50-FOOT ROBOT. She never worked evenings. In fact, Meryl couldn't remember a night when she'd been out past the boy's bedtime and the thought was filling her with a strange mixture of excitement and trepidation. But the store was holding a special midnight sales event and as the assistant manager it was important for her to be there. She paused at the door expectantly. Rose and Alexander were curled up together on the couch, absorbed in some nature documentary about baby animals and unaware of her angst.

"Well, I'm off," she said.

Alexander bounded over and hugged her around the knees, which helped lift her mood, at least momentarily. "Maw-mee, when coming home?"

"You'll be asleep when I get home, little man," she said, running her fingers through his soft, smooth hair. "But I'll come check on you, okay?"

"Kay."

"We'll be here all night," Rose reassured her, "so just call if you need to chat or anything."

Meryl nodded and left quickly, afraid that if she lingered she'd just end up staying. By the time she arrived at the comic book store, Cameron was already setting up for the sale, perched on top of a folding ladder and hanging signs from the ceiling tiles.

"Hey, boss with boobs," he said. "I didn't know you were working tonight. This may be a first."

"It is a first," David interjected as he appeared from the stock room carrying a large cardboard box stuffed with rolled T-shirts. "It's the first midnight sale where David gets to go home and be with his lovely wife instead of being here with not-so-lovely Cam."

"Dude, that's not cool," Cameron retorted.

David ignored him and smiled at Meryl. "Everything all set for tonight? Alexander's good?"

"He's good," Meryl answered, wondering if she sounded convincing. "Rose's watching him for me."

"I can go down and check in on them if you want?"

Meryl shook her head. "Thanks, but that would totally make me look like 'hysterical mom' and that's not who I wanna be. Besides, Rose taught elementary school for thirty years. I'm sure she can handle Alexander for a few hours."

"True enough," answered David. "And you're okay with handling tonight's festivities?"

"That's why I have all this awesome managerial power, right?"

"Right." He set the cardboard box on the floor. "Before I forget, all these shirts are overstock, so I need you guys to really push them out of inventory, okay?"

"I think we would sell a lot more if Meryl wore one that was about two sizes too small, maybe with a nice pair of shorty-shorts," Cameron suggested.

"Isn't that sexual harassment?" Meryl asked David.

"You want to file a complaint?" David grinned.

"Hey!" Cameron objected, "That is not sexual harassment. It's a tried-and-true marketing tool. Pretty girls in tight clothing having been selling crap to people since the ancient Greeks were around. Don't punish me because I'm trying to keep The ROBOT successful."

"I think maybe we should put the male employees in the tight T-shirts?" Meryl suggested.

Cameron balanced himself on the ladder and grabbed his paunchy belly with both hands, giving the folds of flesh a firm jiggle. "Yeah," he snorted, "I'm all kinds of sexy. The only thing this huge gut will sell is barf-bags."

By ten, the store had begun to fill with customers, most of them college students who were sacrificing that week's pizza and iced latte money to stock up on comic books and posters to decorate their dorm room walls. There was a smaller contingent of high-school and middle-school students: boys in woolen caps with their skateboards tucked under their arms; slender girls with heavy eye-liner who lingered over the Manga comics; ashen-faced young gamers who were taking a few hours away from online fantasy worlds to purchase all the related merchandise.

"Hey," Cameron whispered to Meryl as she worked the cash register, "are you with us tonight?"

"Huh?" she frowned.

"You seem miles away."

Meryl stiffened, realizing that her mind had been wandering back and forth between her conversation with Tess, the strange one-hundred year old book, and the residual apprehension that someone besides her was tucking in Alexander for the night. "Sorry," she chuckled, "So much for my promise not to be hysterical."

"Girl, you're a long ways off from hysterical. Just kinda distracted."

"Sorry."

"No worries, but the kid's four years old, Meryl. Cut the cord already," he joked.

"Shut up, dumb ass."

"Besides, he's in good hands. Rose is a righteous old girl, right?"

"Yeah..." her voice trailed off. Then she said suddenly, "You know why she came to Oregon? She told me that it was to seek her fortune."

"That's cool. She gonna grow weed or something?" Cameron asked.

"She didn't say exactly."

Cameron waited for more but was disappointed. Finally, he sneered, "Wow, what an outstanding story, boss lady. You should write novels or something."

"Don't I have the power to fire you?" she retorted.

"Go ahead and do it. I need this job like I need a second asshole."

"Cameron, you are definitely the equivalent of two assholes."

"Ooo. Burn. Now is there more to that story or what? I mean, is granny-panties about to knock over a bank or something?"

"I don't know what she's up too, actually. It's like one day she woke up, decided her life in Arizona wasn't working for her and drove to Oregon. She didn't know anyone or have a place to stay once she got here. You have to have some big plans in mind if you're going to take a risk like that."

"She's creeping you out?" he suggested.

"No. Really. She's not. I mean, she's a really nice person. Like insanely nice. I guess I'm just kinda fascinated about these mysterious plans of hers. Shit, that sounds so lame."

"You totally need a boyfriend."

Meryl rolled her eyes. "Gosh, Mom, no I don't."

"Yes, you do. Know how I know you need a boyfriend? Go ahead. Ask me how I know."

Meryl squeezed his hand, looked deeply into his eyes and with exaggerated ardor asked, "Cameron, can you please tell me how you know what's better for me than I do? Pretty, pretty please?"

"'Cause what you're describing is the need for a little excitement, a little wind blown up your skirt, something to get your panties in a twist. The biggest thrill in your life right now is giving Alexander his nightly bath. You're in some desperate need of crazy, mindless fun and adventure."

"That's why I have you, Cam. Every moment I spend with you is chock full of fun."

He shrugged and sighed loudly. The gesture was only partly for effect. Both of them knew he was right. "While I am an indescribably awesome person, it's not the same and you know it."

"Let's change the subject, okay?"

He slumped over and lightly banged his head against the countertop.

"Don't damage your brain," Meryl said. "You can't afford it."

Cameron was about to deliver a scathing rejoinder when he paused, distracted by something at the back of the crowded store.

"What?" Meryl demanded.

He whispered, "You see the dude two rows over, next to the T-shirt display? The skinny guy in the black hoody? Check him, he's totally digging on you."

Meryl glanced up. A college boy was staring back at her. He had a long, narrow face with a rounded chin and thin lips. He wore his curly auburn hair long, shaggy and brushed forward so it completely covered his forehead with a few wisps falling into his eyes. Meryl had to wonder if he kept it long partially to disguise his big ears. Other than the hair, however, he was unusually well-groomed for a college boy, dressed in a clean, wrinkle-free pair of blue jeans, a green shirt and the black hoody which had the Oregon State University symbol embroidered on the right breast. He smiled and Meryl quickly looked away, suddenly and curiously embarrassed.

"I don't think he's looking at me," she mumbled to Cameron. "I think he's looking at the asshole who's beating his head against the counter."

"That's a dirty lie. Go talk to him," Cameron urged. "He looks like he needs help choosing the right apparel."

Her face flushed. "You're interrupting my story. I'm trying to tell you about Rose."

"You would rather tell me about the old bag of dust you live with than go talk to the walking, talking pinup loitering in aisle two? What the hell's wrong with you?"

"He's cute, but he's hardly pinup material."

"Are you kidding me?" Cameron said, deliberately raising the volume of his voice. "He's very pretty. If I were a different kind of guy, I'd help him try on T-shirts myself."

Meryl ignored him. "So what kind of fortune do you think a sixty-year old woman would be seeking in the middle of Oregon?"

"Don't know, don't care. The only sixty-year old woman I know is my mother and the only thing she seeks is lemony-fresh laundry. Why don't you just ask her if you're so insanely curious?"

Meryl shrugged. "I guess that seems too pushy, like I'm getting too personal with her."

"Babe, the old lady's watching your kid. That's pretty personal."

"True."

"Okay, so just be friendly about it. People always want to talk about their big plans. Maybe she's some kind of business guru or something?"

"I don't think so. She seems to be doing a bunch of research. Her room's filled with all these papers and maps."

"Maybe she's writing a book?"

"Could be, I guess. But why would you need to come to Oregon to do that?"

"Oh, he's looking again!" Cameron whispered, glancing back over her shoulder at the boy in the black hoodie. "My god, he is sooooo pretty."

Meryl resisted the inclination to look and asked urgently, "What do you think these numbers mean?" She snatched a pen and discarded receipt off the countertop and perfectly reproduced the two lines of numbers and symbols she'd found written on the adhesive note inside Rose's copy of *The American Boy's Adventure Reader.*

Cameron frowned and said, "A combination maybe? I bet she's gonna rob a bank!"

"Those look like coordinates," another voice offered. The young man from aisle two had sidled up to the counter and quietly laid a small stack of merchandise near Meryl's hand. He smiled at her again. His mouth was long and filled with rows of perfect white teeth. The type of teeth you get only from years of expensive orthodontia and professional whitening services, Meryl thought to herself. She immediately felt bad for being so negative, blushed and tried to look disinterested.

"What's that?" Cameron asked quickly, eagerly.

"Geographic coordinates," the young man repeated. "You know, latitude and longitude. The first set of numbers is the latitude, or the distance of a place from north to south, divided into degrees, minutes and seconds. The second set is the longitude, or the distance from east to west."

"That's soooo awesome," Cameron replied. "Are you some kind of brainiac or something?"

"No," the young man chortled, clearly either missing Cameron's sarcasm or being too polite to acknowledge it. "I do geocaching so I'm really familiar with finding coordinates."

"Geocaching? What's that?" Cameron asked, placing his chin on his knuckles and fluttering his eyelashes. Meryl, still mute, felt compelled to kick Cameron gently on the ankle.

"It's kind of an online treasure hunt using the global positioning system," he replied, his gaze still fixed on Meryl. "People hide different objects in public places and then post the GPS coordinates online. Other people go and find what's hidden. It's like a big game."

"Wow," Cameron said with feigned awe, "that's way too smarty-smart for me. But, you know, my friend Meryl here is very interested in learning new things related to geography and coordinates and stuff to do online that have nothing to do with pornography. Please enlighten her." And with that, he mock-hobbled away and left the two of them staring wordlessly at each other.

Meryl swallowed hard and forced herself to speak. "Sorry. He's a jackass."

The boy shrugged, and this time his disregard for Cameron's behavior was clearly an act of courtesy. "Not a problem, but I'm glad he left," he smiled sheepishly.

"Most people feel that way about him."

"Lemme see your note there," he offered, pointing to the discarded receipt.

Meryl slid the scrap of paper across to him and watched with amusement as he studied it intently. With his head tipped forward, she was able to quietly examine his face. Under the bright fluorescent lights, his hair clearly had streaks of blond in it, the result of sun-bleaching. A band of freckles ran from the ridge of his nose, across his high cheekbones to his short sideburns, but they were almost imperceivable beneath what was clearly a deep but fading tan.

No way he's a native, Meryl told herself. No one in Oregon has a tan like that.

Then she asked meekly: "So... in geocaching, do people hide anything... valuable?"

The young man shrugged. "Usually it's just crap. The fun's in the search." The corners of his green eyes crinkled. "Pretty nerdy, huh?"

"It's a little nerdy," Meryl agreed, laughing, "but then again you're hanging out in a comic book store on a Saturday night so you're already covered in nerd stink."

He turned his face slightly to the left and Meryl realized he was blushing. He quickly composed himself and retorted, "Now what about you? You work in a comic book store. What's that make you if not a nerd?"

"Desperate for money and friends with the owner."

His laughter was quick and sharp-sounding. "So it's nepotism, not nerd-ism?"

"Pretty much. I'm actually a pretty poor excuse for a nerd." She leaned closer to him and whispered, "I don't know shit about comic books."

He smiled like she'd just told him her deepest, darkest secret. In fact, her appalling lack of knowledge about The ROBOT's stock was well-known, but David kidded her that she made up for it by being exceptional at filling out the day sheets, scheduling staff and processing invoices.

"So I trust you won't hold my more nerdy qualities against me?" the boy asked.

Meryl took a long pause, like she was really considering it, then answered, "If you help me figure out what these coordinates lead to, I'll overlook it."

"That sounds fair."

Meryl's cell phone began to ring in her pocket. She reluctantly excused herself and answered it.

"Maw-mee, me going sweep now," Alexander said on the other end.

"Are you, sweetie?" she replied. "Did you have fun with Rose tonight?"

"Yes uh-buh me sweepy."

"Okay, I'll be home in a little while and then I will check on you."

"Kay. Night, maw-mee."

"Good night, little man."

Rose's voice interjected. "Everything's fine here. How's the sale going?"

"Busy," Meryl replied, glancing up at the young man who was now absently browsing through a tray of bumper stickers.

"Then we won't keep you. By the way, we made a blanket fort in the living room so don't be surprised when you get home."

"Sounds like fun."

"Yeah, it was. If you guys are interested, don't you think it would be fun to take few road trips or go camping? You know, use a tent that isn't made out of blankets? I feel like I haven't seen much of Oregon at all."

"Sure. I'd love that."

"Okay. I'll talk to you about it later. Good luck with the sale."

"Thanks." She hung up, turned back to the young man and apologized.

"Not a problem," he said. "You have a kid?"

Meryl felt a lump growing in her throat. Historically, this was the point where her pleasant conversations with attractive members of the opposite sex would come to a screeching halt. She knew she shouldn't feel defensive about that question, but her shoulders tightened anyway.

"Yes," she replied. "My son, Alexander. He's four."

"Cool." He seemed sincere. "I have a little brother who just turned four."

"You do?" she gawked.

"I know. He was a bit of a surprise to Mom and Dad. Nothing like being sixteen years older than your sibling, right?"

"I guess you won't be sharing any hand-me-downs with him."

"Heh, heh, not likely. But he's great. The shitty part is I'm attending school here and he's living back in San Diego so I don't get to see him very often."

Ah, San Diego, Meryl smiled with satisfaction. That explained the tan.

"Yeah. I'm Meryl, by the way."

He brightened. "Ike," he said, grasping her hand and shaking it gently. Meryl noticed his palms were sweaty. "So, do you want me to plot these coordinates for you? I could come back tomorrow and let you know where they land."

The lump in her throat was gone. "Sure," she replied. "That would be great. Now, can I interest you in a collectible nerd T-shirt?"

CHAPTER FIVE

Just before noon, Ike materialized in the doorway of The
ROBOT. He was dressed in a white linen shirt, tan slacks with sharp
creases running down the front of each leg and had a backpack slung
over his right shoulder. Around his neck, which Meryl noted was
longer and more elegant-looking than most mens', he wore a curious
fishhook-shaped pendant on a braided fiber cord. He'd clearly spent
some time taming his shaggy hair as she could now confirm he had
eyebrows. His face was freshly shaved and, most important of all, he
smelled good. Although Ike's efforts lacked any kind of subtly, Meryl
had to indulge in a private smile. It had been a really long time since a
guy had tried to impress her and she was enjoying every second of it.

"Hey!" he waved from the doorway. "This a good time?"

"Absolutely," she beamed, immediately worrying that she
sounded too enthusiastic. She gestured him over. "Did you just come
from class?"

"Yeah, I have a two hour break and then I go back for my
statistics class."

"You never told me what you're studying," she said.

"Computer engineering," he grinned. Meryl raised her eyebrows.
"I know, it explains a lot huh? First this guy's playing some weird
treasure hunting game, and now you discover he's really into
computers, too."

It felt as though his self-deprecating attitude was rehearsed, but Meryl found it charming nonetheless. She imagined Ike was, by nature, awkward around girls and compensated through preparation, considering each word and gesture as carefully as he planned out his wardrobe choices. "It's a good choice," she said. "I don't own a computer but in theory I'm in favor of them."

"What? How do you not own a computer in this day and age?"

"Well, crushing poverty helps."

"Oh. My bad. Sorry."

She touched his arm conciliatory and immediately felt self-conscious about it. "Don't be," she stammered. "It's all good and I survive just fine. Besides, any extra money I have right now is going into the bank so I can start classes next term."

"That's awesome."

"And once you graduate, then what?" *Oh god*, she blanched, *did I just ask him what his future plans are? I sound like such a parent.*

Ike took a deep breath and ground his teeth. "I know this will probably terrify you, but I want to design video games. Which explains partly why I hang out in comic book stores, I guess."

She nodded. "What kind of video games?"

"Well, being a dude, I'm kind of pre-programmed to design really graphic, violent ones. You know, the type our parents blame all of society's ills on."

"So plenty of heads exploding and such?"

"You got it. My games will just hemorrhage all over the players. Is that totally repulsive or what?"

"You know that I work in a comic book store, right? Most of the merchandise in this place drips blood on your shoes."

"You don't like that?"

"Well, being a girl, I'm kind of pre-programmed that way. But, I've gotten used to it."

Ike was just about to reply when David appeared from the back room, carrying a handful of rolled quarters. The older man pretended not to notice the abrupt halt in their conversation and simply offered a cheery "Good afternoon!" as he placed the quarters in the cash register.

"Hey," Ike replied politely.

Meryl stood awkwardly and waited.

"Do you want to take your lunch break?" David asked her, as nonchalantly as he could muster.

Meryl felt a surge of panic. David was not a stupid man. She knew he had said that on purpose, perhaps even timed his appearance after he'd spent a few moments listening to their conversation. "Ummmm," she stammered, "okay." She looked at Ike and asked, "Have you eaten?"

"I could definitely eat," he replied.

Her panic faded. She grabbed her purse and they headed toward the Willamette River and then north along the river walk. They ended up at a small sandwich shop where she ordered a ridiculously small salad and a short iced coffee, which Ike insisted on paying for. She picked at the greens with her plastic fork and regretted her earlier comment about living in "crushing poverty." It wasn't true of course, especially since Rose had moved in and assumed half the expenses which she always paid promptly and in cash. The truth was Meryl had more money in the bank now than she ever had and she hoped Ike wasn't feeling sorry for her. She couldn't stand it if he was.

Ike noticed the way she was turning the lettuce leafs almost with disdain. "Do you want something else?" he asked.

"Huh?"

"It's like you're on a starvation diet there," he laughed. "Have some protein."

"Oh, no," she answered firmly, "I just don't have a huge appetite. You should really let me pay for my own lunch, though."

He shook his head, just as firmly. "Don't worry about it. It's my pleasure."

A long moment passed with nothing said, then Meryl asked about the pendant around his neck.

Ike immediately touched the fishhook, stroking its curved barb with his fingertips. "It's Hawaiian," he said. "My parents took us there on vacation several years ago. This little old lady was selling them down by the beach so my mom bought one for me and one for my brother. The old lady made them out of bone so they looked just like the fishhooks used by ancient Hawaiians. She blessed them for us and told us that we needed to keep them in a special place when we weren't wearing them."

"And where's your special place?"

"A box my brother made for me in preschool."

"Nice."

Ike shrugged. "Well, you know the types of crafts preschoolers make. Too much glitter and elbow macaroni, but I still think it's awesome."

Meryl thought about the myriad of artwork decorated with glitter and hard pasta all over her apartment and then replied, "That's a funny coincidence. When I finally get to OSU, I plan to major in marine biology and move to Hawaii."

"Ever been there?" he asked.

She shook her head. "I've never been anywhere."

He looked skeptical. "Really? Not even on family vacations?"

"My parents were kind of homebodies. Their idea of vacation was filling up the inflatable pool in the back yard. Actually, when I moved from Portland to Corvallis it was a major, major deal for me."

"And your family still lives in Portland?"

"My mother does. My dad died several years ago."

Ike surprised her by not acknowledging her father's death. She was used to people suddenly looking away, even apologizing to her as though they were somehow responsible for the massive heart attack that had killed her father on a downtown sidewalk. Instead, Ike asked if she had any brothers or sisters.

"Nope. It's just me."

"That's cool," he replied. "You see your mom much?"

"No."

He nodded and didn't probe further. She could tell by the crinkle running across his brow that he was searching for a new topic of conversation. "Oh, hey," he said suddenly, "I mapped those coordinates for you." He opened the front pocket of his backpack and pulled out a folded sheet of paper.

"That's awesome. Where'd they end up?"

He smoothed down the paper on the tabletop and answered, "Nowhere. They ended up in the middle of nowhere."

She inspected the printout. Ike had drawn a tiny black "X" in the middle of a patchwork greens, blues and browns. "Is this a forest?" she asked.

"Yup. Your coordinates are right smack in the middle of a national forest. These are the mountains" — he lightly drew a finger along the paper to indicate the position of the different landmarks — "rivers, the valley, and of course, the ocean."

"So these coordinates are close to... What?"

"That's what I mean. These coordinates aren't close to anything. There's not even a road nearby."

"That's so weird."

"Can I ask where these numbers came from?"

She blushed. "I'm embarrassed to tell you, but my roommate's doing some kind of research and she had these numbers written down. But just so you don't think I'm completely nosy, I wasn't trying to memorize them. My brain just kinda works that way."

"Do you have a photographic memory?" he smiled.

"For some things, I guess. I see certain details, patterns and numbers — and they just stick. I'm really good with puzzles. Sudoku is my bitch."

"Okay, I'm going to test you."

"Ah, c'mon..." she protested.

Ike grinned mischievously and insisted. "Close your eyes."

"Okay. They're closed."

"What color shirt am I wearing?"

"Easy. White."

"And my pants?"

"Tan slacks. Which you ironed this morning, by the way."

"Shoes?"

"Black. Skechers, I think."

"Nikes, actually."

"Dammit."

"Socks?"

"How the hell would I know what color socks you're wearing?"

"You're supposed to have a good eye for details, so tell me what color of socks."

She paused briefly to think, then replied, "Tan. Poly-blend."

He laughed. "You nailed it. How the heck did you know that?"

She opened her eyes and said, "That was a total guess. You're a really tidy guy, so I figured you'd match the socks to either the pants or the shoes. I had a fifty-fifty chance of guessing it right."

"You should be a detective."

"My dad used to say that too. He told me that he and my mom never bothered lying to me about Santa Claus because they knew I'd figure it out anyway. But when I get to the university, I think I'll stick with marine biology."

"It's the same thing," he said. "I mean, it's all about observing and understanding behavior, whether it's human or animal. A biologist

59

may try to figure out why animals do what they do, and a detective does the same with people."

Meryl smiled. "Wow, you just blew my mind."

"You're teasing me," Ike blushed.

"No, I'm not. Seriously. That was very insightful. I'd honestly never thought of it that way." Meryl suddenly found that she couldn't hold his gaze. She looked down at her lap.

"Sorry I couldn't clear up the mystery for you," Ike sighed after a few awkward seconds.

"What?"

"The coordinates. Sorry I couldn't tell you more about them. I even pulled up some topographical maps of the area, but it's pretty much the forest primeval out there."

That term caused Meryl to stiffen. *"The forest primeval?"* she asked.

"Yeah. Literally the middle of nothing."

CHAPTER SIX

On her next day off from work, Meryl found herself standing at the doorway to Rose's bedroom. She acknowledged that she was taking the coward's way out, ignoring Cameron's advice to ask Rose directly about the growing accumulation of maps, charts, books and hand-scratched notes which now nearly hid her desk and laptop from view. It wasn't paranoia which had led Meryl to stand motionless in the doorway. She certainly didn't think that Rose was up to something criminal, it was just that she was up to, well, *something*. And somehow, so she told herself, if she just stood in the doorway and looked, her curiosity wasn't intrusive. Cowardly, but not intrusive.

The computer screen-saver beckoned to her with floating images of the South Pacific. A forested atoll melted into a spiny starfish, melted into a ruby-colored sunset, melted into the elegant curl of a breaking wave. Next to the monitor, Meryl noticed the now-familiar tattered edge of *The American Boy's Adventure Reader*. Even as the strange clutter in Rose's room shifted daily, the book never left its place next to the computer. Its position there seemed significant, maybe even reverential. Meryl turned and looked toward her own room. She could see parts of Alexander sticking out of the tousled bedsheets, his hair glinting like tarnished bronze in the sunshine, his small shoulders rising and falling slowly as he slept. Nap time was her only chance to investigate, to violate her own rule without Alexander catching on.

She stepped across the threshold.

I'll just read the story I started the other day, she told herself, carefully pulling the old book clear of the jumble without dislodging anything else. The pages immediately fell open to the chapter's beginning:

The Cursed Gold Mine

In the deep forest primeval of Oregon, there lies a gold mine forgotten by all of Mankind. None will venture there and even the Red Man will refuse to approach its crumbling portal. Some say the mine is cursed, for many a brave adventurer, seeking his Fortune without regard to the perils of the wilderness, has laid down his life in the pursuit of its riches.

The mine lies in the dark shadow of a rocky peak, not far from the banks of a roiling stream. Many years ago, two prospectors named Mr. Sykes and Mr. Bittle established a claim here after panning for gold in the nearby creeks and enjoying much success. Mr. Sykes and Mr. Bittle understood from years of wandering the forests of the American frontier that rivers filled with gold ore often meant great treasure lay hidden in the surrounding hills, waiting to be excavated by shovel and pick ax. With their claim papers in hand, Mr. Sykes and Mr. Bittle hired trustworthy and hearty men to help dig out the tunnels and passageways of their mine. Mr. Bittle was a stern but fair foreman who ensured that every man worked hard and was justly rewarded. Under his watchful eye, the mine was transformed into a small but profitable enterprise. In his turn, Mr. Sykes and a few of his most trusted men handled the business of transporting the gold to the coast, where it would be placed on steamers and sent to the mints in California. Every few weeks, the friends would look forward to loading bags filled with gold-rich ore onto the horses for the journey west.

At the start of one such sojourn, Mr. Sykes clapped his dear friend on the shoulder and promised a quick return. "I shall travel as swiftly as the rain and the mud will allow," he said with a hearty laugh.

Mr. Bittle responded in kind. "O I am not anxious! The hills are full of gold and the men are both strong and honest. With each trip, dear Friend, we all become rich men indeed!"

But the march through the forest was long and dangerous. There were no roads, not even the most primitive of mountain trails used by the Red Man. Mr. Sykes and the men who accompanied him had to battle not only the rugged and unforgiving landscape, but constantly guard against attack by Indians and forest beasts of all description. It took weeks for the party to reach the coast, sell their gold, buy provisions and start their long journey back into the wilderness.

Upon his return to the mine, Mr. Sykes found the camp vandalized and eerily quiet. There was no sign of human activity — not the clank of metal against rock, nor the rumble of ore carts as they were pushed along their rails. When he had departed weeks earlier, Mr. Bittle and a dozen men were busily tunneling into the nearby hills. But now every soul had vanished! At first, Mr. Sykes imagined that his men had fallen victim to the Savages who wandered the hills and valleys, but there were no arrows nor spears nor other gruesome indications his men had been massacred. Mr. Sykes searched for any trace of the missing men, but the rain and wind had long erased all prints and what remained of the camp had been ransacked by wild animals.

When next the frightened men climbed the hillside to the gold mine, they found it was also abandoned but otherwise intact. Inside the mouth of the mine were the remains of a barricade, hastily built and violently destroyed. Nearby they discovered the shattered rifles and spent cartridges of some futile battle. But a battle against whom? Perhaps it was Indians after all? Or bandits? Or something else entirely?

"They have all been killed! Murdered!" one of Mr. Sykes's companions insisted. He was a stout man with a heavy beard and not the sort who would frighten easily. But Mr. Sykes could see fear burning in his dark eyes.

"No!" insisted another, a thin man who tended the pack horses. "They must have run away! Had they perished here, surely we would have found their pitiful bones!"

The third man offered a different opinion. "They were spirited away! See how their barricade was smashed from the outside? Someone broke through and overpowered them, then kidnapped them all! Certainly this is the work of Savages!"

The men erupted into a fierce argument fueled by their great and sudden dread of the forest. Mr. Sykes held up a hand and they quieted themselves. "Silence now," he commanded. "When the morning comes, we will continue our search and resolve this great mystery, but for now, we must prepare for the coming night. Repair the barricades and stoke a fire! Load the rifles and bring the horses and supplies to the top of the hill! Tonight we sleep in the mine!"

As darkness fell, Mr. Sykes and his compatriots sat guard around a roaring campfire at the mouth of the mine with rifles slung across their laps. All around them, the wilderness seemed particularly forbidding. As the night progressed, the campfire dwindled to embers but no one dared to venture out to gather more wood. Instead, Mr. Sykes left one man alert to guard the others as he searched the mine tunnels for scraps of wood. He lit a lantern and stumbled through the narrow passageways, gathering up anything he could burn. Presently, the horses, which had been tethered at the mouth of the mine, began to whinny and cry in a most unnatural way. This was quickly followed by several gunshots and the panicked shouts of his three compatriots. Mr. Sykes dropped the tinder he had gathered and wielded his rifle before him. He ran as quickly as the narrow tunnels would allow as the din grew louder and louder — and then suddenly ceased! By the time he returned to the mouth of the mine, the barricade again lay in ruins and his compatriots were gone. Vanished as though by an act of sinister magic.

Confronted by the apparent tragedy, appalled by a fearful mystery, Mr. Sykes could do nothing but cower in the mine, his rifle poised and his finger on the trigger. But what to shoot? The darkness provided no answers.

At dawn's first light, it became clear that some unseen and malevolent force was at work! Fearing for his very life, Mr. Sykes mounted the fastest horse, abandoning the rest, along with his mine and his Fortune. His flight from the wilderness took many days and when he arrived at a small coastal village he was a disheveled and pathetic sight. The townsfolk took pity upon him and called for a doctor. Despite the physician's care, no one could calm Mr. Sykes's panicked nerves nor comprehend his strange story.

Mr. Bittle and the other miners were never seen again, and over time the people who were familiar with this strange tale assumed they had fallen victim to *either unforgiving Nature or blood-thirsty Savages. Some suspected Mr. Sykes had murdered them all for his love of gold, but he never returned to his claim nor revealed the location of his accursed mine. His heart filled with grief, Mr. Sykes bought passage aboard a steamer and left Oregon forever.*

True believers, whether they be hungry for Gold or Glory, or simply foolhardy in their love for adventure, insist that the cursed mine still awaits discovery somewhere in the shadows of the mountain peaks. By now, its entrance has surely been reclaimed by the forest and would be near impossible to detect. Inside, a fortune in gold awaits those strong and fearless enough to extract it. But if you go, be warned — for the forest holds many mysteries and great dangers!

Meryl rolled the book around in her hands, reading Rose's numerous sticky-notes and the childish doodles which decorated the margins and were particularly profuse around the gold mine story. Inside the cover, written in the same immature hand, was the name of the book's original owner: *Elijah Robert Comstock, Newport, Oregon, Age 11.* On top of this Rose had placed a note which simply read: "Frostwood Lane, Benton County" but this street was unfamiliar to Meryl. Another note had the word "Newport" written on it, surrounded by dozens of question marks.

She carefully slid the book back into its spot on the messy desktop and glanced at the laptop. Almost every morning she heard the soft *ticka-ticka-ticka* of the keyboard echoing through the wall between their bedrooms. Immediately after, Rose would disappear for hours, then reappear in the late afternoon without explanation. Meryl lightly brushed the touch-pad and clicked to view the browser history. A long search-string filled the monitor, containing phrases like "gold prospecting," "Oregon gold mines," "rivers" and "national forest." So what Rose had said that night they had sat together at the kitchen table was true — she had come to Oregon to seek her fortune. But Meryl never imagined Rose meant it so literally. Gold prospecting seemed like a vestige from another, long forgotten time and Meryl was embarrassed for the old woman. What could Rose possibly be thinking? After all, she was an educated and intelligent woman and it wasn't the nineteenth century anymore where anyone with a mule and a pickax could stake a claim in the uncharted Oregon wilderness. Even if the mine in the story was based on a real place, surely there were laws preventing people from going into national forests and carting out gold ore on a whim?

Meryl swiveled slightly in her chair and surveyed the rest of the room. Her eyes lingered on the nearby bookshelves now so packed with mementoes. Two shelves seemed dedicated to Rose's teaching days and included a tiny archive of student photos, notes written on sloppily folded construction paper and garish crayon renderings. Another was stacked with books about Oregon's history and geography, many marked with the telltale sticky notes. The next was neatly lined with small framed photographs of Rose, in every case standing in front of some great monument or natural wonder. Alone. No friends, no children, not even that ex-husband she sometimes spoke of so acerbically. The shelf below the photographs held a large champagne glass from a Nevada casino half filled with commemorative plastic poker chips and strands of glass beads. Around its base was a collection of shot glasses, each inscribed with the name of a different casino in a half-dozen different states all over the country. At the back of the shelf and partially concealed by shadow was a small wooden box shaped like a pirate's chest.

No doubt containing Blackbeard's treasure, Meryl thought with an involuntary snort.

If she allowed herself the conceit, Meryl could spend hours snooping through Rose's room, inventing some mysterious significance for every object she found. But the truth of her roommate's past seemed both obvious and ordinary: Rose liked to gamble. And it was likely her search for a lost gold mine was just another gamble in a string of get-rich-quick-schemes from someone unsatisfied with a teacher's pension. That revelation made Meryl both pity Rose and feel ashamed of her trespassing. If she had discovered anything with her snooping, it wasn't that Rose had dark secrets, but rather that she suffered from a great frailty.

As she rose to leave, her knee bumped against something underneath the desk. There was a loud rattle and then a *whump* as two cardboard boxes tumbled forward and partially spilled their contents over her feet.

"Shit!" she growled, quickly pulling the desk chair back and getting down on her hands and knees. They were packing boxes, similar to those Rose had stuffed into her car when she first arrived but clearly much older. One had a large water stain on the outside and both had warped lids like they'd sat out in the elements at one point. They were labeled in faded black marker — reading TOSS OUT and CHARITY respectively — but the handwriting was not Rose's precise, teacherly script. Meryl righted the bottom box, noticing it was filled with sheaves of papers before replacing the lid. The upper box wasn't as full and contained what appeared to be a man's personal effects. Since the only man Rose had ever mentioned was her cheating ex-husband, Meryl assumed the belongings must be his. But with closer inspection that seemed unlikely. Among the clutter were Oregon road maps dated to the 1940s and 50s, a broken compass, a dog-eared wilderness gazette, a worn leather wallet, the mileage log to a 1963 Oldsmobile, and a pocket knife so dull and rusted it must've seen decades of hard use before it found its way into the carton.

"Mah-mee, wad do in Robe's rube?"

Alexander's small voice so startled her than Meryl fumbled the box and scattered its contents a second time. "Dammit, Alexander!" she snapped.

The boy looked confused. "I wote up," he said, then added with conviction: "Not uppose ta be in Rode's room witout pamission."

Meryl sat there for a moment, unsure if she should feel like a scoundrel or a hypocrite. She interrupted her discomfort by quickly scooping the items back into the box, stacking it and pushing the chair back into place.

"Okay," she said, "let's get out of Rose's room." But even as she said this and scooted Alexander down the hallway, she was aware he had stood obediently in the hallway the entire time.

"Not uppose ta be in Rode's room witout pamission," he repeated.

Meryl was suddenly relieved that his speech was often unintelligible, just in case he said something when Rose got home. She couldn't ask him to lie about what he had seen, and doing so would only confuse him more. Instead, it was Meryl who lied: "I was just cleaning up."

Alexander didn't respond, and Meryl wasn't sure if he didn't believe her or just didn't care. She ushered him back down to their bedroom and he crawled groggily back under his furry blanket and fell asleep. She wondered if Rose ever stood at their doorway, analyzing it for clues to their past. Granted, there wasn't much to analyze. Compared to Rose's loaded shelves and cluttered walls, her's and Alexander's space was almost spartan.

Like anyone, Meryl had her collection of mementos — the photos, trinkets and bobbles everyone collects over a lifetime — but for reasons she didn't spend too much time scrutinizing, most of them were still packed away in boxes she hadn't touched since leaving Portland. Boxes and more boxes. Maybe boxes were how human beings organized time, made it manageable and gave it meaning, she thought. What you packed was important. What you unpacked was valuable. What you left packed was painful. She moved quietly across the room and slid the closet door aside. Toward the back, partially hidden behind her clothing, were her boxes. She carefully lifted one out of the pile and broke the tape seal. Inside were the remnants of a life which now seemed exceedingly distant.

As she quietly sorted through the contents, she felt glad Alexander had been too young to really remember their life before what David, Rachel and Tess all referred to as "The Great Escape." One day far in the future, when he could understand it better, she'd explain it all to him. But for now, she kept it hidden inside cardboard boxes.

She set aside a stack of high school yearbooks and the pile of notes she and Tess had always exchanged during Language Art class. Underneath a smiling face stared up at her behind a cracked pane of glass. She hesitantly lifted the frame, dislodging a large splinter of glass which hit the bottom of the box with a *thunk*. The sound startled her, but perhaps not as much as the photo itself.

A handsome boy with a bad complexion studied at her with dark blue eyes. His face was perfectly faceted, like a stonecutter had carefully shaped it from a block of marble. Dark, stringy hair hung over his wide, spotty forehead in limp tendrils. He had prominent cheekbones, a strong jawline and a long mouth with thin lips. His smile was lopsided, more of an insolent smirk. It was perhaps the kind of smile a man might use to get things he didn't really deserve. A smile that could melt hearts and beguile minds if you let it.

She suddenly remembered why she hadn't touched these boxes in over a year and quickly repacked everything.

For the remainder of the day, Meryl kept herself so occupied with meaningless activity she eventually forgot all about *The American Boy's Adventure Reader*, the old boxes filled with men's belongings under Rose's desk, and the mocking portrait hidden at the back of her closet. At dusk, she and Alexander walked down to the public library for a toddler's storytelling hour. They returned to find that Rose had made a big pot of spaghetti with homemade meatballs. This was followed by television together and Meryl finally crawled into bed around 11 p.m.

to the sound of rain thrumming against the basement windows. She closed her eyes just as her cell phone buzzed on the nightstand. Reluctantly she read the screen:

TESS: TOM CAME BACK.

Meryl didn't sleep a wink.

CHAPTER SEVEN

When Meryl told Ike she hadn't been anywhere outside of Portland, it wasn't an exaggeration. For the majority of her life, her lack of contact with the world outside of the city limits hadn't mattered much. Portland was, especially for a young girl, its own world with enough adventure to fill a lifetime. That changed the morning Meryl woke up, looked around the bedroom she'd grown up in, and found everything to be persistently unsatisfactory. Not just unsatisfying, but *persistently unsatisfactory*. There was a difference she found, and it was a profound one.

She explained it to Tess like someone eating a meal: "A person can have an unsatisfying meal in their favorite restaurant but still return to enjoy that restaurant over and over again. Unsatisfying can be a one time thing, a fluke. *Persistently unsatisfactory* is more like eating every meal in a very bad restaurant with a rude waitress, finding a booger stuck to your fork and realizing you have no other options."

So that morning, Meryl lay in bed for a long time, stared at the ceiling, listened to the little fussing noises Alexander made in his sleep and decided that persistently unsatisfactory was no longer something she — no, *they* — could accept. Right afterwards she sent David and Tess the same text message which consisted of two words: PLEASE COME.

The next morning, half an hour after her mother had left for work, Tess was at the front door, holding a bundle of cardboard boxes and spools of packing tape with tears streaming down her face. Meryl had rehearsed the "Great Escape" so many times in her head that it took her and Tess less than an hour to pack everything she wanted to take, bundle up Alexander in his jacket and wool cap, and position themselves on the front porch just as David and Rachel pulled up in their big blue SUV. She didn't remember anything more about leaving the house she'd grown up in, the house which had turned into a hollow and hostile place ever since her father had died. She didn't even look back as they drove off into the gray, rainy morning.

The distance from Portland to Corvallis was less than a hundred miles, but for a girl who hadn't been anywhere it might as well have been on the other side of the planet. Even through the rain-streaked and foggy windows, Meryl's first glimpse of open road was thrilling. The sight of orchards with neat rows of trees and sprawling farms with ramshackle barns partially hidden behind wandering banks of rain was almost ethereal. She barely said a thing the entire trip, just pressed her face to the window and watched the world unfold in front of her. Only the chirping of her cell phone broke her dream. It was Tess.

MERYL: MISSING ME ALREADY????

TESS: HELLS YA!!! SURPRISED UR PHONE'S STILL WORKING.

MERYL: HAHA TEXT FAST. ONCE MOM FINDS OUT IM GONE THE SERVICE WILL BE CUT OFF. U CAN CALL ME ON DAVIDS PHONE THO.

TESS: LOVE, U SURE THIS IS THE RIGHT THING TO DO?

MERYL: TOO LATE NOW, BUT YES. IT IS

TESS: UR MOM WILL NEVER SPEAK TO U AGAIN

MERYL: SHE DOESNT SPEAK TO ME NOW

TESS: WILL SHE KNOW WHO U WENT TO LIVE WITH?

MERYL: YEA BUT ITS ALL GOOD. SHE HATES THEM SO SHE WONT COME AROUND.

TESS: WHY???

Meryl really couldn't explain her mother's strong aversion for David and Rachel — whom she typically referred to as "your father's friends." Perhaps it was enough that David had known her dad since childhood and enjoyed a friendship with him that wasn't based on the twisted sense of ownership her mother always mistook for affection. Although she didn't know this for a fact, Meryl assumed that David had opposed her parents' marriage. Certainly he was uncomfortable that her mother saw the world in a very proprietary way, and felt herself uniquely qualified to run every life that intersected with her own. Maybe he had watched in silence as his boyhood friend had slowly been beaten down until, one day while returning from his lunch hour, he dropped onto the sidewalk and just died? Almost immediately after, her mother forbade Meryl from having any contact with David and Rachel. No reason was given and no dissent was allowed.

But all of this was too convoluted to put in a text message, so Meryl just replied to Tess with: IDK. CUZ SHE'S CRAZY.

TESS: U TELL TOM?

MERYL: YEA, LAST NITE

TESS: AND????

MERYL: NOT MUCH REACTION AS USUAL.

TESS: WAT IF HE WANTS TO SEE ALEX?

MERYL: HE NEVER DROVE 10 BLOCKS TO SEE HIM SO NOT WORRIED ABOUT IT.

There was a long pause until the next message arrived, which Meryl interpreted as Tess collecting herself. GOD MISSING U SO MUCH ALREADY HUN.

Meryl felt her own anguish rising in her chest, like a bubble passing through murky water, but she didn't allow it to come out. She had kept her grief at bay by focusing more on her anger and the purposefulness it created. She replied: U WILL HEAR FROM ME!!!

TESS: WONT BE THE SAME

MERYL: TESS, THINGS HAVENT BEEN THE SAME IN A LONG LONG TIME.

The memory of her mother and that rainy day when she escaped from Portland to Corvallis were at the top of Meryl's mind as she stood on the crest of sand dune and looked out at the gray Pacific Ocean. Alexander had squatted down at the base of the dune and was digging holes with a piece of driftwood. Rose had wandered some distance down the beach to snap photographs of a collection of Herring gulls who were scampering in and out of the surf. And for a moment, Meryl felt both alone and happy. A ship's horn sounded and she glanced back at the interlocking iron arches of the Yaquina Bay bridge and the quaint white lighthouse which stood on the hillside above her. She could now honestly say that she'd been *two places* outside of Portland and it felt like progress. But Rose had promised much more for their day together, having mapped out an ambitious road-trip which would take them north along the winding Pacific Coast Highway toward Astoria, with multiple stops along the way to enjoy the rocky beaches, cliff-top vistas and lush river valleys.

"Smell that air?" Rose called as she trudged back through the grassy drifts of sand. "Does it not just rejuvenate your soul?"

Meryl smiled and said quietly, "Yes, I guess it does."

Rose stopped a few steps below the dune on which Meryl was standing and gazed up at her. "Is this your first time seeing the ocean?"

"Not the first time. Just the first time this close up."

"Huh! Fancy that! The would-be marine biologist who's never been to the sea."

Meryl stretched her arms wide and let the cold wind blow across her, billowing out the shoulders and sleeves on her jacket. Her reply was almost giddy: "But that's not true anymore. Here I am. At the sea."

A broad smile crossed Rose's face. "Next trip, let's actually take you out on a boat. It's one thing to stand on the beach and marvel at the ocean. It's another thing to feel all that raw power beneath you. I think there are whale-watching tours depending on the time of year. Plus, it might be a good idea to see if you get sea-sick before you dedicate your life to studying the ocean."

"Rose, how do you know more about the state I grew up in than I do?" Meryl asked.

The older woman shrugged. "Honey, you're so very young yet. You have plenty of time to fill that marvelous brain of yours with all kinds of information."

"It just seems like I've wasted a lot of time already."

"Oh, that's complete hogwash, child. When you're young you need your parents to interpret the world for you. But when you become an adult, that becomes your privilege and opportunities present themselves like never before. You just have to be brave enough to seize them."

Rose turned toward the sea and hummed softly. Over the weeks they had lived together, Meryl had become used to Rose's more mystical moments. She hadn't decided yet if the woman was just eccentric or operating on plane which was higher, more complex and ultimately much more interesting than her own. Meryl watched with amusement as her housemate noisily sucked in several lungfuls of sea air, stretched like a cat rising from a nap and smiled sleepily.

"Perhaps we should move on?" Rose suggested. "There's still much to see. Are you ready to go back to the car, Alexander?"

"Yet we cam," the boy answered, kicking sand back into the holes he had spent so much time digging.

They climbed the steep steps back to the parking lot and Rose paused on the landing to take a photo of the lighthouse on the wooded hill above.

"You know, they say that place is haunted," she remarked absently.

"Really?" Meryl replied.

"My hand to God. The legend is that a hundred years ago a young, beautiful girl — just like you — crept inside and vanished forever. At the time, the lighthouse was abandoned and a very dangerous place to visit. The people from Newport came up here in droves and searched every corner of the building, but the only thing they ever found was her handkerchief."

"So what happened to her?"

Rose widened her eyes and lowered her voice in mock dread. "No one knows. Some say she became lost in the secret passages rumored to lie beneath the lighthouse. Others think that pirates, using those same tunnels, abducted her. For years though, people have reported seeing her ghost wandering past the windows."

Meryl chortled. She was not generally impressed by ghost stories, considering herself too scientifically-minded to believe in phantoms. Still, she couldn't resist asking: "Do you think it's true?"

"I think all legends have some element of truth to them," Rose responded. "Even the most fantastic tale still draws upon the experiences of the teller. And places like Newport are filled with all kinds of strange tales. So yes, I can believe that the lighthouse is haunted."

Meryl's mind skipped back a few days to when she had found the sticky note with the word "Newport" written across it and secreted inside *The American Boy's Adventure Reader*. She almost dared to ask Rose about the book, the notes, the charts, her real reason for being in Oregon. But her courage failed her again.

They drove north along the meandering highway in an automobile that, to Meryl's ear at least, sounded like it was just a few miles short of the scrap yard. Rose assured her there was no need for concern. Despite appearances, the battered sedan had successfully transported her from the desert plateaus of Arizona to the forests of Oregon without incident and thus had demonstrated that it was mechanically sound. This was faulty logic, of course. Just because something hasn't happened before doesn't mean that it can't happen. She wondered if this was another example of Rose's mystical side, where she seemed to trust her car's reliability more to a Higher Power than a reliable mechanic. Regardless, they managed to cover over two hundred miles in the sputtering vehicle, most of it in reverent silence as they circumnavigated huge inland bays where strange rock formations, capped with wind-blasted trees, protruded out of the cold water. They crept through quaint seaside villages which looked like they hadn't changed in over a century — at least if you were able to ignore the restaurant and coffee shop chains. Alexander had managed much of the long trip without incident but had finally grown tired and cranky. Rose turned back after the boy had thrown a first-class tantrum at the edge of a tide pool on a public beach. The fit had exhausted him and he fell asleep in his car-seat almost immediately.

Somewhere along the way — Meryl wasn't sure when or where — Rose left the Pacific Coast Highway and headed inland. The road was narrow and twisted, and almost immediately there was a noticeable decrease in traffic where long periods would creep by without the passing of another car or any other sign of human life. The trees grew so tall, and the stands so thick, that Meryl frequently lost sight of the sun. Dark shadows crisscrossed the road like spiderwebs.

Meryl squirmed in her seat. "Don't take this the wrong way, Rose, but are we lost?"

"Not in the least," Rose laughed. "I just thought a change of scenery would be nice for the ride home."

Meryl rolled down her window a few inches and a cold stream of fragrant air blew across her. "What a beautiful place," she said. "I had no idea that this forest was here. It just goes on forever and ever."

"Honey, you really do need to get out more," Rose snickered. "This is what Oregon was like before the modern age, when all this was still a wild frontier."

The car entered a dense thicket of feathery Douglas fir and stout western hemlock trees. The sun vanished and the car's interior darkened. Rose turned on the headlights, drove a short distance more and then pulled off to the side of the road.

"What're you doing?" Meryl asked.

Rose answered with a smile, "You have to seize opportunities when they present themselves, child." She opened the car door and stepped out onto the pavement.

"I can't leave Alexander," Meryl protested.

"Don't worry, girl, we aren't going anywhere," Rose assured her. She stepped confidentially to the center of the road and pulled a small yellow device from her sweater pocket.

"What's that?" Meryl asked, following her reluctantly.

"It's a GPS thinga-ma-jig," Rose answered, poking at the device's buttons. "I bought it just before I left Arizona and have been trying to learn how to use it ever since. It'd be easier to learn how to fly an airplane, I'm afraid. My mind is not attuned to technology."

"That's funny. I just met this guy at the comic book store who is very interested in GPS. He even plays some game with it."

"I don't suppose he taught you how to use these things?"

"Sorry."

"No matter," Rose said, "we'll find out if I can manage this in a few seconds anyway."

Meryl stood there quietly and ached. At this point, she almost felt like Rose owed her an explanation. It was a stupid feeling, based largely on her sense of shame. If Rose actually told her what was going on, she wouldn't have to pretend that she knew nothing. She wouldn't have to muster every ounce of self-control to keep her mouth shut. Perhaps she wouldn't feel so guilty, as well.

"Oh, fudge," the older woman said, "I don't know if I'm using this correctly or not. It shows me where I am, but I want to see where I'm going."

Meryl asked quickly, "Where's that?"

"At the moment, to the top of that hill. Come on. We won't lose sight of the car."

Rose strode across the pavement and climbed the steep bank on the opposite side with ease. This mountainous terrain was the first place where her tall, gangly body didn't seem awkward or clumsy. Meryl followed obediently and upon reaching the summit found herself looking across thousands of acres of untouched wilderness.

"Amazing, isn't it?" Rose asked breathlessly.

"Yes. But what're you looking for?"

"A needle in a haystack, I'm afraid."

Meryl sighed and Rose heard it.

"Okay," she whispered, "I'll tell you if you can keep a secret."

"Rose, we're in the middle of nowhere. Who am I going to tell?"

"Well, I mean later you see. No breathing a word of it to the landlords or friends or anyone, okay?"

"You're making this sound so ominous."

"It is a little ominous, I suppose," Rose said. "It's about old myths and lost treasure, so you can understand the need for secrecy?"

"Okay, I promise," Meryl assured her, although based on what she already knew, it seemed like Rose's great secret was safe from being believed by, well, almost anyone.

"Years ago, when I was still living in Arizona, I came across this old story book in a used book store. Probably the type of book you'd expect children in some one-room Oregon schoolhouse to be using to practice their reading skills. I bought it as a curiosity, but as I begin perusing it, I found that the child who originally owned it had filled it with all kinds of notes. The child's name was Elijah and he was fascinated with a story about a lost gold mine."

"And you believe that this gold mine is out here?" Meryl asked, gesturing to the forest with a broad sweep of her arm.

"Child, I know it is out here," Rose stated firmly.

"How?"

Rose raised an eyebrow. She seemed a little offended by the question.

"I mean," Meryl added quickly, "if this was just a story in a book, it's probably fictional right?"

"Remember what I said earlier about all legends having some foundation in fact? This young boy — Elijah — was convinced that the story was real. The more I looked into it, the more convinced I became that the story was based on real events and Elijah knew it. His words, written almost one hundred years ago, convinced me." Meryl was about to object again, but Rose stopped her. "This is why I came to Oregon, you see. I've been waiting years for this opportunity. I came to find Elijah's secret. I came to find the gold."

Meryl nodded sympathetically. She'd finally been given an explanation — the very one she'd expected — and it sounded insane.

"That's a pretty interesting way for someone to spend their retirement years, Rose," she said, hoping her words didn't sound too flippant, but certain they did.

Rose set her jaw and gazed back at the forested valleys and mountaintops. "You remember that ghost story I told you about at the lighthouse this morning?" she asked.

"Yeah."

"Is that story fictional?"

"I don't know. Probably. Most ghost stories are probably fictional."

"But the lighthouse is real. It stands there on that hill. We saw it. And if the lighthouse is real, then maybe the girl was real, and if she's real then maybe the tragedy is real and her ghost is real too."

"And I agree with that," Meryl replied. "But you can't see this gold mine like we saw the lighthouse so what makes you think it's real?"

"Because when I decided to come to Oregon I had one goal I needed to accomplish before anything else..."

"And what was that?"

"I needed to find the boy who originally owned that textbook. I needed to find Elijah Robert Comstock. And I've finally done just that."

CHAPTER EIGHT

Aside from feeling generally poor about herself, Meryl discovered there were other unpleasant consequences to violating Rose's privacy by snooping through her belongings. The most immediate and tedious of these was spending hours listening to her roommate detail all the points of her long investigation, most of which Meryl was already aware of but unable to reveal. Still, she listened patiently to all of it, even enduring multiple readings of *The Cursed Gold Mine* followed by a full hour of Rose laboriously explaining the genesis of her ten year search. From the frenetic way in which she spoke, it was clear that Rose had an anxious need to not only be believed, but to be congratulated on her tenacity. Meryl responded with carefully chosen words. She certainly wanted to believe that there was a treasure trove hiding in the vast Oregon forest, but she considered herself a realist and Rose was quick to mistake hunches for logic. To Meryl's mind, following Elijah Comstock's childish doodles to the mine's portal was about as likely and reliable as using a dowsing-rod.

"I'm not clear on one major thing..." Meryl confessed gently one night as they labored shoulder-to-shoulder over a sink full of dirty dishes.

"What's that, darling?" Rose hummed.

"Elijah Comstock read about the mine in the *Adventure Reader* and became convinced that the story was true. That's what you think, right?"

"Precisely."

"But why? Why did he become convinced? He must've had much more to go on than just that short little story."

Rose smiled wryly. "Girl, that's why I came to Oregon, you see. I needed to find Elijah in order to find that connection."

"You said you had found him."

"And I did, in a manner of speaking..."

Meryl frowned as the older woman dried her hands and motioned for her to follow. Rose rummaged for a few moments in the stacks of papers on her desk before producing a manila folder. Inside was a photocopy of a newspaper obituary dated June 9, 1998. A grainy photograph of an elderly man with a shaggy beard was accompanied by a headline reading BELOVED PHYSICIAN DIES AT AGE 85.

Meryl read the article aloud: "'Elijah Robert Comstock, M.D., a prominent physician and life-long resident of Oregon passed away on Monday evening. He was 85 years old. Dr. Comstock cared for the families of Lincoln and Benton counties for over forty years. Through the early part of his career, Dr. Comstock shared a practice in Newport with his father, Thomas W. Comstock, M.D. Father and son will both be remembered for their altruistic nature and medical skills. The elder Comstock was instrumental in saving many lives during the 1919 Spanish flu epidemic and the younger for his willingness to travel to even the most rural communities to help those in need. After his father's death in 1928, Dr. Comstock moved to Benton County outside of Corvallis where he continued to practice medicine. He retired in 1974 and devoted much of his latter years to gold prospecting, an interest he carried with him from childhood. Many who knew him recalled his skill as a storyteller, always anxious to spin a wild yarn about his adventures and the strange things he encountered during his wilderness excursions. Although he frequently spoke about his search for a rich vein of gold, he was never successful in finding his "mother lode." Dr. Comstock was preceded in death by his wife, Rose Elizabeth and his sons, John and Charles. He is survived by two grandchildren who reside out of state. Funeral services will be held on Sunday with interment following at the Mt. Union Cemetery.'"

Meryl was impressed and smiled broadly at Rose. "It's so weird looking at this old face and knowing it was the same person who owned your book."

"Now, read the second page..." Rose urged.

"What's this?" Meryl asked, frowning at the other document in the folder.

"It's a copy of an old mining claim," Rose replied breathlessly. "If a gold prospector made a strike, he had to file an official claim to the area or someone else could move in and pirate his gold. Look at the name on the document."

Meryl squinted at the messy, handwritten words. "'John K. Sykes,'" she read. "Really? Is this the same Mr. Sykes from the book?"

"I believe so. The same one who fled from the gold mine and claimed that the whole area was cursed. Once I found his mine claim in the Oregon state archives, I was able to figure out its approximate location and get some GPS coordinates. That's why I'm trying to figure out how to use that silly navigation device. So you see why I don't think this story is completely fictional?"

"I must admit, that's pretty amazing."

"Now imagine this," Rose continued, holding the old green textbook tightly to her chest. "This gold claim was filed by Mr. Sykes in 1908, so you can assume that the ghastly tragedy that befell his men happened soon after — probably in '09 or '10. The textbook was published in 1915. The story says that Mr. Sykes was the only survivor and upon his return to the coast he was placed under a physician's care. Based on where I think the mine's located, one of the biggest port cities close to Mr. Sykes's claim was —"

"Newport," Meryl said quickly.

Rose nodded. "And Newport is where Elijah Comstock's father was the town physician..."

Meryl felt the back of her neck tingle with excitement. "You think that Elijah Comstock knew the story was real because his father treated Mr. Sykes after he escaped from the forest?"

"Natch! To every other young boy, this was probably just a scary story in some silly adventure book. But Elijah knew better because he had some inside knowledge. Elijah would've been around six when Mr. Sykes was under his father's care, living in his house for days or even weeks."

"But all your evidence is circumstantial, Rose. Unless you can prove that the Mr. Sykes in the book is the same one who's on the mine claim and was, at some time, a patient of Elijah's father."

"Circumstantial is the best I can hope for considering how many years separate me from these events," the older woman smiled dolefully. She anxiously paced the length of the small bedroom. "But I know this is true. I know this mine is out there and these people and events were real."

Meryl's next question was obvious, but she hesitated in asking it. "Why?"

Rose stopped and a strange look crossed her face. It was the same expression Meryl had seen when they stood on the Newport beach and stared out at the ocean. It was as though Rose had her own source of inside knowledge, or at least thought she did.

"I know because something put this book in my hands," she said, caressing the tome's spine with her long fingers. "Something wanted me to follow this trail, to solve this mystery."

"You're talking about what? Fate? Destiny?"

"Yes, yes!" Rose exclaimed. "Elijah Robert Comstock probably held onto this book right up until his death, and then it was given away by his family because they didn't understand what it was. And somehow it found itself in a used book store in Arizona. It's like a treasure map that floated for years in a bottle on the ocean. One day it washed up on the beach and landed at my feet. That is Fate, pure and simple."

There was something about how Rose spoke, the confidence she had in unseen and benevolent forces, that both inspired and disturbed Meryl. Perhaps it was simply the substantial age difference between the two women which allowed Rose to feel comforted by the idea of Fate while the same concept intimidated Meryl. If everyone's future was preordained, Meryl had to wonder where the events of her own life were leading her and if anything she did really made a difference on the outcome. Her father had died, her relationship with her mother was irreparable, the father of her child was invisible, and she was struggling to make it on her own before she had even reached her twentieth birthday. If Fate was real, it had a wicked sense of humor she decided.

"Let's say the gold mine is absolutely genuine," Meryl suggested.

"It is." Rose sounded somewhat irritated.

"You know that because you have the GPS coordinates to it?"

"Well, I have approximate coordinates to the larger area Mr. Sykes registered as his claim."

"So even if you got in to the larger claim area, you'd still have to search for the mine on foot?"

"Most certainly."

Meryl exhaled slowly. "Okay, then. Let's say you actually find the mine, which would be like finding a needle in a haystack I think, but let's say you do it. Then what? I doubt if the U.S. government is going to let you go in there and dig out any gold. It's a national forest, after all."

"What if they don't know about it?"

"Huh?"

"Well, this mine is in the middle of nowhere. Who's going to notice some old coot like me carrying out some ore in my backpack? It happened all the time during the frontier days. Miners would stuff a nugget or two into their boot and walk out with it. It was called 'high-grading the gold.'"

"And if they caught you, they'd hang you?"

"Yes indeed."

"And what would they do to you today?"

"Prison, I imagine," Rose said with a casual shrug.

"It just seems much more complicated than walking in and picking up gold nuggets off the ground, Rose."

"But walking in and picking gold up off the ground is all I have to do."

"You'd have to dig for it, Rose."

"No, Meryl, think about the story. Mr. Sykes leaves with some of his men to take a shipment of gold ore to the coast to sell. They returned weeks later to find their camp destroyed and the mine abandoned, but it's obvious that some of the miners barricaded themselves inside the mine before it was overrun by Indians. Now during all those weeks Mr. Sykes and the other men were gone, Mr. Bittle and those left at the mine were still digging. Day in and day out, dig, dig, dig. Somewhere in that mine, forgotten by everyone, are sacks of raw ore waiting to be collected."

"What if it was bandits, not Indians, who overran the mine?" asked Meryl. "They would've taken any gold they could find, right?"

Rose shrugged. "Unlikely it was bandits. Miners knew how to keep their strikes secret, but Indians would've lived in the area and could've cared less about gold. As I figure it, I just need to creep in a few of times and haul those ore bags out."

"Seems kind of dangerous, Rose."

"Not if you were with me, Meryl."

"What?"

Rose sat down next to Meryl and took her hand. "You're the only person I've told about this," she said urgently. "I've seen over these past few weeks what a good person you are, so I know my trust in you is warranted. You're right, it's dangerous to do this alone. But together we could. Imagine if you had a magic pot of gold, and every time you need a little extra ching-a-ling to get you by, you could just go to the pot and pull some out?"

Meryl managed a weak chuckle. "That's a nice idea," she said, "but the gold wouldn't even be usable. Doesn't the raw ore have to be processed somehow to get the gold out?"

"Oh, I have that covered! I know people," Rose said proudly. She then leaned close and whispered, as though afraid someone might actually overhear her peculiar plan: "What do you have to lose? You're living in someone's basement and have a job you're not particularly keen on. Imagine what you could do with all that money? Your college tuition would be paid for with plenty of extra to give Alexander the kind of life he truly deserves."

Meryl shook her head. "I've got to tell you, Rose, there're probably much easier ways to get money for college than looking for an old gold mine in the middle of the Oregon forest."

"There may be an easier way to get money, but probably not *this much money*." There was a sparkle in Rose's eye Meryl had never seen before, as though a little fire had ignited inside of her. It wasn't clear if her excitement was more about the allure of great wealth, or the search to find it. Meryl imagined that same sparkle was there every time Rose pulled the handle on a slot machine. If all those casino mementos on her book shelf were any indication, her fascination with money was about more than just getting rich. It was about the game, and the gamble, of getting rich.

"And what about the curse?" Meryl asked.

"Pardon?"

"It's the one thing you haven't explained. This mine's supposed to be cursed, remember? A bunch of men vanished and it drove Mr.

Sykes insane. If you're talking about Fate, aren't you tempting it by trying to find this place?"

Rose dismissed her. "Oh, good grief! There was never a curse, darling. Prospectors were always telling stories to keep interlopers away from their claims. Where you have gold mines, you almost always have stories about ghosts and evil spirits and curses."

"But that obituary said that Elijah Comstock encountered weird things in the forest while looking for this same mine."

"It also said Elijah was known for spinning a wild tale or two. I'm sure he did see all kinds of strange and fantastic things, because nature's full of the strange and fantastic. But that's different from curses, which, of course, don't exist."

"I'm just saying that if you believe in Fate, then it can be both good and bad, right? If some higher power brought Elijah Comstock's book to you, it doesn't mean that it was for a good reason."

"Oh Meryl," Rose groaned, "you are taking me much too literally. I wasn't referring to Fate in the 'Hand of God' sort of way. Just that the book fell into the hands of someone who could appreciate its true value." She patted Meryl's back. "Goodness, you are so jaded for someone so young."

Although she didn't show it, Meryl took that comment hard. Ever since Alexander was born, she had made a concerted effort to be both positive and productive, even when she didn't feel it in her heart. Over time, playing the role of a strong, determined woman had become second nature, a mask that she put on every morning. In the months since leaving Portland, she'd not allowed herself to cry, to mourn, or even to worry. If those feelings began to creep in on her, she had a variety of techniques to push them out again. She'd clean the entire apartment until she was exhausted. She'd pull an extra shift at work. She'd take Alexander on a long outing to the playground or the library. Anything to occupy her mind until the feeling withered away. But at the end of the day, these were still just tricks. They didn't change the fact that Meryl was, at her core, lonely, heartbroken, and frightened nearly all the time. And that she was, in fact, jaded.

The next morning, Meryl found her techniques for staying positive failed her. Instead of talking with Alexander about what kind of nuts squirrels like best or why birds can fly but small boys cannot, they walked to the daycare in silence. Then there was the long, solitary walk downtown to open The ROBOT, where she'd work alone until lunchtime. All of it provided too much time to regret, too much opportunity to think about how her and Alexander's lives would be so different if there was just a little more money in the bank...

Finally, after spending an hour standing at the shop's front door, watching a soft rain patter against the sidewalk outside, she shook off her melancholy and made the phone call she'd been putting off for over a week.

When Cameron appeared for his shift slightly before noon, he found Meryl already dressed in her coat and holding her purse.

"I'm not late," he declared.

"I didn't say you were, idiot. But I'm meeting someone for lunch so do you mind coming on just a little early so I can go?"

"Not gonna if you call me an 'idiot.'" he quipped.

"Cameron, I'll kick your ass."

"Flirting with me isn't gonna help you, boss lady," he answered, throwing his backpack in a graceful arch over the front counter and onto the floor. The he screwed up his face like he was thinking long and hard about something and exclaimed, "You're meeting someone? You never leave the store!"

Meryl was embarrassed but hid it. "Today I am," she said coyly. "And shut up."

"Who is it?" Cameron pressed.

"Cam... c'mon. Do a girl a favor."

"Oh, I will totally do you the favor, but you have to tell me who you're meeting first."

"Cam…"

Cameron began to move with exaggerated slowness toward the checkout counter. "Caaaan't… take… ooooo-ver… until Meryl… spilllllllls… her shit," he said.

"Ike has a couple of hours between classes so I asked him to meet me."

"You asked him?"

"Yes. Girls can ask guys out, you know. It's the twenty-first century, after all."

Cameron snorted. "Can they? No one's ever asked me."

"Clearly most women are oblivious to your charms."

"Okay, now you're just sucking up," he responded. He waved her off playfully. "Go, go… Take as long as you want. I got this bitch covered."

Meryl didn't even stop to thank him before she bolted for the door and hurried toward campus.

Ike had arranged to meet her in the Memorial Union, the immense domed building which was both the symbolic and geographical center of the university. It sat at the far end of a grassy, tree-lined quad, looking more like a temple erected to ancient gods than a hub for campus life. The grounds were empty, which Meryl thought strange until she entered the building's rotunda and found it crowded with students avoiding the rainy weather. The place smelled distinctly of wet hair and warm neoprene. At the top of the grand marble staircase, she stood for a long and awkward moment to survey the main lounge. She'd only been inside the Memorial Union once before, during summer break when the place was abandoned. Now large clusters of students congregated on the couches, talking about their studies while they sipped huge paper cups filled with coffee or read thick text books or tapped away at tablets or laptop computers. On the far side, near a line of towering bay windows, someone was playing a piano. The whole scene seemed so sophisticated, so contrary to what she had known in high school, that for a moment Meryl felt profoundly inadequate.

I could just go, she told herself as her stomach fluttered nervously. *Before I find him or he finds me. I'll just tell him something came up. It'll be easier that way.*

But before she could flee, Ike waved at her from across the room and smiled brightly with those perfect rows of white teeth. He was slouched against the piano with a handful of other students, all of whom were gazing admiringly at the small Asian woman playing flawlessly from memory. The walk across the crowded room felt like it took forever and that she was scrutinized by everyone in the room. In truth, however, no one noticed her or cared.

"How are you?" Ike whispered, putting his arm around her wet shoulders and squeezing them gently. She smiled but didn't reply. Talking during the performance seemed inappropriate, even if it was in the middle of a crowded room where dozens of other conversations were ongoing regardless of the music. She, Ike and the others gathered at the piano, listened attentively until the performance had finished and was followed by a smattering of applause and a few appreciative hoots from the room.

"You must be Meryl?" the young woman at the keyboard asked.

Startled, Meryl just gawked at her. Ike quickly stepped in and introduced everyone in the small group that ringed the piano. "Shiho, Phillip, Ryan, Regina... this is my friend, Meryl. I told you about her."

The young man named Phillip nodded at her and declared, "You work at the comic book store."

Meryl said, "Yeah, I'm the assistant manager."

"No wonder Ike likes you. Have you seen his dorm room? Dude's a major nerd."

"She knows that already," answered Ike. "I came clean about my sordid past of action figures and comic books ages ago."

Phillip squinted at Meryl. "And you find that attractive, huh?"

She shrugged. "I can't really judge, can I? I spend most of my day around nerds."

"Leave them alone," Shiho, the pianist, chimed in playfully. "You work as a bagger in a grocery store, Phil" — then with an appreciative smile she turned to Meryl — "It's very nice to meet you. Ike's said great things."

Great things? Meryl thought. *How much could he know about me in such a short time?* She immediately felt both flattered and uncomfortable and decided the best course of action was to change the subject. "You play beautifully. Are you a music major?"

Shiho laughed and replied, "No, political science actually. What you've just heard is actually the product of many years of compulsory piano lessons."

"Well, it was amazing."

"Thanks. Ike says you hope to start classes next semester. Do you have a major yet?"

Meryl didn't know if these strangers' detailed knowledge of her life should be worrisome, but unlike the string of college girls she'd interviewed as potential roommates, there was nothing judgmental about the question.

"Yes," she answered. "Marine biology."

"Well, you came to the right place! Have you seen the wave research lab here?"

Meryl shook her head. "Not yet. I hear it's amazing."

"Mind-boggling is more like it. And there's the campus out on the coast too if you're doing research. Have you been out there yet?"

Meryl shook her head sheepishly.

"Are you going to plan her entire academic career for her, Shiho?" the girl named Regina asked with a sigh.

Shiho straightened her back and cocked one eyebrow. "I'm just asking questions."

"Shiho's like our collective life coach," the boy called Ryan explained. "If you ever goes off the rails, she'll get you back on."

"No appreciation for my mad organizational skills," Shiho sniffed.

"We totally appreciate you," Ryan insisted. "If it weren't for you, we'd all be giant slackers."

"You are giant slackers, just not completely useless ones... thanks to me."

"Ouch," Ike laughed.

Shiho shrugged. "Sorry, gang, but sometimes a doctor has to cut to cure."

As Meryl stood there and watched them interact, hurling insults yet without a trace of true maliciousness, she realized that she didn't have this kind of relationship with anyone in Corvallis, except maybe Cameron. In fact, she hadn't had a close group of friends since high school, and most of them had long since stopped speaking to her. Except for Tess. Tess. The only true friend she had left, reduced to voice on the phone or exchanged text messages.

After a few more moments of friendly banter, Ike was able to coax Meryl away from the piano and to a pair of overstuffed armchairs. He brought them cups of steaming Chai tea and then asked casually, "So not to sound too much like Shiho, but when are you gonna start classes?"

Meryl shrugged. "I'd like to start next semester," she said. "But honestly, there's a lot of stuff to figure out."

"Money stuff?"

"That's a big part of it. The rest is time, I guess. I think about how I'm going to work everything I need to do into twenty-four hours, and it's like something has to go, but I don't really have anything I can give up."

Ike was silent for a moment while he practiced his next question in his head. "Can I ask about your, uh, situation?"

"My... uh... situation?" Meryl parroted him. "That's a diplomatic way of... uh... putting it."

"You can tell me if I'm being a douche bag for asking. It's just not something you've ever mentioned. I guess I'm curious."

To her surprise, she was neither offended nor self-conscious about his curiosity. Now that she'd been somewhat ingratiated into Ike's social circle, the question didn't seem invasive. She smiled sheepishly. "My roommate called it the '800-pound gorilla in the room.' It's that thing everyone's aware of but shy to mention."

"Huh. I haven't heard that saying before."

"Me either, but Rose has lots of little gems like that. It's like she learned to speak by watching old movies or something."

Ike grinned. He seemed so perfect, from his flawless skin to all those white teeth to the tiny crinkles next to his green eyes. She forgot for a moment that she had a long and disastrous history of mistaking beauty for character.

"Okay," she said, "I'll nutshell it for you."

"Cool. Nutshell away."

"I was a freshman in high school and I met this smokin' hot guy and I fell in love with him in about five seconds. We got serious really fast and a year later Alexander was born."

"Wow. That was some damn good nutshelling. Your whole life's story in two sentences."

"The details are embarrassing."

"He wasn't a nice guy — Alexander's father, I mean?"

"No, he's a nice guy. But he's not father material or even boyfriend material for that matter. Let's just say that he wasn't going to let fatherhood interfere with his big fat high school experience, you know?"

"Don't take this the wrong way," Ike said cautiously, "but you... don't seem... you know... like the type of girl who would get into a situation like that."

Meryl felt a smirk spreading across her lips. She wasn't offended by anything Ike was saying, mostly because he was so tragically awkward about it all. "You mean... I don't seem... like a slut?" she mimicked him as before.

Ike recoiled as if she'd just thrown her hot chai in his lap. "Shit, I didn't mean it that way!"

She shook her head. "Don't be stupid. I understand what you're saying."

"It's just that you don't seem, I mean, you seem so responsible that... Shit. I'm a douche and I'm gonna just shut the hell up now."

"Yeah, you're really not very good at this," she laughed.

"I should've taken Mom and Dad up on those etiquette lessons, I guess."

"Really, you're not offending me. I know it's hard to talk about. People are always searching for the right word to describe it. You called it my 'situation.' I think that's the most polite term I've heard. Others have called it my 'error,' my 'lapse in judgment,' my 'lack of responsibility.' If you were my mom, you would call it my 'complete and utter destruction of life as I know it.'"

"And what do you call it?"

"I like the word 'surprise,'" she answered after a moment's thought. "Surprises are always unexpected, but they can also be good. And Alexander was the best surprise I've ever had in my life."

"He must be an awesome kid."

"He is."

"And is the father still in the picture?"

"He was never in the picture. Tom was, um, how to explain him? Have you ever been really, really into someone, but when you look back on it later you kind of realize that what you saw in them was all in your mind because you were just really, really into them? That was me and Tom."

A psycho-analyst would find it significant that Meryl's relationship with Tom sprung up just months after the death of her father. That analyst would certainly draw the same conclusions Meryl had reluctantly come to on her own — that grief-stricken from the loss of one important man, and receiving no support from her withdrawn mother, she went out and found an inferior substitute. Tom had made her feel loved and important at the darkest hour of her life, and at the time that's all that mattered. But she couldn't say any of this to Ike, who was still thinking about her question anyway.

After a contemplative moment, he shrugged and said: "I guess the closest I've been to being really, really into someone is admiring girls from afar because I was too terrified to speak to them. Which, if you hadn't guessed it, was my situation from sixth to about eleventh grade."

"You don't seem to have any problems now, so what changed? Did your balls finally drop or something?" Meryl snorted.

Ike blushed. "For the record, my balls dropped ages ago, but in high school it's like I sprayed on girl-repellent every morning. I finally got over my senseless fear of women, at least enough to talk to them."

"Was it a fear of women or a fear of rejection?"

"Oh no, I totally get rejection. I've had a lot of experience with rejection. But you girls are scary. If you're a guy, you just don't understand how girls work."

"It's okay. We don't understand guys, either."

His toothy grin returned. "I'm sure that's true."

Meryl then added, "You know, being a nerd is kind of fashionable right now. I could see plenty of girls being into a nerd."

"So says the chick who works in the comic book store. But to answer your original question, about being totally into someone, I guess I'm still waiting for that experience to happen."

"Maybe you'll be lucky and avoid it."

"It was that bad?"

"At the time it was awesome because I was in this total fog, but then reality set in and the next thing I knew most of my friends couldn't relate to me anymore and my mom had stopped looking me in the eye."

"That sucks, Meryl."

She shrugged. Despite the unpleasantness of the topic, she found her conversation with Ike was making her feel good. She wanted so badly to tell him everything, to believe that someone who seemed so perfect would listen and empathize and not give those disapproving or pitying looks she got from others. "I guess it was to be expected. I mean, who wants to chill with the pregnant teenager? It kind of cramps everyone's style. And as for my mom, well, she had big plans for me. Now ruined, of course."

"I'm thinking she envisioned you as graduating Magna cum Laude and then going onto a Ph.D. at Yale?"

"Yeah, something like that. Instead, I graduated high school early, got a job and then as soon as I could, I got the hell out of Portland. That completely pissed her off. Mom likes to be in control, and when I took that away, she pretty much lost her mind."

"It's not a Ph.D. at Yale, but that's still a pretty amazing accomplishment."

"You're right. It was. Oh! That sounded totally stuck up, didn't it?"

Ike shook his head.

"I think I just violated one of the main rules girls use to get guys to like them," Meryl said with a dramatic cringe.

"Wait," Ike exclaimed with mock excitement, "*there are rules?*"

"Ike, your dad never told you about the rules?"

"The bastard never mentioned rules. Shit. No wonder I have such a miserable history with this."

"Well, the rule is that I act like a moron so you won't feel intimidated by me."

"Do I have to act like a moron, too?"

"No, you have to act like an asshole. You know, ignore me whenever it suits you. Forget my birthday. Lie to me."

"Wow. Those rules suck."

"Yup."

"So," he said provocatively, waving a plastic stir-straw at her, "have you ever done that?"

"You mean have I ever acted moronic to impress a guy?"

"Yeah."

"Ike, how do you think I wound up with a four-year old?"

He laughed. "So the father — Tom, right? — he responded to that?"

"With Tom, acting like a moron was more of a lifestyle choice. But it works for him. He's a very successful moron."

"Your mom must've hated him."

"Nah, she loves him. Aside from being passive-aggressive, the other thing Mom does really well is hypocrisy. Of course, it helped that he's gorgeous and pretty damn charming too. Mom figured that if I was knocked up, at least it was good that the father was easy on the eyes and kind of cool. Never mind that he couldn't even remember Alexander's name."

Meryl suddenly noticed a deafening silence from the other chair. Ike was just staring at her.

"You're not feeling sorry for me, are you?" she asked sharply.

"No," he lied. "I just can't imagine all you've been through. Other people would've just collapsed."

"Collapse isn't an option," she answered. "Although, it would be kind of awesome. Like a mini vacation, y'know?"

They spent the remainder of the hour talking about more pleasant things. Ike regaled Meryl with stories from his boyhood — about boogie-boarding in the warm California surf, the summers he spent working as a lifeguard on a public beach, and backyard pool parties complete with smoking barbecues and flickering tiki torches. He confided his addiction to watching Internet videos of people hurting themselves on skateboards and building Lego spaceships with his little brother. He spoke of a family that was close, loving and so very different from Meryl's experience that he might as well have been describing quantum physics to a child. And as Meryl sat there and listened, she realized that Ike never once apologized for his past or his good fortune. She admired him for that. He didn't lie or dumb down his life in order to make her feel better about her own. He refused to act, well, like a moron in order to impress her.

After, he walked her back to The ROBOT and neither one noticed the rain or the chilly temperature. When they entered, Cameron met them with a look that was both surprised and uncomfortable.

"Everything okay?" Meryl asked.

"Yeah," Cam answered softly. "You have a visitor."

She turned, confused, as a tall man walked toward her. His body was a sculpted mass of muscle — a massive torso squeezed into a tight shirt but with a tiny waist and spindly legs that made him look strangely top-heavy. "Hey," he said.

The man's face was so incongruous with the environment she'd kept clean of reminders of her past that it took a few seconds for her to place him. And in that instant, her good mood vanished completely.

CHAPTER NINE

"You surprised to see me?" Tom smiled with an air of confidence which seemed completely inappropriate for the circumstances.

Meryl had spent months getting used to walking the Earth without seeing him. It had not been an easy process. She had to face the fact that her infatuation with Tom had too much to do with physical attraction and too little with understanding how that attraction blinded her to certain realities. She had worked hard not to blame him for how things had turned out, and to accept that a young man who had difficulty keeping a minimum wage job and barely made it through high school probably wasn't going to be a serious competitor for either Boyfriend or Father of the Year. Meryl's expectation that somehow Tom would spontaneously change into who she wanted him to be had always been a major obstacle in their relationship. It was a foolish notion, guided by emotions which at the time had left her exasperated.

In the months since leaving Portland, she'd played out the scenario of seeing Tom again a thousand times in her head. It always took place years in the future, when she was living in Hawaii with some as-yet-to-be-identified husband who worked as a world-famous nature photographer. Alexander would be in his teens by then. He'd have Tom's height and good looks, but Meryl's personality. He'd be old enough to understand how he'd come into the world and mature enough not to mourn the absence of a father who had never been there in the first place. He'd have a close and loving relationship with his step-father, the nature photographer, and this would be the man he called "Dad." He'd dismiss Tom with a look and it would crush him. Yeah, that was how it was supposed to go down. But now that she was actually confronted with Tom, she was overwhelmed by a sense of panic which showed on her face in a twisted and painful frown. They stood there, both quietly gauging each other's expression and body language, seeing who would be first to make the next gesture.

It was Meryl who was finally able to reply grimly, "Yes. I'm surprised."

Tom shifted his discomfort from one leg to another. The smile had vanished. "A good surprise?" he asked obtusely.

"It's a surprise, Tommy. I don't know what else you want me to say?"

He looked hurt. She tried not to care. "Can we talk?" he mumbled.

Meryl glanced around and every single person in the store was staring back at her. Cameron seemed fascinated be it all, like he was watching some kind of science experiment unfold in front of him. Ike looked apologetic, embarrassed by her embarrassment. She felt a little disappointed when Ike quietly excused himself.

"Thanks for the tea," she replied. "I had fun."

"Me, too," he smiled, sympathetically. Meryl believed him when he told her that he was not very experienced with girls. But she also knew he was smart enough to know that old boyfriends showing up unexpectedly is a game changer. His departure added sadness to all the other emotions rushing through her body.

"Cam, would you mind watching the store for a few minutes more?" Meryl asked.

He nodded. "It's cool."

Meryl led Tom into the stockroom at the back of the store and closed the door behind them. The room was small, cluttered with boxes of T-shirts and dusty piles of action figures, and poorly lit by florescent lights which crackled overhead. Tom smiled again, more confidently this time though it was undeserved. Then he pushed a little further.

"Can I get a hug?" he asked.

"No," she said. Unlike Ike, Tom was a guy who knew the "rules of dating" by heart and played the game very well. He slumped and thrust his hands deep into his jeans pockets like a little boy denied an ice cream cone. Meryl's irritation increased.

"How'd you find me?" she snapped.

"You told me you were moving here, remember?"

"No, I mean how did you find out where I worked? Corvallis is a small town, but it's not *that* small."

"Your mom," he said.

"Well, that figures."

"Hey, your mom's been like my only source of info on you and the kid since you stopped talking to me," Tom replied defensively.

Meryl immediately bristled, but she didn't attack. "She always liked you, no doubt about that. She told you I worked here?"

"She told me that the people who were helping you had been friends of your dad and they owned a comic book store. I put the rest together. Not a huge number of comic book stores in this town."

"Got it."

"I think she misses you, Meryl."

Meryl shuddered. "Please don't do that."

"Do what?"

"Please don't act like my mom's press secretary. I can assure you that you have no idea what motivates my mom. It'd take a team of psychologists working 'round the clock to even get close."

"I didn't realize that's what I was doing," he replied glumly. "It just seems that way to me is all I'm saying."

"In her own way, I'm sure she misses me. But doesn't it strike you as fucking messed up that you're the one she has a relationship with? You're the dude who knocked up her daughter. In a normal universe she'd hate your guts. In this universe she hates mine."

Tom didn't answer for a long moment. There was no debating with Meryl on this subject, as there was nothing to debate. It was a fact that the mother had blamed the pregnancy entirely on the daughter and contorted it into some act against her parental authority. Tom didn't try to understand the old lady's acutely chauvinistic attitude. He didn't care why Meryl's mother seemed to love rather than resent him. He was only relieved that it made his life easier.

Wisely, he decided to change the subject. "Did Tess tell you I went by and saw her?"

"She told me."

"You'd be proud of her. That chick's like a bank vault. I couldn't get shit out of her."

Meryl ducked her head down to hide her involuntary smile.

"Are you still pissed at me?" he asked.

"Tom, do you even know why I was pissed at you to begin with?"

"Because I was a total asshole. I get that. You needed me to be there for you and I wasn't. I shirked my responsibilities and I will totally own that."

"Wow, that sounded so completely rehearsed. Were you practicing that little speech in the car all the way down here?" she snarled.

"Are you kidding me?"

"Are *you* kidding *me*? You 'shirked your responsibilities?' Do you even know what 'shirked' means?"

"Oh, 'cause I'm too retarded to know a big word, right? Damn, be a bitch much?" he shot back despite himself.

"You're just trying to say what you think I want to hear."

He took a breath. "Let's just chill, okay," he said softly. "I'm being serious. I just wanted to see you and Alex."

"Alexander."

"Whatever. I just wanted to say hi and see how you were doing. That's the total fucking truth, whether you want to believe it or not."

"Since when?"

"Since always. You were the one who moved away, remember? If I'm not seeing you guys it's because of you."

"We didn't move to the moon, Tom."

He paused to calm himself. In all the time they had known each other, Tom hadn't won an argument yet. It wasn't looking good that this would be the first time. "You didn't leave me an address."

"You found me without one."

"And your cell phone was shut off."

"That was my mom. I was on her plan and when I left Portland she shut me off."

He arched his back like a cat about to pounce on a bird. "*You* never called *me*," he said resolutely.

"That's because I didn't want to see you. That's why I moved away. Get it?"

He looked frustrated. "So this is some kind of bizarre girl logic, right? You take off so you never have to see me again, but you're pissed because I didn't chase after you? And now that I've shown up, you're pissed off because I found you? So no matter how you cut it, it's my fault, right?"

"Right," Meryl quipped.

He ran a hand through his stringy hair, pushing it out of his dark blue eyes. "Look, I'm not gonna pretend that I understand that, but you don't have to bust my nuts either. I just wanted to see you and my son. If I came too late or my gesture is too lame, I'm sorry but it's the best I can do right now."

Meryl felt admonished and it irritated her. Thirty seconds earlier she had been destroying him, but his sudden contriteness had taken all the fun out of it.

"Okay," she said softly. "I don't really want to fight either."

He smiled at her, roguishly. "Yes, you do."

"But I won't," she replied quickly. "What is it you want?"

"To see you and Alexander. I mean that."

"I have to work right now and he's in day care."

"Well, I didn't mean this exact second. Later would be fine."

"What time are you driving back to Portland?" Then, hoping Tom was wondering about the college boy she'd walked into the store with, she added: "I may have plans tonight."

"I don't have to return right away. I thought I'd stay a few days."

There was a tinge of panic in Meryl's reply. "Stay a few days? What's that mean? Where?"

He shrugged. "I was kind of hoping I could crash with you."

She snorted. "Fat chance."

"Again, don't bust my nuts, girl. There's nothing to that. I don't have enough cash for a motel."

"That's not my problem, Tom. I have a roommate. I can't just bring some guy home to spend a few days."

"Like your roomy doesn't have boyfriends stay over, huh?" he smirked.

"First, you're not my boyfriend anymore. Second, she doesn't actually. She's in her sixties and really not into bringing guys home."

"Seriously?"

"Seriously. She's a retired school teacher."

"So she'd be offended by you bringing me home?"

"That's not the point. I don't think it would be appropriate. I don't know how I'm even going to explain you to Alexander."

"What the hell are you talking about? What's to explain? I'm his daddy."

Meryl's anger was quickly resurfacing and she knew she had to end this conversation soon or it would draw on into the night like all their arguments. "Tom, he hasn't seen you in almost a year. I hate to break this to you, buddy, but you're a stranger to him."

Tom flinched in mock pain, grabbing the front of his pants with both hands. "Oh man, there goes the other one!" he grimaced.

"What the hell are you talking about?"

"My left nut. You just crushed it. It's gone. Pulverized."

Meryl shook her head. "You're a fucking jerk."

"So, you gonna let me crash on your couch or what?" he asked again.

"No fucking way. If you wanna see Alexander that's cool, but it's gonna be somewhere else. We can meet you at the park or go to a restaurant or something."

"Okay, but you're leaving me homeless for the night."

"Stay warm."

He sauntered to the doorway and paused. "You gonna at least give me a phone number where I can reach you?"

"No. Come back here tomorrow around four. After I'm off work you can go with me to see Alexander."

"Okay. But really, girl, I'm down to one nut. I can't take much more of this abuse, okay?"

Meryl wasn't impressed. "At four, Tommy. Don't be late."

CHAPTER TEN

Once, in a moment of anger, Meryl had insisted that if you discounted how handsome he was, the most interesting thing about Tom was that his last name was spelled "Jekyll" but pronounced *JEE-kill*. Where this pronunciation came from was not clear, even to Tom and his family. But the name lent itself to all kinds of mutations, both favorable and unfavorable, ingenious and foolish. It was his teammates on the junior varsity basketball team who started referring to him as *"JEE-killer"* and it was a sobriquet that stuck. A year later, when it became common knowledge that Tom was the father of Meryl's unborn child, he became known as *"Lady JEE-killer."*

In a strange way, the pregnancy had allowed Tom to enjoy a level of high school celebrity he had never really earned. Despite what Meryl might have said when she was so furious she couldn't see straight, Tom was not stupid nor unkind nor unfeeling. He did not, as Tess often suggested, work so hard on sculpting his body because he had no other assets worth noting. However, he could occupy a space without defining it and was content to move from day to day with as little effort and accomplishment as possible. His high school academic's counselor once told him that he had never met someone so dedicated to mediocrity. And whether it was the string of unremarkable grades he earned; the fact that he graduated 201st out of exactly 402 students in his class; or that he never kept a job longer than six months because of his exceptionally poor attention span, Tom's entire life had been defined more by underperformance and missed opportunities than anything else. By the time his high school career was winding down, the only things notable about him were his looks and that he had had a child at a very young age.

Meryl was also remembered for having had a child at a very young age. But while Tom was congratulated, usually in the most lewd ways imaginable, Meryl became invisible and whatever popularity she had enjoyed abandoned her as quickly as her friends. Her last year in school had been an exercise in loneliness. The only thing that got her through it was the promise of seeing Alexander at the end of the day and that all those extra credits she started accumulating as far back as middle school would earn her an early diploma. Ironically, she had graduated from high school only one month behind Tom, although for her there was no gown or mortar board, no commencement ceremony, not even a feeling of accomplishment. She got her diploma in the mail, but she didn't care. The end of high school meant escape from a life that had become increasingly intolerable.

As she paced at the front of The ROBOT, Meryl was itemizing and agonizing over all these little high school memories. She checked the time on her cell phone and began to fume.

"How late is he?" David called from across the room. He'd never met Alexander's father and was almost as anxious about Tom's arrival as Meryl. Plus, there was an understandable curiosity on his part to see the individual who, as much as anybody, had compelled Meryl to leave her childhood home and move into his basement.

"Twenty minutes," she replied. "I'm gonna have to leave in a minute or two or the daycare will charge me that stupid late fee again."

David smiled. "If he shows, what do you want me to tell him?"

She squared her shoulders and slung her purse over her arm. "Tell him I left with no forwarding address."

"You got it."

The twenty minute walk from the comic book store to Alexander's daycare helped dissipate some of her anger. She felt relieved that she hadn't mentioned Tom to the child yet, even though she'd spent the last twenty-four hours rehearsing an explanation for him. The child was in a good mood and wanted to swing on her arm as they walked home, which calmed her more. They had made it as far as the end of the block when a dark brown Jeep Cherokee shot by only to brake suddenly in a cloud of vaporized rubber.

"Hoob dat, Maw-Mee?" Alexander asked, dangling lazily from Meryl's fingertips.

"Hey!" Tom bellowed. "You didn't wait for me."

"You were late," she replied tersely.

"I got lost. I don't live here, you know. I went by your store and some old dude chewed me out."

"That was my boss, Tommy."

"I figured. Anyway, sorry, my bad. You wanna ride?"

Meryl pulled Alexander into her arms and stepped slowly off the sidewalk and up to the Cherokee's passenger door. The vehicle was an older model with torn vinyl seats and soiled floorboards littered with discarded hamburger wrappers and empty energy drink bottles. The red-and-blue tassel from Tom's high school mortar board hung from the rearview mirror. The vehicle's engine rumbled so loudly Meryl could feel it reverberating through the pavement and into the soles of her feet.

"Where'd this come from?" she asked.

"I bought it a few months ago. Used, of course, but it's a four-by-four. I can scale a mountain in this thing."

"That must be very useful in the big city," she taunted him. Then she noticed Tom's eyes had fixed on Alexander.

"Hey, little dude," he smiled. "How's it going?"

"Dop pop-op," Alexander replied.

Tom frowned and looked at Meryl. "What did he say?"

She shrugged. "Sometimes he just makes noises."

"Get in. We can go for a ride," he urged.

Meryl glanced around the interior of the Jeep and noticed a nest of wrinkled clothes on the back seat. "Did you sleep in here last night?"

"Uh, someone wouldn't let me sleep on her couch, remember?"

"For fuck's sake, Tommy, you could've frozen to death."

"It wasn't that cold. Around four a.m. I found an all-night diner out on the highway and nursed a cup of coffee until the sun came up. So, you wanna go for a ride or what?"

"You don't have a child seat, Tommy."

"No."

"Then we can't."

"Seriously? We don't have to go far. We can just go down the block to the park."

She thought about this for a moment. In her mind, she'd already drawn certain lines in the sand when it came to dealing with Tom. There were rules that couldn't be bent, favors that would never be granted. But as was usually the case when she dealt with Tom "Lady JEE-killer" Jekyll, the problem was not in establishing boundaries but in keeping them. She hated that his mere presence was making her feel weak even when she vowed to stay strong. Almost without knowing it, she began to give a little.

"We live up two blocks and then left," she told him. She sounded angry, exasperated. "It's the big white house on the right with the dark red trim. We'll meet you there."

He nodded and roared off down the road. She set Alexander back on the sidewalk and he resumed swinging on her arm as they walked. For a few seconds, Meryl hated herself.

"Hoob dat?" he asked again.

"That's your daddy," she told him.

He was quiet for a moment but otherwise didn't react. Then he began to tell her about the cookies he had enjoyed at afternoon snack break.

By the time they reached the house, Tom was sitting on the hood of the Jeep and chatting with Rose. The latter had been filching flowers from David and Rachel's garden again, as she had a bundle of dahlias and daisies lying across her arm. Meryl had been uncomfortable with this practice from day one, just as she still worried that Rose tapping into the landlords' WIFI signal without their knowledge was somehow a form of stealing. But since neither David or Rachel had said anything about the strangely disappearing blooms, or had any complaints about diminished Internet bandwidth, Meryl had decided not to make an issue of it. There was a part of her, however, that continued to think such practices were strange for someone of Rose's age, intelligence and background. After all, she wondered, weren't school teachers supposed to tirelessly promote honesty and virtue?

"I see you've met," Meryl said as they approached.

"Yes, yes, yes," Rose cooed. "Tom was just showing off his Jeep to me."

He shrugged, embarrassed.

"It can climb a mountain, he tells me," Rose continued.

"So I've heard," Meryl answered.

Rose gave her a strange look. "That could prove handy in a place like Oregon."

Meryl changed the subject. "Tommy, you can come in for a while and hang out with Alexander if you want, but then we got things to do."

"What things?" he smirked.

"We're writing a screenplay together," she growled. "You have half an hour."

"You're giving me half an hour? Are you kidding me?"

"You could've had more if you had shown up on time."

"I was twenty minutes late."

"Thirty minutes late. Three. Zero."

"Daaaaang. You're so strict," he moaned, giving her a well-practiced grin that once would've made her crumble.

Instead, she just glowered. "Thirty." She turned and led him and Alexander down the narrow steps to the basement.

Despite its modest size and humble decor, Tom was impressed by Meryl's subterranean home. Yes, the floor was scattered with toys, the furniture was all secondhand and their was a sizable mountain to dirty laundry that needed washing, but it was still *her place.* By comparison, Tom still lived at home and was primarily supported by his parents due to his notoriously unreliable income. Not bad for a girl who was a year younger than him, he thought with some sense of pride.

Tom was not a petty person and he had always hoped Meryl's departure from Portland would be good for her and Alexander. In the most honest sense, he knew he wasn't up to the task of being a reliable partner and parent so the more successful she was, the less he had to be. Or at least that's what Tom told himself.

"Alexander," Meryl said to the child, "why don't you show Tommy your toys."

Excitedly, the boy pulled a laundry basket filled with plastic and wooden toys to the middle of the room and dumped it unceremoniously into a large pile. Tom joined him on the carpet, sitting cross-legged as be began to sort the child's dinosaur collection into piles of "plant eaters" and "meat eaters."

"What're we gonna play, buddy?" he asked, quickly adding, "In the twenty-four and a half minutes we have left?"

Rose caught Meryl in the hallway and whispered, "Does the daddy really only get thirty minutes with the boy?"

Meryl was immediately annoyed. "Rose, stay out of it."

"It's just so little time... and he came so far."

"Unannounced and uninvited. Gimme a break. He doesn't get to just roll into town and upset everything. Plus he totally stood me up this afternoon."

"For pity's sake."

"Rose, it's not your concern."

The older woman held up her hands in a gesture of supplication and nodded. "You're right, you're right. I stand rebuked and humbly withdraw the suggestion."

She returned to the kitchen and Meryl wandered down to her bedroom, lingering at the doorway where Tom couldn't see her but she could overhear he and Alexander's play. The child was laughing, but it didn't mean anything. It was the same laugh he used whenever he saw a bird splashing in a rain puddle or his favorite cartoon played on television. The man who was making plastic dinosaurs rampage across the living room floor was an oversized playmate and that was all. For a second, Meryl felt sorry for Tom.

Five minutes before she planned to ask Tom to leave, Rose called to her and she found everyone seated around the kitchen table. A large plastic cup filled with the flowers Rose had stolen from David's garden was set in the middle of the table. Tom and Alexander were already seated.

"What's this?" Meryl asked.

"Dinner. What do you think?" Rose replied absently.

"I think Tommy needs to be on his way, Rose."

"Darling, where I'm from, we never send anyone out into the cold night without a hot meal. Take a seat, please. I insist."

Once everyone was settled, Rose presented what she called "Impossible Pie," a fluffy mixture of eggs, onion, cheeses and sausage. It was rich, greasy and delicious. But Meryl felt ambushed and could barely bring herself to pick at it.

"So, Tom," Rose said genially as they ate, "what is it that you do? Sorry, I called you Tom. Do you like to be called Tom, Thomas or Tommy?"

"Tom," he answered. "Meryl calls me Tommy but she's the only one who does." He shot her a quick grin which was met with indignation. "What do I do? Well, I graduated a year ago and now I just work, I guess."

"You guess? You don't know if you work or not?"

"It depends on whether you're asking me or my boss," he chortled.

Rose grinned broadly. "Since your boss isn't here, I'm asking you."

He moved stiffly in his chair. Alexander was gazing up at him, as though anxious for his reply. "Right now, I'm between jobs."

"I'm so sorry. What happened?"

"I was working at this sandwich shop, but they changed shifts on me and I kind of forgot when I was supposed to go in."

Rose laughed.

Tom shrugged. "It's no biggie. That job bought me my Jeep and now I have time to cruise down here for a visit."

"The *mountain-climbing* Jeep," Rose noted.

"Right. The mountain-climbing Jeep."

"So, tell me... Have you ever actually climbed a mountain in it?"

"Not yet, but I'm aching to try. Did you see the tires I have on that beast? They can chew up anything! I have these buddies who want to go whitewater rafting down on the Rogue River. We're trying to get a whole group together for that."

"But that's not a mountain. That's a river. You're just gonna park that Jeep on the riverbank while you raft? That's no fun."

Tom raised an eyebrow quizzically. "You have a better idea?" he asked.

"No, she doesn't," Meryl interjected.

"Hush up, child," Rose scolded her. "I have a much better idea."

"Rose..."

"Wait, wait," Tom said quickly, "I wanna hear the idea."

Rose said proudly, "It so happens I have a little camping trip I want to go on and I don't have an appropriate vehicle for that. I have that old clunker out front of the house, which is pretty much the disgrace of the American automotive industry. Maybe you saw it? I love that hunk of junk, but no way it can go off-roading."

To Meryl's relief, Tom's reaction was less than enthusiastic. "Is there a mountain involved in this camping trip?" he asked.

"Over the hills and through the woods," Rose sang. "There are some backcountry roads for part of the way, but then the rest of it would be true off-roading, perfect for a Jeep four-by-four. I've been trying to talk Meryl into going with me. This poor child hasn't seen anything of this beautiful state. And I think she has a friend who understands GPS?"

Meryl's simmering irritation now came to a boil. She'd come to understand that there was a certain degree of pushiness to Rose — whether it was taking other people's flowers or always coordinating the dinner menu — but somehow the older woman had just managed to include Tom *and* Ike on a crazy expedition even she hadn't agreed to be part of.

"Rose," Meryl said as firmly as she could without sounding completely hateful, "Tom's leaving and Ike's busy with school. I'm afraid you may be asking too much."

Rose let out a thunderous laugh. "You don't know if you don't ask. And Tom can always say no if he wants to."

"I'm saying no," Meryl said bluntly. The rest of the meal was held in near silence, except for those moments when someone would offer a strangled comment in the hopes of alleviating the tension. It didn't work.

After dinner had concluded, Tom and Alexander placed the toys back into the laundry basket.

"They're just precious together," Rose whispered in her ear, ignoring Meryl's obvious anger. "And that Tom, oh my, he is so good-looking, isn't he?"

Meryl was trying not to think about Tom in that way, so she didn't reply immediately. Instead, she pulled Rose aside and said, "What were you thinking? First you invite him to dinner and then on your little gold-hunting excursion? Are you crazy?"

"Darling, imagine how much easier it will be for us if we have a vehicle that can actually get us in and out of that forest," she replied.

"My point is that I never agreed to do this with you, Rose. And I certainly never agreed to have my ex-boyfriend involved."

Rose looked regretful, her thin white eyebrows pulling together over the ridge of her nose. "Oh, I do apologize. When he showed up here and told me that you invited him over, I figured your relationship was a cordial one."

"We don't have a relationship, Rose. Cordial or otherwise. We had one, but it's been over for a long time. Why would you think I'd want him to come along on this or any other trip?"

"So you are coming?"

"Geeze, stop doing that!"

"What did I do, for Pete's sake?"

"That thing where I say something and you read six layers of meaning into it that just aren't there. I didn't say I was going on your treasure hunt, either."

"I think you did," Rose hummed, seemingly amused.

"Shit, you are so bossy sometimes. Are you even hearing what I'm saying to you?"

Rose reached out and with a warm hand gently squeezed Meryl's elbow.

What a school teacher thing to do, Meryl thought. It didn't work but the attempt was second nature to Rose.

"I do hear you," she said tenderly. "And I promise that I won't mention it again, but..."

Here it comes, Meryl winced.

"...I just think you should consider it. After all, we're talking about one weekend. Two days. If we find the mine — terrific. If we don't, well then you and Alexander had a great weekend in the forest telling campfire stories and drinking hot cocoa and making s'mores."

"Well, that's another thing... I don't know if I want to take Alexander on something like this. It might be dangerous."

"Dangerous?" Rose snorted. "We're just going to have a little look-see. It won't be any more dangerous than camping out in your own back yard."

"But why would you want Tom in on it? You don't even know him. Or my friend who knows about GPS, for that matter. I thought this was some great secret only you and I would know about?"

Rose dismissed this with a wave of her hand. "Who says they need to know any of the details?" she whispered. "I'm guessing both of these young gentlemen would come simply because you invited them. That's how it works between men and women."

"What the hell, Rose?" Meryl gaped. "What are you suggesting I do? Ply my feminine wiles to get them to go along with your insane plan?"

"Really, Meryl, you are so dramatic sometimes," Rose sighed, noisily dumping a stack of dishes in the sink. Meryl couldn't tell if she was really angry or just feigning exasperation. With Rose, it was often impossible to tell sincerity from performance. "We're not asking them to rob a bank or kidnap someone. One of them just helps us find a spot on the map and the other helps us get there in his big four-by-four Jeep. Easy-peasy. If we don't fill them in on all the particulars, well, that's our business. 'Feminine wiles' have nothing to do with it. They'd go just because you asked them to."

Meryl said, more calmly this time, "Just do me a favor and don't make any more plans for me and Tom, okay?"

"Absolutely. Cross my heart."

"Thank you."

"I'm sorry if I violated any boundaries."

"Okay."

"But he's still sweet on you, you know?"

"Tom likes girls. It could be any girl. I just happen to be in close proximity, that's all."

"Say what you will, but you have history and a child in common," Rose smiled. "That counts for something with men, even those who aren't real daddy material. He drove all the way from Portland to see you."

"Hardly a major sacrifice on his part. It's a ninety minute drive and not one he's bothered to make in almost a year. Plus, he's here to see Alexander, not me."

"You and Alexander are a package deal. He sees one, he sees the other."

Meryl glanced quickly back at the adjoining room where Tom was driving a plastic dump truck up Alexander's arm and into his tousled hair. The child was laughing loudly.

By midnight, the play had long since ceased and Alexander had fallen asleep on the floor with the dump truck tucked under his arm. Meryl scooped him up and carried him into the bedroom. She slipped the socks off his tiny feet and tucked the blankets in around him. He didn't stir, other than the gentle fluttering of his eyelashes as Meryl's caress over his feet induced a dream about running barefoot in ankle-deep grass. As she rose from his bedside, she started to see Tom standing at the doorway, watching her.

"You're really awesome with him," he whispered.

She shrugged. "Years of practice helps," she replied. "You should probably head out, Tommy. It's late."

He squared his shoulders and grinned impishly. "Seriously? You're going to make me sleep in my car again?"

"I didn't make you sleep in your car the first time," she retorted. "You have free will."

"Come on, babe," he replied. The smile broadened and he moved closer to her, but the movement was almost imperceptible. "I've been good, right? We're all getting along. Don't make me sleep in the cold."

Meryl paused in her reply, but it was purely for effect. "Please reference my previous comment about you having free will and all. If you don't like the cold, I suggest you go get yourself a motel room."

His eyes moved, jumping across to her bed and then quickly back to her face. Like his small encroachment into her personal space, the gesture would've been undetectable to anyone else. His motions were well-practiced, almost second nature to a man who was used to getting what he wanted without much effort. But Meryl caught it and her mind immediately flashed back on what she had told Rose in the kitchen: Tom liked girls. A lot. It's not like he had gone without female companionship in all the months since their breakup, silently pining for the "one who got away." Meryl knew that she'd never been "the one" and she seriously doubted that "the one" even existed for him. But his subtle intimation, the way he was lingering at the doorway, was intolerable. Meryl flushed.

"*Seriously?*" she barked.

"What?" he chuckled. "Is there something wrong with that?"

"How do I begin to answer that question? You have more nerve than a toothache."

"*I have more nerve than a toothache,*" he laughed. "What is that? Where did you hear that?"

She shook him off. He was trying to deflect her attention. "When you live with Rose you start picking up these weird little phrases. How about if I'm just fucking blunt with you? No fucking way in a thousand fucking lifetimes."

Tom was unfazed. His smile broadened. "Wow. That's a lot of fucking lifetimes."

"You got it."

"You didn't mind once upon a time."

"That was a long time ago, Tom."

"Not so long."

"Look," she took a deep breath and conjured up a tone like an adult might take with a disobedient child, both stern and somewhat condescending, "you're gonna blow this, buddy. It's bad enough that you show up unannounced, but if you think that you're gonna crash at my house and take privileges like that, you need serious help from a trained professional. It ain't gonna happen."

His smile didn't disappear, but it twisted into something more uncomfortable, the reaction of a man who from experience knew that women could be both offended and flattered at the same time. "No problem," he said. "You can't blame a guy for trying, right?"

"Go to your car, Tommy," she grumbled. She escorted him to the front door and held it open for him. She saw Rose peek in at them from the kitchen, but she quickly vanished once Meryl spotted her. .

"So I can come by and see Alexander again tomorrow?" he asked.

"I would suggest you call ahead of time to make sure it's convenient," she responded.

"Shall I call your secretary and make an appointment or are you actually going to give me your number?" he snickered. This time, it was Meryl's turn to be unimpressed. She quickly wrote her number on a scrap of paper and handed it to him. Then, without another word, she closed the door and turned out the exterior light before Tommy had even made it to the top of the steps.

Again, she didn't sleep a wink.

CHAPTER ELEVEN

By 10:00 a.m. the following morning, Meryl found herself lying on her back in a nest of pillows with her legs propped straight up against the wall. She wiggled her toes and for a moment wondered how it would look if she painted her toenails bright green. The thought didn't linger, however, and her mind quickly turned to Ike.

If she was being honest with herself, Meryl couldn't say whether she wanted to see Ike because she was interested in him or because it was a way to avoid Tom. She knew that part of her sleep issues had to do with Tom's proximity, even if he was camped out in his Jeep on the other side of town or wherever he decided to hole up for the night. It was this emotional melange — the combination of resentment and an uncomfortable but lingering affection for Tom — which finally compelled her to snatch up her cell phone and dial Ike's number.

By the fourth ring, Meryl was feeling deeply remorseful, certain that Tom's presence had somehow scared Ike off. Then the ringing abruptly stopped.

"Hey, you," Ike chirped. "How you doing?"

Meryl blurted out:. "What are you doing for lunch? Do you want to meet me?"

"Oh, me? Why, yes, I'm doing fine? Thanks for asking," " Ike replied sarcastically. "And how are you?"

"Smart ass."

"Well, come on. No 'hello, how are you' or anything? Didn't your mommy teach you any phone manners?"

"Ike, if you'd been paying attention to any of my stories about my mother, you would realize how completely retarded that question is."

"'Nuff said. How are you?"

"I'm okay. Sorry I haven't called earlier. That was probably pretty rude."

"Nah. I figured you were spending time with your friend." He stumbled over the word 'friend,' which made Meryl smile.

She snorted. "He's Alexander's father, but that doesn't mean he's my friend."

Ike's voice raised an octave. "Oh. That's cool. So what's up?"

"I have the day off from work and I'm gonna walk down toward campus. Wanna meet me at that Hawaiian cafe? You know what I'm talking about?"

"Sure," Ike replied. "How about at eleven-thirty?"

"Actually, I was hoping you could meet me sooner, like in the next thirty minutes? Would that work?"

"Uh, yeah, I guess so. It'll take me about that long to get ready and walk over there."

"No problem. I'll get a table and meet you inside." She hesitated and then added, "I wanna talk to you about that whole geocaching thing, if that's okay?"

"You thinking about starting it up?"

"No, but it's related. Well, kind of. I have something that I may need your help in finding, let's just put it that way."

"Wow. Spooky."

"I didn't mean it like that," she assured him. "I'll try not to be such a babbling idiot and explain better when I see you."

"Okay, no problem. See you soon."

Meryl hurriedly dressed and struggled to get Alexander ready although the child seemed quite content to stay in bed. He fussed and whined and ultimately they left the apartment nearly thirty minutes later than she had wanted. Her urgency was completely contrived. She knew Tom would eventually show up and she wanted to be busy when he did. As they left the basement and stepped into the mid-morning sunshine, she immediately spotted Tom's Jeep parked along the street nearby. She could see him nested in the back seat in a pile of blankets and decorative pillows which were clearly borrowed from Rose's bedroom.

A part of her was relieved that Rose hadn't snuck him back into the apartment and onto the couch. There was another part of her that was intensely irritated that she'd snuck the pillows out to him. "That bitch," she said under her breath.

Alexander caught it. "Wub Mah-mee?" he asked.

"Nothing, sweetie. Let's go this way," she replied, directing him quickly down the street and away from the Jeep.

By the time they arrived at the restaurant, they were nearly forty minutes late. Ike had waited. Meryl knew he would. For a moment, he looked confounded by the presence of the small boy clinging to Meryl's hand and she suddenly realized that she hadn't mentioned bringing him.

Alexander looked up at him and blinked.

Ike recovered quickly, "Hi, there," he grinned. "I'm Ike. What's your name?"

The child beamed and replied, "'Skander."

Ike nodded but he didn't understand. "His name's Alexander," Meryl interpreted.

"Awesome. I'm very glad to meet you."

"Dat okay," Alexander said dismissively as he climbed into a chair next to Meryl.

"Sorry we're so late," she said to Ike. "I didn't get a lot of cooperation getting out of the house."

"Not a problem. I haven't ordered yet."

A waitress quickly presented herself, distributing glasses of ice water and a coloring sheet and a basket of crayons for Alexander. The boy began to scratch dark waxy lines across the paper.

"What're you coloring?" asked Ike.

"Da fiss," Alexander answered, turning the sheet to show Ike a school of fish now partially blotted out by his heavy slashes of green and yellow.

"He doesn't color inside the lines yet," Meryl said. "Not enough hand-eye coordination at his age."

"I'm kind of the opinion that coloring inside the lines is really overrated anyway," Ike replied. He glanced around the restaurant, taking in the cluttered decor of old fishing nets strung with twinkle lights, battered surfboards, artificial palm fronds and fiberglass sea creatures suspended from the rafters. "You must've chosen this place on purpose?" he smiled.

"Yeah, I guess it's all part of my stupid Hawaiian fantasy," she confessed.

"You'll make it there. Once you get that degree in marine biology, anything will be possible."

Meryl felt embarrassed and replied quickly, "Actually, that's kind of what I wanted to talk to you about."

"Really?"

She let out a soft groan and covered her eyes with her hands. "I can't believe I'm telling you this, especially since we just met."

"Hey, if you're gonna ask for tuition money you came to the wrong guy," he joked.

"No, it's actually a lot crazier than that."

"You need a kidney?"

She suppressed a giggle. "No."

"Ninja assassins are out to get you and you need me to take you on a daring cross-country drive to sanctuary in Mexico?"

She was laughing openly now, but was still covering her face with her hands. "Crazier," she said.

"Wow. Ike is intrigued," he replied. "How about you just tell me? I'm assuming it has something to do with geocaching, right?"

She took an unsteady breath. "You know those coordinates you helped me find?"

"Sure. The coordinates to nothing in the middle of nowhere?"

"Turns out they weren't to nothing. Turns out my roommate believes that they'll lead her to a gold mine. A lost gold mine."

Ike let out a single awkward guffaw. Meryl and Alexander were staring at him expectantly. The child flashed a large grin. "Okay," he replied, "I so wasn't expecting that."

"Crazy, right?"

He shrugged. "I guess I'd say *different.*"

"Are you being polite?"

"No, I'm being honest. I figured there had to be more to those coordinates than you let on. I wasn't expecting a gold mine."

"Neither was I. My roommate — her name is Rose — kind of sprung it on me." Meryl paused to let the waitress take their order and then continued: "It turns out this is why she moved to Oregon. She's been doing a lot of research and she's convinced that there's this nineteenth century gold mine hidden out there somewhere."

"Well, she doesn't sound any crazier than anyone else who goes treasure-hunting. Even if you don't find anything, a lot of people just enjoy the search, you know? And the mystery of it all."

"Kind of like people who do geocaching?"

Ike tipped his water glass to her. "Yeah, just like them," he chuckled. "So what can you tell me about the mine?"

"Not much. It's a gold mine. It was abandoned due to some kind of curse and no one's ever been able to find it again."

"So it's like the Lost Dutchman?"

"What's that?"

"The Lost Dutchman is a very famous gold mine legend from Arizona. This gnarly old prospector found a rich vein of gold hidden in the mountains outside of Phoenix but never shared the exact location with anyone. He ended up taking the secret to his grave. People have been trying to find the Lost Dutchman ever since and some have died or disappeared in the process, which I suppose is what led to the legend that the mine is cursed."

Meryl suddenly felt very uncomfortable. It showed on her face.

"What?" Ike asked.

"Rose is from Arizona."

"Oh. So?"

"Do you suppose she would have known about the Lost Dutchman?"

"I don't know how anyone looking for gold *couldn't* know about the Lost Dutchman. It's a very famous legend."

"Shit," Meryl grumbled.

"Why? What's the problem? Do you think your roomy is bullshitting you?"

"I don't know. She's shown me a ton of stuff on it but I also don't know her too well and, well, there are other issues too..."

"Spill it," he commanded.

"I don't have any proof of anything, okay. It's just that she seems like she's hiding something. She retires from being a school teacher and then one day moves half-way across the country to go looking for a gold mine. She gave up everything to come here. Her home, her friends, whatever... And showed up on my doorstep with whatever she could stuff into her car. And she's old too. She's in her sixties."

"Is her being old one of the weird things?"

"No, I just think it's strange for someone her age to be looking for a gold mine."

"I guess it's not typical, but then I have grandparents who went backpacking in the Andes for their fortieth wedding anniversary."

"Okay, how about this: she won't get a post office box because she says she doesn't get any mail. And she doesn't have a bank account because she says she doesn't trust banks."

"How does she pay her rent then?"

"Everything's in cash."

"Does she have a mattress stuffed with money?" he chuckled.

Meryl shrugged.

"Sounds to me like she's trying to stay off the radar," he offered. Then he gasped, "Shit, do you think the Ninja assassins are really after *her*?"

"Shut up. I'm being serious here. Do you think I should be worried about that?" Meryl answered.

"About ninjas?"

"Ike. C'mon."

He shook his head slowly. "I don't think refusing to get a mail box or a bank account is illegal or immoral or anything. Maybe she's an anarchist?"

"A retired public school teacher, Ike?" cackled Meryl. "That's about as far from anarchy as you can get."

"You don't know she's a retired school teacher."

"Huh?"

"Did she show you her teaching certificate or snapshots from her retirement party?"

Meryl knew he was teasing her and she began to feel self-conscious about her own paranoia. "Of course not. It never even occurred to me to ask. I mean, how would you work that into casual conversation?"

He arched his eyebrows and cried dramatically, "So what kind of reference check *did* you do on this maniac before you moved her into your home?"

Suddenly Meryl felt stupid. She replied sheepishly. "I let her move in because she was the only person I interviewed who didn't take one look at Alexander and treat me like I was a leper."

"Good enough," Ike nodded.

"Maybe it was a mistake?"

"Maybe it's nothing. I'm not advocating for over-reaction here, but if you're really curious, why don't you just check out her story?"

"How do I do that? It's not like I can hire a private investigator."

"You don't have to do anything that elaborate, but you could check out the gold mine story pretty easily without relying on what she's shown you. Do you know who owned it?"

"Nothing more than his last name. Rose found his original mining claim — or at least what she said was the original mining claim — but the owner's kind of a big mystery. I know more about this boy from Newport who went looking for the mine as an adult but never found it."

Their Hawaiian-style hamburgers had arrived, smelling of smoky beef, sweet grilled pineapple and mango sauce. The waitress shuffled around their plates and then set a basket of large fried chicken strips in front of Alexander. The child looked bewildered.

"Those look kinda big for you," Ike said to him. "Do you want me to cut those up for you?"

Alexander nodded and waited patiently as Ike diced the meat into small chunks.

"It's really hot," he said to Alexander. "Do you know how to blow on it to make it cool?"

Alexander blinked twice and smiled. "Hot?" he asked.

"Right. Hot. You can blow on it. Watch." Ike skewered a piece of chicken on Alexander's fork and raised it to his lips and blew gently. Alexander took the fork and imitated him with slightly more saliva than Ike had intended.

"Great," Meryl beamed, "you just taught my son to spit on his food."

Ike shrugged. "I just impart knowledge. I don't claim any responsibility for how it's used."

Alexander tried again, and again with sloppy, unappetizing results.

"Your tongue needs to stay in your mouth when you do that, kiddo," Ike told him. He then turned back to Meryl and asked, "What were you saying about Newport?"

"This is how Rose found out about the mine," explained Meryl. "She found a child's storybook from the early 1900s which had a story about the mine. If you read it, you just think it's a creepy kid's story. But the boy who originally owned the book — his name was Elijah Comstock — had made all these notes in the margins. He clearly thought the mine was real and apparently spent his adult life looking for it."

"And this Elijah Comstock lived in Newport?"

"Originally. His father was the town doctor and later he became a doctor too. Rose believes that the man who owned gold mine was one of Elijah's father's patients and personally told Elijah details about the mine."

Ike brightened. "Okay, so there's your lead. If you can find out more about Dr. Comstock then you can find out more about the mine."

"Dr. Comstock's been dead for over twenty years, Ike," Meryl frowned.

He shrugged. "Hey, you're the one with the curious mind. You figure out where we need to go, and I'll drive us there."

Meryl was surprised. "You have a car?"

"Is that so unusual?" Ike laughed.

"I've never seen you drive, I guess."

"Yeah, I live in teeny-weeny Corvallis. Who needs to drive here when everything's a five minute walk from everything else? But I'm serious, if you want to take a road trip, I'll act as chauffeur."

"That's really nice of you, Ike."

He shrugged. "It's no biggie. You have me interested now."

"Would you be interested enough to help me with one other thing?"

"What's that?"

"I kinda told Rose how you know all about maps and GPS and such... And she kinda wanted me to ask you to help us find the mine."

"If the mine's real, you mean?" he asked.

"Of course. Like I said, the mining claim seems to be real. She showed the paperwork to me. That's how she got the GPS coordinates I gave you, although it's safe to say those are pretty imprecise. Rose has a GPS thingy like yours, but she has no idea how to use it."

"You know, the mine could be something as small and hard to locate as a hole in the ground."

"I guess I didn't think of that. The storybook made it sound like it was a pretty big operation, using lots of men."

"I think the best I could promise you, Meryl," he said, "is to get you to the claim site. But you'd still have to search the forest to find the mine entrance and that might be impossible after all this time."

Meryl smiled, coyly. "So is that a 'yes?'"

"I'll reserve my answer until I know a little more, okay? Maybe after we learn more about your dead doctor."

"Okay. I know he lived in Benton County up until his death, so maybe he still has family around?" Meryl said. "I have tomorrow off too. We could go then if it doesn't interfere with your classes? I'd have to bring Alexander, though. I can't afford to put him in daycare if I don't need to."

Ike leaned close to the boy, who was still diligently blowing on every chunk of chicken although they had long since cooled to room temperature. "What do you say, kiddo?" he asked. "Do you want to ride in my car? You can even listen to my iPod."

"Ride in your cah?" Alexander said, wide-eyed.

"Yeah," beamed Ike. "He's in."

After lunch had concluded, Ike walked with Meryl and Alexander back to the large clapboard house with the dark red trim. Tom's Jeep Cherokee had disappeared from the street, which both relieved and disappointed Meryl. There was a part of her that wanted him to wonder where she was, maybe even to be worried about it. Certainly he'd wonder if she was with that college boy he'd seen her with the other day. Maybe the thought of it would even hurt Tom a little. Meryl smiled at the thought of that.

The basement was dark and quiet when they entered. The bedding Rose had obviously loaned Tom was now neatly stacked on the couch. Alexander pushed the blankets and pillows aside as he searched out the television remote control and began flicking through the channels.

"Come here," she said, touching Ike's elbow fleetingly. "Let me show you something in the bedroom."

Ike blushed immediately.

"Oh, God," Meryl cringed. "Sorry. I totally didn't mean it to sound like that."

He composed himself. "I totally didn't take it that way."

Meryl ignored his lie. She even found it charming. She led him into Rose's room and allowed him to quietly soak up its character. For a small space, Rose had crammed a lot into it and Ike quickly inspected all the photographs, diagrams, charts and maps which covered the desk and decorated the walls.

"Wow," he said softly. "She's really into this, huh?"

"That's an understatement. What do you think? Does this seem like the room of a psycho?"

Ike's gaze flicked from place to place. "I'd say she's overzealous," he answered. "But that's not psycho. Where's this book you were talking about?"

Meryl retrieved *The American Boy's Adventure Reader* from its usual spot next to Rose's laptop and handed it to him. He thumbed quickly through the dogeared pages and read some of Elijah Comstock's notes aloud. "Dr. Comstock and your roommate seem to have similar obsessions," he stated.

"Tell me about it."

"So what else do you know about this dude?"

"She showed me his obituary, but that only had general information about his life. It did mention that he was an avid gold prospector who spent a lot of time traveling through the Oregon forests." Suddenly her eyes widened. "Wait a second... she had a sticky-note on one of the pages in the book with a partial address on it, I think. I didn't think much about it the first time I saw it."

Ike flipped through the pages and quickly found the scrap of paper. "Frostwood Lane, Benton County," he read as he slid into Rose's desk chair and tapped his fingers against the touch-pad on her laptop. With a few skillful keystrokes he mapped the address. A colorful satellite view of the Oregon countryside, crisscrossed with roads and labeled with tiny pins and photographs unfurled across the monitor. He tapped the touchpad twice and image blurred, enlarged and refocused. The photograph was difficult to interpret, but appeared to be a bird's-eye-view of a large house and several outlying buildings located at the end of a twisted dirt road.

"That can't be his house," Meryl said disbelievingly.

"Well, this is the address listed for him. Does he have any surviving children?"

"He had two sons and a wife, but they all died before him."

Ike took out his smartphone and entered the house's address and GPS coordinates into it for future use. "Well, if the family members are all dead, I don't know who's living in this house now, but it seems like we need to check it out tomorrow."

"You mean just show up on their doorstep?"

"Why not?" he grinned. "If they don't want to talk to us, they'll tell us. But if the house's current occupants knew poor ol' Elijah, maybe they'll be able to tell us where he was prospecting and what he found. In any case, it's an objective source for confirming your roommate's story."

Ike quit the web browser and reset the laptop to the same state in which he had found it. He picked up *The American Boy's Adventure Reader* and sat for a long minute, quietly contemplating its worn spine. Then he rose and wandered over to the bookcase, tapping the book gently against the shelves. Meryl could see his eyes darting back and forth, scrutinizing everything. There was a strange warmth which rose inside of her as she watched him, a mingling of admiration and curiosity. Aside from Tom, Ike was the only man she'd felt anything close to a serious attraction for, even if their relationship could only be counted in days. Her pregnancy and Alexander's subsequent birth had kept her from experiencing so many of the rites of passage young women enjoyed, including the simple delights of dating. It was odd that snooping through her roommate's belongings with a boy she barely knew seemed like a date, but then Meryl knew she had little to compare it to.

"She's a gambler?" Ike murmured.

"Hmm?"

He tapped a fingernail against the oversized champagne glass. It chimed softly. "She's spent a lot of time in casinos," he said. "And it looks like she won a few times, too."

"I noticed that too. What do you think that means?" Meryl asked.

He shrugged. "I suppose it means she likes money and wants to be rich."

"Who doesn't?"

"Exactly. But it also explains why she's looking for a lost gold mine. She wants to get rich. Filthy rich." He crouched down and inspected the lower shelves, his fingertips sliding across the various knickknacks as he assessed them. "Yeah," he said, almost inaudibly, "she definitely likes money..."

He reached for the wooden chest partially hidden behind the champagne glass. Meryl had noticed it the first time she'd searched Rose's room, but didn't bother to open it for the same reason she hadn't open any drawers or cabinets. It seemed like it was less of a violation of privacy if you were just inspecting what was sitting in plain sight. But opening things?

"Wait!" she cried just as Ike began to lift the chest's lid.

He frowned at her. "What's wrong?" he laughed.

"Maybe we shouldn't open things?"

"Why not?"

"Does it cross some kind of weird line, do you think?"

Ike's frown deepened. "Really?"

"It just seems like if you put something inside a little treasure chest you probably don't want people looking in there."

"Well of course you don't," he replied. He sounded almost sarcastic about it. "But I guess if we're already snooping through someone's room we shouldn't be total hypocrites here, Meryl. We're already being shitty. Might as well go for broke." He didn't wait for her to reply and immediately raised the lid and let out a slow, deep whistle.

"What?" she asked.

"Check it out," he said, whispering for some reason.

She tucked herself up next to him and he raised the chest's lid a little more. Inside, neatly arranged in rolled bundles, were piles of cash. From what Meryl could see, it appeared to be mostly twenties and fifties bound up with rubber bands.

"So this is why she doesn't have a bank account," mumbled Ike.

"Holy shit."

"Yeah."

Meryl was just about to reach for one of the bundles when there was a sudden burst of noise coming from the living room. She heard the front door bang into the wall and loud voices echo through the basement rooms.

Alexander shouted happily: "Rode! Tommy!"

CHAPTER TWELVE

In the wave of panic which washed over her, Meryl found herself momentarily frozen. Ike was staring at her, his hand still resting on the edge of the wooden chest filled with the bundled cash.

From the outer room, Tom's voice: "Hey, Alexander! Where's your mommy?"

Then Rose: "Meryl! We need help! We got a car full of groceries!"

Forcing herself to move, Meryl grabbed Ike by the wrist and led him quickly and quietly out of Rose's room and down the short hallway to her own.

"Act casual," she whispered to him, sounding simultaneously stern and ridiculous.

"Really?" he whispered back. "I was thinking I would act Scottish. I do a really decent Scottish brogue."

"Fucking smart ass."

He looked at her with amusement, then startled when he realized he was still holding Elijah Comstock's tattered book.

"Meryl?" Tom called again, louder this time. "You here?"

Almost instinctively, Ike tucked the book into his pants at the small of his back and pulled the hem of his shirt down to hide it. Tom appeared at the end of the hallway. The three of them stared at each other. Silently.

Ike spoke first. "Hey, man. How you doing?" he asked. There was a distinct tinge of cockiness in his voice which Meryl hadn't heard before. When these two young men had first encountered each other in the comic book store, Tom had the advantage of surprise. This time, Ike held that advantage and he was clearly enjoying it.

"What's up, Turbo?" Tom replied, grimly.

Meryl took Ike by the elbow and led him over. "I guess you guys didn't get a chance to meet," she said, hoping her nervousness wasn't evident in her voice. "Ike, this is Tom."

"How you doing?" Ike repeated, extending his hand.

Tom took it without pause and gave it a firm shake. "I'm fantastic," he said. "You?"

Ike shrugged nonchalantly. "Awesome."

"Wow. That's super."

"Yup. Sure is."

"It's like two dogs sniffing at each other through a garden gate," Rose interjected. She shouldered her way between them and grinned broadly. "Did I hear that you're Ike? The fella who knows all about these GPS thing-a-ma-jiggies?"

"Uh. Yeah," Ike stammered.

"Brilliant. We will so need to discuss that, but right now I have a bunch of groceries that need to be put away. Come give us a hand, please."

Rose proceeded to organize the three of them like she was lining up her students for recess and marched them out to Tom's Jeep. Once the groceries had been unloaded onto the kitchen countertop, Ike drew Meryl aside.

"I gotta cut out," he said. "I have a class in forty-five minutes and I still need to go back to my dorm room and get my textbooks."

"No problem," Meryl smiled. "Thanks for everything."

He turned to leave when she caught him by the sleeve.

"Ike, you still have Elijah's book down your pants," she whispered urgently.

"Nah," he smiled impishly, "when everyone was busy unloading groceries I put it back next to the laptop."

Meryl cocked an eyebrow. "You're smooth."

He laughed. "I was trying to make up for teaching Alexander to spit on his chicken tenders. See you tomorrow morning. I'll pick you up at nine."

"Perfect."

When she closed the door and turned, she found Tom waiting for her.

"That's the same dude you were with at the comic book store," he said rhetorically.

"Yeah."

"He seems cool."

"He is."

"Let me guess... computer nerd?"

"Don't be a dick, okay? You don't even know him."

"I don't have to know him to guess Turbo's rocking Star Wars underwear."

"Why are you still here, Tom?" she asked, brushing by him and heading toward the kitchen.

He followed. "What do you mean?"

"You visited with Alexander and this's your third day here. Isn't it time for you to head back to Portland?"

"Wow, if I didn't know better I'd swear you were trying to get rid of me," he chortled.

"I don't mean to sound rude, but it seems like you've done what you wanted to do."

He shrugged. "Kind of," he answered, "but I figured I'd hang around for a few more days, maybe through next week."

"I don't remember inviting you to stay another week."

"I don't remember needing your permission. I have free will, remember?"

"Actually, I invited Tom to stay a while longer," Rose interjected sheepishly. "I didn't think it would be a problem."

Meryl seethed. Her whole body felt like it was tingling and her fingertips began to twitch. She turned away from them and absently shuffled several cans of corn niblets.

"Why are you pissed off?" Tom asked obtusely. "If you're afraid I'm gonna cramp your style with homeboy there, you don't have anything to worry about. I'm not hanging around for you, Meryl."

"Then what are you hanging around for?" she growled.

"I want to spend some more time with my son and I'm gonna help Rose with her project."

"Project? What *project*?"

"I told him about the mine," Rose answered. "Tom has generously and gregariously agreed to provide the transportation in return for a cut of any profits we make."

Meryl felt her mouth drop open. She glared at Rose. "Profits?" she gawked. "We don't even know where this mine is. It's a big forest out there, you know. Elijah Comstock spent years looking for it and still came up empty."

"Elijah Comstock didn't have the advantages we have," Rose answered. "He had to cover all that territory on horseback or on foot. He didn't have the global positioning system and off-road vehicles like Tom's Jeep."

Meryl turned back to Tom. "So that's it? You think you'll hang around for a few more days and come away a millionaire?"

"Maybe. Couldn't hurt to try," he said, flashing his trademark, infuriating, lopsided smile.

"And that's the only reason you're staying?"

"That and Alexander, like I said."

"*Really?*"

Tom smiled again, but this time it wasn't playful or roguish. It was arrogant. "That's it. Sorry if you were expecting something more."

Time had caused her to forget how, from their first meeting at a high school assembly years earlier, Tom was someone who absolutely refused to be controlled by anyone. It was taking every ounce of her restraint not to unleash on him, to remind him of every thoughtless, selfish act he'd perpetrated over all those years. She clenched her teeth and swallowed those memories. She swallowed the fact that he hadn't been at his own son's birth because — so he claimed — his cell phone had been mysteriously switched off and he hadn't received any of her panicked voicemails. She swallowed that it had been more important to him to befriend her scheming mother rather than support her. She swallowed down the realization that her son had no real memories of his father and one day she'd have to explain why that was without making Alexander feel culpable in the whole situation. She swallowed everything down. She couldn't control what Tom did, but at least she'd deny him the knowledge that he could still hurt her.

"You're not staying here," she said bluntly.

"Meryl, be reasonable," Rose answered in her best sing-song teacher's voice.

"No, Rose."

"I live here too, Meryl. I pay half the rent, half the utilities. I don't think it's appropriate for you to tell me who I can and cannot offer the couch to on a completely temporary basis."

"Are you just trying to piss me off? You know how I feel about this. How can you think this is okay?"

"There will be rules," Rose said. "The first of which is a full and complete understanding that no one gets in your way. Isn't that right, Tom?"

He nodded stiffly. "I meant what I said. I'm just gonna help Rose out and visit with Alexander when it's okay with you. That's it.

You and Turbo can go off and have a big fat geek wedding for all I care."

There was an instant when Meryl fantasized about grabbing Alexander by the hand, storming out of the apartment and not reappearing until Tom had returned to Portland. The fantasy quickly faded, being both childish and impractical. As satisfying as such of display of self-righteous indignation might've been, she had nowhere to go and therefore no luxury for being so dramatic.

"Darling, I really didn't mean to spring this on you," Rose insisted. "Tom and I discussed it while we were at the supermarket and we had every intention of talking to you about it. Tom just let the cat out of the bag faster than I expected. But I want to assure you, this is just a business arrangement. Tom drives me in, Tom drives me out, Tom goes home. Easy-peasy."

Meryl didn't reply. Or more to the point, she couldn't reply. It was taking all her focus to keep from exploding.

"It just seems like Meryl might have other ideas about my motives," Tom said. "I hope I've cleared that up now?"

"Yes, Tom," Meryl responded coldly, "I think I understand your motives completely."

CHAPTER THIRTEEN

True to his word, Ike knocked on Meryl's door at exactly 9:00 a.m. holding a cardboard carrier with four cups of coffee and a juice box for Alexander. He was nicely dressed, maybe overly so for just a long drive through the Oregon countryside. But again Meryl assumed part of that was for her benefit, and part of it was for Tom's. She hadn't told Tom about the outing. Still fuming from their argument the day before, she took some measure of delight in seeing him look acutely embarrassed that Ike had not only caught him sitting around in a pair of gym shorts and a ratty T-shirt, but had also made the gesture of bringing him coffee.

Ike extended a cup to him and smiled. "Sorry, I hope I didn't wake you. Coffee?"

Tom shook his head. "No, thanks," he replied. "I try not to drink too much. The caffeine's bad for the heart."

Ike shrugged and handed a cup to Rose who accepted it eagerly. "Aren't you a sweetheart?" she cooed. "Are you and Meryl spending the day together?"

"And Alexander too," Meryl replied quickly. "Ike's taking us out for a day trip."

"What kind of car you got?" Tom asked. He felt the need to stay a part of the conversation, and asking about cars was usually a safe subject among guys. Plus, he was counting on Ike knowing nothing about them.

"A Nissan Juke," replied Ike.

"Really. What kind of engine's in those things?"

"Internal combustion, I believe." Ike turned his back to Tom before he could catch his sneer.

Rose frowned. "I don't know what kind of car that is. Is it a four-wheeling dealy-bob like Tom's Jeep?"

"Not likely," Tom snorted. "You wouldn't get far off-roading in a Juke."

"That's true," Ike said. "My parents bought it for me as a high school graduation gift, but I don't think they intended for me to take it on safari or anything."

"Meryl," Tom interjected, "I thought I might spend the day with Alexander?"

Meryl felt her anger rising again. "You never mentioned that to me," she said curtly.

"Sorry. I didn't know I needed to make a reservation to hang out with my boy."

"Well, you do," she snapped. "And his calendar for today is full."

Rose acted quickly to avert another argument. "That works out just fine," she said, "because I was really hoping Tom would help me with some important errands anyway. So you three have a great day out and we'll see you later." With arms outstretched, she began herding them toward the door like they were a wandering flock of sheep.

Tom called to the Alexander: "How about a hug for your dad before you leave?"

The boy looked befuddled but he obediently crossed to Tom and imparted a brief and awkward embrace. Whatever Tom had hoped to accomplish by the gesture, it seemed to have the opposite effect. Everyone in the room suddenly felt very uncomfortable. Except for Meryl. Meryl felt smug.

The weather forecast called for rainstorms and they'd barely left the Corvallis town limits when drops began to patter against the roof and hood of Ike's car. It was the kind of storm typical of the Pacific

Northwest, where the clouds settled over the valley floor like swathes of dark fabric, their edges bending and curling on the stiff air currents as they dropped shifting walls of mist across the highway. The low hills and woodlands dissolved into a blurry patchwork of greens and browns. Oncoming traffic became a broken string of fuzzy headlights. Solitary farmhouses melted into soft gray shapes, only to reveal themselves a moment later when the clouds shifted again and allowed a shaft of sunlight to dance across their peaked roofs and weather-beaten shingles. Meryl watched it all through a rain-streaked window, filled with that same sense of awe she'd felt standing on the Newport beach and staring at the ocean.

Ike had plotted the directions to Frostwood Lane into his GPS unit and mounted it to the car's dashboard. The meandering route would take them down the edge of the Willamette Valley and into the forested foothills. Meryl watched with amusement as the pulsing blue dot which represented the car slid along digital roadways while an electronic, but distinctively feminine voice provided driving instructions.

"*Turn right at the next intersection,*" the voice commanded. "*Proceed one quarter of a mile and merge left.*"

"That's so weird," Meryl smiled.

"Really?" Ike asked. "I find her kind of comforting."

"Her? You call it 'her?'"

"Actually, I call her 'Miss Margaret.'"

"'Miss Margaret?'"

"Yup."

"I'm dying to hear the story behind that one."

Ike smiled. "'Miss Margaret' was my second grade teacher. Actually, her name was Margaret Ankundinov, but good luck trying to get second graders to pronounce 'Ankundinov,' so we just called her 'Ms. Margaret.'"

"And you had a serious case of puppy love for Miss Margaret and that's why you named your GPS thingy after her, right?"

"Actually, it was because Miss Margaret was always telling us what to do."

Meryl sniggered. "Freak."

"Show some respect, will ya? 'Miss Margaret' might end up making you a very rich woman."

"Well, if 'Miss Margaret' does that then she'll get every bit of my respect. Right now, all she's doing is barking orders."

Ike grinned, paused, then asked abruptly, "Am I causing some tension between you and Tom?"

Meryl glanced back at Alexander, but the child was happily watching the cartoons Ike had loaded onto his iPod, oversized headphones propped precariously on the crown of his head. "Tom and I just come with tension," she said. "He's just acting really territorial right now. He shouldn't. He has nothing to be territorial about."

"I guess that's what I want to be clear on," Ike answered. "If there's something still between you and him, just let me know, okay? You don't owe me anything. Except the truth, I guess."

"In all honesty, Ike, there's nothing between us. We have Alexander in common but that's it. Tom blew it with me a long time ago and there's no going back as far as I'm concerned."

Ike nodded but said nothing. The news pleased him, but he thought it tacky to show it.

Anxious to change the subject, she asked, "What do you think about curses?"

He was used to her strange questions and ideas and didn't bother to even look up from the road. "Are you talking about dirty-word-type-curses or someone-killing-a-chicken-in-a-room-filled-with-black-candles-type curses?"

"That last one."

"Mmmmm. I don't know if I have an opinion on that, actually."

"Do you think those kinds of curses are real?"

He shrugged. "Only to the person who's cursed, I suppose."

"Huh?"

"Well, I don't think that curses are something supernatural, if that's what you're asking? But I think if someone believes in curses, and believes they are truly cursed, then they start looking for proof in everything around them."

"Like how?"

"Well, let's say that you believed you were cursed to die at a young age. Every time you got the sniffles or a headache, you'd probably worry it was going to be the end of you. Maybe, subconsciously, you'd even do things to make yourself sick or shorten your own life. I think curses work because of the fear factor."

She turned and looked pensively out the window.

Ike asked, "Are you wondering if this gold mine's cursed? Like maybe it's Oregon's version of the Lost Dutchman?"

"Well, it was the name of the story in Elijah's book — *The Cursed Gold Mine*," she said.

"Yeah, but the story doesn't really say that there's a curse on the mine. It's not like some forest witch-doctor cast a spell on it or anything. Those people just had a lot of bad luck and bad luck leads to belief in curses."

"You sound like Rose."

"Hey, she's an educated woman. There's no reason for her to believe in curses either."

"Just in stories of lost gold mines, huh?"

Ike chuckled. "But the mine is real. She's proven that, I think."

"I guess that's my point, Ike. Elijah Comstock was real, Mr. Sykes was real, the mine was real, the gold was real... But the curse? The curse is just make-believe?"

"*Reduce your speed*," the electronic voice on the GPS unit interrupted, "*turn right in 300 feet...*"

Ike steered carefully onto a narrow and unpaved country road. They began to bounce roughly over the deeply-rutted road and Ike slowed the car to a virtual crawl. The sun had finally broken out from behind the rainclouds and it flickered as the forest canopy began to envelope them.

Ike asked morosely, "Why are you worried about this curse stuff?"

Meryl felt terribly self-conscious. She wasn't superstitious and she certainly didn't want Ike thinking she was frightened of such things. She replied firmly, "I just find it odd that Rose believes in everything else about the story *except that*. Hell, she even told me that she believes in ghosts, but not curses for some reason."

"That's because the idea of a curse doesn't fit in with her plans. It's an obstacle, so she's chosen to ignore it. I noticed she has ways of getting around obstacles."

"You noticed that from meeting her twice, Ike?"

"Hey, she doesn't understand GPS, meets me and immediately wants me to give her lessons on it. I'm a total stranger to her, but it doesn't matter because I can help her get past an obstacle. She did the same thing with Tom, right? I mean, hasn't he agreed to drive her into the forest looking for this mine? Yeah, this's definitely a lady who's figured out how to get her way. So even if there was curse, I don't think she'd ever admit to it unless it was helpful to her."

Meryl frowned. "Maybe 'curse' is the wrong word? It's too... Maybe 'mystery' is a better word? It just seems like there's a huge part of this story that's being completely ignored."

"You're talking about what happened to the original miners?"

"Yeah. Think about it, Ike: Mr. Sykes and his buddies come back from selling their gold on the coast and the mining camp's abandoned, right? They find evidence the miners had a gunfight with someone before they disappeared. Then, in the middle of the night, Mr. Sykes' buddies vanish too. But the story never gives any clues as to what actually happened to all those people."

"Probably no one knew. The forest was a lot bigger and more mysterious a hundred years ago, Meryl. It probably swallowed up people all the time and no one ever had any idea what happened to them."

"There was one eyewitness who survived."

"You mean Mr. Sykes?" he said with a sly grin.

Meryl nodded. "If Elijah's father took care of Mr. Sykes after he escaped the forest and made it back to Newport" — she glanced at the back seat where Alexander had removed the headphones and was listening intently to their conversation — "Elijah would've been just a boy a few years older than Alexander — and boys are very curious. If Mr. Sykes told Elijah about the mine, then maybe he told him what scared him so much that he gave up a fortune in gold."

Ike didn't reply and seemed to be thinking about it.

"*Turn right and proceed 500 feet. The destination is on the right,*" said 'Miss Margaret.'

The car creeped down a heavily overgrown driveway and into a thick stand of hemlock trees, stopping in front of a gray clapboard house. Immediately Meryl felt her spirits fall. At one time the two-story dwelling must've been magnificent. Its quaint form and elegant scrollwork were a testament to early twentieth century architecture when houses were unique feats of design and engineering. Wide wooden steps led up to a gabled porch with spindlework pilasters. The roof was steeply slanted with two narrow brick chimneys at either end. Thick ivy, untended for years, had covered the entire facade of the home up to the dormers on the roof. Dozens of birds had nested in the growth and they dispersed skyward in a chattering cloud as Ike, Meryl and Alexander exited the car and slammed the doors behind them.

"I'm thinking no one's home," Ike said.

"Maw-mee, whose house is dit?" Alexander frowned in response.

"It used to belong to a doctor, honey," she replied, taking the child's hand and leading him up to the porch steps. "But I guess the place was abandoned after he died."

"Judging from the state of the road, I'm thinking it was abandoned a long time ago," Ike said absently.

"Elijah's obituary said he was survived by two grandkids, but they lived out of state."

"I guess they weren't interested in moving back to the ancestral home, huh?"

"Maybe this's why?" Meryl answered, reaching into the dense carpet of ivy and dislodging a plastic sign faded by rain and time. It read: PROPERTY CONDEMNED. NO TRESPASSING. She handed it to Ike who carefully propped it up on the sagging porch steps.

Ike mumbled, "Okay, so Elijah's house is a death-trap. Got it."

"It was probably awesome once."

"Yeah, a hundred years ago..."

Meryl led Alexander up the creaking steps and peered through the dusty windows. "There's still some furniture and stuff inside," she said.

Ike opened the mailbox mounted next to the front door and extracted a short stack of leaflets, all of them curled and faded with age. He read one aloud: "'Estate sale, Saturday and Sunday, June 27 and 28, 1998. Furniture, clothing, art, kitchenware and household goods of all description. Everything must go! Two days only!'"

"That's probably how Elijah's story book made it into Rose's hands. Someone bought it, sold it and it finally ended up in Arizona," Meryl said. "It's a little sad, though. A whole life boxed up and sold off to strangers."

Ike wasn't listening. He was staring at the front door and said, "Someone's been here."

"Huh?"

Ike pointed to the window on the front door, the lower pane of which had been broken out. He turned the door knob and it clicked open. "Shall we go in?" he asked.

She hesitated. "Isn't that breaking and entering?"

"Actually, I think it's just 'entering' since someone else did all the 'breaking.'"

"Smart ass. You know what I mean."

"What harm is there? Obviously no one lives here, so it's not like we're violating Elijah's personal space or anything."

She still didn't move.

"Come on," Ike urged. "Have a little adventure."

"You stay right next to mommy," she told Alexander as they stepped across the broken window glass just inside the threshold. The house's interior was dark and musty-smelling. The living room was asymmetrical in shape with a warped hardwood floor and a beautiful red brick fire place at one end. The charred fragments of several logs still sat inside the hearth and Meryl wondered if they were the remains of the last fire Elijah had ever enjoyed in this home.

"Look here," said Ike, squatting down to inspect the muddle of shoeprints in the thick layer of dust on the wood floor. A larger mark in the dust — roughly rectangular in shape — seemed to be the spot where a sleeping bag had been rolled out.

"It was Rose," Meryl said absently.

"You think?"

"Yup. I bet she was up here days after arriving in Oregon. That's why she had the address written down. Plus, I found some boxes hidden under her desk. They were filled with men's belongings, but at the time it never occurred to me that stuff was Elijah Comstock's."

"Wow, the old girl actually broke in *and* jacked stuff," he chuckled. "There's a lot more to her than meets the eye."

"Hey, you were the one who pointed out how she's good at getting around obstacles."

"True that. But if that's the case, then our trip here was probably for nothing," he said dejectedly. "Whatever wasn't sold off in 1998 she's already rummaged through. We won't find anything new."

Although Meryl felt Ike was probably right, there was no way she could just walk away now. "We're here," she replied, "so let's have a look around. You never know what you might find?"

She took Alexander by the hand and they wandered passed the fireplace and toward the back of the dwelling where there was a dining room with a large bay window. A small wooden table with a formica top still occupied the area and was strewn with a handful of discarded styrofoam cups and plastic cutlery, presumably remnants of the 1998 estate sale. A fleeting ray of sunshine streamed through the dirty, cracked window panes, sparkling off the flecks of dust their movements had stirred to life. Beyond the glass, stretching out for as far as Meryl could see, was the forest.

"Rose thinks she's fated to find this mine." Meryl wasn't sure why she felt it necessary to mention this.

Ike laughed at her. "First curses and now fate. Are you trying to creep yourself out?"

She shrugged. "To be honest, I didn't spend a huge amount of time ever thinking about these things until I met Rose."

"Curses and fate are similar. It's all about the believer."

"So if curses are inspired by fear, what inspires someone to believe in fate?"

"Hope," he said simply.

"So was it hope that let us find Elijah Comstock's house with the front door unlocked?"

Ike guffawed. "No, that was the Global Positioning System and Rose, in that order."

The rain started to fall again, tapping hollowly against the panes of the bay window. Meryl took a few steps closer until her nose almost touched the cold, dirty glass. As with the house itself, the wilderness had begun to reclaim most everything that Elijah Comstock and his family had built in their many years occupying this remote plot of land. She could see an old stone well, now covered with a sheet of warped plywood and a pile of rocks to keep it weighted down in the wind; and what looked like a giant pile of pick-up-sticks that must have once been a small barn. Saplings were growing in a deserted vegetable garden surrounded by a meandering barbed wire fence and obscured by thick clumps of weeds and nettles. At the end of the fence line was a small gate which led into the forest beyond. It was padlocked shut with a chain so rusted its brown patina made it almost indistinguishable from the wood. Meryl couldn't help but wonder if that was the gate Elijah used every time he set off to look for Mr. Sykes' gold mine, his private portal into the mysterious wilderness beyond. An unfamiliar and uncanny feeling swept over her and for an instant she believed in both curses and fate.

"Is it weird that whenever we're together we always end up snooping through other people's stuff?" she asked.

"It's been awesome," Ike replied, flashing his rows of perfect white teeth.

It wasn't the answer she expected and it reminded her how little she actually knew about Ike and how, invariably, first impressions are almost always wrong. From day one there'd been a part of her that saw him as being out of her league in both intellect and opportunity. From the conversations they had enjoyed, Meryl knew Ike came from an affluent and tight-knit family, the kind where the members were as much friends as they were kin. Even when it had been intact, her family had never known that kind of closeness. Certainly she had vague memories of loving parents, but all those recollections belonged to a time before her father had died and her mother had retreated into herself. When she allowed herself to think about it, Meryl could still conjure up vivid memories of chopping vegetables with her father for the pot of chili he made every Fourth of July. Or being lulled to sleep by her parents watching late-night reruns of *Sienfeld*. Or awakening to the aroma of pancakes frying downstairs. But these were fragmentary recollections and they never amounted to what she imagined Ike had grown up with — a true sense of belonging and acceptance. Meryl hadn't found that until Alexander had come along and looked up at her with eyes filled as much with fascination as with love.

She called to the child: "What do you think about this house, honey?"

"Dirty," Alexander replied as he kicked a broken piece of wainscoting across the floor.

"Do you wanna go upstairs and look around with me?"

He nodded eagerly and ran to her side.

"Do you think it's safe?" she asked Ike.

"Just be careful where you put your hands and feet. I'll finish poking around down here and then meet you up there."

When Meryl and Alexander reached the landing above, she could smell fresh rain-scented air. At the far end of the hallway, a branch thick with feathery foliage was protruding from a bedroom doorway and half way into the hall. As outlandish as the sight was, Meryl found the scattered pine cones and tiny mushrooms growing between the floorboards to be stranger still.

"There's a tree up here," she called down to Ike.

Some old disturbance, whether it was wind, lightning-strike or landslide, had pushed the trunk of a fir tree through the corner of a small bedroom. But the tree had continued to grow, eventually cracking apart the ceiling and carpeting the floor with a thick bed of needles and puddles of foul rain water. It was almost as though Nature had reached out with a great hand and was trying to drag Elijah Comstock's abandoned house down into the earth. Nearly hidden beneath the bough was a rusted bedstead and the cotton and steel skeleton of a moldering mattress. The needles on the tree twitched as the wind blew through the crack in the house and coursed over she and Alexander. She was shivering by the time Ike reached the top of the stairs.

"Are you cold?" he asked.

"No, just creeping myself out."

He chuckled and stood shoulder-to-shoulder with her. She could feel the heat of his body warming her arm and could almost hear his heart beating in the space between them. Or was that her heart? She wasn't sure. They stood there looking for a long time and it was as close to a perfect moment as she could recall having with anyone outside of Alexander. But as was usually the case, the moment was transitory.

Alexander had wandered to the bedroom door opposite the fallen tree and groused, "Maw-mee, it too messy."

The room was obviously a makeshift storage space filled with packing boxes and a few pieces of unremarkable furniture draped with mold-covered bed sheets. Most of the containers here had been unceremoniously dumped onto the floor, rummaged through and then tossed aside.

"I guess the estate agent got tired of packing up Elijah's crap?" Ike muttered.

"This wasn't the estate agent," Meryl corrected him, her eyes flicking from the piles of refuse to the scratches on the walls to the scuffed footprints left on the dusty floor. The same footprints as were on the dusty living room floor. Meryl lifted the edge of a box labeled PERSONAL PAPERS with the toe of her shoe. Empty. She took a deep breath and smiled. "Rose would be looking for maps and journals and stuff like that, right?"

"Sure," he agreed. "Something useful that would help her find the mine."

"Right, because as you said earlier, if it doesn't fit in with her way of thinking, then she's going to ignore it."

"I'm not sure where you're going with that?"

Meryl turned and surveyed another stack of boxes labeled CLOTHING which appeared to have been left unmolested. "I wonder what happened to all Elijah's prospecting gear?"

They tipped out the boxes and began to sort the old garments and supplies into piles. Most of the items were frustratingly ordinary and indicative of a frontier doctor: tattered linen shirts with missing buttons, moth-eaten wool jackets, two crushed felt hats, a tangled bundle of thin ties and well-worn leather shoes. The second box contained clothing of a more casual nature, including several nightshirts, a pair of denim overalls, underwear and heavy galoshes. It was the third box that intrigued Meryl most. It contained a jumble of gear which seemed more typical for an outdoorsman. A wicker basket held Elijah's handmade fishing lures and a tin can filled with small barbed hooks that still smelled faintly of bait. There were wide-brimmed hats stained by sweat and rain, work gloves, belts, a pair of red suspenders, rubber waders and cowboy boots with soles worn thin by years of wandering over the rugged and mountainous countryside. Finally, there was a flat tin pan, a portable lantern and a long T-shaped metal pick like a geologist might use to crack apart rock samples. Meryl sat back on her haunches and sighed.

"Sorry, nothing useful" Ike said gently. "It was a long shot."

Meryl nodded and ran her fingers through Alexander's hair as the child continued to rummage through the mounds of clothing, lost in a private game of dress-up. He put a weathered belt around his waist and fumbled to secure it. Along its length were a series of hand-drawn symbols mixed with single words written in neat block-like letters. The boy quickly grew tired of it and dropped it on the floor. Meryl laid it out lengthwise so she could see the entire line of strange doodles, all of which had been scratched into the leather surface with a sharp instrument like a pocketknife. Most of the figures were extremely simple, a mixture of geometric and organic forms. About half of them were labeled with one or two written words but the rest had no explanation at all.

┌TRAIL /\\ PASS ⊖ ⋏ ▽ ≋
⊙ STOP!! ⅃ ⌣ ⇀ WATER
TRIBE ⌐⌐ °₀° 𝝅 △⌣

Ike squatted down next to her and mumbled, "Strange things to decorate a belt with..."

"They're not decorations, they're notes," Meryl replied. She quickly wrapped the belt around her waist with the line of symbols positioned upside-down. "Look, if you were hiking through the forest and you had something important you wanted to remember, you wouldn't write it down on paper because paper would get destroyed too easily. But if you had your notes scratched onto your belt, all you have to do is look down" — she lifted the edge of the belt so the symbols appeared upright to her — "and boom!"

"Dannnnggg," Ike laughed. "You must be pretty impressed with yourself right now?"

"I'm actually more impressed with Elijah," she answered, spreading out the belt again. "Whatever all this means, he clearly thought it was so important that he wanted it wherever he went. And look — some of the words and symbols have been scratched out and rewritten. He changed things, made new notes."

"Maybe he was coding the forest?" Ike suggested.

"What do you mean?"

"Prospectors did that all the time. If they were hiding a fortune, they knew it might be years before they could come back to collect it.

Since a person's memory can fade after all that time, they'd mark rocks or trees with symbols only they understood. It was like leaving a permanent trail of breadcrumbs."

"If that's the case, then if we find his symbols they might lead us to the mine."

"It's possible, right? Except that finding these symbols after all these years probably won't be any easier than finding the mine itself. It's still a bunch of needles in a haystack."

"True," Meryl replied, coiling up the belt and sticking it in her jacket pocket. "But I think I'm taking this with me anyway."

CHAPTER FOURTEEN

Rose and Tom had been busy. When Meryl returned home from her trip to Elijah's decrepit house, she was greeted by a stack of boxes and supplies inconveniently located in the center of her small living room.

"Mah-mee, what is dat?" Alexander cried with a mixture of curiosity and suspicion.

She grumbled in response, "Camping supplies."

Privately she corrected herself. It was perhaps more accurate to say that Tom and Rose had bought supplies only people with no practical knowledge of what camping entailed would think appropriate. Judging from the packaging and the quantity alone, it looked like Rose was provisioning an army rather than preparing for a three-day excursion. Some items made sense, like the two igloo-shaped nylon tents, the sleeping bags and the large carton of high-protein trail bars. However, she was unable to explain the need for a full-sized shovel, the eighteen pack of toilet paper, two nylon bags stuffed with more oranges than anyone could possibly eat in three days, or the large plastic jug of cinnamon-flavored candy.

For the next two hours, she struggled to ignore the pile, busying herself with the rare opportunity to cook dinner and do her laundry without Rose's inevitable assistance. As the evening drew on, however, her mood soured as the lopsided stack of supplies irritated like a pebble in her shoe that was slowly but persistently rubbing her foot raw.

By the time Rose and Tom came through the front door, laughing, her irritation had turned into a boil.

"Hello, darling," Rose chimed, adding a bag filled with colorful plastic rain slickers to the supply pile. "Did you eat yet? I can whip something up for all of us."

Meryl responded with deliberate coolness: "It's almost ten o'clock. We ate ages ago."

Rose didn't seem to notice her acerbic inflection and quickly checked her watch. "Is it really? Good grief. We got so involved with what we were doing that I totally lost track of time."

Meryl took Alexander's hand and grumbled, "Maybe you two can hold down the volume? It's already way past his bedtime and I need to get him settled for the night."

This time, Meryl made sure her tone and demeanor were undeniable and Rose wilted away as though someone had thrown a bucket of cold water on her. Tom, who had more experience with Meryl's moods, lingered by the front door as though he was planning to make a run for it. It angered her further that neither bothered to follow or call after her as she half-carried Alexander down the hallway and placed him under the covers. She sat in the dark on the edge of the child's mattress for a long time, letting the slow rhythm of his breathing calm her. In the outer room, she could hear Tom and Rose talking softly. Her emotions were a stew of resentment, rejection and territoriality.

After nearly an hour, Tom appeared at the doorway, his broad figure dimly illuminated by the single bare bulb burning in the hallway. "I'm coming in, okay?" he said. "Don't shoot."

Meryl sniggered in spite of herself. "Don't wake Alexander."

He crept across the room and sat cross-legged on the floor near her feet, almost like he was prostrating himself before an angry monarch. "I'm gonna cut out tomorrow morning," he whispered.

Meryl stiffened automatically. "I thought you were going to take Rose into the forest?"

"This isn't working," he said. "I'm just pissing you off, Meryl. This was a bad idea. I shouldn't have come."

"What about Rose?"

"I'm sure she'll handle it. It's not like I'm contractually obligated or something."

"But you're going to disappoint her."

In the dim light, she could see him squirm, then square his shoulders. "Don't do that," he objected.

"What am I doing?"

"Don't play those games that girls are so good at." He anticipated her protest and added quickly: "And don't tell me how I'm being sexist or insensitive or something. You know what I'm talking about."

"No, I don't. What're you talking about?"

"I'm talking about how I can't ever win with you. I came to see you and you're offended. I tell you I'm leaving and you're offended. No matter what I do, I'm screwed."

"I thought you came to see Alexander? That's what you told me."

"Actually, I said I came to see you both, remember?"

"And you've spent more time with my sixty-year-old roommate than you have with either of us," she sniffed.

Again, Tom paused in his reply. In the dark, he was just a soft contour. She couldn't see his eyes narrow or his brow knit, but she knew he was bristling. She could feel it in the empty space between them. When he finally spoke, the strain of containing his temper was evident in his voice. "I'm not playing this with you," he said slowly.

She pressed her challenge. "Playing what?"

"This game where you always put me in a maze and then dare me to find my way out like I'm some kind of retarded lab rat."

"Gee, Tommy, this is turning out to be a pretty piss-poor apology."

"That's because I'm not apologizing. I don't have anything to apologize for, except for maybe showing up unannounced. That was my bad and I'll totally take the blame for that one. But the rest is just me telling you that I'm leaving for Portland."

"Really?" she chuckled, mockingly.

"Really. I haven't been honest with you much in the past because it always seems to get me ripped up, but I figure there's nothing really to lose. I just think it's messed up that you're on me for not spending time with you and Alexander when you took off for an entire day with Ike."

"We're not together anymore, Tommy. You don't get to pop in and reorganize my schedule or determine who I spend time with."

"I'm not arguing that…"

"I know you've been with other girls since we broke up. Tess told me that much."

"I'm not arguing that either."

"Then what's your point, Tom?"

"My point," he replied, enunciating each word with great care, "is that you can't have it both ways. I'm not going to take a beating for being the bad ex-boyfriend and rotten deadbeat dad and then when I make an effort you beat me up again for trying. I get that you think I'm a complete fuck-up, but I'm really not. You're like impossible to please. You always have been. No matter which way I turn in your maze, I always hit another wall and I'm tired of it. So I'm gonna leave because I figure the memory of me will be less upsetting than the sight of me."

There was a moment, albeit fleeting, when Meryl considered stopping. To the rational part of her mind, there was no need in pressing an assault when her opponent had already surrendered and was preparing to retreat. But whether it was the lingering memory of all of Tom's past transgressions, or just that her circumstances over the last year had trained her to never back down, it was suddenly important that Tom feel more than humbled. She needed him to feel beaten.

"You know what pisses me off the most about your little field trip to Corvallis?" she seethed.

"Hmmm. Dunno. That I didn't die in a fiery car wreck on the Interstate before I even got here?"

She didn't pause to recognize his ridicule. "It pisses me off that you're pulling the same crap with Rose that you pulled with my mom, Tommy. Damn, if I didn't know any better I'd swear you have some... *thing...* for old ladies."

"Are you kidding me?" he asked, incredulous.

Part of her was screaming to stop, but she let her raw emotions carry her on. "Don't act like you don't know what I'm talking about. When we found out that Alexander was coming and I needed to you be in my corner, you comforted my mom. And then after Alexander arrived, and she made every second of my life a living hell, you just ignored it. You were more concerned about being her buddy than being my boyfriend and Alexander's daddy."

"You know," he answered, feeling almost sorry for Meryl at this point, "most girls would be happy if their boyfriends made an effort to get along with their moms. In case you hadn't noticed, moms usually don't care for the guys who knock up their little princesses."

"Fine, but in case *you* hadn't noticed, while you were campaigning for the Bestest Mom Buddy of the Year Award, my mom was treating me like a fucking slut."

"Yeah, sorry your mom was a total bitch to you, but that was going on long before I ever came into the picture, Meryl. I didn't realize you were having a bunch of mommy issues and Rose was some kind of weird surrogate."

Meryl gasped. "She's not a surrogate, you asshole." Her volume had risen and Alexander stirred, turned toward the wall and grumbled something incomprehensible.

Tom paused, but only briefly. "Really? Why not?" he asked. "From what I've seen, she's a hell of a lot nicer to you than your mom ever was. This old gal even makes you dinner every night. I think I saw your mom toast a bagel for you once. So what exactly is your problem with her and I being friendly? Or is it just because it's me?"

"Yeah," Meryl replied. "It's because it's you."

His voice faltered and he lowered his head to conceal his pain. There was a long, anguished silence between them.

Then Meryl whispered, "Why did you have to come back, Tommy? I was just getting everything sorted out. I didn't feel like I was in constant pain anymore."

"And now you do? 'Cause of me?"

"Yeah. I guess so."

"And that's why I'm leaving in the morning."

He stood up and crept out, shutting the door gently behind him so as not to disturb Alexander.

Meryl heard Rose rise early the following morning and begin her morning routine in the kitchen. Pots and pans began to clank followed by the soft sizzle of bacon. The salty aroma roused Alexander and the boy kicked off his blankets and stuck his legs straight up in the air.

"Look, Maw-mee," he chirped, "I stand on my het."

"I see that, baby," she replied groggily, mustering a weak smile in response to his acrobatics. There must've been a time when she'd been able to bounce that cheerfully out of bed in the morning, but at the moment she couldn't remember when. Maybe it had something with being a kid and your biggest care in life was what toy to play with first, she thought. Unintentionally, she reminded herself of the vacuuming she'd yet to complete, her late-afternoon shift at the comic book store and the fact that she still had to face Tom and Rose one more time.

For an instant she thought about sending Tess a text message to fill her in on the argument with Tom, but quickly abandoned the idea. Tess had always been the one friend solidly in Meryl's corner through all the drama, but Meryl didn't believe even Tess would support her now. She felt ashamed, pulled the pillow over her head and squeezed her eyes tightly shut. Alexander knelt down next to her and giggled softly. His small hand snaked underneath the pillow and his fingers curled around her nose.

"Hey," she whispered, "that's my nose."

"Ding!" he chimed in a high, piercing voice. He pinched softly.

"I'm going to need my nose back, Alexander. I have to use it later today."

"Ding! Ding!"

"Why's my nose making a dinging noise?"

The giggling turned to peels of joy, followed by "Ding! Ding! Ding!" He carefully lifted the edge of the pillow and peeked underneath. "Maw-mee, why you hiding?" he asked.

She didn't know how to answer him. After the initial exhilaration of rebuking Tom had faded, she'd spent the rest of the night feeling utterly conflicted about him, about Rose, about the allure of a lost gold mine. And about Ike too. But there was no simple way to explain that to Alexander, no easy way to confess that her problem with his father was actually much more about her roommate. Somewhere over the past few weeks, Meryl had stopped thinking about the gold mine as just being Rose's and had started thinking of it as something she had a personal investment in, whose strange history had become intertwined with her own. But when Rose revealed her secret to Tom after knowing him for only a day, Meryl had felt betrayed. Rose had become another — and Meryl cringed to use the term — "mother-figure" who seemed more interested in being friendly with Tom than loyal to her.

"Maw-mee?" the boy asked again, having not received an answer. Suddenly he gulped with excitement and cried, "Somebody here!"

Beneath the pillow Meryl hadn't heard the doorbell and Alexander had bolted out of the bedroom before she could even push the blankets off of her. "Alexander," she called, "Rose or Tommy will get it. You know you're not supposed to open the front door." But he was already gone. She stumbled out into the hallway just as Rose was letting Ike into the apartment.

"It Ike!" Alexander squealed. "Hi, Ike!"

"Hey, big guy," Ike smiled as he ruffled the child's hair. He glanced at Meryl and then across at Tom, who was still nested in a pile of bedding Rose had prepared for him on the couch, his hair twisted into an ugly corkscrew shape. "Sorry," he said. "Am I early?"

Tom grumbled his protest: "What is with you and the early morning visits, Turbo?"

"I just really like seeing you sitting around in your nasty old underwear, dude," Ike retorted instinctually.

"Early for what?" Meryl asked, cutting short what had now become and expected and somewhat tiresome exchange of insults between the boys.

"Breakfast, of course," Rose offered. "And no, you're not early, darling. This is just a house filled with lazy bones. Come in, come in!"

Meryl quickly caught Ike by the elbow and pulled him out into the stairwell and closed the door behind them. It was raining again and the pavement was freezing against her bare feet. She shuddered partially from the cold, partially from suddenly feeling very self-conscious as she stood in front of him dressed in threadbare sweats with uncombed hair.

"My idiot roommate invited you?" she asked.

Ike looked shocked. "I don't understand," he stammered. "She called me on my cell phone last night and invited me over. She made it sound like you knew about it. I thought you gave her my number?"

Meryl shook her head slowly. "I didn't give her anything. She just knows how to get what she wants, right?"

"She hijacked my phone number? Damn, I'm so fucking embarrassed right now."

Meryl smiled sympathetically. "Don't be. It's all on her, Ike. Did she say why we're all having breakfast together?"

"Something about finalizing plans for a camping trip. The trip to find the gold mine."

Meryl blinked, dumbfounded. "Shit. She's amazing. I came home yesterday and she and Tommy had filled the apartment with camping supplies. Didn't ask. Just did it. Sorry, Ike, but there's not gonna be a trip. Rose got you here under false pretenses."

Ike bit his lip. "Bummer. I was looking forward to it, actually. What happened? I thought you were getting into this whole thing?"

"Did she tell you she had invited Tommy as well?"

"No, but I figured as much."

"Yeah, well let's just say I have some mixed feelings about that part."

"Oh," Ike grumbled.

"Don't worry. He's driving back to Portland this morning. That's why the trip's off, you see. Once he goes we won't have any transportation."

"Damn, that old woman totally played me," he groaned.

"You should've known better," she teased him.

"Maybe I should just leave?"

Meryl caught his hand, suddenly aware of how cold her fingers must've felt against the warmth of his. "Just stay. Rose is a good cook and Alexander's excited to see you. You might as well get breakfast out of it."

Meryl had not exaggerated about Rose's cooking abilities. The meal she'd prepared had clearly been designed for young men and included a skillet heaped with fried potatoes and onions, fluffy mounds of scrambled eggs, a pile of bacon and fresh muffins crammed with

Oregon blueberries. The entire meal was a hot, aromatic bribe... and Meryl wondered if she was the only one who noticed.

There was little conversation except for Alexander and Ike, the only people at the table who weren't feeling generally miserable. They discussed Legos and why dogs had wet noses.

Once the empty plates were cleared from the table, Tom stretched and said, "Thanks for the grub, Rose, but I better hit it. It's a long drive back."

Rose smiled in a way that seemed both inherently sad and slightly manipulative. Ike cautiously offered to help Tom load his bags and was quickly rebuffed.

"I'll help you load," Meryl volunteered, jumping up and throwing Tom's backpack over her shoulder. "Let's go!"

Tom stooped down to give Alexander an uneasy hug, but the boy was uninterested and pushed him away. Humiliated, he left quickly without another word to Ike or Rose. Outside, he found Meryl sitting in the passenger seat of the Jeep Cherokee.

He glowered at her before swinging himself inside the cab. "Unless you're going with me, you better get out," he snapped.

"If I let you stay, and we go on this camping trip, I just want to know what's in it for you," she said bluntly.

He shook his head slowly. "Gimme a break, Meryl. Are you kicking me out or not?"

She shrugged. "I haven't decided yet."

"So what? You're having a change of heart and you came out here to save face in front of Rose and your college boy? That's so lame."

She said firmly, "Ike's coming too, you know? Rose invited him last night."

"Yeah, I figured that out for myself when Turbo showed up at the door this morning."

"And you can accept that?"

He took a quick look at her and snorted loudly. "What do you want me to say?" he asked. "I'm not in this for you, Meryl."

"Then what is it? Really?"

He looked at her incredulously. "I just want the gold."

"That's all. Just the gold?"

He moaned. "Holy fuck, you're exhausting me."

"Look, I'm reconsidering all this because, frankly, you have the only vehicle that'll get us close to the mine. If you don't go, none of us can and I want to know what's there as much as anyone. But if you go, if we're crammed together for days, I just think we need to be clear where we stand with each other."

"I'm clear. You're the one who's having a recurring meltdown over all this."

"Tommy," she said, her voice sounding unusually deep and sombre, "it hurts me having you here. I don't know how else to put it. After a year of not seeing you, I was beginning to feel normal again, and then you pop up and ruin it all."

He tightened his hands around the steering wheel until his knuckles turned white. But he didn't seem angry. It was more like remorse. He replied with a simple, "Sorry."

She nodded slowly. "So just level with me and tell me why you came."

He turned his face away from her and seemed to be intensely examining a nearby tree. "Okay," he said, "I wanted to see if there was anything left between us. Is that what you wanted to hear? You got me to confess, okay. I didn't like how things had ended and as the year went on it bothered me more and more. So I came to see for myself, okay? That's why I'm here."

Meryl had expected to feel smug, but in fact she only felt relieved. They'd spent days circling each other like two dogs disputing the same yard, and now that the truth was out Meryl felt like she could finally lower her hackles, even if just a little. "You know we can't go back to the way it was?" she asked gently. We were a hot mess together, Tommy."

"True that." He turned back to face her and his eyelids looked moist. "So, if I'm not overstepping my bounds here, can I ask if you and Turbo are... involved?"

"Nah. Just friends. I really don't know him very well yet."

Tom seemed a little relieved by the news and offered graciously, "He seems like a decent guy."

"Yeah. So if this trip happens, I assume you'll treat him decently?"

Tom laughed. "Not even a little bit."

She grinned almost by reflex. "How about you treat him decently in front of Alexander, then?"

"I can do that."

"And you could stop calling him 'Turbo,' too."

"Oh, no way. 'Turbo' stays. But I promise I won't call him anything worse. At least to his face."

"I can live with that."

"And in return," he said, "if you and *Turbo*" — he put deliberate emphasis on the name if only to annoy her — "decide to venture off on some great love affair, maybe you can wait until after I've gone home?"

Meryl blushed. "I can live with that, too."

She stepped out of the Jeep and felt warm despite the cold rain beating down on her. She ran back to the apartment. Tom stayed in the Jeep for the next thirty minutes until he had regained enough composure to walk back into the apartment and pretend that absolutely nothing had happened.

CHAPTER FIFTEEN

The following morning the rain stopped after nearly a week of continuous drizzle. There were even moments when Meryl could catch a fleeting glimpse of blue sky, which she took as a good portent. It didn't even occur to her that she was once again, and quite involuntarily, thinking about fate.

Despite the early hour and the cramped conditions, the mood inside the Jeep was almost festive as they departed Corvallis and headed toward the wilderness beyond. Meryl was relieved that Tom and Ike, who were seated next to each other in the front so one could drive while the other navigated, were chatting without the usual barbs or sarcastic inflection. Rose had brewed a large thermos of hot chocolate and was passing out cups to everyone except Alexander who was dozing in his car seat. Meryl cradled the hot styrofoam cup in her hands and shivered. She pulled up the collar on her bright orange jacket and noticed the garment smelled faintly of wood smoke. David had lent her the coat the night before and the aroma was clearly a remnant of his and Rachel's many camping excursions. She had expected an interrogation to accompany the jacket, but it never came. Perhaps it was David's respect for her father, whom he had known much longer and much better than Meryl herself, which kept him from ever playing the role of parent. Instead, Meryl and Alexander enjoyed Rachel's all-vegetarian cooking and David's humorous anecdotes about roughing it in the Oregon backcountry.

After dinner was over, David had presented her with the jacket. It was covered with zippered pockets and Velcro bands to keep out the water and the wind. Meryl slipped it on and pulled the hood down over her forehead. David clapped his hands gently around her shoulders. "That's actually not a bad fit considering," he smiled.

"It's super warm," she replied.

"Do you have some good hiking boots?"

"They're good enough," she replied, although it didn't sound too convincing and David frowned.

"How about warm, waterproof clothing?"

She nodded. Not being an outdoors enthusiast in any way imaginable, Meryl had packed herself a strange ensemble of mismatched clothing including numerous sweaters, a knitted cap with padded ear flaps, a couple pairs of wool socks she'd borrowed from Rose, and the worn leather belt that Elijah Comstock had inscribed with those cryptic symbols. "It's good enough to get me through a weekend," she assured him. She rubbed her hand over the sleeve of the jacket and added sarcastically, "Dang, David, couldn't you find a brighter color? It's making me tear up."

"First lesson of surviving in the wilderness is having the ability to be seen, kiddo. You can get lost very easily out there. One tree begins to look like another after a while."

"Well, I left a map to where we're going on the fridge," she told him. He smiled approvingly and it made her feel bad. In fact, at Rose's insistence the map on the fridge was intentionally imprecise in its details. For a moment, Meryl wanted to blurt out everything, to tell David about the entire plan, about the mine, about how she might just return home inconceivably wealthy. But she knew he'd be pragmatic, as he was about everything. He'd tell her exactly what she already knew but was trying to ignore — that the mine was probably little more than an old lady's pipe dream and she was crazy to waste a weekend beating the bushes with her ex-boyfriend and a guy she barely knew in tow. Yeah, she told herself, David's pragmatism would kill her excitement — a feeling she hadn't known for a long time and now guarded jealously. So she said nothing.

"Oh!" David exclaimed, "I have a few other things for you..."

He led her and Alexander into the house's narrow attic space and pointed across to the opposite wall. "That big red backpack over there is for you too. It has an aluminum frame, so it's very sturdy but lightweight. And then there's this..." He took her wrist and fastened a small nylon pouch to it with a thin Velcro band.

"What is?" Alexander demanded, grabbing at the strange item.

"It's a flashlight," Meryl said, pulling the device from the pouch and snapping it on. A braided cord kept the flashlight secured to the pouch.

"Having done it a few times, there's nothing worse than taking those nighttime potty breaks and dropping your flashlight," David smiled. "And I figured this would be a better, less embarrassing option than getting you one of those hats with the spotlight on the front of it. You'd look like a miner or something."

Meryl quietly noted the irony of David's words and gave him a quick kiss on the cheek. The man blushed and then looked down at Alexander, who was quietly awaiting his own gift and hoping it too would be a flashlight. Instead, David slipped tiny green mittens onto his hands which, when he clenched his fingers shut, looked like the heads of Tyrannosaurus Rex. The boy was pleased and almost immediately his hands engaged each other in fierce, primeval combat.

The Jeep bounced over a pothole and it brought Meryl's mind back to present. The quiver of excitement returned as the forest's boundary rose before them. Obscured by the shifting mist, its jagged contour reminded her of a great fortress wall complete with parapets and towers. She felt almost inconsequential as they zipped down the winding highway and penetrated the tree-line. Tom clicked on the headlights and filled the interior of the car with a soft green light. Alexander fussed in his car seat.

"Mah-mee, where duh sun goat?" he asked.

Meryl smiled. "There are too many clouds and trees, baby," she replied. "The sunlight can't get through."

Ike tapped a couple of buttons on 'Miss Margaret,' his GPS unit. "We're getting close," he announced to the group, sounding very much like a flight attendant delivering a pre-flight safety lecture. "Rose's coordinates to the mining claim are in the middle of nowhere, but according to my maps there should be an old logging road along here that'll get us into the area."

"Do you think the road might actually lead to the mine?" asked Rose.

"We won't be that lucky. It's going to be a primitive road and probably pretty hard to spot. Most of them were cut years ago by the logging companies and aren't maintained."

They drove on for some time in silence but for the hiss of the tires on the wet asphalt and the *plink-plink-plink* of raindrops hitting the roof.

"Reduce your speed. Prepare to turn right in three hundred feet," 'Miss Margaret' instructed them mechanically. Tom immediately slowed the Jeep and Meryl pressed her face closer to the window.

"Turn right in one hundred feet..."

He braked and carefully pulled the car onto the loamy shoulder of the highway. A few yards ahead, the headlights illuminated a break in the trees where a narrow dirt road curved gently to the right and disappeared into the mist. Had the GPS device not alerted them to its location, they would've easily zipped right past without even noticing. There were no fresh tire tracks in the dirt and parts of the road were being reclaimed by thick grass and colonies of feathery ferns.

"It doesn't look like it's been used in a long time," Meryl mused.

"Ages," Ike agreed.

Tom took a deep breath and said, "Tighten your seat belts and hold on. This is gonna get bumpy."

He turned the Jeep and they began to slowly roll down the rutted path. Their progress was slow, and by the second hour, had become somewhat painful as well. The constant jostling had given Meryl a sore rear end and an anxious bladder. She tried to ignore her discomfort, reminding herself that they had expected the journey to be a difficult one. She also found herself relieved that Tom was there. His boasts about the Cherokee hadn't been exaggerated. Every time the vehicle roared through a pool of stagnant water or blasted up a spray of thick mud as it climbed a slippery hillside, she became a little more grateful that Rose had invited him along.

By late afternoon, they came to a large semi-circular clearing. The sun had broken through the clouds and streaked the meadow with gold. A stiff wind rolled across the thick carpet of grass and shook the clusters of blackberry bushes, their branches loaded with dark fruit.

"Beautiful," Rose sighed.

"This may be a good place to set up camp for the night," Ike said. "According to my map, this road goes on for several more miles but we're already inside Mr. Sykes' claim."

"So that means the mine could be around here somewhere?" Rose asked excitedly.

"It's going to be a bitch to find," Tom answered, frowning at the border of thick trees which encircled them.

"Let's get out, then," Meryl moaned. "My butt's killing me."

Ike began to fiddle with the GPS unit again. "Let me mark this place real quick."

"Pin dropped," 'Miss Margaret' stated as a bright red "X" flashed on the GPS monitor. *"Location recorded."*

Tom turned off the engine and Meryl was about to open her door when Alexander chirped, "Mah-mee, I seed the monkey."

Meryl looked at him quizzically. The child was leaning forward in his seat and staring intently toward the front of the car. "You see a what, honey?" she asked.

"Monkey," he repeated, pointing.

They all turned to look, but the meadow was empty. The clouds had shifted again and the forest had receded into twilight. To Meryl's right, the prickly fingers of a blackberry bush scratched at the car door.

"Did he say he saw a *monkey*?" Ike asked.

"Yeah. You know, the famous Oregon mountain monkey you've heard so much about," snickered Meryl. But her joke seemed lost on everyone as they were all leaning forward in their seats, gaping into the woods.

"I don't see anything, do you?" Rose asked no one in particular.

"Nope," Tom answered.

He flicked on the car's high beams and a wide disk of light struck the trees on the opposite the Jeep. A vague, dome-like shape appeared, positioned just to the edge of the roadway. From that distance, with the mist and a foggy windshield obscuring any details, it was impossible for Meryl to determine the animal's species other than it was large and covered in fur.

"Hey, buddy," Ike said brightly to the child, "I think you spotted a bear."

Meryl squinted. "Really?"

"It was probably eating blackberries. Pretty cool, huh?"

"Actually, seeing a bear in the same area you plan to camp is not cool at all, Ike."

"It'll take off. No wild animal's gonna stay around if humans show up."

While Meryl knew this was generally true, it didn't make her feel any better. She hesitated. "Are you sure that's a bear?"

Ike looked again. "Definitely."

The animal moved. It seemed to extend several feet in height and then slipped further into the trees and vanished.

"Yeah, definitely a bear," Ike said confidently. Meryl didn't debate it with him. She couldn't say what the animal had been, only that it was certainly not a monkey.

No one moved or spoke for several seconds. Then Tom turned in his seat and glanced around the Jeep's interior. "So, we getting out or what?"

"What if that was a bear?" Meryl asked.

"I think they live here," Tom quipped. "But it's gone now."

Still, no one moved.

"Christ, people!" he lamented. "Did we really come all this way to hide in the car?"

"Tom's right," Rose said decisively. "Come on, you grumbling gusses! We'll build a big fire and that ol' bear won't dare to come back."

The old woman opened her door and stepped out into the gentle rain, then crossed to the back of the Jeep and raised its lift-gate. Sheepishly, everyone followed. "Here's the tent for you and Ike, my darling," she said to Tom, hoisting a green nylon bag into his arms.

Tom suddenly looked panicked. "Me and Ike's tent? There's no way in hell I'm sharing a tent."

"You're not willing to share a tent, or you're not willing to share a tent with me?" asked Ike.

"Either."

Rose was unfazed and glanced over at Meryl who gave her a look that clearly said, 'See, I told you there were going to be problems like this and you didn't listen to me.'

"Do the math, Tommy," Meryl quickly responded. "There's five of us and only two tents."

"Okay, so do the math another way," he growled. "Why can't I share a tent with someone besides Turbo?"

Ike was trying not to be offended by Tom's protestations, especially since they'd spent the last few hours chatting amicably and he was actually beginning to think of him in more positive terms. "What's the issue? You have a problem with nocturnal flatulence or something?"

"Not usually, but if you're in the tent with me I'll make an exception."

"Bring it."

Meryl interrupted: "Tommy, the women are sharing one tent and Alexander's in with us. That leaves the other tent for you and Ike. Deal with it."

"That's just sexist," he sneered. "Why can't my son and I share a tent?"

"And where's Ike gonna sleep?"

"He can build a nest in a tree."

"Tommy, if you choose to sleep in your Jeep or somewhere else, that's fine. But Ike has at least one half of that tent."

Tom grumbled something incomprehensible and tossed the rolled tent to Ike. "You get to set it up," he said.

Ike shrugged. "No problem. I understand why reading instructions might be a problem for you."

"Whatever."

"Boys, let's get started," Rose suggested. "No one will be sleeping at all if we don't get these tents up before sundown."

They set about their various tasks, which considering their cumulative ignorance took much longer than any of them expected. Once the tents were up, Tom and Rose dug a fire pit while the others scoured the stump-filled clearing for dry tinder. As she wandered its length hand-in-hand with Alexander, Meryl realized that the glade wasn't natural. Clearly, the trees here had once been as thick and tall as the rest of the forest, but decades before humans with chainsaws had destroyed all that and had left a swath of stumps as wide and as long as three football fields.   It would be hundreds of years before the towering forest had reclaimed this spot, but smaller trees, grasses and forbs had already repopulated the site.   Alder patches ringed many of the stumps and had begun to fill in the gaps between the dead roots. As beautiful as it was, Meryl also found it a little sad. They seemed so far away from humanity here, yet even this place had been touched by men. But of course, she reminded herself, the loggers who had cut down this forest hadn't been the first people here either. Somewhere, perhaps sitting in its own clearing, being slowly reclaimed by the trees, was Mr. Sykes' now legendary mine.

Rose walked over to where Meryl and Alexander were happily clambering over the stumps. She looked irritated. "Those big sacks of oranges I had... I can't find them," she said.   "You didn't happen to move them, did you?"

Meryl shook her head. "What do you mean you can't find them?"

"I mean poof — they just disappeared — like into thin air."

"Welcome to the wilderness," Meryl smiled. "Somewhere a raccoon's having a good laugh on us."

"Surely a raccoon couldn't have taken both bags," Rose argued. "They must've weighed ten pounds each. Shoot. They were darn good oranges, too."

A small shiver ran up Meryl's back. "You don't think that bear came back?" she whispered so Alexander wouldn't hear.

"Oh darling, we'd notice that," Rose whispered back. "It's not like such a grand animal could stroll incognito into our campsite."

"Yeah, I guess. David told me that we should lock all the food up in the car or hang it from tree branches or the forest minions will raid us all night long."

Rose sighed loudly and began to walk back toward the campsite. "I guess I'll go stand guard on the rest of the food until we can figure out how to secure it," she called over her shoulder. "It'll be an awful long weekend if we don't have our munchies."

Alexander continued to climb from one stump to another, providing a monologue of broken English as he imagined himself scaling towering castle walls or leaping from mountaintop to mountaintop. Within a few moments, the anxiousness Meryl had felt while squinting at the woolly shape caught in the Jeep's high-beams returned. It was like an itch in the back of her throat she couldn't scratch. It was in that instant that she knew they were being watched.

She climbed onto the flat top of a nearby stump and surveyed the ragged edge of the trees, where the original forest still grew dark and thick. The late afternoon sun cast a latticework of shadows through the branches and it was impossible for her to distinguish one shape from another. But still she waited, unblinking, like she was picking out everyday shapes in a bank of clouds. Her skin began to tingle, but she wasn't sure if it was from the warmth of the sun, the tickle of the breeze across the back of her neck, or that she was becoming more and more convinced that something was staring back at her. Then, from just inside the tree-line, something dropped. At first, Meryl thought it was a dead branch dislodged by the wind. But it didn't hit the ground nor make any noise. Instead, it looked like someone standing in the shadows had lowered a raised arm to their side. She let out a small gasp.

Alexander looked at her, puzzled. "Mah-mee, what doing?"

She didn't answer him, afraid to look away. The eyes her father once described as being those of a natural-born detective began to discern shapes from the clutter of shadows — the curve of a shoulder, a bent knee. Her anxiousness suddenly turned to fear and she grabbed Alexander by the hand.

"Come on, baby," she said as gently as possible, "it's about time to start cooking dinner."

She'd become well-practiced over the last year at tempering her emotions, so she walked with purpose without betraying anything to the child. Her mind whirled as it struggled to put a reasonable explanation to what she'd seen.

Once they reached the camp, she left Alexander with Tom and pulled Ike to one side. "Does anyone live out here?" she whispered. "I mean, on your maps, are there any towns or anything?"

The peculiarity of the question immediately put Ike on edge. "Why would you ask me that?" he grimaced.

"I think I saw someone in those trees. A man. Watching us."

He blinked at her, but didn't reply.

"I didn't see him at first because he wasn't moving, but then he put his arm down and I could see him standing there."

"Well, who was it?" he gulped.

"How would I know, idiot?" she barked. "That's why I'm asking you if there are any towns on your maps."

"Towns? There are barely roads out here, Meryl."

She paused, frustrated. "Will you come take a look with me?"

"You want me to come over to the trees with you to see if there's some creepy stalker in them?" he leered.

"If I'm seeing things, wouldn't you prefer to know that now than wonder about it after the sun goes down?"

He nodded and they slowly crossed the clearing to the breach of trees. A pair of grey squirrels fled at their approach and scampered up the scaly side of a maple tree, but otherwise there was no sign of animal life at all. They paused to listen and the forest greeted them with only the soft rustling of leaves.

"Maybe we should spread out?" Meryl suggested.

Ike was quick in his reply: "Forget that shit, babe. Haven't you ever seen a horror movie? You *never* split up. Never." He gave her a lopsided grin. "Is it possible you didn't see what you thought you saw?" he asked.

"Of course. But I've had this really creeped out feeling since we arrived here."

"It was that bear, wasn't it? You've convinced yourself that poor Yogi and Booboo are hiding in the woods, lusting for human blood."

"You say it was a bear. This wasn't a bear. It was standing upright, like a person."

"You know bears do that, right? They can even walk upright for short distances."

"Not like this. It was leaning against a tree trunk with its arm. Like this..." She demonstrated the posture and Ike made a mumbled comment about it being a very relaxed bear. "And bears don't concern you, Ike?"

"Meryl, if you don't mind my saying, I think you creeped yourself out before we even got here. All these ideas you've had about fate and curses. You can't ever turn off your brain and it's doing a number on you now. You were doing the same thing when we visited Elijah's nasty old house. And *The Cursed Gold Mine* story probably didn't help either."

She looked at him intently. "What if all those stories Elijah told people about strange things he saw in the forest weren't bullshit?"

"What if? That was *over one hundred years ago*. Whatever he encountered out here certainly isn't around anymore. Besides, Elijah wasn't a stupid man. He might've spread a lot of tall tales for the same reasons all treasure-hunters do — because he didn't want anyone else looking for the mine."

Meryl shrugged, but remained unconvinced. The idea of the curse, the disappearance of the original miners, the reason Mr. Sykes fled his own claim and never returned still nagged at her. Unanswered questions signified the uncontrollable nature of the universe, a concept Meryl generally found irksome.

They ventured further into the trees until they lost sight of the tents across the field. Meryl scrutinized the area for anything that might resemble the shape she'd seen among the trees, but there was nothing. Even the rocky ground denied her the opportunity to find footprints.

After a few more steps, she stopped and wrinkled her nose. "Well, something stinks."

Ike sniffed loudly and asked, "Is that a skunk?"

"I don't think so. I know what a skunk smells like. Maybe something died around here?"

"If that's the case, then you might've seen some animal scavenging off a carcass."

"But then where's the carcass?" she asked, taking him by the wrist and leading him further into the trees. As they walked, it became clear that the pungent, musky smell was the emanation of a living animal, not a rotting body. The itch at the back of Meryl's throat returned.

Ike seemed to sense her nervousness. "Maybe it's a better idea if we return to the campsite?" he suggested.

"I wanna find it," she protested.

"Tomorrow then. The sun's almost down and we won't be able to find our way back if we stay out here much longer."

Meryl unzipped the pouch attached to her wrist and flicked the tiny flashlight on and off quickly. "I got us covered."

"Wow, couldn't you find a smaller, more useless flashlight?" chuckled Ike.

"Don't be a hater. It was a gift. It's my pee-pee flashlight."

"Well, whatever. Let's go back. Rose had the right idea anyway. We stoke up a big fat bonfire and nothing's gonna come close to our campsite."

Reluctantly Meryl agreed, but the stink continued to burn in her nostrils for the next hour.

As night fell, she and Ike deliberately built a much larger fire than was necessary. They all sat around its edge, warming their feet as they enjoyed a feast of chipped beef over rice, roasted corn and pound cake with fresh strawberries. Meryl began to enjoy herself again, even indulging with the others in some wild speculation as to what she would buy first if they actually retrieved any gold. A house, she told them, where Alexander could have his own room with a big toy box shaped like a pirate's chest. And a college education too. For a moment, that marine biology degree didn't seem so impossible. By the time the evening ended and they all withdrew to their tents anxious for sleep, Meryl had forgotten entirely about the strange shape in the trees.

CHAPTER SIXTEEN

Meryl awoke suddenly to find she couldn't move. She could feel Alexander beneath her arm and hear Rose snoring softly on the other side of the tent, but for whatever reason her body was rigid under the covers and she was inexplicably holding her breath. As her senses cleared, she became aware of a strange warmth against her back which permeated through the side of the tent and her heavy sleeping bag. For one panicked moment, she was certain they'd forgotten to extinguish the campfire and what she was feeling was actually a building inferno. But there was no flickering fire light, no smell of smoke, only the gentle patter of rain falling in utter darkness. After several seconds, she was able to gulp in several breaths of frigid air and turn her head toward the side of the tent. She strained to see, but nothing was there. The rain clouds had blotted out the moon and although she still had the tiny flashlight strapped to her wrist, that arm was tucked under Alexander's head. She arched her back slightly, pressing against the object and found it soft despite its weight. Then, as slowly and silently as she could, she moved her free arm and tucked her hand between where the small of her back and whatever was pressing against her through the tent. The heat of the object radiated through her outspread fingers like she was warming them against a hot towel. She squeezed gently. Instantaneously, silently, the sensation was gone.

It took nearly ten minutes before Meryl could muster the courage to move again, frozen by the realization that whatever had been pressing down on her from outside the tent had been something alive, some animal which had moved away when it felt the press of her fingertips. But moved to where? Did the animal flee back into the forest, or just move far enough away that Meryl could no longer feel it? Whichever was the case, sleep was no longer an option so she fumbled for the small flashlight strapped to her wrist and snapped it on. Alexander and Rose's faces were immediately bathed in a bluish-grey light. Both were lost in a deep and untroubled sleep. As quietly as possible, she pulled on her shoes and jacket, unzipped the tent and stepped outside.

With no moonlight to see by, the forest was a vacuum in space. There was no point where the field in which they were camped ended and the tree-line began, nor where the horizon met the sky. In fact, in the dead of night in the middle of such an expansive wilderness, there was nothing to the world beyond the small disk of battery-powered light Meryl was swinging quickly around her. The rain still fell as a thin mist which tickled her cheeks and the smell of damp earth filled her nose. Placing her feet with great care, she moved around to the left side of the tent, to the spot where she'd felt the heat and weight pressing against her body, but the flashlight's beam revealed nothing beyond a thick understory of plants glistening with dew and several flat-topped stumps like all the others which filled the meadow. The exterior of the tent was undamaged, but the grass on its left edge was crushed down into an irregularly-shaped depression, as if some large body had paused there to rest. Meryl's chest tightened as the fear she'd experienced inside the tent returned. Again she moved the flashlight's beam quickly from side to side, but it wasn't strong enough to reach more than a few feet and even then the rain distorted what she could see.

Wild animals run from people, she reminded herself. *So even if there was some animal here, the moment I started to move around it would've taken off.*

But she didn't feel reassured. After all, the two other wildlife encounters they'd had in the past twelve hours seemed to contradict her logic. Neither of those animals — or were they the same animal? — had fled in terror at their approach. The thing Alexander had called a "monkey" simply withdrew into the trees where they could no longer see it; and the tall figure Meryl had spotted standing at the edge of the clearing hadn't even done that much. If anything, it stood its ground, then moved as if to confirm its presence. Wild animals didn't behave this way. Only people behaved like that.

Something shuffled behind her and Meryl spun just in time to see Rose, dressed only in woolen long-johns and a quilted coat, awkwardly extricate herself from the tent. The nylon and aluminum shell had really been too small to accommodate all three of them, and this was painfully obvious as Rose half-shimmied her way through the zippered flaps and stumbled to her feet.

"Well, there goes some dignity," she mumbled to herself, snapping on her own flashlight and moving it toward Meryl. "Are you all right, darling?"

Meryl whispered, "There was an animal in our camp."

Rose mustered a weak "Oh my!" and moved quickly to her side. "Are you sure?"

"I'm positive. It was right next to the tent. I could've reached out and touched it." She didn't bother to mention that that was exactly what she'd done.

"I don't suppose the little dickens brought back my oranges?" Rose joked weakly. Meryl didn't respond, just pointed her light toward the spot where the grass was crushed flat. Rose stooped to look. "I don't see any footprints."

"Neither did I," Meryl frowned as it occurred to her that she couldn't explain how the animal had moved away yet left no tracks on the muddy ground nor a trail of similarly flattened grass to mark its passing. There were no nearby trees to climb, so did it leap away like a frog? Or fly off? Or — and this was the thought which again sent a cold shiver up Meryl's spine — was it just hiding in the darkness nearby.

Strangely, the lack of footprints seemed to comfort Rose. "It was probably just some little furry critter looking for a quick nibble. You'd think they'd be full after all those oranges." She moved back toward the tent but paused when Meryl did not follow. "Whatever it was, it sniffed around and left," she said with a smile. "Why don't you go back to bed, hun? We have a big day ahead of us."

Meryl grudgingly obliged and curled herself a little more tightly around Alexander. Slowly her fear receded, but the lack of tracks continued to bother her. For the next few hours, every creak and rattle the forest produced caused her body to stiffen. She was anxious for the sun to finally break through the trees and chase away whatever still lingered there from the night before. She knew it was a ridiculous thought. Sunshine didn't dissipate danger any more than a child's nightlight kept monsters from creeping out of the closet. All the dawn really provided was a sense of security, but Meryl wanted it nonetheless.

When dawn finally broke, it was Rose who was the first to crawl out of the tent. Her movement roused Alexander who rolled over, rubbed his eyes and smiled. Of the three of them, he was the only one to sleep through the entire night.

"Mah-mee, weed eat beckfuss now?" he asked.

Meryl's whole body ached from sleeping on the ground and she felt so drained that the last thing she wanted to think about was food. "I think Rose's already cooking it," she muttered, keeping her eyes closed.

"Mah-mee?" the child said again.

"Go back to sleep, Alexander. We don't have to get up yet."

"Mah-mee, gotta poop," he said, somewhat more urgently this time. She helped him pull on some clothing, then helped him out of them again to use a latrine she hurriedly dug behind a copse of trees. It was a process the child found hysterically amusing. When he was done, she doused his hands with antiseptic gel before tucking them back inside his dinosaur-shaped gloves. By the time they returned to the campsite, Tom and Ike were engaged in a heated debate over the best way to restart the fire since no one had thought to throw a plastic tarp over the firewood before going to bed. Rose offered them a bag of corn chips which, she had read, made excellent kindling. But even with this, Tom produced only a single tendril of flame and disproportionate amount of smoke. In frustration, he began to threaten the fire, catching himself in mid-curse as he noticed Alexander.

He looked sheepishly at Meryl and muttered, "Oops. Sorry."

Meryl ignored it and said, "Everyone fan out. See if you can find something dry to burn."

She, Rose and Ike all took different directions and began to collect what dry wood they could salvage from the field, while Alexander squatted down next to his father to help blow on the flames. Quite intentionally, Meryl walked back toward her tent and then out toward the forest. If the animal from the night before had fled at her touch, this was the shortest route back to the cover of the forest. An animal of any size would've certainly left a path in the wet vegetation, especially if it retreated in a hurry. But there was nothing. Not a single crushed plant, not a single mark left in the soft earth. It was only at that moment, as she had replayed the incident for the hundredth time through her mind, that she realized she never heard the animal leave. As her fingers had reached out, the warmth and the pressure moved away. But soundlessly. She listed off what kind of forest animals she knew might have the size and the stealth of whatever had nestled down next to the tent. Cougars — not bears — were the only thing that made sense. But if a large predatory cat had actually crept into their campsite, why didn't it attack them as they slept?

What kind of cougar curls up next to you like it's some kind of overgrown house cat? Meryl wondered.

A weary cheer rose out of the camp as Tom finally got a good blaze going in the fire pit. After a quick meal of bacon and eggs, Rose and Ike sat shoulder-to-shoulder by the coals, he fiddling with his GPS tracker and Rose with *The American Boy's Adventure Reader* lying open in the palms of her hands like it was a hymnal she was using in church.

Rose stated: "The story says that *'the mine lies in the dark shadow of a rocky peak, not far from the banks of a roiling stream...'* In his notes, Elijah calls it a 'crick,' but I assume he meant a 'creek.'"

"What's *roiling?*" Tom asked.

"It means turbulent," Ike replied, "which I assume means this creek is rather large. A little forest stream wouldn't roil."

Tom arched his eyebrow and began to nibble on his sixth piece of bacon. "So big's easier to find than small, so that's good."

Ike shrugged. "There's a lot of 'cricks' out here, Tom."

"But there's also 'the dark shadow of a rocky peak,'" Rose added. "This is logical because we know Mr. Sykes and Mr. Bittle discovered the gold by panning the stream first, which is usually an indication that the surrounding hills have gold in them. So, if they panned the stream and found gold, then they would've built the mine on the banks nearby."

"So, we need a big stream near a big hill," Tom offered.

"I would think so," Rose agreed. "In the margin of the book, Elijah wrote that the sun rises behind the peak."

"That means the peak is to the east of the stream," Ike mumbled, holding the tracker up so Rose could see the illuminated display. "Okay, here's us... and the largest, potentially 'roiling' stream is to the northwest about two miles."

"Oh, that's not far!" Rose replied happily.

"It's not far until you have to beat your way through the bushes to get there," Tom said. "'Cause I'm assuming we can't drive?"

Ike shook his head. "Nah. We're going to have to do this on foot."

Meryl had listened quietly to the entire exchange, but at this point asked, almost rhetorically: "Could things have moved in the past one hundred years?" Everyone stared at her, perplexed. "I mean," she stammered, "creeks can change their courses, right? A creek that flowed near the mine at the beginning of the twentieth century might not be there anymore."

"I doubt things will have changed that much in just a century," Ike replied. "Not unless there was some huge geological event like an earthquake or a major landslide. I think we have to worry more about the place just being so overgrown that we could walk right by it and never notice."

"So looking for the 'roiling stream' and the 'dark shadow of a rocky peak' are still our best clues?" Rose said.

Ike looked right at Meryl when he answered. "Unless Elijah left us any other clues..."

Her fingers immediately ran across the worn leather belt hidden beneath the edge of her jacket. She had forgotten about it up to that point and had not intended to make its existence known to the rest of the party. This wasn't out of deceit, but because revealing it would mean telling Rose how she and Ike had rifled through her room and backtracked her investigation to Elijah's crumbling old house. There was no need to upset things now that everyone seemed to be getting along, she figured. Even Ike and Tom had made it through the night without bloodshed. Besides, the belt was probably a dead end. If Elijah Comstock had marked trees and rocks as a way of guiding himself through the wilderness he had spent a lifetime exploring, such indicators would've vanished long ago. Still, she was comforted by its presence, like this thin strip of cowhide connected her to part of the mystery known only to her, Ike and Elijah.

Within an hour, they had set out for the creek across a forest which had flourished unimpeded for thousands years. This continuous cycle of growth, erosion and decay had resulted in vegetation at times so tightly tangled it forced them to weave, climb and sometimes crawl through the trees. Their progress was further hindered by the toddler who'd grown weary of the outing almost immediately and fell into an extended pout. Ike, Meryl and Tom took turns swapping their backpacks for the child, which reduced his whining but increased their exhaustion. Everyone was relieved when the creek was finally spotted through a break in the trees.

They rested at the edge of a large pool fed by water tumbling down from three rocky terraces. Rose passed around sandwiches and Meryl helped Alexander off with his shoes and socks so he could wade at the creek's edge and chase silvery fry with his toes.

"I think he's happy now," said Tom, gesturing to the child with a half-eaten peanut butter and jelly sandwich.

"It won't last," Meryl replied.

"This seems a little too much for him," Ike agreed.

The comment irked Tom who quickly retorted, "Nah. He'll totally go the distance. That kid's a champ."

"That kid's four," said Ike. "His little legs can't keep up with all this."

"Yeah," Meryl answered, "it was a big fail on my part, guys. I didn't think this hike would be quite so challenging. Depending on how he's feeling after lunch, I may have to head back with him."

"It grieves me to hear that," Rose said. "I so wanted you to be a part of this."

Meryl smiled weakly. "I'll have to be the part who tends to the camp while you guys search." No sooner did she say this than she regretted it. She had no real desire to stay in the camp alone with Alexander after the previous day's experience, but she had to be pragmatic about the situation. Despite Rose's assurances, the weekend had proved to be more than just another camping trip and certainly much more than a toddler could manage. In the long run, she figured dealing with a wild animal nosing around the camp for a quick meal was still easier to deal with than a frustrated four-year-old.

"If you need to go back, I'll go with you," Ike volunteered.

"Thanks. But Rose needs your GPS expertise."

"I have my own GPS thingy," Rose offered, pulling the device out of her backpack. "Ike can set it up so we can find our way back and then Tom and I can continue on. We'll stay by the creek and return before nightfall."

Meryl rolled her eyes. "Rose, did you ever learn how to use that thing?"

The older woman bit her lower lip as she inspected the device. "Well, no. But I'm sure Tom could figure it out just fine. Your generation's more comfortable with electronics anyway."

Everyone turned to Tom, who was only half-listening as he watched Alexander attempting to fish using a strand of grass he had tied to the end of a twig. "What?" he asked. "Oh, yeah. Sure. That works, I guess."

"You shouldn't if you're not sure," Meryl pressed. "This forest is too big and it's too easy to get lost."

"If you want, I can give you a quick tutorial," Ike added. "Let's climb up to the top of the falls and we can get a better lay of the land."

"Excellent idea," Rose grinned.

Leaving their packs in the shade, the five of them began to clamber over the rocky jumble toward the uppermost terrace. As they climbed, Rose offered a commentary on the landscape, alternately using a long branch she'd retrieved from the stream bed as a walking stick and a teacher's pointer. "Now any of those hilltops up ahead could be the one Elijah referred to, as the sun would rise behind them... And see how the stream has all these little waterfalls? This's a perfect environment for someone who'd want to pan gold... The mine would inevitably be located close to the water, as water was a necessary component to separate the gold ore from the sediment around it..."

Whether Rose was actually pointing out relevant features of the terrain or simply seeing what she wanted to see was debatable, but she sounded so confident in her dissertation that by the time they reached the summit everyone was feeling more optimistic. Even Alexander, who preferred climbing to walking, reached the top without complaint and immediately occupied himself by tossing rocks into the cascades. Below them the terrain sloped gently away to the broad expanse of the valley, with the highway barely visible as a pale band of gray winding through a swathe of unbroken green. To their right, the mountain peaks rose sequentially with great white mantles of fog spilling over their summits. And to their left and backs was the creek, the forested hills and maybe — just maybe — the mine.

Ike gestured across the landscape with his arm. "So, we're looking south right now, okay? And we're roughly hiking north and our campsite is roughly to the southeast of us. That make sense? Yeah? Yo, Tom. You listening to this? I'm doing this for your benefit, dude."

"What the fuck," Tom mumbled, but for once it wasn't at Ike's expense. He was faced away from the others, staring intently at the opposite shoreline. Meryl prodded him on the leg with the toe of her shoe, but it didn't move him. That eerie feeling she had the previous day when Alexander had played in the stump-filled clearing suddenly returned. It was the feeling of being watched.

"Nice, dude," Ike sneered, "great language to use around the kid."

Tom ignored him. Or maybe didn't even hear. He turned wide-eyed to Meryl and asked, "Do you see that?"

"See what?" she asked slowly.

Everyone was now looking at the far bank, but aside from the narrow cobblestone beach and a tall line of feathery evergreens, there was nothing to see. Or, perhaps more accurately, whatever Tom was seeing was not immediately obvious to the rest. Still, Meryl instinctively placed a reassuring hand on Alexander's shoulder. The child dropped the rock he was holding, turned and reached up for her. She lifted him onto her hip and he whispered in her ear: "Monkey."

"What, baby?"

"Did he say monkey?" Ike gaped. Unlike his reaction in the car the previous day, this time Ike looked truly alarmed.

Tom crouched and pointed straight ahead. "Right there!" he growled, sounding almost angry. "Can't you see it? It's right there."

"What?" Rose asked, annoyed that their attention had been taken away from the landscape and the mine she was now certain lay just a few yards ahead.

"You see those two big boulders on the other side?" Tom responded. "Now look to the right about six feet. Right there."

Ike squinted and replied, "It's a tree stump, dude."

"The fuck it is."

"What did you see, Tom?" Meryl asked.

"It's a tree stump," Ike repeated.

"Tree stumps don't move, Turbo."

"Then you're seeing things, Tom. There's nothing there."

"I'm not imagining it, Ike!" Tom reached down and plucked a large stone from the shoreline. "Watch as I make this fucker jump," he said, launching the rock in a long, smooth arch across the creek and landing it just inches from what appeared to be a broken stump with rough brown-gray bark.

But as the stone bounced and clattered, the stump transformed instantaneously, unfolding like flower petals reacting to sunshine. Limbs appeared as it uncoiled itself from a tight ball. Long arms stretched out for the trees above as powerful legs with wide, flat feet and long toes gripped the rocky shore like hands. Even its furry pelt seemed to transform, no longer imitating craggy bark, but instead puffing out like a cat bristling for a fight. It was harder to identify the animal's head, which was small compared to its massive shoulders, but once it perched itself on a stony outcrop and turned directly toward them, it revealed a blunted but alarmingly humanlike face.

"It's a fucking gorilla!" Tom gawked.

"That's not a gorilla," Meryl answered, immediately tightening her grip on Alexander and stepping away from the shoreline.

"Who gives a shit what it is," Tom snarled. "Goddamn ugly thing needs to get the fuck out of here!" He scooped up another handful of muddy stones and began to launch them at the creature. The animal had now put enough distance between them that most of the stones felt short. But when one careened over its head, it almost effortlessly reached up and snatched the stone from the air with five long fingers. It lowered the projectile to its face and sniffed it, apparently finding Tom's scent much more concerning than stones themselves.

"Help Tom! Scare it away!" Rose commanded suddenly, beating the tree branch she was carrying against a nearby log and hollering at the top of her lungs like she was trying to frighten off a stray dog: "Scat, you! Shoo! Shoo!"

"You guys, we need to leave," Meryl said. "We need to leave right now."

Tom and Ike sent another volley across the stream, but this time the animal didn't respond at all. It just watched them intently as it gently fingered the stone it had caught in mid-air. It was the creature's indifferent attitude which bothered Meryl the most. She couldn't imagine that even a bear or a cougar, the largest predators living in this part of Oregon, wouldn't flee before a group of screaming, branch-beating, stone-throwing human beings. But this animal not only seemed unconcerned by the display, it almost seemed amused.

"Guys, we need to go!" Meryl bellowed, but her voice was drowned out by the hollow *whump–whump–whump* Rose was producing with her swinging tree branch. Then the thumps took on a different pattern, and for a moment it seemed like an echo. It took Meryl a few seconds to realize that the new sounds were coming out of the forest, the sound of wood knocking against wood. The others paused, straightened and cocked their heads to listen. Four different rhythms rose out of the trees, each with a unique cadence as though it was disembodied voices talking simultaneously.

"What the hell?" Ike murmured. His face had gone ghostly white.

"We're leaving!" Meryl hollered, scrambling back down the terraces to the spot where they'd piled their backpacks. She didn't pause to see if the others were following until she and Alexander had reached the second terrace. But again they had hesitated, transfixed on the opposite shore where two more animals had appeared out of the woods. Smaller and lighter in color than the first, they were similarly built with powerful shoulders and arms, switching effortlessly between walking upright, leap-frogging over boulders and swinging from tree limbs. Their movement reminded Meryl of how a spider might climb a woodpile, with each appendage working independently and often in different directions, generating great speed even over a deeply rutted surface. She screamed again, but the other's seemed transfixed and didn't actually turn to flee until the creatures had reached the creek's edge and had started across. Only Tom held his ground, hurling another armful of stones and landing several against the animals' thick bodies which, though it didn't seem to hurt them, did slow their crossing.

"Tommy, move your ass!" Meryl screamed up at him. He obediently turned and scrambled down behind them, his feet slipping in his his haste and prompting another string of mixed obscenities.

By the time they had all reached the middle terrace, the animals were no longer visible.

"Did we scare them off?" Rose panted. Her voice had a tinny quality Meryl had never heard before, as though the only thing keeping her from panicking completely were years of practiced control. They stood in a huddle for a long moment, listening to the sounds of the forest — the creaking of the trees moving in the breeze, the chattering of birds and the incessant gurgling of the stream.

"They're gone," offered Tom.

"Yes, yes," Rose agreed, although she sounded more hopeful than convinced.

"Wait," Ike whispered. He stepped softly to the edge of the rocky lip and peered over, only to lurch back, trip over his own feet and fall hard against the cobblestones. "Oh, fuck!" he bellowed, recovering quickly despite the pain he was clearly in. He snatched Alexander from Meryl's arms and swung the boy effortlessly onto his back, then grabbed Meryl by the elbow and pulled her roughly toward the tree-line. Everyone followed, this time without hesitation.

As Meryl crossed from the sunshine of the stream bank into the darkness of the woods, she paused to glance back just as the head and shoulders of the first animal they'd spotted was rising over the edge of the rocks from the sandy spit where they'd left their backpacks. Curiously, it didn't pursue them, just perched on the top of a rock and watched with its head tilted slightly to one side. It was now close enough that Meryl could see its face clearly in the sunlight. Despite Ike's earlier description, the animal was clearly more humanlike than apelike. There was a broad but distinct nose which disappeared beneath a prominent brow-ridge. The entire face was covered in soft fur, which grew in long, drooping locks near the corners of the mouth and over eyes which were an almost unnatural shade of yellow-green. But what Meryl realized as she lingered there, overcome with both fear and fascination, is that the animal's most humanlike feature was the mouth with its prominent lips which, as she stood and watched, curled upward into a long, amused grin.

CHAPTER SEVENTEEN

"Where's Rose?"

It didn't register that Ike was asking her until Meryl turned and noticed him staring at her expectantly. They'd maintained an unsteady loping pace through the forest for twenty minutes — the best they could do considering the terrain and the small boy clinging anxiously to Ike's back — and had lost track of the other members of their party in the process. In her panic, getting away was the only thing to occupy Meryl's mind during those interminable minutes. That and wondering how long Ike could continue to carry Alexander, and once he collapsed, how long she could. Only when Ike forced a pause, setting Alexander on the ground but keeping one reassuring hand on the boy's shoulder while he mopped his wet face with the other, did Meryl turn to examine the woods around them.

Where was Rose? And Tommy for that matter? The fact that neither could be seen produced a vague feeling of relief, since Meryl carelessly assumed if they weren't with her, they must be together. Surely Tom was helping the oldest member of their party navigate the wilderness just as Ike had with the youngest? Surely.

"Mah-mee, where Rode ann Tommy?" the child parroted.

She pulled the boy in next to her hip and then whispered to Ike, "Do you think we should call for them?"

Ike was so exhausted his legs were visibly shuddering and he couldn't draw enough breath to answer. He braced himself against the trunk of a fir tree with his hands resting on his knees, and for a moment Meryl was certain he was going to be sick all over his shoes. There wasn't anything she could do to assist him. There wasn't even any water to offer him since they'd abandoned their packs at the bottom of the cascades. When he could finally bring himself to speak, his words came out as a string of croaks. "I don't think... it'll make... any difference.... Whatever those things are... I'm sure they can... smell us on... the wind."

After a brief hesitation, she screamed as loud as she could manage: "Tommy! Rose! Where are you guys?"

Nothing answered her except the creaks and clacks of the trees shifting in the wind. She continued to call for the next ten minutes, and had finally decided to give up when something moved to the left, slightly downhill from their position but definitely heading toward them. They were just silhouettes in the dappled afternoon light, but both tall and long-limbed. It wasn't until one of them stumbled and almost pitched headlong into a woody snag that Meryl recognized it as Rose. Of all of them, she was the least graceful, with a body which seemed a constant impediment to negotiating the forest landscape. She was walking with a slight limp, with one hand resting on Tom's shoulder while he held her around the waist, trying to keep her upright on the uneven ground. She looked terrible. Her dark, flawless complexion was an extraordinary shade of burgundy, as though every drop of blood in her body had bubbled up into her head. Like everyone else, she was dripping in sweat but still clutching her jacket around her like a child might hold fearfully to a favorite stuffed animal when the nightlight had burned out and the closet door had been left ajar.

Rose swung her arm above her head though it was obvious they'd seen each other. Meryl was immediately annoyed. Not so much by the gesture as by the jaunty "Ahoy there, mateys!" which accompanied it. How like Rose, she thought, to cap off a harrowing encounter with some previously unknown hominid with the same chuckling relief you'd expect from someone you'd briefly lost sight of in a department store. But contriteness set in when Meryl noticed that Rose had clearly fallen during their flight from the stream. The front of her trousers were covered in mud and the palms of her hands were bleeding.

"Holy shit, Rose, are you okay?" she called, repositioning Alexander next to Ike as she went to assist Tom.

"No one panic," Rose remarked, almost phlegmatically. "The old gal just took a tumble and scuffed up her knees and hands. Haven't done that since I was a kid. But, come to think of it, haven't had to run through the woods since I was a kid either."

Meryl tucked herself under Rose's right arm and helped steer her to Ike and Alexander's resting place. Just for a second she caught Tom's eye. He looked furious but she didn't have the energy to deal with it so quickly looked away.

"I can't move as fast as you all," Rose groaned as they helped her sit against a mossy log.

"I'm sorry," Meryl replied. "We should've slowed up. I just didn't think. I just needed to get out of there" — her eyes immediately flicked toward Alexander who was still cowering under Ike's arm.

Rose held up a bleeding hand. "Quite right, darling. No explanation needed. Getting the little one to safety should be everyone's first priority."

Tom, who up to this point hadn't made a peep, snorted loudly through his nose. Everyone turned toward him. "Sorry," he caviled, "but from where I was standing it looked like Turbo turned tail and ran. I guess I was supposed to fight rear guard, huh?"

Ike, who was still stooped at the waist with his head tilted toward the ground didn't even bother to look up. Meryl couldn't tell if he was too exhausted or just cared so little about Tom's opinions at this point that it wasn't worth his effort. "Fuck yeah, I turned and ran," he snarled into his chest. "Carrying your son on my back I might add. What the fuck was I suppose to do?"

"How about wait to make sure the rest of us got the hell outta there, too?"

"Shut the fuck up, Tom. I ran because that's what people do when they're scared out of their minds."

"Please, stop," Rose interjected. "No recriminations, okay? We made it out and that's what counts and now we need our cooler heads to prevail, yes?"

Meryl added, "Rose's right. Let's figure out where we are and we'll just all stay together from this point on. Safety in numbers and all."

"Well, since nobody's asking this question, I guess I will," Tom said, still simmering. "What the fuck are those things?"

No one answered him. No one could. But ultimately it was Rose who explained, again in that teacher's voice which seemed so unsuitable to the setting, that a discussion about the animals' taxonomy might be better at another time and with some wildlife experts in the room. Meryl nodded her agreement, deciding privately not to mention how the one creature had smiled at her. *Smiled.* She wasn't a biologist yet, but she couldn't think of any animal on Earth outside of humans that smiled. Apes and dogs could sometimes simulate it, but really they were just showing their teeth. Nothing save *Homo sapiens* had the proper facial muscles or emotional complexity to produce a smile, and seeing it filled Meryl with more dread than anything else to happen since they entered the forest twenty-four hours earlier.

But there was more than the animals' evolutionary history which bothered her. The words from Elijah's storybook were replaying in her head now. She wished she could remember all the details, but wasn't there something about the tents being ransacked by animals? And barricades being crushed? And a whole camp of well-armed men vanishing forever?

"We need to head back to the car and get outta here," she stated with sudden vigor, to which Ike sheepishly replied that his GPS tracker was in one of the backpacks left abandoned next to the stream.

"Fucking dumb ass," Tom snapped. "Why didn't you just put the stupid thing in your pocket?"

"You try climbing through this forest shit with that thing in your pocket," Ike retorted. "It was crushing my balls, and frankly, I wasn't expecting my lunch break to be interrupted by hairy monsters!"

"Rose, you have your GPS thingy, right?"

The older woman shook her head. "Backpack," she said.

"Well, we can't just sit here," Meryl said. "The last thing we need is to be stuck out here after dark."

"I agree," Ike replied. "But which way do we go?"

There was a long pause as everyone quietly considered their options. Again, Meryl turned to survey the woodland but everything was quiet, still, tranquil. "Do you think we should head back to the creek and get our stuff?" she asked no one in particular.

"Risky," said Ike.

"Maybe they left?" Tom offered. "They didn't seem to chase us once we left the stream. Maybe they lost interest?"

"I don't think so," Meryl said, glancing nervously at Ike. "I think they've been watching us since yesterday. There was that thing in the woods that Ike thought was a bear. And then I saw something in the trees when I was playing with Alexander on all those stumps. And..."

"Last night?" Rose interjected, her eyes widening with sudden realization.

"Yeah."

"Last night? What the fuck happened last night?" Tom asked.

"Something came into our camp. It was right outside our tent," Meryl replied.

"Something? What something?"

"Well, I don't really know that Tom. Rose and I got up to look, but it was gone by the time we got outside the tent."

"Why didn't you tell us?" Tom snapped.

Rose interrupted again. "We need to stay focused, kiddos," she said. "It doesn't matter what was in the camp last night. Right now, let's just go back for the packs, find the mine and log it on the GPS. That's our primary objective right now."

"Screw that," Ike answered. He'd finally recovered enough strength to get to his feet. "My primary objective is to not be eaten alive."

"Don't be silly. That won't happen," answered Rose with a supercilious flick of her wrist.

Ike just stared at her, his head cocked slightly to the left with his mouth partially open.

"It's a simple fact that wild animals flee at the sight of humans —"

"—Rose, I don't know where you've been for the last hour, but they didn't flee from us!" Ike shouted.

"Well, if we see them again, there are things you're suppose to do around wild animals, correct? We roll up into balls and pretend we're dead, right?"

"That's for bears, Rose."

"Well, they're bear-like, aren't they?"

"Bear-*like*? I'm not gonna take a chance with something that's bear-*like*, either."

"Ditto," said Meryl. "There's no way I'm continuing on. We need to get Alexander out of here. We *all* need to get out of here. We can think about coming back later."

Rose glanced at the boy clutching Meryl's waist, his cheeks streaked with tears. For the first time since they'd gathered back together, her well-practiced and typically flawless composure began to slip. "It's now or never," she said, her voice quavering.

"It's not," Meryl answered. She tried to sound empathetic instead of what she really was — afraid, frustrated and angry, too.

"It is. It's so late in the year already, Meryl. When we go back home, Tom will return to Portland, Ike will go back to school. Winter will come. *Snow* will come. At that point, it'll be easier to move a mountain than get us all back in the same place at the same time. If we're going to do this, friends, if we're going to know once and for all if the mine's out here, it has to be now."

Tears began to sting Meryl's eyes. "I'm sorry, but I can't take that chance with Alexander here." When she looked around at the other faces, flushed and damp, she felt almost mutinous with what she said next: "I vote we head back to the creek, see if we can find our packs. If not, we can at least find the route we hiked in on from there. Ike, you think you can follow your nose back to the campsite?"

He nodded confidently. "If we get back to the bottom of the falls, I can get us back out whether we have the GPS units or not."

"Well, if we're voting, then I say we head back to the creek, continue up its bank for a while to see what we can see, and then head back to camp," Rose countered. At this point, she looked right at Tom, whom she clearly considered her closest ally in the group, and said firmly, "Wouldn't you agree?"

For an instant, Tom looked like one of Rose's students caught unprepared when she called upon him to finish an equation in front of the class. As a rule, Tom hated making decisions, especially if there was the possibility of him choosing wrong and looking ignorant in front of others. But there was no way to get out of replying, so he said almost apologetically, "I agree with Meryl. We need to leave."

Ike broke the tension by reminding them that daylight was limited and they had a long way to go to get back to the camp. Rose said nothing, turning her body partially away from the rest of them.

"What do you suggest?" Meryl asked Ike.

"We go back as quietly as possible. Everyone arm yourself with something you can use as a club, stick together, keep your eyes and ears open."

Alexander, who up to this point had listened to the adults quietly, responded to the idea of returning to the creek with a succession of racking sobs. Meryl immediately pulled him into her arms and he buried his wet, snotty face in her hair.

The forest acknowledged the child's wails with a renewed chorus of knocks, the same proficient drumming they'd encountered at the creek. The strange acoustics of the wilderness made it nearly impossible to tell which direction the sounds were coming from, but they were quickly followed by movement among the trees on the slope below them. Once again, it was as though the animals pulled themselves out of the light, shadow and shape of the landscape. It was almost like a conjuring trick, Meryl thought, and it made her wonder if the animal who'd hunkered down next to the tent the night before had actually left when she went outside to look around with the flashlight. Considering their ability to camouflage themselves, it now seemed probable that it was there all the time, hidden to her eyes.

"Shit!" Ike cried upon seeing the animals emerge from the trees.

"Head uphill," Meryl commanded. "Get to some higher ground."

They began moving again, half-walking, half-climbing through the jumble of trees, shrubs and boulders. Meryl could clearly see all three creatures following them up. The largest, the dark brown brute who'd snatched the rock out of the air and smiled at her, was on their left flank, clearly positioning himself so they couldn't return to the creek. The other two, who were of similar size and had a more silver-colored fur, were swiftly winding their way through the trees, creating a slowly tightening net around the scrambling humans.

After a few moments, they came to a rocky precipice which completely blocked their retreat.

"We can climb it," Meryl insisted.

"I can't," Rose wept. Her legs wobbled visibly beneath her and Ike moved quickly to prop her up.

Meryl looked to where the largest creature had slowed to a stop. Beneath its dark heavy brows, she could see its eyes flashing as it assessed the cliff and their failing bodies. She had Alexander climb on her back and then immediately began to scale the rock-face. It wasn't as steep as it appeared from below, but the previous night's rain and a thick layer of moss made it difficult to find safe finger- and toe-holds.

"Climb, goddammit!" she barked down to them. They were slowed by both their fear and their fatigue, but followed nonetheless. Tom and Ike went up last, helping Rose climb when she began to weaken.

At the top of the ledge the terrain softened into a more gentle slope and the trees grew thick on the left edge, creating a natural barricade which seemed to offer them some shelter from the biggest creature but would also prevent any escape in that direction. Meryl swung Alexander off her back and sat him down in the grass. He cowered beneath the lip of a boulder as she snatched up several heavy rocks. She stood at the edge of the precipice and with what strength she had left, flung the stones over the other's heads at the creatures prowling closer to the cliff's base. Her arm was neither as strong nor accurate as Tom's, however, so the salvo did little more than create a terrible noise as stone cracked against stone, thumped against fallen wood and created small avalanches of sediment, pine cones and fallen leaves.

As soon as Ike pulled himself over the lip of the precipice, the largest animal made a series of agile leaps and attached itself effortlessly to the rocks about thirty feet below. As Meryl stood above the massive animal, hefting another stone over her head, it gave a defiant snarl and lunged toward her. She hurled the rock which impacted with the creature's shoulder but didn't seem to injure it.

Instinctually she stepped back, grabbed up Alexander and covered his small body with her own. The boy shrieked in what was the longest, most pitiful noise she'd ever heard from her son, the sound of abject terror. Vaulting to the top of the rock-face the creature made a failed grab for Tom who'd quickly positioned himself in front of Meryl and Alexander. Long fingers with hooked nails snatched at the edge of Tom's sweatshirt, causing him to pitch backwards and fall against the rocks. His head made a sharp cracking noise as it impacted with the dark stone and he crumpled to his knees. Meryl rolled to her right, cradling Alexander as she did. She grabbed Tom's arm and pulled him to the far edge of the precipice where Ike and Rose were standing and flinging both stones and obscenities, neither seeming to have any effect. Meryl called to all of them to head into the trees to the east, but she was stopped short as a fourth creature suddenly emerged before her.

A hulking female with pendulous breasts, she stood just within the tree-line and made a rapid clacking noise with her tongue. Meryl was so stunned that she stood gaping. The female trilled like a bird, producing a series of husky notes broken into discernible clusters, almost as though she were forming sentences. The big male snarled in return, its long fingers curling around the end of a fallen tree branch which it raised over its head like a club. Almost simultaneously, both animals charged into the huddle of exhausted humans. Meryl curled herself around Alexander, squeezing her eyes tightly shut and holding her breath. She waited for pain to follow. Or would it be a brief sensation of weightlessness as the two animals flung them like rag dolls over the edge of the precipice where they'd break apart on the trees below? But all that came was a hot rush of a passing body as the female brushed by without touching her. Instead, the creature launched herself onto the big male, perching on his back with her feet while grabbing both sides of his head with her massive hands. The male's makeshift club fell as he lost his balance and toppled off the boulders. The two of them tumbled down the rock-face, slowing their descent by grabbing at ledges or swinging from cavities until they rolled head-over-head in one great heap through the trees. Several of the smaller saplings snapped like whips as they smashed through them. One cracked in half and collapsed with the roar of shattering wood. They finally landed in knot of bushes at the bottom of the precipice. they didn't move for a long time. The male stirred first, but to Meryl's amazement made no aggressive moves toward the smaller female. Instead, he leapt back into the trees with the female fast on his heels.

For a long moment, the forest was quiet but for everyone's soft weeping. Rose was doubled-over on the ground with her arms flung across her head. Tom and Ike were half-crouched nearby, both wielding rocks which, in retrospect, would've done nothing to save them from the creatures. Meryl collected Alexander into her arms and stepped cautiously to the edge of the cliff. The two silver-colored creatures still stood at the bottom, staring at the spot where the big male and female had disappeared back into the trees. They appeared confused. One made a high-pitched chattering noise to which the other responded with a deep grunt. They turned and stared up at Meryl but made no attempt to climb the rocks. Seeing their hesitation, she reacted quickly.

She turned to Tom, Ike and Rose. "Everyone up!" she snapped. "Run!"

CHAPTER EIGHTEEN

When Meryl roused herself, she had no exact memory of the previous hours, only sensations fueled by fear and adrenalin. She remembered that night had been darker than any she'd ever known — darker than she ever imagined nighttime could be once you left the constant and comforting glow of the city lights. There'd been a persistent but gentle rain falling upon her face, and the feeling that her back was both wet and icy cold while her feet and legs stung with a prickly heat. But what she remembered most was the small, shivering body tucked inside her coat and the feeling that if she could just run a little further she'd somehow find a safe place for all of them to stop and rest. A place where no monster could threaten Alexander.

At the end, however, it was simple exhaustion rather than feeling secure which forced them to stop. This time, they'd managed to stay together as they fled, holding onto each other's sleeves and coattails in the darkness. Rose was the first to fall, bruising her already injured knees, but no one had the strength to pull her back onto her feet again. Meryl remembered snapping on the small flashlight she still had strapped to her right wrist and crawling on all fours. They followed her into the hollow pocket beneath the drooping limbs of a giant hemlock tree and fell asleep in the cold midden of fallen needles and broken cones.

As her senses began to reengage, Meryl could see the misty glow of the rising sun to her left and feel the loamy bed of conifer needles beneath her. Her fingertips found the soft mass of Alexander's hair and she instantly pulled him deeper inside her jacket, using her body to keep him off the ground as much as possible. He was sleeping fitfully, his right leg twitching as though he were running from something in his dreams. She lifted her head slowly but the view didn't improve. Near her feet, Ike and Tom lay strewn unceremoniously, curled up into tight balls and shivering in their sleep. Rose was sitting to her right, pressed against the tree's trunk. If she'd slept at all, it wasn't evident in her face. Her eyes were so red and puffy that for a moment Meryl thought they must be infected. It was more likely she'd simply been weeping and rubbing at them for hours while everyone else was unconscious.

"Are they gone?" Meryl whispered.

Rose answered with a flick of one finger. Meryl followed the gesture with her eyes but it seemed to lead to nothing. Beyond the hemlock branches, a dense fog had reduced the forest to a pattern of flat gray shapes, making it almost impossible to discern distances, assess sizes or identify individual objects. But as her gaze lingered there, some of the shapes began to shift, like watercolors bleeding into each other on a sheet of damp paper. She watched fascinated as the ragged contour of a sword fern transformed into a towering behemoth. Despite the lack of details, Meryl could tell from the contour of the animal's sagging breasts this was the female who'd come thundering out of the trees and sent the larger male tumbling down the hill the day before. Once the animal stretched, it moved slightly to its left, hunkered down and disappeared again. After a few seconds, Meryl couldn't tell where the bushes ended and the animal began.

It was unclear to her if this ability to blend with the environment was some evolutionary adaptation or an act of intelligence. Meryl remembered reading about fish who'd bury their flat, speckled bodies into the sand on the ocean floor and virtually disappear. And there were marine invertebrates who could manipulate their own skin cells to imitate the natural patterns around them , camouflaging themselves in the time it took a person to blink. But what the animal half-hidden among the sword ferns did was tremendously more sophisticated. It was as though her race had a particular set of body postures they'd use depending on the terrain, contorting both their size and shape. They could even bristle or flatten their fur to simulate the texture of a bush, a rock or the trunk and foliage of a tree.

She rested her head back into the fallen needles, closed her eyes and felt strangely calm. If the animals had intended to kill them, she figured they would've done so by now. Even Tommy, for all his height and strength, would've been easy to dispatch in his sleep. And what kind of fight could any of them offer being both exhausted and hungry? They'd had no water for almost twelve hours and her own body was already showing all the signs of dehydration. Her limbs felt like they were on fire and her tongue seemed to have shriveled up inside her mouth.

Rose's scratchy voice broke her tranquility. "You know what I was thinking about this morning?" Meryl wasn't sure if the question was rhetorical, but she opened her eyes, looked at the older woman and shook her head anyway. "I was remembering the dream I had the night before I arrived in Corvallis," the older woman continued. "I dreamed of spirits swirling around me like this fog. I remember it so well because it's not the type of dream I usually have."

Meryl asked, "Spirits? You mean ghosts? Like the missing girl at the lighthouse you told me about?"

"No, not like that. They weren't the spirits of people. They came out of the ground and the plants and the trees. I was so startled by it that I just sat inside my sleeping bag and shivered for the longest time. I felt such the fool, like a little girl spooked because my mother and father had forgotten to shut the closet door before I went to bed. What do you think about that?"

Meryl took her right hand from Alexander's back and gently stroked Rose's arm with her fingertips. Rose attempted to force a smile, but failed miserably. "It was just a dream," she said, trying to sound comforting.

"Yes. Just a dream," Rose nodded.

"Were you camping?" Meryl asked as casually as possible.

"No. I was squatting,"

"What's that mean?"

"It's when you sleep somewhere you're not really allowed to sleep. I found an abandoned house by the side of the road so I went inside. No one had lived there in a long time, so I don't think I was breaking any laws really." At this point, Rose began to cry again for some reason. "I was just so darn exhausted from driving and I couldn't find a motel room. I just wanted to lie down and stretch out and sleep forever. But those damnable dreams wouldn't let me. Those spirits vexed me all night long."

The fact that Rose was talking about being in Elijah's house sent a cold chill up Meryl's spine, but she suppressed it and replied calmly, "Don't scare yourself more. Remember, you're the one who told us we need cool heads."

Rose wiped her eyes on her sleeve and mumbled, "I'm trying. I really am trying. It wasn't supposed to go this way, you see. I've had this trip mapped out in my head for ten years. Everything was falling into place, just how it was supposed to go."

Meryl patted her arm, hoping the gesture didn't seem patronizing. She wanted to be comforting if she could, but even more she wanted to keep Rose from falling back into another long rant about fate and such. The last thing any of them needed was to start believing their destinies were already mapped out and nothing they did out here would change their circumstances. If Rose truly felt she was destined to find this gold mine, then so be it. But for Meryl, the fact they survived the night meant they had another chance to escape and get home. She quickly changed the subject and said, "We need to find water."

"Little chance of that. It's not like these *things* are going to let us wander around."

"Can you tell how many there are?" Meryl asked.

"I've counted four," the old woman shivered.

Meryl nudged Tom with the toe of her boot who in turn roughly roused Ike, causing him to bolt upright and crack his forehead on a tree branch. The quick movement and sharp noise produced a weird chattering from the animals. Ike glanced around, dazed and disoriented, then moaned, "Shit. They're still here."

"No one panic," Meryl whispered as the two young men crawled closer to her and Rose. "It looks like we never lost them. But they haven't made any moves either. They're just sitting out there, watching us."

"Strangely, that doesn't make me feel any better," replied Ike tersely.

At this point, Alexander stirred, buried his small face in his mother's neck and keened, "Mah-mee I wanna go home."

"I second that," Ike said, patting the boy on the back.

"Everyone check your pockets and see what we have to work with. I don't suppose anyone has a cell phone?"

After some searching, Tom was able to produce his phone which still had battery life, but no reception whatsoever. Instead, he turned into the fog and recorded several seconds of the strange chattering still rising up around them. He looked at Meryl and mumbled, "For *National Geographic.*"

She smiled, but honestly didn't care much if they got out of here with proof of the animals' existence. She just wanted that phone to work. If she could get off one successful text message to Tess or David, she knew they'd gather rescue forces within an hour. Silently she kicked herself for leaving that misleading map on her refrigerator door for David. That was so stupid. She shouldn't have listened to Rose's paranoia any more than she should take seriously all her mumbo jumbo about spirits and fate.

"Why don't you turn the phone off for now," she told Tom. "Save the battery in case we get reception later."

Tom nodded and obediently powered down the device. "Anyone have any idea where we are?" he asked.

"No," Meryl said, "but before we worry about that, we need water."

She gently lifted Alexander over to his father and rose onto her knees, not daring to stand in case the animals in the fog would see this as aggressive. The increasing light revealed new details. They were in a small glen dominated by a tall stand of hemlock trees. A variety of ferns carpeted the forest floor and grew almost as tall as the tops of their heads when they were seated. She didn't recognize the mountain slopes which were just beginning to emerge from the mist, nor could she hear the creek that had been their original starting point. The animals were positioned around them in a loose circle, with the large female being no more than one hundred feet away. The brawny male was positioned far off to the left, appearing no worse from his plunge down the hillside, with his body half-turned toward the forest beyond. Clearly he was watching them, but only from the corner of his eye. Mostly, he seemed to be manipulating something with his big hands, something which was hidden behind the tall ferns. The two silver-colored creatures were on the opposite side of the clearing, wandering in and out of the trees and gathering things off the ground, some of which they'd pop into their mouths. Their proximity and apparent passiveness after the incident at the creek confused Meryl. It was almost like they'd been given a command to watch but not approach, and for an instant she felt like she was an insect captured in a glass jar being studied by a group of children.

She crawled out a little further, just enough so her head and the tops of her shoulders were clear of the hemlock boughs. This produced another long whine from Alexander but she quickly assured him she'd go no further. Now close enough to reach the thick fern beds, she carefully shook one of the fronds and watched the collected dew spill onto the ground in large drops.

"Find me something we can use as a cup," she commanded and the others began to rummage through their pockets again. Finding nothing suitable, however, Ike pried some strips of bark off the tree trunk and handed them to her. They were shaped more like shallow platters but were sufficient to hold a few mouthfuls of water at a time. As she crawled from plant to plant, she passed back the strips, making sure Alexander and Rose received the first portions. This continued for nearly an hour.

"You got the chick-monster's attention," Tom whispered, mostly as a warning.

Meryl paused and looked over the tops of the ferns to where the female had risen to a squat and had intently watched the entire water-gathering process. Her gaze met Meryl's and she produced a low rumbling noise in her throat, almost like she was talking to herself.

"I guess she's the alpha monster," Ike added.

"Perhaps. But take a look at them. They all know each other," Meryl replied. "Maybe they're some kind of family group?"

"They must be apes, right?" Ike asked.

"Primates of some kind," Meryl responded.

"See, I totally called that one," Tom stated with a smirk. "They're gorillas. Oregon gorillas."

"Oregon doesn't have gorillas, Tommy."

"Like hell. There they are. Four of them. One, two, three, four."

"I said they were primates. I don't think they're gorillas."

"What the fuck's the difference?"

"You're a primate, Tommy, but you ain't a gorilla."

217

"He kinda is," Ike said, but he was ignored.

"Well, they're sure as fuck not humans," Tom insisted.

Meryl's reply was almost wistful. "No, they're something new."

Rose interjected. "Excuse me, but how does any of this speculation help us? We should be plotting our escape."

"Rose, we don't even know where we are," Ike said. "Our trackers were in the backpacks, remember? If we take off running, we're just gonna get more and more lost. And we won't go far without food and water anyway."

Rose's face fell and she offered no more comments.

Alexander, who'd now received most of the scavenged water and was feeling more alert, squirmed his way out of Tom's grip and crawled out to his mother. He did not immediately see the animals across the glen, and perhaps, at least for a moment or two, had forgotten about them. But when the rays of the sun landed on the broad wooly shoulders and crimped face of the large female, he started to scream. Meryl instantly clapped her hand over his mouth and struggled to quiet him. To her surprise, however, the big female seemed bothered by the child's howls and immediately dropped low into the bushes. There was nothing about the beast Meryl regarded as beautiful. Like the others who had pursued them along the banks of the creek, her face was blunt, hairy and rutted. Overall, her fur was softer and more reddish in color, especially in full sunlight. The hair on her face was also shorter and she didn't have the tufts above the eyes and near the edges of her mouth; and for the first time Meryl could see small, very humanlike ears set low on the sides of the head. Maybe it was the deep creases around her green eyes or the white wisps of hair near her temples, but Meryl also felt that this creature was considerably older than the others.

As Alexander wept, the big female crept along the ground and averted her eyes so as not to meet Meryl's gaze. Her tiny ears twitched like a cat's, as she caught the boy's low wails. She began to pace, slowly closing the distance between them.

"What the hell's it doing?" Ike muttered. He and Tom both stiffened and began to pat around in the woody debris beneath the tree for something they could use as weapons. They found nothing more than handfuls of dried bark and withered cones.

The creature's stench, the same overpowering musk that Meryl had smelled before, swept across them. Rose immediately shielded her nose with her shirt sleeve and closed her eyes tightly, as if awaiting the inevitable attack. Instead, the female extended one monstrous hand and set a small collection of items in the grass. Then, almost humbly, she withdrew. No one moved except Ike who slowly crawled over to examine the objects. He grimaced.

"What is it?" Meryl asked.

"I guess you'd call it food," he replied. "I'm not sure what I should do with it."

Tom rolled his eyes. "What do you mean? If it's edible then bring it over, Turbo."

"You gonna eat the dead squirrels, Tom?" Ike retorted.

"It brought us dead rodents?"

"She's trying to feed us," Meryl said.

"Yeah, to fatten us up for the kill."

"I don't think so."

"What the hell? You're not suggesting we eat a raw, dead rodent are you?"

"Of course not, but look at her..." Everyone glanced over at the creature, who'd now returned to her original position and seemed oddly pleased with herself. "She's waiting to see what we do with them. Ike, bring them over."

Ike gingerly picked up the small mangled carcasses along with a collection of fresh blackberries, dandelions and fiddleheads.

"They must be omnivores," Meryl said absently, prompting a rude snort from Tom. "What's your problem?"

"*Omnivores*. Is that today's vocabulary word, Meryl? Why are you approaching this whole disaster like it's a high school science fair? Do you get the deep shit we're in here?"

Meryl stiffened. "We can't outfight them, we can't outrun them, we're in their habitat and they know it. The only way we may get out of this is to outthink them."

Tom grumbled something unkind under his breath and turned away.

"Come on," Meryl urged, "let's be buddies and dig in." She bent in low to pantomime eating the food. Alexander joined in, but not understanding her intent, quickly snatched up the blackberries and gulped them down.

Ike squatted and poked at a limp squirrel with a finger. "Mmmm," he said facetiously, partly for Meryl's sake, partly for the sake of the hairy behemoth watching across the field. "That's some damn fine vermin. Delicious!"

Rose joined their circle but made no attempt to touch any of the food. Instead, she whispered anxiously, "Meryl, let's figure out a way to get these things to go away so we can get out of here. We have got to be on top of that mine, but we'll never find it sitting here."

Meryl was incredulous. "Rose, if we escape, we need to get back to Tom's Jeep. It doesn't make any sense to go further into the forest when we've lost our transportation and our supplies and are surrounded by big forest monsters."

"Primates," Tom corrected.

Rose was unswayed. "I didn't come all this way to give up."

"I didn't come all this way to die," Ike replied.

There was a sharp metallic clink from the far side of the glen and everyone turned toward the big male who was holding one of the backpacks over his head and watching with great curiosity as the items within spilled out onto the ground.

Tom slowly rose into a standing-crouch. "Sonofabitch," he grumbled. "That big ugly one has our things."

"All of them?" Meryl asked.

"Not sure, but I think so. They must've gone back for them after we took off."

"If he has the packs, then he has the trackers too," Ike said.

Tom stretched and teetered on his balls of his feet. While their attention had been centered on the female, the large male had proceeded to disassemble the packs and scatter their contents among the trees. "We just need a diversion," he said to no one in particular. "Does anyone have anything on them that these creatures might finding interesting? Like a banana?"

Ike's face flushed with anger. "Dude, does everything you say have to be sarcastic? Seriously, those trackers are our only hope for getting home. Not to mention that our packs had all our food and water, too."

"And toilet paper," Rose said.

"Hells yeah, that too."

Tom responded: "Sorry, Turbo. I'm under a little bit of stress here. Sarcasm is my coping mechanism, so just deal with it, okay?"

"And maybe you can stop calling me that?"

"Turbo, Turbo, Turbo..." Tom chanted.

"For god's sake," Meryl sighed, "it's like listening to a couple of children. Take a lesson from the toddler who's actually here, boys, and shut the hell up already."

Rose, who'd been ignoring the entire exchange, had managed to produce a crumpled foil package from her shirt pocket. "I have gum. It's very fruity smelling. They might like that?"

There were only three sticks left and they'd become soggy and smashed, but Meryl couldn't imagine the creatures would care. After all, she thought, what was important was the friendly gesture. Fruit-flavored gum in exchange for dead squirrels and a pile of berries seemed like a good exchange. She took the small parcel and stepped to the outside of their circle.

"What the hell are you doing?" Tom asked.

"I'm going to give it to them," replied Meryl.

"You're insane. They'll kill you."

"I don't think they will. I don't think the big female will let them."

"Let me do it, then," Ike said. "You need to stay with Alexander."

Meryl shook her head. "It's because of Alexander that I should go. Have you noticed how the female watches me? Watches him? I think she's interested in us." Meryl took the boy by his small shoulders and tucked him in next to Rose who put a reassuring arm around him. "Don't worry, honey," she whispered to him, "I'm just going right over there. You'll be able to see me the entire time. Do you understand?"

Alexander answered with a whimper.

Meryl looked up at Ike. "As soon as they are all focused on me, you and Tom need to grab as much of our stuff as you can. Stay low. Move slowly."

"Got it," he replied.

By the time Meryl had made it ten feet into the center of the glen, all the creatures began to stir. Even the two silver-colored beasts had abandoned their foraging activities and took an interest. wandering in a wide arch to watch her. She walked as far as she felt was safe, and then imitating the large female's gesture, set the package of gum on top of a large, flat rock. She then withdrew several feet and waited. At first the animals made no attempt to investigate, and after five or ten minutes the silver-colored creatures lolled back into the grass and didn't seem to care any more. The big female and the male who'd scavenged through their backpacks both began to move however. The female lumbered partly into the clearing while the male abandoned the scattered backpacks entirely and circled around to Meryl's left, staying safely behind the trunks of the trees. After a few minutes more, the female wriggled over to the rock and began to stroke the gum packet with a curious finger.

"If she blows a bubble with the stuff I'm gonna freak out," Tom said, perhaps too loudly.

Ike took that as their cue and pulled Tom down into the ferns. They crawled on all fours over to the packs which, to their mutual surprise, hadn't been shredded as they would've expected from a bear or raccoon. Instead, the male had figured out how to manipulate the various snaps, buckles and zippers and had thoroughly rummaged though and discarded their contents. Most of their supplies were tangled up in the fern beds or partially sunk in the mud, and everything had been drenched by the previous night's rain. Like they were scrambling through some weird Easter Egg hunt, Ike and Tom both grabbed a pack and began to collect as much as they could. But even as Ike rapidly stuffed his bag with the stray canteens, a flashlight and several unmolested granola bars, it was painfully clear to him that it simply wouldn't be enough to sustain them for long. Their tents, sleeping bags, most of their food and all of their clothing were at the original campsite or inside the Jeep. Within a day or two, he thought, the dead squirrels might begin to look good.

By the time they had gathered up every stray item they could find and returned to Rose and Alexander, Meryl was still sitting in the middle of the field with only a few yards separating her from the red-haired female. The animal had spent a great deal of time smelling the gum, going as far as actually sticking the pack half way up her left nostril. When she seemed satisfied that it was edible, she turned slightly and made a strange trilling noise. The fern blades nearby suddenly began to tremble and Meryl almost lost her balance and toppled backwards as a fifth creature rose from the vegetation like a whale surfacing from the waves. Smaller and obviously much younger, its fur had an unusual variegated pattern, as though imitating the natural patterns of light and shadow which covered the forest floor. More startling was the realization that the young animal had lay still and silent for hours, just a few feet from the female, and no one had noticed. The female handed the gum packet to the younger creature who popped it, wrappers and all, into his mouth and swallowed it down. Meryl couldn't help but indulge in a smile. The large male, who was watching from the nearby trees, seemed displeased and grunted loudly before wandering away.

Meryl returned to their circle where the others were already rummaging through the clutter of their soaked belongings. "Five," she said, excitedly. "We're now up to five monsters."

"Primates," Tom said, again.

"Which means there could be more," Ike said.

Meryl nodded grimly and then turned when she heard a stifled whimper. Rose was slumped over in the pine needles with Alexander patting her gently on the head. She was weeping again, but this time producing deep, mournful sobs. "Rose? What is it?" Meryl asked gently.

The old woman unfolded a soggy wad of papers in her hands. It was *The American Boy's Adventure Reader*, now soaked through and through and smeared with mud, the childish notes and cryptic clues written in the margins rendered unreadable. Meryl's heart sank, but not because she had any affection left for the book or what it represented. She'd come to think of the *Reader* as being the root of all their problems, but at least its existence meant Rose could try again sometime in the future. If there was such a thing as fate, Meryl thought, it had just punched Rose in the gut by destroying her treasure map in the middle of some uncharted meadow.

No one said a thing until Rose shrugged, wiped some of the mud from the book's cover and sighed, "No matter. I guess it did what it needed to do. It got us this close. It wasn't going to be of any additional help anyway." She glanced up at the grey sky and blinked rapidly as the rain began to fall again. "What a strange time and place to suddenly feel so sentimental," she said.

"I don't know," answered Meryl, "I've found myself feeling the same way. I can't tell you how much I miss that crappy little apartment of ours."

"It goes without saying, darling."

"We'll get out. Sooner or later, they'll either lose interest in us or drop their guard and then we can leave."

"But without finding the mine?"

"The mine doesn't matter anymore."

"Meryl, yes it does. You don't comprehend how far I've come and how valiantly I've sacrificed to be here. There's no way these hairy beasties are going to stop me. They'll have to kill me first."

With those words, Rose suddenly reminded Meryl of her mother — her inflexible, single-minded, selfish mother — and she automatically recoiled. Her thoughts were interrupted by an unexpected and involuntary *whoop* from Ike. He scrambled across to them.

"We caught a break!" he said excitedly. "I found two lighters and our trackers."

"Are the trackers working?" Meryl inquired.

"Yes. Mine's about half-charged, but Rose's has a full battery."

"Can you tell how far we are from the Jeep?"

Ike was already massaging the device's buttons. He smiled. "It's not as bad as I thought. We're about six miles northwest of the camp."

"So we could walk there in a few hours?"

"It all depends on what the terrain's like between us and the Jeep. Plus, we're fooling ourselves if we think these creatures are just going to let us walk out."

Tom punched him playfully on the shoulder. "Don't be a spoilsport, Turbo. You just became my favorite person in this whole forest, except for everyone else of course."

Meryl began to convulse with laughter, which she quickly stifled for fear that the creatures around them would react badly to the sound. She pulled her jacket up over her head and laughed quietly into the sleeve. It went on for much longer than it should have, much more than Tom's joke deserved. But for Meryl, it was the first time in over a day that she actually felt something besides fear.

CHAPTER NINETEEN

As their first day in captivity — or so Rose called it — drew on, Tom amused himself by strolling around in front of their tree or in the general direction where Ike had indicated his Jeep was located. Each time he moved, the animals immediately became alert, pulling themselves into squatting positions or moving to block him. Meryl watched the process with interest and noticed that the big female rarely stirred, but would make small twitches with her head or shrugs with her shoulders, as if directing the actions of the others. After trying this for nearly an hour, everyone was resigned to another night in the wilderness and began to scavenge dry wood for a campfire. Ike constructed a small rain shelter between two of the hemlock trees using the nylon ties off a backpack and three plastic slickers which doubled for catching rainwater and replenishing their canteens. He let Alexander assist, if only to keep the child occupied and entertained.

Their captors watched their activities with varying degrees of interest, but hadn't made any attempts to interfere with their construction or foraging activities as long as they stayed within the boundary of trees. The two silver-colored animals continued to root around on the far side of the woods, sometimes disappearing for up to an hour and then returning with handfuls of food. Some of this bounty was shared with the other creatures, some placed almost like tribute for Meryl to retrieve and bring back to her group. Large quantities of blackberries were produced, mixed with handfuls of bright yellow salmonberries and smooth, dark huckleberries. A dead hare was also offered up, which was more palatable to everyone than the squirrels had been, but proved useless when no one could produce a knife to skin it. Ultimately, it was discarded along with the spongy lobster-red fungus no one could identify nor wanted to eat even if they were certain it was harmless.

The big male didn't participate in any of the foraging activities and seemed the least curious of the bunch. There were times when Meryl felt he was displaying an almost humanlike indignation, as though so offended by their presence that nothing they did would possibly engage him. It almost seemed like he was pouting.

"Maybe when it's dark, we can sneak away?" Rose suggested as they stoked the fire. "Or we could make torches and scare them off. All animals run from fire, right?"

"We're about to find out," Meryl answered as she glanced back at the big female who was now watching them, completely motionless and sitting shoulder-to-shoulder with the juvenile. The wood smoke had already drifted through the trees and was rising above the canopy, but this prompted no reaction from the animals other than a curious sniffing at the air.

"I guess that answers that," Tom grumbled. "If they were afraid of fire, they'd be hightailing it outta here right now. They want to keep us here."

"Or at least the one who keeps bringing us the food does," Meryl remarked.

"'Big Girl,'" Ike said absently as he arranged more tinder on the fire.

"You named them?" Tom railed. "What the hell for? They're not your goddamn pets, are they?"

Ike was now so used to Tom's constant sarcasm that he just smiled and replied calmly, "If we need to discuss them, how are we going to know which one we're talking about? We can't call them all 'big ugly monster,' can we?"

Tom shrugged. "It's accurate, isn't it?"

"I think Ike's saying that by naming them, we have a common way of discussing them. Am I right?" Meryl interjected.

Ike nodded and grinned.

"For fuck's sake," Tom moaned.

Naming the creatures hadn't occurred to Meryl, although she'd found herself thinking of them more and more as individuals. She even wondered if they had named each other, using some kind of language that had been lost to history, except in this isolated clearing in the middle of the vast Pacific Northwest. "So let's hear the names," she said to Ike.

He was careful not to point to the creatures as body-language was clearly something they watched carefully and could misinterpret. Instead, he gestured with slight nods of his head. "That big male over there, the one who doesn't seem to like us," he said, "I'm calling him 'Thunderman' for obvious reasons. He's the policeman of the group. He doesn't make up the rules but he's keen to follow them, which is why he's so pissed off at us. The two with the more silver-colored fur, they're the twins — 'Romulus' and 'Remus.'"

"One of them's a girl, Ike," Rose said. "Correctly stated, Romulus and Remus from mythology were both boys."

"I didn't say my naming system was perfect," he quipped, "and I don't think they'll care. The girl's 'Remus,' by the way."

"How about the younger male?" asked Meryl.

"'A Quart Short.' He's the teenager of the bunch. He's also a mama's boy. Or mom's overly-protective, I haven't figured out which. But there's some reason she never leaves him, even though he looks pretty capable to me."

Meryl glanced over at the hulking female. "And she's 'Big Girl?'"

"That's right."

"'Big Girl?'" Tom snorted. "Big waste of time. Thanks, college boy, way to help us escape. At least we can call them by name when they murder us."

Again, Ike ignored him. "I haven't quite figured Big Girl out yet," he confessed.

"She's the one in charge," Meryl said. "As you pointed out earlier, she's the alpha monster."

"No way," Tom replied. "That big gorilla over there—"

"Thunderman," Ike interrupted.

"—That *big gorilla* could rip her up if he wanted to. He's like twice her size."

"I don't think his size matters," answered Meryl.

"Sure, all girls say that."

Meryl rolled her eyes at Tom. "If he wanted to rip her up, then why didn't he yesterday? He wanted to kill us, but she chased him off. I'm telling you, she's in charge."

Rose threw a handful of pinecones into the flames and asked testily, "Who really cares which one of them is in charge? Maybe if we spent less time naming them and more time..." Her voice trailed off.

"What?" Ike asked defensively. "Go ahead. Speak your mind."

Rose didn't answer.

"You think we should be doing something more maybe? You wanna make a run for it? You won't get very far, old lady."

Again Rose didn't reply, but Tom gaped at him and snapped, "Dude, now who's being the asshole here?"

During their short association, Meryl had never seen Ike exhibit any real anger, but she understood why he was flaring up. After all, this had been Rose's expedition, Rose's grand plan. No one was openly blaming her for their predicament, but Rose's continuing insistence that they escape — not to reach safety but rather to find the mine — was grating on everyone. It had reached the point where Meryl was truly beginning to wonder about the woman's sanity. Her earlier comments about the animals killing her before she'd give up her quest for the mine even had Meryl wondering if Rose had some kind of death wish.

"Do you suppose anyone else on Earth knows these animals are out here?" Meryl asked.

"I bet Elijah Comstock did," Ike snarled, glaring almost accusingly at Rose. "He spent years roaming around out here and you're the expert on him. What did he know about these things?"

Rose was immediately annoyed. "What do you mean? There's absolutely nothing in any of his stuff about these" — she sputtered to find a suitable word — "*assholes* being out here!"

"Well, that's really not true," Ike retorted. "Even his obituary mentioned that he stopped coming out into this forest because he thought it was too dangerous and he was encountering all sorts of weird things."

Rose's eyes widened. "His obituary? I never showed you his obituary."

There was a moment of shocked recognition on both Ike and Meryl's faces as they simultaneously realized that they could no longer recall what they knew because Rose had told them, and what they knew from rummaging through her room. Rose figured it out quickly and responded with practiced reserve: "I see. Just how much of my stuff did you two rifle through?"

"It wasn't like that," Meryl insisted. "We just had a lot of questions and, frankly, you didn't seem very interested in giving us answers."

"So you think I've been hiding some secret information from you about these animals? You read Elijah's notes in the storybook. He wrote about mountains and streams and distances. There wasn't a thing about monsters."

"He wrote most of those notes as a schoolboy, long before he probably ever came out here. But even the storybook talks about the mining camp being overrun by *something*."

"Indeed. By Native Americans."

"It doesn't say that, Rose. In fact, the story makes of a point of noting that there wasn't any sign of attack by Indians. Not a single arrowhead. So we need to know what else you know. I'm sure you have information that you never shared with us. Stuff you withheld to make this whole trip seem more appealing and less dangerous."

Rose arched a thin, white eyebrow. "My goodness, dear, don't say anything I might take offense at."

Tom interjected. "Meryl, no one forced any of us to come out here. We all chose to come."

"Well, that's kind of the beauty of being a con-man, huh? You make your victims believe that everything was their idea," Ike said.

"Geeze, paranoid much?" Tom guffawed.

"Don't defend her," Meryl retorted quickly. "You don't know, Tommy, because she tells you things and you just accept it. But I saw all that stuff in her room from the casinos. How much you want to bet that Rose here has some massive gambling debts or something? Is that why you left Arizona? Is that why you're so anxious to find this fortune?"

Rose recoiled at her words and flushed. "Oh my goodness! How ridiculous you sound! Should I even mention what a huge invasion of privacy that was?"

Meryl refused to acknowledge Rose's hurt feelings. Now that their mutual dishonesty was being addressed, Meryl was intent on getting answers to some of those questions which had bothered her from the day Rose had moved in. Even the old woman's smaller act of chicanery — like highjacking David and Rachel's WIFI signal or stealing flowers from their garden — suddenly took on new importance. But the question she asked first was why Rose paid for everything in cash.

Rose shook her head. "What? I don't understand?"

"You don't have a bank or checking account. Everything's in cash."

"I don't trust banks."

"Apparently you don't trust the phone company or the postal service, either."

"What's that mean?" Tom asked.

Meryl clapped her hands, inadvertently causing Thunderman to growl. "I've finally put all this together," she cried, her eyes fixed on her roommate's face. "I don't think you hate banks, I think you're just trying to stay off the radar. That's why you won't get a new driver's license or replace your broken cell phone or put any of the utilities in your name. You're hiding."

"Who's she hiding from?" Tom pressed. He had no idea who's side he should be taking in all this, but he knew Meryl well enough to trust her instincts. As much as he might loath to admit it, she was good at figuring about people's unspoken motivations. Maybe, he figured, it was just a survival skill she'd picked up from living with her mother for so long.

"From ruthless mobsters, apparently," Rose sneered. She was clearly furious, but still managed to maintain her composure, speaking with that untroubled manner teachers used when confronting a rowdy classroom.

Meryl looked at Ike for support and he obediently offered it. "Meryl's right. Your story is too... Weird."

"Just so I can be crystal-clear on this matter, you're calling me a liar, yes?" Rose asked.

"You're very good with these awesome stories about how we'd go on a weekend camping trip and come home millionaires — and we were retarded to believe it — but I still agree with Meryl that you must know a lot more than you ever said."

"And what would you have me tell you, Ike? That during all those years of researching the mine, I occasionally read an old article about some frontier family who spotted some strange animal in the mountains; or a couple of prospectors who were chased off by something they couldn't identify? Yes, I found things like that, but those stories were over a century old. Those frontier folk were ignorant and superstitious. And those stories had nothing to do with a gold mine which I know to be absolutely, indisputably real."

"Except that the monsters turned out to be real, too," Ike said.

Rose shrugged haughtily. "If you expected me to know that, you're out of your mind. What rational kind of person would believe that?"

"Elijah Comstock?" said Meryl.

Rose shifted uncomfortably.

"But you suspected that too, didn't you?" Rose didn't reply so Meryl pressed on. Weeks of suspicions and frustration poured out of her mouth. "You knew that Elijah Comstock, an intelligent man, a medical doctor, had given up coming into the woods because of what he thought was out here. He was afraid of *them*."

"He was old and befuddled."

"*He was right!*" Meryl roared.

Rose squared her shoulders and said calmly, "We don't really know what Elijah knew and what he didn't and he's not around to ask. But kindly don't play so high and mighty with me, Meryl. If you suspected all this, if you thought me such a villainous charlatan, then why did you come on this trip and bring Alexander, too? You came because, like the rest of us, you hoped we would find the gold and all go home rich The only difference between you and me, Meryl, is that I'm willing to admit to my motives for being out here."

Meryl felt anger course through her body like an electric charge. But she wasn't willing to consider her own choices. She'd been struggling with her guilt over bringing Alexander along for an entire day now, but it was simply more satisfying to blame Rose. "Yeah, I was curious," she agreed. "And you're right, I did agree to come but it was all based on what you told me, and everything you say is a half-truth at best. It had to occur to you that there was more to this forest, more to the disappearance of the miners one hundred years ago, than originally met the eye?"

Rose wrinkled her nose. "I repeat: not once did Dr. Comstock writing a thing about big hairy monsters. You're an utter fool if you think I had some clairvoyant knowledge that these animals were living out here and I chose not to share it with you."

Tom, who'd been listening quietly to their harsh whispers, finally stirred with irritation. "Hey, would you two shut up already? You both give me and Ike shit for arguing and now you're doing it too."

"Yeah, I agree," Ike muttered. "Just drop it. You can hash it out later, once we're home."

Tom lifted his eyebrows in surprise. "See what you've done?" he snarled at the women. "It's to the point where Turbo's now agreeing with me. How messed up is that?"

Ike glanced at Tom and looked confused.

Tom continued: "Meryl, you're being totally paranoid. Seriously. There's no way anyone could've known what was waiting out here. If there had been, we would've all seen the documentaries on the nature channel, right?"

"Shut up, Tommy," Meryl shot back. "Frankly, I've had a little more experience dealing with manipulative old women than you have."

"No argument here. But you shouldn't be confusing Rose with your mom."

"Different women. Same bullshit."

He sighed loudly. "Nope. Different women, totally different bullshit. Let it go, girl."

Tom's knowledge of her past, and his ability to conjure up old memories with a few carefully chosen words, were the two most inconvenient aspects of having him around. Living on her own had forced Meryl to mature quickly and she'd managed to hide her past as an insecure, heartbroken teenager from most everyone in Corvallis. But Tom knew all about the Meryl who existed before her exodus from Portland. He remembered the pretty freshman girl with the chocolate-brown hair and olive complexion who kept staring at him in the school corridors. Girls whispered about how they'd make a beautiful couple — she was dark and exotic, and he was fair and All-American. Boys whispered how she was too smart and probably not worth the effort. But mostly everyone whispered about her dead father. Right before Thanksgiving, as the story went, her dad dropped dead downtown. Apparently his body lay on the sidewalk for nearly an hour while the paramedics tried to revive him. At the time, Tom didn't know if the story was true and part of him didn't care. He could be as sympathetic as anyone, but at sixteen years of age, he was mostly just intrigued by how she followed him around the school, often hiding herself in the crowd or gawking at him around corners. Their relationship had been stormy from the very beginning. She was head strong and an overachiever. He was widely considered a slacker who hated people telling him what to do. But their basic incompatibility did nothing to stop them from becoming sexual almost immediately and the following year Alexander was born.

Meryl had spent more hours than she could count trying to figure out her relationship with Tom. She'd always been fascinated by puzzles, but why she'd chosen this boy to be her first great love was a riddle without an adequate solution. The simplest answer was he was good-looking and it had always been about physical attraction. Most of her friends, including Tess, had speculated that their relationship was a reaction to her father's death, a period of intense vulnerability where Tom had been a convenient distraction. Privately, Meryl had never accepted either explanation. Despite what she said in moments of anger, she'd never really thought of Tom as a bad or stupid person. As he had just demonstrated, he understood her in a way few others did. So Meryl indulged in her pout, saying little as the night drew on and they all huddled together around the campfire trying not to think about what was sitting in the darkness, watching them.

CHAPTER TWENTY

A large mound of blackberries had been piled on top of a flat rock during the night. No, not piled Meryl thought. Arranged, almost in a pyramid shape, and trimmed with muddy tubers and what she assumed was a handful of edible flowers. Curiously, there were no more dead hares or squirrels and she guessed that the creatures must've recognized their repulsion at seeing the previous carcasses and didn't bother to waste more valuable food.

Big Girl and the other animals had become more active once the sun went down, and for hours Meryl could hear them lumbering through the woods and occasionally engaging in the strange gibberish that seemed to form their language. They never approached the fire, but Meryl hadn't decided if that was due to an innate fear or because they were too busy scavenging for food. At one point, very early in the morning, there had been a terrible uproar from the darkness followed by the distinctive howls of Thunderman. With the light of dawn, it had become obvious that the big male had been hunting, as the partially consumed remains of a deer was strung from the branches of a spruce tree on the far side of the clearing. The sight of the fresh meat actually calmed Meryl's fears. Clearly, she reasoned, if they saw the humans as food they wouldn't be hunting deer. Her logic, however, didn't help the others and the morning's conversation again revolved around escape.

Ike looked at Meryl and asked directly, "What do we do?"

His question made her feel both flattered and anxious. She hid her doubt and replied with conviction: "The only way we can leave is if they let us. And the only way they're going to let us is to gain their trust."

"So we're back to your 'let's be friends with the monsters' idea?" Rose asked impertinently. She and Meryl had barely spoken since their argument the day before, and the older woman had abandoned her typically solicitous demeanor for something more defiant.

Meryl controlled her anger and replied evenly, "I'm open to suggestions, Rose, as long as they're somewhat more useful than 'let's just sneak away.'"

"They don't seem to mind if we move around this little meadow," Ike volunteered. "They let us gather firewood without interfering. They just don't like it when we try to head for the trees."

"They also brought us more blackberries," said Meryl, "so they clearly want to keep us alive. The canteens are nearly empty so they'll need to take us to get water. Maybe they'll lead us back to the same stream where we first saw Thunderman?"

"Maybe, maybe, maybe..." Rose grumbled.

As the day dragged on, Meryl decided that the most intolerable thing about their forced captivity was the long periods of inactivity. The clearing had grown smaller and smaller, especially as she and the others grew more hungry and thirsty with few options to collect their own supplies. There were also growing issues with what Rose delicately referred to as "toilet concerns." The concept of privacy had vanished altogether in a largely open area and among animals who were uncomfortably interested in nearly everything the humans did. More often than not, as soon as one of them had finished relieving themselves, one of the animals would stalk over to examine what they'd produced.

"That's by far the grossest thing I've seen them do," Tom had sneered. "I feel like it's only a matter of time before they're sniffing me in uncomfortable places."

More and more, Meryl began to see these actions as something quite deliberate. She was now certain they were being studied.

By late afternoon, Big Girl had left her usual spot near A Quart Short and was wandering around the area's perimeter. She finally hunkered down near a large stump about fifty feet from the huddled captives. Like most wild animals she seemed uncomfortable with direct eye-to-eye contact, yet she was clearly watching them. Her manner reminded Meryl of how zoo animals would watch passersby — through quick glances from the corner of her eye. This was a behavior she only demonstrated with the humans however, as she had exhibited no problem staring down Thunderman or, in moments of almost human intimacy, nuzzle and caress the faces of A Quart Short or The Twins.

Alexander had taken a stalk of milkweed and was dragging it across the tip of Meryl's chin, like he was painting a landscape on her face. Big Girl seemed particularly interested in the child's actions, plucked a blade of grass and began to dandle it against the tree stump. There something wistful about the creature's actions, more than simple mimicry. She seemed almost sad. For a second, her eyes connected with Meryl's but she quickly looked away, turning her face toward the sky as though she was considering something very important floating amongst the clouds. When Meryl looked up again, Big Girl was standing. The creature turned, took three or four large strides toward the tree-line, then paused. Waiting.

Meryl looked around quickly for the others. For some reason, she felt like she needed witnesses but Tom and Rose were gathering firewood on the other side of the clearing and Ike was busy checking Tom's cell phone for a signal everyone else had long since given up on. Alexander was also unaware of the creature's actions and was amusing himself by trying to insert the stalk of milkweed into Meryl's left ear. Big Girl glanced back at her and slumped her shoulders. It was a gesture remarkably similar to one Tom had made regularly when they were dating, whenever Meryl was taking too long to do something and he had grown impatient.

She led Alexander over to where Ike was sitting and said, "I need you to do me a favor. I'm gonna fill our canteens. Would you keep Alexander company for a little while?"

"What are you talking about?" he frowned. "Where're you going?"

Meryl glanced over her shoulder. The giant female was now squatted down, still watching her.

Ike's expression transformed instantly. "Seriously?" he gaped. "Are you actually trying to kill yourself?"

"Be a little more dramatic, will you?" she whispered harshly, clapping her hands over Alexander's ears. Ike began to protest again but she cut him short with a scowl. "You know if they wanted to hurt us they could do so at any moment."

"And how do you know this isn't your moment, Meryl?"

Again, Meryl looked back at Big Girl. The creature rose, turned three times in a circle like a cat positioning itself for a nap, and squatted down again. "I guess I'm taking that on faith," she said. "But it doesn't matter. We need water. Hand me the canteens and a backpack, please."

Alexander was trying to pry her hands off his ears. "Mah-mee, stop," he commanded.

"Please," she said urgently, "trust me on this."

Ike grimaced and was clearly rankled as he passed her the empty canteens into one of the knapsacks which she quickly slung across her shoulders. Ike took the boy from her arms and balanced him against his knee. "What do you want me to say to Tom and Rose?" he whispered.

"Nothing."

"Because you know they'd stop you?"

"Because I don't need another argument over every little thing."

"Mah-mee, where going?" inquired Alexander.

She cupped his small chin in her hand and kissed him on his nose. "Mommy's gonna go get some water for us, sweetie," she said. "Ike will stay with you until I come back, okay?"

The boy seemed to accept that explanation, mostly because he didn't realize whose company Meryl would be keeping. Ike quickly distracted the child by digging holes with him in the soft earth and Meryl crept off without him taking a second look. As she rapidly wove her way between the trees, she noticed A Quart Short dozing in the sun some distance away. Her footfalls roused him and he rolled indolently onto his side to watch her pass. He made no attempt to intercept her and seemed no more concerned about her actions than he did those of the squirrels darting about on the tree limbs overhead. Meryl had to wonder if her leaving the clearing was somehow sanctioned by Big Girl, so the other creatures wouldn't interfere. She walked on, and in a few yards more A Quart Short had lost interest entirely and had fallen asleep face-down in the ferns and pine needles.

As Big Girl effortlessly snaked her away between the trees and along slippery ridges, she revealed the practicality of her species' odd, neckless build. Meryl had anticipated that the landscape would require Big Girl to move more like a great ape, dropping to all fours when navigating through thicker vegetation or along steep inclines. But the beast maintained an upright and very human deportment for the entire journey. She never seemed to slip or stumble, due to a more bowed posture and disproportionately long arms which she used to lift, pull, anchor and push herself along. Her immense physical strength was centered in her shoulders and back; and coupled with a low center-of-gravity, she reminded Meryl of the great mechanical cranes which unloaded cargo ships in the Port of Portland. Unlike the other large mammals of the wilderness, Big Girl had the ability to manipulate her environment, not just react to it. In this sense alone, she was unlike anything Meryl had ever encountered.

They meandered their way up to a narrow chute in the rock face to where a ribbon of icy water was cascading into a deep pool. Meryl was certain this had to be the same creek where they'd first encountered Thunderman as they had crossed no other, but at a higher elevation and perhaps closer to its headwaters. Meryl stooped at the water's edge and the large creature did likewise several yards upstream.

"I'm going to get us more water," Meryl said to her, making the creature's small ears quiver. "Don't freak out or anything, okay?"

She removed the canteens from the backpack and dipped them in the frigid water. Big Girl watched, almost bemused, as bubbles rose from them and popped on the stream's surface. With one meaty finger, the creature made several swipes in the mud at the creek's edge and clicked her teeth together.

"I know you don't understand me," Meryl continued, "but I figure if I talk you won't think I'm up to something. Plus, you make me fucking nervous and talking helps, okay?"

Once the canteens were filled and repacked, Big Girl clicked her teeth again, turned and lumbered off. She'd stop every few feet to ensure her captive was following. As Meryl passed the area where the creature had been crouched, she noticed three figures were scrawled in the damp earth. The mysterious diagrams weren't language, not as humans understood it anyway, but it was communication. Deliberate, thoughtful communication. Moreover, they were something Meryl recognized. She lifted the edge of her jacket so she could see the old leather belt. Elijah Comstock had been a much larger person than she and the loose end of the belt wrapped around nearly to the base of her back. She had had to feed it twice through the loops on her pants to keep it from dangling. But the excess also made it easier for her to see the strange pictograms scratched there decades earlier. Only one of the figures in the mud — a horizontal line intersected by two diagonal lines — matched a symbol on the belt, next to which Elijah had written 'WATER.' Her knees wobbled with excitement. She squatted, dabbed her finger into the silt and redrew the symbol on a flat rock where Big Girl could see it. Then, to reinforce that she understood the symbol's meaning, she cupped some water in her hand and let it trickle out between her fingers. The creature clicked her teeth approvingly.

"I think I get this now," Meryl said softly. "At first I thought these doodles were something Elijah had created. But it wasn't him at all, huh? It was your people. He was writing down your language, trying to figure it out."

Big Girl tilted her head to the left and snorted. Then she turned and quickly scrambled along the stream's rocky edge, heading north.

They continued on for nearly another hour, hugging the creek's bank until the trees thinned. Many of the towering pine and hemlock had been deliberately cut and were piled haphazardly nearby. It was clear that the felled timbers had been there for a very long time, as they were thickly overgrown with ferns and lichens. Meryl wondered, albeit briefly, if Big Girl and her kind had been responsible for this tiny pocket of deforested land.

Then she realized where she was.

The mine entrance was a great, ugly cavity in the hillside. Contrary to Ike's prediction, nature had done little to disguise the opening. In fact, over a century of continuous erosion had actually collapsed much of the rock-face above making the entrance significantly larger than it had been when gold-hungry miners had originally excavated it. What had been reclaimed by the forest were the other human artifacts scattered around the pit, in particular a strange array of wood pylons encrusted with thick moss and a lattice-work of splintered beams which had partially toppled into the chasm below. Meryl paused at the edge of the debris field, afraid. Big Girl didn't share her hesitation, swinging her massive body through the fallen timbers with the same ease as she had navigated the forest trees. When the creature reached the lip of the crater, she glanced back and snorted. Meryl was suddenly aware of the challenge, and the choice, contained within that snort.

Either the area is safe since this giant monster just walked through the middle of it, Meryl thought, *or she's just unaware of the potential danger and was lucky. Either way, I could be walking across the top of a cracked eggshell.*

The creature settled onto her haunches and snorted louder. This time, the sound seemed like something closer to encouragement. Meryl stepped into the debris field. When she could, she placed her own feet into the deep impressions left by Big Girl's massive strides, like a soldier following footprints through a snow-covered minefield. As she moved around the back of the pylons and the web-like timbers which connected them, she realized the structure had been some kind of elevated rail system which fed into the mine at a steep, forty-five degree angle. Rusted iron tracks, similar to a railway, were still in place at the top of the framework. Where the lip of the mine had partially collapsed, the rails were broken and hung over the precipice like fangs dripping with orange rust. Meryl leaned in as much as she dared and peered down. The entrance to the mine was roughly bowl-shaped and perhaps half the length of a football field if you measured straight across. Some fifty feet below was the other end of the rail system, now a twisted jumble of metal and rotting wood, half-submerged in mud and blanketed with brilliant green foliage. Off to one side was a small iron ore cart, upended with its wheels pointing skyward, painted a bright scarlet-orange by decades of accumulated rust. And beyond the wrecked cart stretched the mine's interior. With the sun being high in the sky, Meryl was able to see hundreds of feet inside. The terrifying gullet was choked with rocky detritus which had blocked nearly half of the entrance and crushed the lower parts of the rail system into a twisted tendril of dark metal. Protruding from the rubble, Meryl spotted a handful of decayed wooden ladders and support beams which had been stripped from their original locations and swept down the shaft by rainfall and landslides, forming an impenetrable blockage about three hundred feet into the chasm. To her surprise, her heart sank a little. The obstruction meant Rose's dream of walking into the mine and extracting gold nuggets by hand was clearly impossible, perhaps even suicidal.

Meryl moved to within six feet of Big Girl and squatted down, imitating her slumped posture. The stench of the creature overwhelmed her, but she resisted wincing and forced herself to say: "You knew about this place? Why'd you bring me here?"

As before, the sound of a human voice seemed to fascinate Big Girl. The creature's gaze brushed gently across the young woman. Meryl did her best to follow suit, looking at Big Girl's shoulder instead of her face, keeping her voice soft and limiting her hand gestures as she might do when meeting a strange dog. The massive animal turned away from her slightly, lifting her head upward and contracting her lips as the sunshine warmed her face. Her right hand wandered among the thick clumps of grass and weeds which grew along the crater's edge. She lazily plucked a twig from the ground and without looking drew a crude circle in the damp earth. She then poked two holes in the center of the circle. A chill ran up Meryl's back.

She scanned through the images on the old belt quickly until she found the same symbol with the word 'STOP!' written next to it.

Meryl picked up a twig and drew the same symbol in the dirt.

Big Girl watched but pretended not to, her chartreuse eyes widening as she recognized what Meryl was doing. She gently patted the circle she'd drawn, hauled herself upright and continued to scuttle along the edge of the pit. Meryl paused and looked back at the belt.

'STOP!'

The word itself was puzzling and ambiguous. Was it warning about proceeding further? Or was it indicating that she'd reached an important destination? The creature grunted and Meryl followed obediently, her fascination overwhelming her fear.

At the furthest corner, where the edge of the mine met the hillside, Big Girl dropped down and proceeded to scrabble along the steep embankment. At times, the creature would go down on all-fours, placing her hands flat against the spongy dirt floor and using her arms to steady herself on the rutted terrain. She seemed to understand Meryl's uneasiness and would pause more frequently to allow her to catch up along a route which had clearly been used before as it was not nearly as steep or treacherous as it had looked from the opposite side of the pit. In fact, there was a visible trail here, a series of gentle switchbacks which had been worn down over the years by the feet of giants.

"I don't suppose it would matter if I told you this looks pretty dangerous?" Meryl called. The creature's girth and apparent lack of a neck required her to rotate the entire top half of her body, but she met and for the first time held Meryl's gaze. Then, almost like she was putting an end to any additional protests, she smacked her lips loudly and continued on.

They came to rest on a rocky ledge some seventy-five feet below the mine's rim. It was a flat piece of granite large and solid enough it could've accommodated Big Girl and two others like her with room to spare. Meryl immediately felt like she was sitting on the tongue in a giant mouth, hoping she wouldn't be swallowed. Her nose filled with the smell of the raw earth, the rotting timbers, the rampant fern beds and the rocky fissures filled with stagnant water. But there was another smell here as well. Something which overpowered even Big Girl's natural stink. Something terrible.

Big Girl sidled up to the very lip of the granite shelf until her long toes hung over. She'd turned her body so Meryl could only see the crest of her pointed skull and her left ear. With her right hand she scooped out a gob of wet earth and lifted it to her face. Then she groaned in a way Meryl hadn't heard from any of the creatures before. It was low and plaintive and reverberated so loudly in the enclosed space that Meryl could feel it course through her body like an electric shock. It was the sound of grief.

Meryl sat cross-legged and waited in complete silence. It took a long time before Big Girl turned back to face her. The handful of earth she'd scooped up was smeared across her face, creating four muddy bands which ran from the bony ridge over her left eye, across her nose and mouth and to the end of her massive jaw. She looked down into the chasm, then back at Meryl.

"You want me to look down there?" Meryl asked.

Big Girl stuck out a fat index finger and drew in the mud on the surface of the rock. A circle with two dots in the middle.

Meryl began to crawl toward her, whispering encouragement to the rock beneath her: "Please don't collapse, please don't collapse, please don't collapse..."

She came within inches of Big Girl's shaggy hide. The smell was almost unbearable, but the stench rising from the chasm was even worse. On her hands and knees, Meryl peered over. The mine shaft dropped precariously, a one-hundred foot fall to the partially flooded floor below. A large dark shape lay in the brown water, barely visible in the dim light. Its arms were splayed out to the sides and Meryl could see deep grooves in the earthen walls where desperate fingers had tried to dig or claw or pull their way to safety. The legs, as massive as tree trunks, were curled into a sickening and unnatural fish-hook curve. The body had clearly been there for a while. The hide had separated from the bone and the soft tissues had long since dissolved into the gooey stew in which it lay. The skull, now devoid of eyes, was tilted back as though the creature had died longing for the sunshine above.

There was no way for Meryl to understand what relationship had existed between Big Girl and whoever lay at the bottom of the chasm, and in a way it didn't matter. Whether the body had been a sibling, a parent, a mate or a child, Big Girl's anguish was palatable. Grief rose off her body like static electricity, jumping from the tips of her wiry fur to the soft hair on Meryl's arm. Involuntarily, Meryl's mind flashed upon the death of her own father, an event she hadn't witnessed but which she had recreated in her head a thousand times over the years. She had often wondered what her father's last thoughts were as he lay sprawled on that Portland sidewalk surrounded by skyscrapers and strangers who called frantically on cell phones for help which would arrive too late. Meryl wondered if her father had thought of her, wished for her and her mother to be with him in his last moments — or if he had just died lost and confused. Now she wondered if the creature at the bottom of the pit had had similar thoughts. Were such emotions even possible in these animals? Meryl's whole body convulsed and for an instant she thought she might vomit into the chasm. But instead, she burst out in sobs and buried her face in her hands. The emotion which overwhelmed her was more than simple human empathy, it was the sudden realization of something much deeper which connected her to the hairy giant perched a few inches away. It wasn't just the inevitability of death which tethered them together at this moment, but the reality of the resulting sorrow. She wiped her tears from her face and happened to glance at the diagram Big Girl had drawn for her twice. The mysterious circle with two dots in the center suddenly revealed its hidden meaning to her. A skull with empty eye sockets. A primitive pictogram for a place of death.

The creature was watching her intently. Meryl knew that tears of grief weren't shed by any animal on earth but humans, yet Big Girl seemed to intuitively understand her reaction to the corpse below. Meryl smeared her fingers in the mud and drew four bands across her face. Big Girl straightened her back and let out a long, deep breath. They sat in silence for a long time until a voice from above echoed down to them.

"Meryl! Meryl! Where are you?"

CHAPTER TWENTY-ONE

Tom appeared at the edge of the crater, jumping recklessly between the buckled pylons. Meryl waved up to him and he froze. With all the history and drama between them, Meryl had once been certain that she'd seen every mood Tom was capable of producing. But it was only in the past few days that she'd seen him scared. And now, she was seeing something else. Something beyond fear. He was terrified to the point of hysteria.

"Holy shit!" he cried. His voice cracked with anguish. "Holy shit! Holy shit!"

Meryl waved again and called up to him, as softly as she could, "It's okay. I'm fine. I'm fine."

"You're sitting in a goddamn pit with a fucking gorilla!" he cried.

"Tom!" she called back, louder this time, "I'm telling you it's okay. She brought me down here. She wanted to show me something. She's not hurting me."

As if to reinforce this, Big Girl made a noise which sounded like a dog's bark — sharp and disapproving. Tom's histrionics were clearly irritating her, which she reinforced by turning her back and refusing to look at him.

"How'd you get down there?" he bellowed.

"There's a little path over on this side. I'm telling you I'm fine. You need to calm the fuck down, okay?"

Tom nodded and squatted. Meryl could see him shaking.

Big Girl stood up and moved away. At first, Meryl was sure it was out of annoyance but once he had quieted himself she seemed no more concerned about Tom than she did the tiny insects buzzing around her. The giant lowered herself off the far end of the granite shelf and onto a narrow path which had obviously been carved by the original miners a century earlier. The walkway led gently down to an adjoining tunnel. The rotted remnants of a wooden safety rail were still in place, but offered no protection to the steep drop beyond. Big Girl seemed to recognize the danger, so she stood between the shelf and the chasm until Meryl had crawled down. They moved slowly until they could stand side-by-side at the mouth of the tunnel.

"Meryl!" Tom shouted from far above. "What're you doing? Don't go in there!"

She turned and waved to him. He stopped shouting but began moving along the crater's edge toward the start of the switchbacks. Meryl waved to him again, urging him to stop, but he ignored her.

She and Big Girl were now so far inside the mine, so far from the diminishing sunshine, that it was difficult to see the passageway. It was obvious from the timber supports embedded in the rock walls that this narrow cleft had been part of the original mine. It was much too small for Big Girl to squeeze through, but clearly she thought this tunnel was important.

The creature stooped and tapped the naked rock where a variety of symbols had been inscribed just to the right of the tunnel entrance. The images were worn down by season after season of wind, rain and snow. A spiral, two intersecting boxes, a long serpentine line, and once again, the circle with two dots inside. Meryl struggled to find the glyphs on the belt coiled around her, but other than the death's-head emblem nothing matched.

By the time Tom had reached the crude trail leading into the mine, Meryl had entered the tunnel and was no longer visible. The only shape which remained was Big Girl, who had now squatted down and was gently rocking back and forth. He paused before stepping onto the trail and wondered fearfully how Big Girl would respond if he decided to climb down to her. The creature clearly didn't care for him and a flick from one massive hand would send him tumbling into the pit. But whether he was compelled by curiosity or the old feelings for Meryl which were suddenly welling up again, Tom stepped onto the path.

Meryl had only taken three steps inside the tunnel when she felt like a massive hand had wrapped around her, slowly squeezing the air from her lungs. She turned to go back but Big Girl's head blocked the exit as the creature sniffed at the stale air inside, as though picking up a century-old scent. She doubted the animal would block her way if she tried to leave, but there was a certain earnestness in Big Girl which compelled Meryl to continue on. Strangely, she felt like she'd disappoint the creature if she didn't at least try to understand what was so important about this particular hole in the rock. Meryl steadied herself, readjusted the heavy backpack strapped to her shoulders, and pulled the small LED flashlight from the pouch on her wrist. The shaft was just over five feet in height and little more than three feet wide. The walls were raw serrated rock, still clearly showing the jagged scars left behind by dynamite, pick axes and chisels. Scattered down the length of the corridor were roughhewn timbers which braced the ceiling and walls. Some had collapsed over the years and others were buckling. Meryl brushed her fingers across one which lay inches above her head and dislodged a cloud of soot deposited there from ancient torches or lanterns. She ducked underneath the beam and continued further into the tunnel. Big Girl produced a distinct *har-rumph* noise, as though issuing a warning. Several feet ahead, the passage widened and heightened considerably but was partially blocked by a crude barricade. The barrier of scavenged timbers and heavy rock almost reached to the ceiling, leaving a gap just a few inches wide at the very top. Near the base were dozens of metallic cylinders, approximately the size and length of Meryl's littlest finger. She hunched down and pulled one from the dirt. It was a bullet casing. Dozens lay about, representing several different calibers of ammunition.

Standing on her tip-toes, she felt around on the top of the pile and accidentally dislodged several stones which clattered down the pile and prompted Big Girl to issue a much louder warning.

"I'm okay," Meryl called back to her. The creature rocked nervously, her ugly, blunted face still filling the end of the tunnel.

Meryl removed the backpack and set it on the ground nearby. She then climbed up on the base of the barricade, clearing away some of the rubble with her hands until she was able to push her head and one arm slightly through the gap. The LED flashlight wasn't strong enough to illuminate anything beyond the sandy floor on the other side. More brass shell casings glinted softly in the flashlight's beam. This time, they numbered in the hundreds.

Tom's voice suddenly echoed through the passage, followed immediately by a sharp bark from Big Girl. Meryl scrambled back to the tunnel entrance. Tom had climbed down to the granite platform overlooking the pit and the gruesome corpse it contained. His proximity had clearly antagonized Big Girl, who was snarling at him and beating the dirt with her fist.

"Tom!" Meryl cried. "Just stop! Stay there!"

He froze.

"Crouch down," Meryl commanded. "Make yourself look small."

He complied, confused, anxious. Big Girl stopped pounding the dirt, but she didn't take her eyes off of him.

"What the hell are you doing?" he gasped. "Are you trying to kill yourself? Come out of there."

"I told you, she's not hurting me. She led me down here. But if you come across she could throw you over the edge. You need to chill out and use your fucking brain."

"Are you kidding me with this?" he growled. "You're seriously gonna play the 'Tom's a moron' card while standing inside a collapsing mine shaft?"

"It's not collapsing and I'm not kidding you. If you come across to this side, what the hell are you going to do? Challenge her to a fist fight or something?"

"I just want you to come out with me." He was almost pleading.

"I can't," Meryl replied. "I need to check something out first."

Tom's cheeks reddened with anger. "This's no time to be stubborn. Can't you ever just do what you're told?"

"Really?" she taunted him. "You're choosing to pick this fight now?"

"This is bullshit, Meryl. What happens to Alexander if his mom gets eaten by a monster here?"

Meryl stood stunned for a moment. The only other person who'd ever accused her of being irresponsible was her mother, and never so loudly as the morning when she'd tearfully told her that she was pregnant. But even then she half-expected that reaction. She knew her mom too well to believe she'd put aside her own emotions and just be, for once, a little empathetic. If her mom regretted what she said she never acknowledged it, even when Meryl had proven her so completely wrong by graduating early from high school and single-handedly supporting her infant son. Responsibility was like a second skin, she wore it everywhere and it was impossible to shed. So if this was a rare moment of great irresponsibility, Meryl didn't recognize it.

She noticed Big Girl was watching her, her head cocked to one side like a guard dog. Maybe she would've attacked if Meryl had signaled it, and not because she was some kind of pet Meryl had trained, but because she was a feeling creature who was becoming more and more annoyed with Tom. Meryl composed herself and lowered her voice.

"Tommy," she said slowly and as adamantly as possible, "I'm going into this little tunnel and I will be back in a few moments. If you decide to come across to this side of the pit, I will just wish you luck and hope that the injuries you receive are not life-threatening."

She marched back to the barricade and crawled up the debris pile until she was able to slither through the narrow gap at the top. The tumble down the other side was both inelegant and painful.

The thick, padded jacket David had lent her was now ripped in several places and something had jabbed her hard in the left leg during her fall. She called out to Big Girl or Tom: "I'm fine! Don't panic! I'm just being clumsy!" She moved the flashlight's beam to where her jeans had torn slightly and her leg was damp and sticky. It wasn't a bad injury, just a deep scrape several inches above her knee.

Her anger with Tom had made her reckless, so she lay for a moment in the dirt and stared into the darkness. There wasn't a sound in the tunnel other than her deep, anxious breaths. Not even the wind made it this far inside the mine. The air was stagnant and had a strange, faintly bitter smell to it which Meryl identified as being from all the copper shell casings.

She sat up and brandished the flashlight in front of her. The chamber was roughly oval-shaped with a ceiling that sloped sharply to a dead end. From the poor quality of the air, it was clear the barricade had been like a cork in a bottle, sealing the room off from the rest of the mine. She didn't have to speculate as to why. The death's-head pictogram Big Girl had drawn twice and all the spent cartridges clinking under her feet told her the whole story. This was the site of someone's last stand.

Meryl took one indecisive step away from the barricade and her foot clanked against something metal. She retrieved a broken lantern from the dirt. The device was designed like a primitive flashlight, with a small basin for a candle and a polished tin mirror behind it. Globs of melted wax and a withered wick were still adhered to its tarnished skin.

She swung her own light in a broad circle around her feet, illuminating for the first time in over a century scattered ammunition boxes, an empty canteen and two cans of beans someone had apparently smashed open with a rock. A second barricade, only a third as high as the first, lay beyond this rubbish. It had been constructed mostly of piled rock and gravel and Meryl doubted that it would've provided much protection from any kind of adversary. The beam from her flashlight skipped along the jagged contour of the rubble and landed on two booted feet with the toes pointed toward the low ceiling. Instinctually she dropped to a low crouch, holding a mouthful of air so she wouldn't choke on it.

The boots were covered in thick dust and the wispy tendrils of an ancient spider's web. Their occupant had clearly not moved, nor posed a threat to any other living creature, in generations. She scowled at her own ridiculousness. Big Girl had warned her with a doodle in the mud that this was a place of death. She had expected to find bodies beyond the barricade, but suddenly she was reluctant to look. It took her a moment to move again, stepping sideways in a great arch until she had rounded the stone obstruction and was positioned just an arm's length from three bodies tucked into a low alcove at the end of the chamber. The man in the dusty boots was lying on the ground parallel to the barricade. The other two men, both dressed in high-waisted overalls, were propped up against the rock pile as though they had fallen asleep there. The exposed areas of the bodies — the heads, necks, hands — were all skeletal. So were the feet of the body furthest from her, a man of small stature who was curled up on his side with his head resting on a large canvas bag. One hand cupped the end of the bag, though three of the fingers were missing or lay scattered in the dirt, obviously pulled off by rodents or other animals which had scavenged on the remains shortly after death. The clothing on all the bodies was still intact but clung tightly as though it had been epoxied to the raw bone, resulting in rigid and unnatural contours. The two men closest to her had several weapons, a combination of rifles and revolver, all now thoroughly corroded. Plus, there were two additional lanterns and what appeared to be the remains of a crudely-made torch. The third man — the shoeless one — had no visible weapons or other property. In fact, his only possession other than the clothes he was wearing was the canvas bag he'd used as a pillow.

There was no unpleasant smell to the bodies, or at least not any Meryl could detect. She assumed, however, that this tunnel must've smelled very differently to the forest animals, including Big Girl and her kin. After all she surmised, the shaggy monsters could've never squeezed down the narrow passageway or seen the three skeletons beyond the first barricade, but clearly Big Girl knew they were there. Even then, Meryl could hear the creature snuffing and snorting at the end of the tunnel, drawing into her nose whatever lingering scent of decomposition still floated in the stale air.

Between the creature who had fallen down the pit and these three bodies, the entire mine must've seemed like a crypt to Big Girl, Meryl thought. She touched the muddy fingermarks she'd made on her own face and shuddered a little.

Maintaining what felt like a respectful distance, Meryl half-crawled closer to the skeletons. What intrigued and bothered her were not the weapons nor the meager belongings nearby, but what was missing. There was no evidence in the chamber of a campfire, no remnants of blankets, bedrolls or even a warm coat. It was cold inside even during the day, so Meryl imagined it would be almost unbearable late at night or when the weather outside turned poor. Other than the lone canteen and the two shattered bean cans, there wasn't even any evidence of food.

And then there was the man without any shoes, concealed as far into the alcove as a person could crawl and cradling the bag. Was he being protected by the others? Or was he, in fact, protecting something? The objects in the chamber began to connect together like the pieces of a jigsaw puzzle. Clearly, whatever had chased the men into the tunnel had been so frightening that they chose to box themselves in and slowly die there rather than attempt escape. But what they brought into this tomb with them was equally significant. No provisions to speak of. Just weapons and one canvas bag.

Big Girl howled. The noise reverberated as it traveled down the tunnel and broke over the top of the rubble blocking the exit.

Meryl rushed back to the outer barricade and called through the gap at the top: "I'm okay. Everything's fine. Tommy, are you still out there?"

"Yes," he replied.

"You okay?"

"I'm fine, but I think you need to give us a shout out more often. Queen Kong appears to get upset if she doesn't hear from you regularly."

"Is she bothering you?"

"Other than giving me the occasional stink-eye, she's pretty much ignoring me. I'm letting her."

"Good. She doesn't like to be looked at directly, so don't make eye-contact with her."

"That's fine. I'd prefer not to look at her at all," he quipped, though his voice was strained. "You planning on coming out of there anytime soon? It's getting late. We need to go soon."

"Just a few more minutes."

"What's in there?"

Meryl glanced back at the far end of the chamber. The vague silhouette of the boots was still visible in the glimmer of her flashlight. "Nothing but a bunch of old mining junk," she replied, "I'll be out in a few."

"Hurry. I'm not enjoying this."

She continued her inspection, moving slightly deeper into the alcove but still careful not to touch the remains. The skeletons began to reveal clues to the men they'd once been: some loose strands of gray hair, a silver tooth, a wool shirt whose missing buttons had been replaced with leather ties. She wriggled toward the shoeless body, tucking her legs under her chin and shuffling like a crab so she could fit beneath the overhanging rock.

Keeping the flashlight level with her right hand while steading herself with the left, Meryl reached for the bag. Her fingertips pushed against the canvas exterior and she was surprised to find it filled with what felt like large chunks of gravel. She repositioned herself for a better grip on the bag's frayed corner and tugged hard. It was deceptively heavy and she tipped forward, catching herself with her right hand but coming down hard on the flashlight. There was a loud crunch and the light was immediately extinguished. She tumbled, her knees smashing through the brittle bones of the second man. The old ribs and vertebrate crunched like breaking wood and her nose filled with the musty odor of damp decay and moldy cloth. She rolled to her right and found herself sprawled between the two corpses, fingers groping frantically for the flashlight but finding only crushed rock and torn fabric. The lens had popped off during her fall and, along with the batteries, was now scattered somewhere among the dirt and bones.

She paused and held her breath. *You're not going to die here*, she told herself. *Not after all this. You're going to get out of this mine and out of this fucking forest. You just need to get a goddamn grip.*

She moved her hands over the debris on the floor, but slowly this time, so as not to scatter the lens cap and batteries any further. Operating completely by touch, she finally found the missing pieces, carefully dusted them off on the sleeve of her jacket and reassembled the flashlight. The light flickered twice and then filled the alcove with a bluish-gray glow. Grime-filled eye sockets and a mouth lined with broken teeth gaped at her. During her fall, the skull of the shoeless man had broken free of the body and was lying just inches from her nose. The lower jawbone had dislodged and hung at a strange angle, as

259

though the corpse was caught in a silent scream. Meryl felt sick. Moreover, she felt ashamed.

"Sorry," she whispered to the man, her eyes welling with tears.

The empty sockets stared back.

As carefully as possible, Meryl pulled the canvas bag free from the skeleton's grip. It was approximately the size and shape of a bread loaf, and even heavier than she first anticipated. Tied shut with a length of rotted leather cord, its surface was discolored by the fluids which had drained out of the miner's dead body a century earlier. It took all her strength to hoist it as high as her shoulders and heave it over the pile of rubble and onto the floor of the outer chamber.

Once free of the bodies, she retrieved one of the tin cans from the chamber floor and used its jagged lip to saw through the leather cords which bound the bag. Inside were chunks of raw ore, most about the size and shape of marshmallows. She extracted one and inspected it. A glistening ribbon of gold ran across the nugget's surface. Even with her injured leg and surrounded by dead bodies, Meryl's heart still leapt.

"You died for this?" she asked the bodies in the alcove. "And you guarded it all these years? Even Elijah Comstock never found you."

"Meryl?" It was Tom.

"Yeah?" she called back.

"Who are you talking to?" Her words, though softly uttered, had still echoed down the passageway.

"Just talking to myself," she answered swiftly. "I'm almost done in here. I'm coming out."

After tying it shut again, she pushed the bag of ore through the crawlspace at the top of the outer barricade and then followed it through. Crouched at the end of the tunnel, she smothered the glow of the flashlight between her body and the rock wall until she'd concealed the ore bag underneath the sloshing canteens in the backpack. It made the pack almost excruciatingly heavy, but she managed to pull it over her dusty, soiled jacket and cinched down the straps. Upon reappearing at the end of the shaft, Big Girl immediately swung her massive body onto the narrow trail which connected the mine to the granite slab where Tom was huddled. She barked angrily at the man and he recoiled instantly.

"What the hell?" he exclaimed, looking anxiously across to Meryl. "Call your pet off, will you?"

Meryl frowned. "Maybe I surprised her?" she said. Then, to Big Girl, she offered gently, "Everything's okay. I'm fine."

The beast's green-yellow eyes were barely visible beneath the thick shag which covered her sloped forehead. She growled, deep and long.

"What the hell's wrong with it?" Tom keened.

"I don't know, but she seems to want to come across to where you are. You probably better get back up that trail and give her some space."

"Yeah, my thoughts exactly," he said, turning and bounding clumsily up to the first switchback.

Big Girl immediately crossed to the granite shelf and hunkered down at its edge. Even when crouched, she was over five feet tall and looked like a coiled spring. This time, she barked directly at Meryl. Angrily.

"Uh, I don't think she's gonna let you cross," Tom said.

Meryl's mind began to flood with all kinds of unpleasant images: of her body lying next to the bones of the giant at the bottom of the gorge, or torn apart with the pieces decorating the clefts and crevices of the mine shaft. She began to devise an escape plan, but there were only two options — to move toward the snarling beast or return to the barricaded tunnel. If she retreated, would Big Girl turn on Tom? If she proceeded, would the creature swat her back as easily as Meryl could flick away an ant?

"What's wrong with it?" called Tom. "I thought she was your buddy."

Meryl glanced down at herself. She was covered in dust and cobwebs and fragments of old bone. Blood had soaked through her jeans from where she'd injured her knee, leaving a dark reddish-brown circle on the denim. She brushed at her clothes and a heavy layer of grit sloughed off. Big Girl raised her head and flared her nostrils.

"I don't think she likes how I smell," Meryl said.

"She's one to complain," Tom bellowed back.

"She's a wild animal, Tommy. I'm sure that nose of her's is picking up all sorts of things you and I can't smell."

"So what do you have on you she's so upset about?"

Again, Meryl elected not to answer truthfully. Instead, she just replied, "I think it's just from all the dust and stuff stuck to my clothes. I must not smell like I did when I went inside and it's freaking her out."

"Take your clothes off," he suggested.

Given different circumstances, Meryl would've considered that a quintessentially typical comment from Tom, but here and now, he was deadly serious. "Then what?" she asked. "Freeze to death tonight?"

"Well, at least take your coat off and then throw it up to me. It's the dirtiest thing anyway. Maybe that'll settle her down?"

There didn't appear to be much choice as Big Girl wasn't budging from her spot on the granite precipice, so Meryl quickly stripped off the heavy backpack and coat. She shook the coat off over the pit, then bundled it into a ball and tied the sleeves together.

"Okay, I'm gonna throw it to you," she called to Tom, "but I'm gonna have to throw it over her head. You ready?"

"I'm ready," he answered. "Just don't throw like a girl."

"Just make sure you catch it, asshole," she retorted. She cocked back her arm and flung the garment as hard as she could.

The bundle made a wide arch over Big Girl and Tom leaned forward with arms outstretched. But the jacket was going to land short and in his desperation to grab it his left foot slipped off the path and in an instant he was tumbling. He rolled in a series of sloppy cartwheels down the slope, pushing an avalanche of rock and sediment before him. He made no sound. Not a shout or a gasp or even a grunt as his body hit the granite ledge just a few feet from the creature, bounced once and then entered the void above the chasm. There was no thought or emotion in Meryl as she watched him fall. There hadn't been time, as the misstep had been so instantaneous that her mind was still processing what she was seeing as Tom's body hung weightless for an instant over the gorge. Then, just as instantaneously, Big Girl reached out with an abnormally long arm and giant hand. There was a loud pop, like a cork being yanked out of a bottle as the creature caught him by the arm, swung him about and tossed him back onto the embankment. Meryl's balled up jacket rolled to a stop just a few inches from him.

It was only then, as Tom lay limp and knotted, his face hidden beneath a grotesquely crooked arm, that Meryl found it in herself to scream. It was a sound Big Girl seemed to understand, being something closer to her own language, which was constructed not so much of words but of sounds indicating need and emotion. Startled, the creature dashed up the path and waited half way to the top of the pit.

Meryl ran across to the ledge, disconnected from her own carelessness by her panic to reach Tom. She could feel him breathing, his big chest palpitating with quick and uneven breaths. His left arm had been pulled from the socket at the shoulder, but it was still attached. Had he time to build more inertia or Big Girl's catch had been less skillful, she might have only succeeded in dismembering him before he plummeted to his death. Meryl gently moved his arm away from his face. He looked peaceful, like Meryl remembered him when he was sleeping. She cupped his cheeks and her tears pelted his face.

"Tommy," she sobbed, "please wake up."

His only reply came in the form of quick, gasping breaths. Meryl looked around quickly and found that Big Girl had retreated even further toward the rim of the pit. She'd turned her massive body away from them, as Meryl noticed all the creatures would when they felt uncomfortable. With her right hand she was plucking long blades of grass and was nervously chewing on the tips. Occasionally, she'd glance over her shoulder but turn quickly away if Meryl noticed.

Meryl wondered if perhaps Big Girl thought she had killed Tom. He must have seemed so small and fragile to her, and as he lay there unmoving with Meryl sobbing over him, perhaps the animal felt somehow remorseful? Beyond the creature, the late afternoon sky was turning dusky and lengthening shadows had nearly swallowed the entire mine. Meryl estimated they had less than an hour of sunlight left. If she wasn't able to move Tom in that time, they'd be trapped on the ledge for the rest of the night. Maybe forever. Her thoughts returned to the *The American Boy's Adventure Reader,* to the story which had led them here, and the curious, almost sentient way the wilderness had been described by the author. What phrases had been used? "Sinister magic?" "An unseen and malevolent force?" At the time, she'd thought those words were just melodramatic flourish. But now, the mine and the forest really did seem like conscious organisms which had lured them to this very spot. And what about these forest giants, she wondered. Were they the cause of it all?

Tom's skin was cool and clammy and she gingerly lifted his head into her lap. "Tommy, you need to wake up. We can't stay here," she whispered to him urgently, as though she could talk him out of his unconsciousness. "We have to walk out. We have to get away from the mine and I can't carry you. Please, I need you to wake up."

His eyelashes fluttered and his pupils rolled forward as he regained his senses, and with it, the full agony of his injury. Far above, Big Girl howled in chorus with him.

Meryl kissed his forehead as he convulsed and gulped for air. If he heard her reassuring words, his pain and disorientation prevented him from answering her.

She pressed her face close to his and it steadied him. "Tommy," she said again, firmly. "I need you to stand up. We need to walk out of here. Do you understand?"

He looked at her and there was a flash of recognition. He nodded only because her voice and face were familiar and because he did trust her. He had always trusted her. Meryl got him to the point where he could sit upright and he immediately vomited into the nearby ferns. She quickly retrieved the backpack and gave him some small sips of water. It did nothing to alleviate what must've been excruciating pain, but at least he was more lucid afterwards. As he rose to his feet, his left arm burned so intensely he nearly fainted on the spot. Meryl quickly moved in front of him, her hands pressing against his chest and shoulders, propping him up. His weight, coupled with that of the pack, nearly toppled her.

"No," she commanded, "we're not going to fall down. We are walking out. Do you hear me? I'm going to help you."

He nodded and stood on his own, wobbling. Meryl scooped up her bundled jacket and cinched it around his neck and over his left arm, holding the dislocated limb in place against his side in a crude sling. He put his right arm over her slender shoulders and she half-pulled, half-carried him up the switchbacks to the rim of the mine. By the time they arrived there, Big Girl had vanished. Meryl knew the creature was probably hidden in the long shadows of the surrounding woods but she suddenly felt betrayed. Again, the malicious mind of the forest seemed to manifest itself around her. The sun had already receded over the mountaintops and the western sky was a ribbon of brilliant fuchsia, but it was quickly fading. She squinted at the landscape around her. Already it was difficult to distinguish the trees from the old weathered pylons. Her chances of finding a way back to the stream, and then back to the clearing, back to Alexander, faded with each passing moment.

She looked up at Tom and smiled, gently touching the whiskers on his chin. Her touch reassured him, but his senses were too scrambled for him to understand that the gesture was deceptive. They were lost.

CHAPTER TWENTY-TWO

They'd not made it any further than the edge of the debris field when the last sliver of sunshine extinguished itself and left them standing in darkness. Meryl felt foolish to have been so surprised by nightfall. Since she and Tom had hobbled out of the mine, she'd run a series of calculations through her mind, determining how long it would take them to walk back to the clearing and contrasting it to how fast the light was fading. Her calculations had been optimistic, even fanciful, relying on ridiculous variables like the magical slowing of the earth's rotation or that the aurora borealis would somehow appear as far south as Oregon and light their way back. But once the forest had sunk into darkness, it became evident that there wouldn't even be a robust moon to travel by. The wilderness melted into a patchwork of soft grey shapes, vertical striations marking the boundary where the debris field met the trees; and above an ocean of stars more clear and more complicated than Meryl had ever seen before. The fact that there were so many stars, and yet their light did nothing to help their situation, only seemed to reinforce her suspicion that the forest was both conscious and duplicitous. Again, she found herself thinking about fate.

Tom shifted uncomfortably and whimpered. "Meryl," he said, "we either gotta move or I gotta sit. I can't just stand here or I'll pass out again."

She helped lower him to the ground and propped him against the base of a pine tree. He'd been able to keep himself conscious since they had escaped the pit, but the constant agony of his injured arm was sapping his strength. She stood there in the gloom for a long time, her mind whirling with ideas as she forced the despair out of her brain. The heavy backpack was making her legs ache and she thought briefly of tossing the gold away but couldn't bring herself to do it. She squatted down next to Tom and clicked on her little flashlight. The beam was growing weak as the batteries were now mostly drained.

Even in his debilitated state, Tom found the tiny light laughable. "Are you planning to walk us back using that?" he asked.

"Sorry," she retorted, "would you prefer we use your flashlight?"

"I don't have one," he grumbled.

"I know you don't, asshat, so why don't you shut up?"

He leaned his head back against the tree trunk, stared up at the stars and sipped some more water.

Meryl crouched over him and began to pat at his pockets. "You don't have any matches or a lighter, do you?" she asked.

"No. I wasn't expecting to be out here after dark. I didn't bring anything with me."

Meryl clicked the flashlight off, stifled a sigh and tucked herself in under his good arm.

"You should take your jacket back," Tom said.

"Nah, you keep it. If I get too cold I'll do some jumping jacks or something."

"We could try walking back?"

"Tommy, we may be the world's worst campers, but let's at least try to learn from our past mistakes. The reason we got lost in the first place is because we went running around the forest in the dark. No, we'll do what they teach children to do and 'hug a tree.'"

"Doesn't that hugging a tree thing presume that someone's gonna come looking for you?"

She sounded crestfallen when she replied. "Someone is looking for us, Tommy. We're overdue getting back. David and Rachel will have raised the alarm by now. It's only a matter of time before packs of search and rescue dogs come howling up this mountain. But tonight, if we walk around, we'll just get more lost. I know I can get us back to that creek once the sun comes up, and then we can locate the others from there."

"Hope so."

"I will," she said tersely. "There's no way I'm leaving Alexander out here."

Had there been a perfect moment for Tom to remind her that she *had* left Alexander, this would've been it. And no sooner had the words spilled from her mouth than she braced for what would've been a logical and deserved repudiation of her parenting skills. Instead, Tom said kindly, "He's not alone. Rose and Ike are with him."

"You know that's not the same thing," she said. Her voice cracked and she felt Tom's hand squeeze her arm, his fingers digging gently into her bicep.

"Just think about all those search and rescue dogs. We just need to stay upright and moving until they show up, you know?"

She appreciated the empathy, even if she didn't feel deserving of it. If Meryl were to honestly assess her long and conflicted history with this man, there hadn't been many times she'd refused an opportunity to tell him what a poor father he was. But of course, she consoled herself, he was a poor father. He just wasn't, as it was turning out, an irredeemable human being.

Tom fell silent and within a few moments his breathing took on the deep, slow tenor of sleep. Meryl's mind filled with new calculations. She tried to determine just how long and how forcefully she'd have to rub two sticks together before they would burst into flame. She wondered if banging two hunks of gold ore together would produce sparks. She estimated how long they had before the air turned so cold that sleep, and then hypothermia, would consume them. And between it all, she repeatedly castigated herself for leaving Alexander, for letting her curiosity bring them out here in the first place, for listening to Rose.

She became so lost in her own thoughts, that the taps echoing out of the forest almost escaped her attention. It was the same rhythmic noise they'd heard at the creek, the sound of wood knocking against wood.

"Tommy, you hear that? The tapping's back." She nudged him to no effect.

She clicked the flashlight on and rummaged in the underbrush until she was able to produce a fallen branch, about the length and width of a baseball bat. She moved away from Tom and whacked a nearby tree trunk five times in quick succession. The tapping from the darkness stopped as though the entire wilderness was puzzled by the unexpected interruption in its nocturnal conversation. The sudden silence was acutely unnerving.

"Hello?" she bellowed as loud as she could. "Can anyone hear me?"

The tapping began again. First one low resonating beat, then two more. It was impossible for Meryl to judge distance or the exact direction from where the knocks were originating, but she imagined that for Big Girl and her kinsmen, this type of communication was as informative as a phone call for a human being. She pounded the tree trunk until her hands grew raw and numb from the reverberation. Twenty beats. Forty. Sixty. The tapping continued all around her, becoming louder as though the forest was triangulating her position.

Then suddenly a different sound — a crack of dried wood followed by the crunching of pine needles. Meryl paused, immediately on edge and raising the branch like a weapon. There was a strange flash of orange light between the trees to her right. It was such an odd sight she was certain she'd imagined it. Then it reappeared, brilliant and flickering, a bouncing point of firelight. Ike's face was gaunt and distorted in the wavering glow of a torch as he broke through the trees and headed toward them. She dropped the branch and ran, throwing her arms around his neck as his free hand pulled her in and rested on the small of her back. His lips met hers and she indulged the kiss, not because the circumstances were even faintly romantic, but because at that moment Ike was as welcome a sight as a pack of search and rescue dogs. When they finished, she took a step back and wept.

"Are you okay?" Ike asked, his hand caressing the knob of her shoulder.

When she answered, it came out unintentionally terse. "What the fuck are you doing here, Ike? Why aren't you with Alexander?"

"He's with Rose. He's scared to death, but I told him I was coming to get you so we need to get back or he'll think I'm a liar and I don't want a little kid thinking I'm a liar."

"Should I ask how you even found us? Did you track us on GPS or something."

"GPS doesn't work like that, I'm afraid. I did it the old fashioned way. I followed your footprints, tracked you to the stream and then north. Then I heard you shouting." He suddenly looked startled, like he'd forgotten something important and added, "Where the fuck is Tom, anyway?"

She quickly led him over to the tree where Tom was still sleeping, now trembling in the cold. She sniffed, "He's badly injured. There's something wrong with his arm. He slipped and almost fell but Big Girl grabbed him. She saved his life but his arm... his arm's completely fucked up."

"Broken?"

"I don't know. Maybe dislocated? He can't stay awake. We barely got out of the mine before the sun set."

Ike looked startled. "The mine? You found that fucking thing? It's real?"

"Yes."

"Where's it at?"

She didn't want to talk about the mine. She didn't even want to think about it. The story in Elijah Comstock's book may have been intended as a fantasy, but for Meryl the curse of the gold mine seemed more and more real as the hours had progressed.   She shrugged nonchalantly, trying to give the impression that there was nothing to be seen without actually having to lie to Ike. "It's back behind us. Big Girl led me there but it's a really long story. I'll tell you about it later. What do we do about Tommy?"

Ike planted the torch upright in the soft ground and squatted down next to the slumped figure. He carefully untied the jacket Meryl had knotted around Tom's shoulders and moved his hands over the man's left arm. The fingertips were dark and swollen.

"Definitely dislocated," Ike confirmed. "He's losing circulation. We have to pop the arm back into place."

"Wait, seriously?" Meryl asked. "How do you know?"

"All those summers of being a lifeguard in San Diego. I had to be certified on CPR and first aid. They covered dislocations in the trainings."

"So you've fixed one before?"

"Sure," he snickered, "a fake one on the guy sitting next to me in class. But since I don't see an emergency room out here, I'm gonna just do my best here."

Tom's head bobbed as he came out of his stupor and he looked up at them groggily. "Ike?" he muttered.

"Yeah, Tom. It's me," Ike replied, almost tenderly.

"I'm happy to see you."

"That's because you're delusional."

"Nah. I'm really happy to see you."

Ike leaned close to the larger man as though he was going to embrace him. He put his mouth next to Tom's ear and whispered — "You've been a total prick to me from the first moment we met!" — then snapped the injured arm up and back. There was a muffled pop and Tom roared in agony, his screams piercing the night and silencing the chorus of knocks which still echoed around them.

"I'm sorry," Ike said, although he sounded unconvincing. It wouldn't have been in his character to make Tom suffer, but there was a little part of him which enjoyed inflicting some momentary pain on the man who'd bullied him for the past week. The fire in Tom's arm diminished and his wails softened to labored panting. He tipped forward and rested his forehead on Ike's shoulder. Ike gaped at Meryl and conjured a perplexed smile. "Look," he said, "we're bonding here."

"Had to happen sooner or later," she replied.

"Yeah, but he'll hate himself in the morning," Ike said.

"I won't," Tom whispered. "Thanks, Turbo."

"Go fuck yourself."

Tom grinned.

"Why don't you rest for a few minutes?" Ike suggested, shifting Tom's head from his shoulder back to the tree. In a matter of seconds, he was again unconscious and Ike guided Meryl off to the side. "He needs a doctor," he said grimly.

"I thought you fixed him?" she asked.

"I popped his shoulder back into place, but who knows what else was damaged, especially if he fell. He could have all sorts of injuries."

"Please tell me you know how to get us back to the others," she said.

"I've been dropping pins," Ike replied with a tinge of self-satisfaction. He reached into his coat pocket and pulled out his GPS unit. He flicked it open and the screen glowed softly. Meryl found something tremendously reassuring in that glow. At the moment, the cell phone-sized piece of technology felt like their own real connection back to the human world. "I dropped a new location pin every few minutes. All we have to do is follow them back, like a trail of breadcrumbs."

Meryl smiled. "You must be feeling pretty good about yourself right now?"

He shrugged. "Honestly, I'm not feeling too good about anything. I can get us back to the clearing and then back to Tom's Jeep, but the batteries on this thing aren't gonna last forever. If it dies, we're screwed."

"Maybe there's another way of getting back so we don't have to use the battery power," Meryl suggested. She picked up the branch she had previously discarded and prepared to strike a nearby tree trunk when Ike roughly grabbed it and threw it into the darkness.

"Don't," he whispered urgently, "you don't know what you're doing."

"Don't you hear all those knocks? It's Big Girl signaling to us," Meryl protested.

"No. It's not. She was at the clearing when I left. When she returned without you and Tom, I knew something was wrong. That's when I snuck away to find you." Meryl couldn't see Ike's face, just the vague outline of his slender body in the torchlight. He was slightly crouched, as though on guard against something.

"You snuck away?" she asked. "Why didn't they stop you?"

"When Big Girl came back, they all got really torqued up, agitated, whatever you want to call it. They weren't watching us so I slipped away."

Meryl paused to listen to the knocks in the darkness. "It is Thunderman?"

"No," Ike replied, "it's something else."

"Something else?"

"There's more of them."

"What? What do you mean?"

"There's more of them, Meryl. More than Big Girl and Thunderman and their little family unit. There's more of them in the forest. I saw them as I was hiking out here. I saw them behind the trees."

The thought that Big Girl's clan was not the only one living in the forest had occurred to Meryl once or twice, but since she'd seen no evidence of others she'd assumed Big Girl and her family were the last of their kind. But now, suddenly, the humans were both outmatched and greatly outnumbered. The realization added an obstacle to reaching Rose and Alexander which was potentially more dangerous than the darkness, the terrain and Tom's medical condition.

"How many?" Meryl asked.

"How could you even know?" Ike answered. "Unless they step into full sunshine and flap their hands over their heads, you never even see them. It seems like they can make themselves invisible whenever they want. There could be hundreds standing yards from us and we'd never know it. I only caught glimpses of the other ones because I saw them moving from tree to tree."

"They weren't hiding?"

"Sometimes yes, sometimes no. They appear to be nocturnal, so there could be a whole forest of them waking up right now and looking for something to eat. And..." He paused and looked over his shoulder at Tom who was still blissfully unaware of their predicament. "And, we have an injured animal with us."

"Ike, you're scaring the shit out of me," Meryl said. Her hand instinctively came up to her mouth as she suppressed a sob.

"We could just wait it out here?" he suggested. "Build a roaring fire. Keep it blazing until morning."

Meryl straightened and swallowed her emotions. "Can't. I need to get back to Alexander. He's probably out of his mind with all of us being away from him."

Ike didn't debate it. He knew that would be her answer. "We need more torches," he said.

They spent the next twenty minutes assembling two more torches, stripping the lining out of Meryl's jacket to create the wicks and smearing it with sap from nearby pine trees. Ike carried one in his left hand while he helped support Tom with his right. Meryl carried two, one in each hand, held out before her as though the shimmering light cast some kind of protective shield around them as they walked. But since the creatures had shown no apprehension for fire, it was just as possible that the torches were acting like a beacon to all those eyes that squinted out at them from the trees and the brush. The tapping continued without pause, following them as they maneuvered their way slowly through the timber, first in front of them, then behind, then to the left, then to the right.

Whenever Tom asked to rest, Ike would click on the GPS tracker and check their direction. Twice they had missed the pinpoints he'd plotted and had to backtrack, but he didn't dare keep the device on for fear of draining it completely.

After an hour of stumbling their way down the slope which had led to the mine and along the rocky bank of the creek, they came to a large meadow. The starlight reflected on the waist-high grass. The breeze had kicked up and made the entire meadow shimmer like rippling water.

"Are you sure we're going in the right direction?" Meryl asked Ike. "Big Girl and I didn't pass through here when she led me out."

He quickly checked the GPS unit and nodded. "I don't know exactly which way she led you," he responded. "I could only follow your footprints to the stream, then I winged it. I'm just backtracking the way I came and we're right on target. Rose and Alexander should be on the other side of this meadow, just beyond those trees."

"Let's go then," Tom offered weakly. "Less talk, more walk."

They started off again, holding the torches high over their heads as they entered the ocean of grass. No longer shrouded by the trees, the wind became colder and the torches began to snap and pop. One of them blew out and sent a long strand of gray smoke snaking across the field. They paused briefly to relight it, but getting the wick to catch again was difficult. Once accomplished, Meryl took two steps forward and stopped.

"Let's go," Tom grumbled, but Meryl refused to shift.

The two men drew closer to her, huddled beneath the dancing firelight. "What is it?" Ike asked.

"Straight ahead and just to the left," Meryl whispered. "Do you see that?"

At the far end of the meadow something was moving. Low and dark with a curved outline, it appeared like a rubber ball floating across the top of a turbulent sea. It was advancing at a slow but steady pace until it came to a spot which blocked their entry into the trees beyond. Then it sank into the grass and disappeared. Meryl might've missed it had it not been for her previous experiences with these animals' unique form of camouflage. From that first afternoon when she saw the man-like shape standing in the trees and watching Alexander play, she began to look for movement which was contrary to the environment, or shapes that didn't quite blend into the patterns around them. In this case, what had alerted her was that the object moving among the grass was traveling uphill and against the wind.

"Is it one of our gorilla buddies? Maybe Big Girl?" Tom asked.

"I don't think so," Ike breathed.

"What are you talking about, Turbo?"

"There are others out here," Meryl replied quickly. "Ike spotted them when he was searching for us. All that knocking we've been hearing since we got out here" — she paused to listen to the taps, the sounds now so faint over the wailing wind — "the knocks I thought Big Girl and the others were making, *it's not them.*"

Tom didn't answer and they just stood there for a long moment, shivering in the wind and silently praying that the torches would't blow out.

"We could make a run for it," Ike suggested.

"Run where?" Meryl asked. "That's the direction we need to go."

With his arm now back in its socket, Tom had regained some of his strength but the persistent pain was making him angrier by the moment. He snarled, "This is bullshit! Let's just keep going." He took a step forward but Meryl immediately blocked him.

"Don't!" she commanded. "We can't afford to be reckless here."

"We can't stand in this field all night either," he replied. "We're sitting ducks out here."

Meryl turned to look at the far edge of the meadow. The strange dark shape had not reappeared, but rather seemed to be waiting for them, nestled down just below the top of the grass where it couldn't be seen. She turned and handed a torch to Tom.

"Are you strong enough to run?" she asked.

Ike immediately protested. "I thought you said running for it *wasn't* a good idea?"

"We're not going to run away," she said. "We're going to run straight to the trees and back to Rose and Alexander."

"Hells yeah," Tom chuckled.

"Okay, that seems like a monumentally bad idea considering what's waiting for us over there in the grass," said Ike.

Meryl wielded her torch like a club. "We're going screaming and yelling and flinging our torches around all the way," she said, her eyes widening with a sudden surge of adrenalin. "All animals run from fire, right?"

"These don't," Ike snapped, "or haven't you been paying attention?"

"Fine. Then maybe they'll run from bat-shit crazy, 'cause that's how we're gonna be acting."

Tom slapped Ike on the back and boomed, "Come on, Turbo, we can do this. We're gonna scare the living shit out of these big monkeys!" He bounded forward, running in an awkward and hobbled manner, holding the torch aloft in his right hand while his left hung limply in its bulky sling. He roared loudly, the sound of a man in excruciating pain and acute desperation.

Meryl immediately followed, leaping through the grass so every step she took fell on the earth with a resounding *thump*. She found Ike following closely on her heels, carrying his torch like a rapier over his head. Tom cut a straight path through the grass, directly toward the spot where the large dark mass had hidden itself. Even in his injured state, he was still an imposing sight and he could make a fearsome noise. Approximately one hundred paces from the tree-line, their charge across the meadow dislodged the creature which reared up like a large black sail catching the wind, over eight feet in height and covered with bristling fur. Instinctively, Tom wheeled back and launched his torch right at the animal. The smoldering branch smashed into the creature's chest with a shower of scattered sparks, briefly illuminating a craggy, nearly hairless face. The beast produced a loud howl and fled to the left, along the edge of the trees and back down the slope of the hill. Tom continued on, barely breaking his stride as he stooped to retrieve the smoking torch and hurled it again. By this time, however, the creature had retreated far enough that the limb landed harmlessly in the brush.

Tom pressed on into the cover of the trees and then stopped there to wait for Meryl and Ike.

"You guys okay?" he gasped, clutching his injured arm which was burning intensely again.

They both nodded, but Tom didn't allow them to pause. He pointed, and they turned to see more dark figures rising out of the grass behind them. They formed a broken wall of fur advancing quickly toward the trees, stretching from the top of the meadow nearly to its bottom edge. Meryl didn't stop to count them. She just turned, and screaming for Alexander, ran as fast as she could.

CHAPTER TWENTY-THREE

Rose had built an impressive campfire and had kept it going for hours by scrabbling around on her hands and knees in the dark, gathering up twigs, pine cones, fallen bark or anything else she could burn. Although built mostly to comfort Alexander, it had inadvertently become a beacon, guiding Meryl, Tom and Ike through the thicket and back to the clearing where Big Girl had held them captive for the past two days. Alexander had heard Meryl shouting his name, and by the time she broke through the last stand of trees he was on his feet and shrieking for her. She knelt down beside him and his small arms wrapped around her, his fingers coming to rest on the backpack filled with canteens and hidden gold. The child was sobbing, but was able to gulp down enough air to chastise her.

"Mah-mee, I'm mad at you," he blurted in a way that, coming from someone so young, might have been funny had he not been so terribly sincere. His words destroyed Meryl and she folded her body over his like she was trying to cocoon him.

"I'm sorry, baby," she whispered, "I'm so sorry. I won't leave again. I promise you."

When she composed herself enough to look up, she found the others scrambling about and shouting commands to each other. Rose was down on the ground, scooping up armfuls of brittle pine needles and dried leaves and dumping them onto the existing fire where they flared brightly and produced a smothering cloud of acrid smoke. Tom and Ike had stoked the remaining torches and were frantically digging shallow basins for two more fires. Meryl peered across the flames at the trees through which they had just fled, but there was no sign of pursuit. The creatures who'd risen from the grassy meadow like ghosts had apparently stopped before they hit the amber glow of the campfire. Or, she reminded herself, they were just hiding. Watching. Waiting.

"They disappeared," Ike said vacantly.

"No, they just stopped chasing us," replied Meryl.

"Not them," he said, "Big Girl and the others. They're not here."

The entire glade was now enveloped in a smoky gray haze. The vapor was making her eyes water, so it took a moment for Meryl to confirm that Big Girl and her tribe had indeed vanished from their usual nesting spots. Even Thunderman, who'd moved from his vantage point only to stretch and defecate, was nowhere to be seen. This development, more than anything, set Meryl's nerves on edge.

She placed Alexander on the ground, ran her fingers through his tacky hair, and whispered to him, "Sweetie, can you help mommy find a good digging rock?"

The child seemed pleased to have something to do and he quickly located one of the pointed stones he and Ike had used earlier to carve tunnels in the soft ground. Meryl immediately began to scratch out a hole at the base of a tree, glancing frequently over her shoulder to make sure the others were not noticing her activities.

"Why use digging a hole, Mah-mee?" the boy asked.

She cupped his small chin and quickly silenced him. "Mommy's going to hide something in this hole, sweetie," she replied. "But it's our secret so you can't tell anyone, okay?"

"Nob Rode?"

"No, not Rose. Not anyone, okay?"

"Nob Ike too?"

"Not anyone, Alexander. I need you to promise this, okay?"

He nodded and squatted down to watch as she slipped the canvas bag out of the backpack and into the shallow hole. She quickly covered it with dirt and detritus.

"What is?" he asked.

"Just rocks, sweetie. Just stupid rocks."

Alexander disregarded the bag with a sniff and moved back to the fire to warm himself. Meryl was grateful for his obedience, having no explanation for why a bag full of "stupid rocks" was important enough to secretly bury. She felt like a liar and worse, like a traitor. Everything about this trip had gone so tragically wrong, yet somehow, through some inexplicable instrument of fate, she'd managed to walk out of a collapsing gold mine with a small fortune just as Rose predicted they would. The revelation that there was gold to be discovered at the mine might've made everything else worth the pain, the fear and the desperation they'd endured for the past forty-eight hours. But Meryl couldn't bring herself to tell anyone of it nor understand her own motivations for doing so. She just felt that if the others knew what she'd carried out of the mine, it would make things worse.

The wind had picked up again and the flames on the bonfire fluttered violently.

"No, no, no," Ike yelled at the fire, "don't you dare blow out!"

Meryl sat Alexander down between the trees and the largest fire and crossed to Tom with the filled canteens. He had removed the sling made from her jacket and was struggling to make his left arm work. His face was damp and as pale as a sheet of paper. She handed him the canteen and told him to rest.

"I can do this," he protested, stumbling slightly as he attempted to shift a moss-covered log.

Meryl touched him on the back and said firmly, "Tommy, go sit with your son. He's terrified and you'll make him feel better. I'll do this."

He looked strangely surprised and glanced over at Alexander, who was rocking slowly with his knees drawn up to his chest. It was the first time Meryl had suggested Tom comfort the child since their ordeal had begun. He didn't know what to make of it, but was suddenly and painfully aware when Meryl had snuck off to the mine with Big Girl earlier, she'd left Alexander in Ike's care, not his. He handed her the bright orange jacket and said, "Put this back on or you'll freeze."

She smiled weakly and did as he commanded. He walked slowly over to the boy, who immediately crawled into his lap. It may not have been a loving gesture from son to father, but rather the response of a scared child to the comforting presence of an adult. Regardless, it was as demonstrative as Meryl had ever seen Alexander with Tom. She allowed herself a second to feel hopeful just as Tom allowed himself a second to feel wanted.

By the time Meryl turned back to the half-finished fire pit Rose was next to her, scooping out dirt with her bare hands. The older woman looked horrible. Meryl always thought she had a kind of light to her, some indefinable energy which radiated off her skin. But now she was haggard and the lids around her eyes had swollen up and were dark with fatigue, hunger and the continual irritation of wood smoke.

Meryl extended a canteen to her. "Have some water," she said. "You look like you can use it."

Rose accepted it greedily and guzzled down several large mouthfuls. She wiped her cracked lips on her sleeve and asked weakly, "Ike said you found the mine?"

Meryl gave her a sad smile. "Yes. I found it. Big Girl led me to it."

Rose seemed close to tears. "They own it?" she croaked with a tinge of anger in her voice.

"They?"

"These —" she choked down the vulgar term she wanted to use "— *monsters*. The mine is their's? They live there too?"

"Rose, I think they've always lived there," Meryl replied.

"What do you mean, girl?"

"In the original story about the mine, what if it wasn't Indians who killed the miners but these animals?"

Ike moved across to them and dumped an armload of kindling into the shallow basin and lit it with his torch. The flames quickly stretched upwards and between the three fires the entire campsite radiated with a misty, comforting light.

"I think that's pretty obvious," he offered. Rose shot him an irritated look.

Meryl continued: "It makes sense, doesn't it? The rumors about curses and strange animals that Elijah told his family about even in his old age... In the original story, doesn't it say that Mr. Sykes thought that the mining camp had been ransacked by wild animals?"

"It does, but I think anyone who reads that would assume he meant ransacked *after* the miners were killed, by animals scavenging for food, like bears or raccoons. That's how I interpreted it, at least," said Rose.

"I think the miners' camp was overrun by these things. The story was wrong about several things. It said that the miners built a barricade but it didn't hold, that it had been smashed. But Big Girl led me down into one of the mine passageways and from what I saw, the barricade was still intact and the miners put up a hell of a fight. There were bullet shells all over the place. I think the creatures were just too big to fit down those narrow tunnels and that's what saved some of them."

"So what happened to the miners?"

Meryl leaned closer to them and whispered, "It was like they were so scared that they sealed themselves into that tunnel and never came back out again. I found three skeletons and it looked like they just laid down and died. Although, more likely I guess, that they died from thirst or hunger."

"It couldn't be these same creatures," Rose replied. "Not unless they are extremely long-lived, which would be doubtful in such a hostile environment."

Ike chimed in again. "No, but it might've been their ancestors. If they live in family groups, this might be their territory and the miners were the invaders. And so are we."

"They haven't tried to hurt us," Rose replied, almost defensively. "Big Girl seems to be in charge and she's protecting us, just as Meryl said."

"But that's the problem," Ike answered.

"I don't take your meaning, Ike."

"She seems to be protective of Meryl and Alexander in particular. Maybe it's some kind of mother-instinct, I don't know? But I also think that's why she's not letting us leave. In Big Girl's mind, she thinks of Meryl and Alexander as being her property."

Up until that instant, Meryl had felt fortunate that Big Girl had been so protective of her. But Ike was right. Thunderman would've likely killed them all on that first day had Big Girl not interceded, and certainly he wouldn't hesitate to do so if Big Girl's attitude ever changed. She turned to look at the blackness which lay beyond their flickering ring of fire and shuddered. The forest creaked and clicked and rustled. She knew there were hidden eyes in that darkness, staring back at her, watching them all, planning the next move...

She said finally, "We all know we have to get out of here. And sooner rather than later. Tom needs a hospital and the rest of us won't last much longer. But I don't think that it's Big Girl and her family who are going to try and stop us."

"Kiddos," Rose's tone was suddenly infused with a motherly inflection which both Meryl and Ike found annoying, "can we really forget about the mine so easily when we are so close?"

Meryl wasn't surprised by Rose's objection. In fact, she had prepared for it. No matter how bad things got, Rose's obsession with the mine hadn't diminished. What was Ike's observation about the woman shortly after meeting her? That she knew how to circumvent obstacles in order to get what she wanted? Her steadfast refusal to give up finding the mine, even in the face of mortal danger, only underscored how right Ike had been. Meryl also knew that if she told Rose about the canvas bag she'd buried at the base of the nearby tree, it would only inflame the old woman's desire to stay regardless of the danger. So instead, Meryl chose to lie. "The mine's a lost cause," she said firmly. "It's in ruins and trying to get inside any deeper than I went would be suicidal. You need to give it up, Rose. There's no gold. This stupid dream of yours is dead."

The old woman shifted her jaw, perhaps to hide the quivering of her lower lip. Then she turned and went back to gathering dried pine needles.

Ike was staring at Meryl from beneath drawn brows. "Ouch," he said.

"What? You think I was too harsh?" she gawked. "After everything, she's still thinking of the gold."

He shrugged. "That's why she came to Oregon in the first place, right?"

"Yeah, but for fuck's sake Ike, there's a point when you just have to stop living in your little fantasy world. I think I reached that point about two days ago. And then when Tommy almost plunged to his death this afternoon. Yeah, I'm done. As soon as the sun comes up, I'm taking my son and I'm walking outta here."

"I get that and I agree with you. I'm just saying it's got to kill her when she's so close and *you* were the one who actually found the mine. Sucks, y'know?"

There was a pang of remorse, but it didn't last. Despite her best efforts, Meryl still found herself blaming Rose for their predicament.

All those little acts of deception and exaggeration the former school teacher perpetrated on a daily basis had been an irritant. But the more Meryl thought about it, the more she convinced herself that Rose had some inkling that finding this particular mine was going to be much more than the weekend camping trip she'd described so glowingly.

"I still say she had to know that there was something dangerous out here," Meryl grumbled. "Something more than bears and cougars, I mean."

"She's confessed to that," Ike replied. "But she chose to see what she wanted to see."

Meryl's body was racked by so many sensations — fear, exhaustion, hunger, and a persistent ache that burned in her lower back and legs from carrying a bag full of gold ore through the forest in the dead of night. At that moment, there wasn't any room in her for sympathy. She was about to reply when Ike grabbed her shoulders.

"Shhhh!" he ordered. He was staring into the darkness over their heads. A quick series of sharp cracks and snaps echoed far above the haze of wood smoke, followed by the rattle of falling bark. Limbs popped and the hemlock's thick trunk shuddered as some great weight struggled to break through the latticework of branches. Ike shoved Meryl back while simultaneously ducking to his right. A great dark object dropped between them, struck the ground with a hard *whump* then quickly deflected into the fire. The tall bundle of burning wood immediately collapsed under the object's weight and sent up a plume of sparks and smoke. The object wobbled to a rest among the coals but didn't burn.

"A rock!" Meryl cried. "It's a rock!"

Ike crept closer and grumbled, "More like a small boulder." He turned defiantly toward the dark forest boundary. "They're throwing shit at us!"

An instant later, more cracks pierced the air and all five people scrambled for the scant protection of nearby trees. Two more stones, each about the size of a small watermelon, bounced through the forest canopy and crashed down inside the camp's perimeter. A handful more — Meryl couldn't tell how many — had fallen short and could be heard clattering in the darkness beyond. Another barrage quickly followed. The projectiles were all large stones and seemed to be indiscriminately cast into the air. Meryl had to wonder if the creatures were doing so only to create the chilling chorus of breaking wood that now drowned out even the incessant whistling of the wind.

"Are you kidding me?" Ike bellowed into the night. Like Meryl, he was now angry at the wilderness which imprisoned them.

"Just stay down between the trees," Meryl said, trying to sound reassuring.

"The fires are letting them see us," Rose noted. "We just painted a target on ourselves."

"The fires are also keeping them out there," Meryl responded.

"Yeah, but now they've pinned us down so we can't even put more wood on the fires to keep them going."

There was a brief lull in the attack and the five huddled people collectively held their breath. Alexander, who'd been clinging to Tom's neck, disengaged himself and pushed his way inside Meryl's jacket until he could hear her heart beating. She tried to wrap it around the boy, to keep him warm now that they were forced away from the flames. But still covered in grime from when she had tumbled onto the skeletons in the mine, and stripped of its lining to make torches, the garment was of little use and Alexander shivered violently.

"Are day coming, Maw-mee?" the boy whispered.

Who did he mean, she wondered? Was he asking about Big Girl and the other creatures who had completely vanished from the glade, or did he know that there was something else in the forest, something that Meryl had little chance of shielding him from? Then a terrible thought occurred to her and she quickly rose and propped Alexander on her hip.

"Get down! Get down!" Tom barked.

"No," she cried, bounding back toward the trio of fires, "you have to move! It's a trick!"

The other three adults did not debate her logic, scrambling back to the edges of the second and third fires with their backs pressed against a massive tree. They panted in unison, great draughts of steam spilling from their lips in the cold forest air. And they waited.

Then something moved just beyond the trees where they were huddled just seconds earlier. Meryl couldn't determine its size or how far away it was, but it moved like the facile shapes which had swarmed after them in the meadow, unfolding itself from the smoky gloom into a humanlike posture and then dodging away through the tree trunks. Two more flashes of movement followed in the same area, but Meryl couldn't tell if it was the same creature or different ones.

"How'd you know?" Tom gasped.

"Because we've all been a bunch of idiots," she replied. "We keep thinking that these creatures are just animals, but they're not."

"They're big ugly gorillas," Tom replied.

"I don't think so," Meryl said quickly. "'Cause your big ugly gorillas just tried to outflank us."

"And that makes them, what? Us?"

Meryl shook her head. "No, not us. But like us."

Tom suddenly seemed angry again. "What the fuck do you know that we don't, Meryl? What the hell did you see in that mine?" he barked.

Meryl turned to find all of them looking up at her expectantly. Even Alexander was staring, his blue eyes twinkling with tears in the firelight. "Big Girl took me to a grave," she started. "There was another creature, a dead one, at the bottom of the mine. It must've fallen in there and broken its legs. It looked like it had been there for a long time, but her reaction to it was weird. It's like she knew it, wanted me to see it, to share her sadness, you know?"

No one answered.

"Look, she drew this on the ground in two different spots" — she snatched up a pine cone and haphazardly drew the circle with two dots inside — "once at the top of the mine, once on the ledge overlooking the dead creature. And then this symbol and a bunch of others were scratched into the rock at the start of the tunnel where I found the miners' skeletons."

"What's it mean?" Ike asked, squatting down to examine the diagram.

Meryl lifted the edge of her jacket to expose Elijah Comstock's old leather belt. "I'm not sure, but Elijah marked the same symbol on his belt and wrote 'stop' next to it. I think Big Girl was telling me that those were all places where someone had died."

Tom and Rose were both befuddled and suddenly angry. "Elijah's belt?" Rose exclaimed. "What belt? Where did you get that?"

"From the same place you got all your materials on him," Meryl snapped. "Ike and I went to his old house. The broken down one in the woods. You were there too, weren't you?"

Rose gaped at her. "I'm speechless," the woman said. "How dishonest—"

"Give it a rest, Rose. It's not like you were going to share any of this information with us. You fed us just enough to get us excited about the gold and kept everything else to yourself. You're a fucking hypocrite."

"Listen," Tom interrupted, "can maybe everyone stop keeping secrets? Our collective asses are on the line here, so man up and spill already."

"You think Big Girl knew about the dead miners?" Ike asked.

Meryl took a breath and answered, "She couldn't possibly have seen them. That tunnel was a tight squeeze for me and barricaded at the end. No way she or any of the other creatures could've made it through.   But somehow she knew those skeletons were in there and she was trying to tell me that by drawing this mark on the ground."

"You think it's some kind of writing? Like a hieroglyphic?"

Meryl shrugged. "Call it whatever you want, but I'm telling you that Big Girl was trying to tell me something important."

"So where's your protector now?" Tom asked. "Where are any of our big forest monkey friends?   First they kidnap us, then they abandon us so we can be hunted by other big forest monkeys, is that it?"

"The one you call Big Girl came back here," said Rose.   "She showed up without you guys and that's when Ike decided to go looking for you while I stayed with Alexander. She talked to all the others, and then they left."

"*Talked to the others?*" Tom exclaimed.

"I don't know how you want to describe it, but that's what she did. It sounded like so much jibber-jabber, but that's what she did."

"And then they all left?" Meryl asked.

Rose nodded. "Ran off is more like it," she said.

A strong, cold gust of wind tore through the campsite and the third fire flickered weakly. The stone the creatures had first hurled at them had crushed most of the tinder and was sitting like a giant smoking bird's egg on a nest of red coals.

"We have to roll that stone out of there and get that fire going again," Ike said blankly.

Meryl nodded and set Alexander back in Tom's lap. She pulled up the collar on her soiled jacket and with Ike took several tentative steps toward the smoldering fire pit. Except for the creaking of timber caught in the wind, the forest was peaceful. They squatted at the fire's edge and using two tree branches broken off by the fallen stones were able to shift the boulder to one side and dump a mound of dried conifer needles on the coals. A great orange plume engulfed the kindling as the needles quickly curled into fragile cinders, but the burst of light was enough to illuminate the nearby trees and the shaggy animal who was stooped there, silently watching them.

Alexander screamed at the sight of the creature and Meryl's body immediately tensed. She resisted turning to run back to the child, to abandon Ike to face the threat alone. Her fingers tightened around the tree branch she had used to shift the rock. The face was familiar with its blunted nose, deep-set eyes and sloped forehead. The skin was leathery and relatively hairless except for silver clumps which started at the edges of the wide, lipless mouth and spread over the mandible. It was difficult for her to gage any emotion in that face or thought behind those eyes. Whatever the creature's intent was in having crept so close to the dwindling fire without being noticed, its face revealed nothing to the petrified humans.

"I didn't even smell it," Ike whispered, holding his tree branch over his shoulder. "Usually you can smell them."

"It's downwind from us," answered Meryl, not taking her eyes off the huddled mass of fur. "They know what they're doing."

"I'm convinced. Now what?"

Meryl rose to her feet, stretching as much as she could in the hopes of appearing taller. She gripped the tree branch with both hands, holding it across her chest like a soldier might hold a rifle. The creature's brows lifted slightly but it showed no fear of the young woman. She heard Alexander whimper behind her, the sound muffled by Tom who had turned the child's face into his body and shielding him with his arms. Meryl dug her heels into the ground and waited. She was no obstacle to the animal if it wished to cut through her to get at Alexander, but she was determined to hold her ground regardless.

The beast shifted, lowering its head slightly and narrowing its eyes like a cat focusing on a songbird. Big arms moved, thick knots of muscle flexing between the shag, and from the shadows it revealed a long spear ending in a sharpened point.

"Shit," Ike gasped, frantically grasping for Meryl but his fingertips just brushing along the dirty cuff of her jacket. "Get down again!"

The creature raised the spear tip toward her. The shaft of the weapon was nearly as thick as the calf of her leg and for an instant, Meryl felt strangely vindicated. Big Girl's curious drawings in the mud, the diagrams at the mouth of the mine tunnel, the disembodied taps on tree trunks, the recognition of death and now the use of weapons... Tom may have derisively referred to them as apes, but clearly they were much more than that. As the creature rose to its full height, its head brushed against the tree limbs above. Meryl closed her eyes as another gust of cold wind cascaded over her, puffing out the pockets of her jacket and whipping her long hair across her face. She heard the creature inhale deeply and opened her eyes just as the behemoth lurched away from her as though he'd been jabbed with a sharp thorn. Nostrils flared wide and the heavy brows sunk down over the eyes. Then it made a half-turn toward the shadows and produced a peculiar clicking noise with its tongue. The forest began to shift. What had appeared to human eyes as the silhouettes of tree trunks or clumps of vegetation suddenly transformed into scattering bodies. The terrible realization that they'd been completely encircled, with some of the creatures being only a few feet outside the ring of firelight, was inconsequential as Meryl realized that nearly every creature was carrying some kind of spear or heavy club. This wasn't a herd of wild animals. It was an army.

CHAPTER TWENTY-FOUR

Three hours before sunrise, Alexander collapsed. He didn't just lie down and go to sleep, but actually toppled over and might've smashed face-first into the ground had Meryl not been there to catch him. He was the only one in the party who actually slept for any real length of time, perhaps because he was the only one who truly felt safe tucked up against his mother. His small hand had instinctively wrapped itself around a long tendril of Meryl's hair and his eyes flickered with dream beneath darkened lids.

None of the adults had spoken since the creatures had suddenly and inexplicably retreated back into the wilderness. Instead, they rested in shifts with at least two people always on watch for shadows moving among the trees and ferns. It was only when the eastern sky lightened to a deep scarlet that Rose wandered alone over to the fires, loaded on extra tinder and began to sort the remaining supplies. Meryl scowled. Even when they were threatened at every turn, the woman still played at being everyone's mother. And this particular morning, Meryl found herself resenting the pretension but also blaming herself for it. Maybe Tom had been right, she thought. Maybe she'd come to think of Rose as a surrogate mother, when really she was little more than a relative stranger whose kindnesses seemed so very manipulative in hindsight. If that was the case, then all Meryl had done was trade one controlling mother figure for another, and it made her feel foolish.

She reached across to where Ike was sleeping and gently stroked his stubble-covered chin. His eyes fluttered open and for a moment he seemed to have forgotten where they were as his lips bent in a curious smile. Meryl wondered what dream she had just interrupted. Whatever it was, it seemed to be a happy one.

"As soon as the sun's up," she whispered to him, "I'm taking Alexander and we're leaving. I need to know if you're in."

He shifted uncomfortably and pursed his lips. "Of course I'm in," he said, "but why're you whispering?"

Meryl glanced back at Rose, who was now puttering around the farthest fire and appeared to be separating out the remaining food supplies. "I'm telling you that we're leaving, no matter what, no matter who argues."

He was astounded. "You think Rose's going to object, even after last night?"

"Don't know, don't care. I'm just saying that my son and I are making a break for it and we need you and your GPS tracker to do it."

"And Tom?"

"We need his car keys."

Ike scowled and sat upright. "We need him too. Right?"

"In case you haven't noticed, Ike, Tom has his own mind. He'll do what he wants to do."

"But we're including him, right?"

"Of course we are. I'm including everyone. I'm just telling you my decision's made, so I don't give a flying fuck what Rose or Tom decide to do 'cause I'm leaving."

"Not that I'm thinking that he'd prefer to stay here in the forest with that messed up arm, but what happens if he chooses not to come?"

"We need his car keys, Ike," she repeated. There was a hardness in her voice Ike had not experienced before.

"Damn, girl," he squirmed, "what's going on with you?"

She looked down at Alexander. "I told you — we're getting out. Everyone's invited if they want to come but if they don't, I'm still going. That's why I need to make sure you're in."

"So we save the child but leave the old lady and the injured guy behind, is that it?"

"Of course not. But I've been thinking about what you said last night about Rose and it's totally true. *This* is why she came to Oregon. *This is her great quest.* If I have to choose between Alexander and that stupid gold mine, which do you think I'm going for?"

"And the same for Tom?"

Even when their relationship was at its worst, Meryl had never truly wished anything horrible to happen to Tom. Naturally, there'd been plenty of fantasies about him living out his remaining days in misery, pining for her into his old age and eventually going to his grave regretting the loss of their relationship. But those were the musings of a teenaged girl in pain and they'd never represented her true, albeit convoluted, affection for Tom. She chose her words carefully before replying: "Let's just say that I'm not going to be slowed down by constant arguing."

He nodded. "Fair enough, but I can't believe any rational person would think that hanging around here is a good thing."

"That's because you're a rational person, Ike."

"And they aren't?"

"Not always," she frowned, sadly. She looked at Rose hunched over the fire and then at Tom who was curled into the fetal position between the roots of the hemlock tree with his stocking cap pulled down over his eyes, oblivious to the world. "I know them better than you."

As the sun began to cleave through the trees and speckle the ground with warmth, Meryl carefully roused Alexander, stood up and stretched. Ike pulled himself up next to her and surveyed the clearing. Other than the occasional songbird or grey squirrel, there was no wildlife in sight. The flattened grassy nests usually occupied by Big Girl and the other behemoths were still empty.

"Where day goat, Maw-mee?" asked Alexander.

"I think they left, they went away," she replied, trying to sound as upbeat as possible.

The child didn't smile, but only said, "Good."

"I agree," Ike grumbled, walking to the edge of the third fire where the large creature with the silvery chin had been crouched just hours earlier. The landscape beyond, for as far as Ike could see, was cratered with large, manlike footprints. There were too many to count, too many to even speculate exactly what their numbers had been. "Look how close they got to us," he shivered. "And we didn't even see them."

"If you're right about them being nocturnal, then we have to go this morning while they're sleeping," Meryl stated.

"I don't think nocturnal means they *can't* be active during the day," he cautioned.

"Maybe not, but the odds will be more even. We can see them coming."

"Meryl," he replied grimly, "we've *never* seen them coming." He pushed the sole of his shoe into a nearby impression. His foot was less than half the size of the creature who'd made the print, and the print was less than ten feet from where they had slept. "Why do you think they left like that? They were so close and we were so defenseless."

That strange moment had occupied much of Meryl's concentration in the intervening hours and she still didn't have a good explanation. She wasn't yet ready to attribute it to the intervention of some higher power, but the beast with the silvery chin had clearly recoiled as she stood to confront it. And then, in whatever incomprehensible language the creatures used, he had ordered his minions to retreat. Having no good answer, she said blithely, "I don't think that big one liked me."

Ike laughed uncomfortably. "No, he didn't. But I can't figure out why. I mean, no offense, but I don't look at you and think, gee, she's one scary bitch."

"Thanks for that, I guess."

"Do you suppose he didn't like the way you smelled?"

"Geeze, speak for yourself, Ike."

"I'm serious," he pressed. "He kind of snorted at you. You know, how a dog will snort when it's caught the scent of something really interesting? Like that."

This was true, and Meryl remembered that Big Girl had behaved similarly when she emerged from the mine. It was a fact that nonhuman animals relied on their sense of smell much more than humans, and she wondered what it was that they found so repulsive about her that they'd actually retreat rather than confront her.

Tom, disturbed by the sound of their voices, turned stiffly on the ground and groaned loudly. The groan suddenly became a bellow and the others hurried to his side.

"Something's wrong," he moaned, struggling to sit upright. His right hand had swollen to nearly twice its normal size and was tinted an ugly grayish-purple. He made an attempt to roll up the sleeve of his thermal undershirt, but the swelling extended up to his shoulder and the garment was so tightly constricted that he couldn't budge it.

Ike carefully ripped the sleeve open along the outer edge. The arm looked like a grotesque sausage and Tom was no longer able to move his fingers. He flinched at the sight of his own injury and a bead of sweat snaked down his cheek and dropped onto his chest. All he could say was, "Oh, shit. I'm fucked, Meryl."

Ike touched his forehead. "He's burning up."

"Shall I make some cool compresses?" Rose offered. "It might relieve some of the puffiness?"

"Puffiness?" Meryl said curtly. "'Puffy' is what my ankles get once a month. This is way beyond puffy."

Ike quickly interceded. "I think we're beyond cold compresses, Rose," he said. "Tom needs a doctor and he needs one today."

Rose nodded grimly and touched Tom's leg with a gentle hand. "Darling, I can bring you one of the granola bars. We have two left. Would that make you feel better?"

Tom didn't reply. He titled his head back against the tree and grimaced.

Meryl, however, was angry again and no longer willing to constrain it. "Are you fucking kidding me?" she shouted at the woman. "You think a granola bar is gonna somehow heal him?"

Rose stood and straightened her shoulders. Meryl was suddenly very conscious of their difference in height, but she had no more fear of the woman who now towered over her than she did of the hirsute monsters prowling the woods around them. She was too tired, maybe too desperate, to feel anything but defiance.

Rose replied amiably, "Whatever we do today, whatever is decided, better to do it on a full belly than an empty one."

"Don't do that!" snapped Meryl.

Rose cocked an eyebrow. "What am I doing?"

"Don't use that goddamn teacher's voice of yours. I'm not a third grader and this isn't a class field trip."

"I apologize if that's how you interpreted my words," she responded with continued aplomb. "I'm only trying to help. I think a hearty breakfast would do us all a world of good."

Meryl quickly stepped around her, walked briskly across to the closest fire-pit and with the toe of her boot began to kick dirt onto the flames. The coal bed hissed as a plume of white smoke spiraled out of the pit and floated up through the trees. When she walked back, the others were gawking at her. Only Tom hadn't reacted to her demonstration, being in too much pain to care.

Surprisingly, it was Alexander who was the first to speak. "Mah-mee," he fumed, "you making too muck noise!"

Meryl reached for him, but he ducked her hand and glared up at her with his arms crossed in front of him in the classic stance of the pouting toddler. She found she couldn't make eye-contact with Rose, although what she said next was most certainly for the older woman's benefit: "Alexander, Ike and I are leaving. This morning, right now. We're not going to stop to cook breakfast, we can eat trail bars and pick blackberries along the way. We're not stopping until we get back to the Jeep and then we're driving out of here."

Tom looked up at Ike, intentionally avoiding Meryl, and said, "Well, fucking nice of you guys to include us."

Ike looked embarrassed, which irked Meryl even more than Rose's strange insistence that they stop to cook breakfast. For the first time ever, he responded meekly to the other man. "Tom, you know we can't stay here like this. The creatures are gone for now, so this is our chance. We have to go."

"I know," Tom said. "I'm just wondering why you and Meryl didn't bother to have this conversation with me and Rose too?"

"We were letting you sleep," Meryl said quickly, but she could tell he wasn't buying it.

"Tom's right," Rose stated. "Frankly, Meryl, I don't remember there being an election where you became mayor of the forest."

"There wasn't a vote," answered Meryl, stoically. "I'm just telling you the facts. We are leaving. Ike knows how to get us back to the Jeep using his tracker. We're going to hike back there as fast as possible and drive the hell out of here."

"Before we've reached the mine?"

"I told you, Rose, I reached it yesterday and there's nothing there. There's no reason to go back."

Rose's demeanor was beginning to slip as she retorted, "You'll understand if I don't take your word for it."

Meryl shrugged. She tried to make it look nonchalant, even though she really wanted to scream at the top of her lungs. "Do what you want. I don't care anymore."

Rose glanced quickly to Tom and said, "I guess it's you and me, kiddo."

"No," he replied, his words were weak and breathless sounding. "I'm going with my son."

In that instant, Meryl felt more astonishment for Tom than she had in all the years they'd known each other. He didn't mention his own pain and failing strength. Had Tom not been injured, his response might've been different and Rose's lavish promises of a fortune in gold might've swayed him. But Meryl hoped not.

Rose barely paused to react to his rejection. "Well, I guess we should divide the supplies?"

"You can have it all," Meryl answered. "We just need one of the backpacks to carry enough food and water to get us to the Jeep."

"And how far is that?"

"About six miles as the crow flies," Ike said. "If only we were crows."

"And you can direct me to the mine?"

Meryl pointed. "How far would you say, Ike?"

He replied: "I plotted it. It's a little less than three miles but if you bring me your tracker I can program the coordinates in for you."

"Thank you," Rose said. She was cordial. And very, very cold.

Everyone set about quickly gathering what they could, snuffing out the fires and searching the brush for anything that could be used as a weapon. Meryl took one of the smaller backpacks and filled it with one of the remaining granola bars, a handful of blackberries, two canteens of water and a few matches. She feigned rummaging through the rest of the scattered supplies until she was able to coax her way back to the spot where she'd hidden the canvas bag filled with gold nuggets and quickly unearthed it. She slipped it into the bottom of the knapsack and turned. Ike had watched her from several feet away, but he said nothing, his face expressionless.

Ignoring him for the time being, she helped Alexander lace up his boots and made sure Tom still had the keys to the Jeep in his pants pocket. Then, once Ike had settled down to program Rose's GPS unit, she hunkered down next to him.

"Should I even ask what that was?" he whispered brusquely.

"Rose hasn't used her GPS unit at all on this trip, has she?" she replied, ignoring his question.

"No. She doesn't know what she's doing. We've been using mine exclusively."

"Switch out the batteries."

"What?"

"We have twice as far to go as she does. Switch them out so your unit is fully charged."

He didn't say anything. He just stared at her blankly.

"If she doesn't even know how to use the device, what difference does it make if it's not fully charged, Ike? Switch them."

He opened the back covers and quickly switched the batteries. "If you let Rose go off on her own, she's dead," he murmured.

"How do you suggest I stop her? Knock her over the head with a rock and carry her out on my back?"

"Go and talk to her. It needs to be you. Tom and I barely know her. If she listens to anyone, it'll be you. There's still time to change her mind."

"When has she ever changed her mind, Ike? She's played us all from day one and she's still playing us. Her innocent school teacher act is a big scam. Her whole life has probably been one get-rich-quick scheme after another and we just got caught in this latest one. Shit, even with his arm that messed up, she still had the balls to ask Tommy to stay and help her. She's freaking crazy."

"Yeah, but you knew all that before you came on this trip, right? Or at least suspected it."

Meryl was deflated.

"Come on, you're a smart girl. You had her figured out a long time ago. That day you and I went rifling through her room we both knew she wasn't on the up-and-up. But we — and I totally include myself in this — still came on her little treasure hunt anyway. She may be a pathological liar, Meryl, but that just makes you and me complete idiots for believing her."

"It was just supposed to be a simple camping trip, Ike."

"Camping happens in campgrounds. Face it, we decided to go roughing it in the middle of freaking nowhere because it sounded exciting and maybe we'd all get rich off it too. The only person who's really been honest about their motivations for coming on this trip is Rose. Seriously, one way or another, she won't survive out here." He handed her Rose's GPS unit and said softly, "Give this to her, will you? Tell her it's programmed with the coordinates to the spot where I found you last night and to the Jeep, whichever she decides to use."

Reluctantly, Meryl walked over to Rose. She straightened her back and said firmly, "You really need to come with us. This mine was meant to remain lost and you need to let it go so we can get out of here with our lives."

Rose was almost resigned in her reply. "Darling, let's not rehash this argument, shall we? We're never going to change each other's minds. We're both too stubborn for that. There's no way I can walk out of here when I'm this close. Not after I've spent ten years of my life getting to this place."

Meryl fought to choke back her tears. Her anger was slipping and she resisted it. Anger was what sustained and energized her. Anger would allow her to save Alexander. She extended the tracker and said: "We've turned it off to save the battery life. Ike programmed it so you can find either the mine or that big meadow where we left Tommy's Jeep. I hope you will choose to go to the Jeep."

Rose took the device and tucked it in her pocket. "I never did learn how to use it properly. I guess I will follow my nose."

"Please, don't." The words came gently and Rose looked almost surprised. "I know we said some really harsh shit to each other, but this is too serious now. I don't want anything bad to happen to you, I really don't. But if you stay here, you'll never get out. The only way we can escape is to stay together."

Rose shook her head. "I'm sorry, Meryl, I didn't mean for things to turn out this way. But I've got to see this through to the end. Don't you wait on me. If you make it back to the Jeep, drive away."

"We'll send help back."

"Don't. This place is mine."

Meryl frowned. "You're wrong, Rose. This place belongs to them. It always has."

Rose touched her gently on the shoulder.

All Meryl could say was. "Please!" The word came out strangled and desperate.

Swinging the backpack onto her shoulder, Rose smiled, turned in the direction Meryl had pointed to earlier, and moved swiftly through the trees. In a few seconds, she had vanished completely from sight.

CHAPTER TWENTY-FIVE

Their departure from the glade was slowed not by Tom, who, despite his injury and fever was still able to walk at a decent pace, but by Alexander who tearfully objected to Rose strapping on her backpack and heading off alone in the opposite direction. No one had any patience for the child's histrionics, nor the words to adequately explain why his friend was leaving. In the end, they couldn't wait for him to cry himself out so Ike loaded the boy onto his back and let him sob into his shoulder blades.

"I can carry him," Meryl insisted.

"No worries," he snapped. "We'll take turns and you have your own pack to carry. Let's move. You'll have a lifetime to explain to him what happened here today."

Ike led the way with both the child and the GPS tracker hanging from around his neck. Occasionally, the computerized female voice would suggest a course correction or offer the revised distance to the plot point where Tom's Jeep was located. The persistent wind which had battered them all night long had softened to a stiff breeze, but every fluttering branch or rustling bush made Meryl jump as she constantly scanned the trees for signs of pursuit. An undulating landscape did little to sooth either her anxiety or her aching muscles. Every bluff and gully was something they had to surmount or skirt, burning both time and energy. Each stand of trees or grassy meadow was likewise a potential ambush spot for a race of creatures that seemed to specialize in stealth. But as the morning progressed, it was clear that they were slowly descending the mountainside. It was hard for Meryl to remember any details of their frantic flight through the woods on that first night, but it had seemed at the time that the creatures had almost herded them uphill, into the foothills where the forest was nearly impenetrable. So the further they descended, the better she felt.

Ike had eventually convinced Alexander, whose grief over Rose was now signified by the occasional sniffle and sad glance over his shoulder, to walk beside him and hold his hand. Meryl would catch Tom watching them, but his face was so deformed by his own suffering she couldn't tell what he was thinking or feeling at the sight of another man comforting his son. Undoubtedly it would be an image Tom would have to live with, the shape of things to come. Meryl didn't know who Alexander would eventually grow to call "daddy," but she was certain that man wasn't here.

About an hour outside of the glade, they paused under some alder trees along the side of a rocky ravine. Meryl removed her backpack and passed around the canteens. Below, great grey slabs of rock buttressed a twisted creek that trickled with brackish water and formed an ugly pool at the base of the cleft. Some distance away, a flock of crows were skipping along the tops of the boulders and squawking loudly.

"Do you want me to carry that pack for a while?" Tom asked.

She shook her head as she stripped off her jacket and knotted it around her waist. "No, I want you to carry you. How're you feeling?"

"Like shit, but I will power through it."

She gave him a slight smile. Then she glanced at Ike, but he had his back turned to her, perhaps intentionally so, and was sharing a peanut butter granola bar with Alexander.

After the brief respite, they scrabbled down the incline and walked along the banks of the stream toward the congregation of birds. The crows didn't seem particularly concerned by their approach and although most hopped to higher perches, few flew off.

Instinctively, Meryl held up a hand and everyone came to an immediate stop.

"What?" Tom panted.

"The birds aren't leaving," she whispered.

"And?"

"That means they are more interested in something up there than they are scared of us."

Tom bristled. "Can we go around?"

"It would mean climbing over all these rocks," Ike offered. "Which I doubt you could do with that arm."

Meryl took a few steps forward and stopped again. Along the left side of the creek were three large, straight tree branches rising vertically from the center of a jumble of boulders. The branches had been stripped of bark and foliage. A single crow, glistening as though it had dipped its head in oil, twitched on the tip of one branch and cawed at them defiantly.

They said nothing, but each of them hefted the various clubs they were carrying and crept forward. The warm, sour smell of death reached them. Laying in the center of the boulders was a large, hairy body that had been bisected by three crudely-made lances. The creature lay with its face half-sunk into the earth and fallen leaves, as though it had been struck down in flight and had crashed headlong into the ground. One of the lances had obviously been thrust through the body once it was down, as it had punched deeply into the earth and had anchored the beast to the forest floor. The kill was fresh. The creature's blood had saturated the ground and stained the fallen leaves a bright scarlet. Beyond the protestations of the crows who had been picking away at the carcass, Meryl could also hear the incessant rustling of insects and rodents beneath all the litter as scavengers of every description swarmed in to feast.

They made a wide arch around the body but it wasn't until they reached the head — or what was left of it — that it occurred to Ike to shield Alexander from the gruesome spectacle. He and the boy quickly withdrew to a nearby pile of rocks and waited quietly. Despite the mutilation of the body, it wasn't difficult for Meryl to recognize which creature it was. The pendulous breasts were enough to identify Big Girl.

"Are these spears?" Tom grumbled. He touched a projectile gingerly, as though it might still have the power to harm him if he handled it too roughly.

"Yes," Meryl replied as she squatted near the corpse's right shoulder. She didn't even try to find the face of the creature who had protected them for the last few days. That part of the head was nothing more than an organic mash of bone and tissue. The same sense of grief and nausea that she had felt at the mine, looking down at the remains of the creature at the bottom of the pit, consumed her again. She held her breath and closed her eyes, resisting the urge to vomit or cry or just run blindly through the forest looking for escape. She remembered the conversation she had had with Rose on that very first night they were trapped in the glen. The only way she and the others would escape the forest was to outsmart it.

She turned away from the head and examined the lances more closely. They did not appear to have been fashioned by tools as she might've expected from primitive humans. Rather they were scavenged objects which had been manipulated by massive hands and strong fingers. The conical tips of each spear had been shaped by grinding the wood against rough stone, but this part of the weapon appeared to be harder and darker than the rest.

"Tommy," she called, "what do you think this is?"

He hobbled over and scraped away the encrusted blood and tissue with a wad of leaves. "It's burned," he said. "After they made the spear tip, they must have hardened it in fire."

"So these guys have fire?" she cried.

"It explains why Big Girl and the others didn't take off when we built that first campfire, why they sat around staring at it like we were preforming some magic trick."

She shuddered. "What it doesn't explain is why they didn't attack us last night? We were assuming the fire was keeping them away. But if they're not scared of fire like other animals, if they can even control it, then something else was keeping them back."

"And that would be what? Our bad breath?"

"I wish I knew..."

"Guys," Ike called from where he was standing on a nearby boulder, "you should come up here."

Meryl and Tom crawled up the rock and stood shoulder to shoulder with Ike and Alexander. Big Girl's body, now seen from an entirely different vantage point, one closer to that of an eight-foot forest beast, took on an eerie new significance. Around the corpse had been scraped a crude circle and near each of her elbows was a small hole. Lost in the clutter of leaves, pine needles and blood, the configuration had not been noticeable when they were standing near the body. It only revealed itself when they stepped away and rose several feet in height.

"A circle with two dots in the middle," Ike whispered. "Now look behind us, to the left and part way up the hill."

They slowly turned to see the body of A Quart Short which had been pinned to the trunk of a fir tree by a spear through the thorax. Unlike Big Girl, his face had not been mutilated and his eyes were still open, their edges wriggling with insects. Above his head, carved in the bark of the tree was the same circular symbol.

"I don't see Romulus and Remus though," said Ike.

"Or Thunderman," Tom noted.

"Shit," Meryl gasped as she jumped down and approached Big Girl's body.

"What is it?" Tom asked.

"We underestimated these things again." With the toe of her boot she poked at the line carved in the dirt and crawling with tiny ants feasting on the unexpected bounty provided by Big Girl's remains. "Elijah Comstock found this symbol and apparently many others during all those years he spent out here. I think he presumed it was some kind of warning to stay away from a particular place, which is why he wrote 'stop' next to it on the belt. I thought maybe it was being used to mark a place where someone died. But we were both wrong. It's used to mark those who are meant to be killed."

"Huh?"

"That's what Big Girl was trying to tell me at the mine. The dead creature in the pit, the miners from a century ago... Don't you see? They were all marked for death."

"It's like 'The Black Spot,'" Ike said softly.

Tom was agitated now, partly from confusion and partly from fear. "What the hell are you two talking about?" he cried.

"Did you ever read Treasure Island?" Ike asked.

"Never."

"It's a book about pirates. If you were a pirate and the other pirates wanted you dead, they'd present you with 'The Black Spot.' It was your death warrant. From that moment on, no matter where you went or where you hid, they'd hunt you down."

Tom looked wide-eyed at Meryl. "You think Big Girl and the other big monkeys with her... were... what? Assassinated?"

"She didn't draw this symbol around her own dead body, Tommy," replied Meryl, "yet at the mine she drew it for me twice and someone or something else had carved it into the stone near the tunnel where I found the dead miners. What if the dead creature she showed me at the bottom of the pit hadn't fallen but had been thrown in?"

"Why?" Tom asked.

Meryl shrugged. "Who knows? Maybe he ate berries off the wrong plant? Or he trespassed into a place he wasn't supposed to go? Maybe they did to him what their ancestors had done to the gold miners over a hundred years ago? And maybe Big Girl knew her own days were numbered?"

Ike added one more grim point of speculation. "Maybe what finally doomed her is that she saved us? Thunderman did try to kill us and she stopped him. Maybe this is a part of the forest where people just aren't allowed to be and she broke some kind of taboo?"

Meryl was running before she had time to even consider her actions, scrambling back the way they had come, back toward the glen where Big Girl and the others had held them captive. She had made it no further than the edge of the stream when strong hands grasped the top of her knapsack and dragged her down to the ground. The heavy bag of gold ore slammed down on her, knocking the breath from her lungs. She rolled onto her back and immediately unleashed all the fury and fear she had kept bottled for days. Her limbs flailed wildly even though she had no specific target for the blows. By chance alone, she landed a solid punch to Ike's left cheek and he toppled off of her.

"What the hell? Are you trying to break my jaw, you crazy bitch?" he bellowed.

She sat up and blinked, dead leaves strewn through her hair and mud smeared along the right side of her body. She didn't know which disturbed her more: that Ike was furious with her or that Alexander was crying again. "Did you jump me?" she retorted.

"Where were you running off to, Meryl?" he demanded. She didn't answer so he repeated the question, more loudly and angrily this time.

"She doesn't know about this," Meryl choked. "She doesn't know what the symbol really means."

"Don't be a fucking idiot, Meryl," he snarled.

"I'm the only one of us who knows where that mine is. It has to be me. You guys can wait here with Alexander until I return."

The freckles that ran along the ridge of Ike's nose and over his cheekbones had vanished beneath the red flush that covered his face. His whole body pulsed with rage. He lowered his voice so only she could hear. "Are you really going to run off and leave your son alone, again?"

Meryl hid her face in her hands and began to weep. But for once, Ike was unmoved by her tears and he made a quick grab for the knapsack which had half-fallen from her shoulders. Within seconds they were grappling on the ground again, this time wrestling for control of the bag. Tom limped over and took a clumsy swing at Ike, but he was too quick and easily dodged away. Suddenly all their legs were entangled and Tom toppled. He rolled to his left to protect his damaged arm, but the mere impact of his body against the ground was enough to have him shrieking in pain. Neither Ike nor Meryl noticed as they continued to scratch and claw for control of the bag. The parcel felt like a wet sack of cement as Meryl struggled to keep her fingers around it, but Ike was taller and stronger and after a few seconds of intense cursing he was finally able to pull it from her grip. He immediately retreated up the hill and hunkered over the bag like a predator guarding a fresh kill.

Alexander ran over to Meryl and threw his arms around her neck. "Maw-mee, stop fighting!" he wailed. She cradled him and sat exhausted and terrified, waiting for Ike to make the next move.

Tom crawled to her side and glared up at Ike. "Give us the bag back," he hissed.

"Or what, Tom?" Ike asked defiantly.

"Dude, I may have a bum arm but I can still kick your skinny ass."

"You can barely stand, asshole."

"I'm not going to let you steal our food and water."

Ike cocked an eyebrow. "Hey, genius, I hate to break this to you but there's a lot more in this bag than just canteens and trail bars."

"What?"

Ike stood and unceremoniously dumped the entire contents of the knapsack out on the ground. The grimy canvas bag hit with a thump. Everyone was quiet. Even Alexander stopped crying as Ike carefully loosened the knot on the bag and reached inside. He pulled out a handful of jagged ore that even in the dappled light of the forest still sparkled with a golden luster.

"What the hell?" Tom said, looking anxiously at Meryl.

"I found it in the mine," she choked, not taking her eyes off Ike. "It was laying beneath one of the skeletons. When the creatures attacked their camp, they must have grabbed what gold they could carry and retreated into that tunnel for safety."

Ike dropped the glittering nuggets back into the bag and tied it shut again. "So you found Rose's treasure and decided to keep it for yourself?" he stated, disgusted.

Meryl was astonished. "That's what you think?"

"I noticed you didn't tell any of the rest of us. I noticed you didn't tell Rose this morning, when it might have made a difference."

"What kind of difference would it have made, Ike? If I had told her that I actually found gold in that mine, would she have been more or less likely to leave with us? You may recall that I kept telling her that the place was a death-trap, that she should give it up? I didn't want her to ever go there. There was no way in hell I was going to tell her that I had actually found gold."

He didn't reply, but after a second Tom said morosely, "Ike, you know Meryl's right. It wouldn't have made any difference. Rose was never going to leave this forest without reaching that fucking mine first. Knowing there was actually gold there would've just sealed her fate faster."

"You don't know that," Ike said angrily.

"Dude, we are under attack by forest monsters and that still wasn't enough for Rose. Show Rose the gold or don't show Rose the gold... The result would have been the same either way."

Ike still looked unconvinced, so Meryl added, "You were right this morning, Ike. We all came here, completely stupid and unprepared, because we believed Rose's promises that we would leave rich people. But you know what, the longer we're out here the less and less I give a shit about that gold."

"That's cool," he replied. "So you won't mind if I hang onto it then?"

"I don't give a shit what you do with it. Just give us back the food and water."

Ike stood there for a long moment as he considered his options. Whatever Meryl's reasons for keeping the satchel of gold a secret, he still felt both outnumbered and outmaneuvered. Finally, he answered, "Maybe I'll just carry the whole damn pack for a while?"

Tom was about to launch into another tirade of threats when a familiar female voice came wafting out of the dead leaves nearby: "*Proceed east for one half mile and then turn south by south-west.*" He carefully fished the GPS tracker out of the leaves and cleaned it on his shirttail. Ike's hand immediately went to his neck where the device had swung prior to his wrestling match with Meryl.

"Throw that to me," Ike commanded.

Tom drew himself to his full height and growled, "Come and get it, Turbo."

"You don't know how to use it. It won't do you any good without me."

"Really? Seems like it's on auto-pilot or something? Apparently Alexander, Meryl and I walk half a mile east and then we turn south by southwest, right? I may not be in college, but I bet you I can figure out how to walk east."

Ike looked terrified and for a long moment the two men glared wordlessly at each other. Then, out of the forest came another familiar sound. Tapping. The beat of a dozen hands drumming their spears against the trees.

CHAPTER TWENTY-SIX

Despite the persistent rasping of wood against wood, everyone stood in place, staring wordlessly at each other. Ike tightened his bearhug on the knapsack and Tom tauntingly hung the GPS unit around his neck. Meryl swung Alexander onto her back and his tiny hands instantly locked around her neck.

"You wanted to know why I didn't tell anyone about the gold?" she barked at Ike. "This is why. Because I knew it would divide us. Keep it if it's important to you, but we've woken up this damn forest with our fighting and now it's time to go…" She turned to Tom and asked, "Which way is east?"

He pointed and Meryl, with her son still hoisted onto her back, began to climb her way out of the creek bed. She didn't look back to see if they were following. She knew they would. She knew that neither the bag of glistening ore nor the rivalry between Ike and Tom would keep them there now that the wood-knocking had begun. Once she reached the far lip of the ravine, the number of trees diminished and for the first time all morning she could feel the full warmth of the sun on her face. She continued east until she came to a steep escarpment.

Tom shuddered as he looked over the edge of the precipice. "I don't think we originally came this way," he muttered. "Ike, what the hell is wrong with your stupid gizmo? It said east and then south."

Ike, who was still intentionally keeping his distance, sneered at him. "It's not that intuitive, genius."

"What do you mean?"

"I mean most GPS devices are going to give you the fastest route between two points. That doesn't mean it's the only or even the best route."

Tom angrily shook the device dangling from his neck. "So it's leading us on a wild goose chase?"

"No, it's telling you the fastest way to get back to the Jeep. What it can't tell you is what kind of obstacles you may encounter along the way. Like a fallen tree or a stream or..."

"A big scary cliff?" Meryl offered.

Ike nodded grimly.

"So what do we do?"

"We adapt. We know that the Jeep is generally to the south of our position, so head south for a while and then reconfigure the unit so it can update the directions for you."

"How?" Tom snarled, poking at the device with an index finger.

"Hey, dumbass," Ike cried, "unless you want to get us all permanently lost out here, how about you don't just start randomly pushing buttons on that thing?"

Standing still was making Meryl increasingly nervous. She felt a compulsion to keep moving, no matter what. "Tommy, give Ike the GPS unit."

"No freaking way!" Tom protested. "He already has the food, the water and the gold. If he has the GPS he'll just take off and let us die here."

"Are the keys to the Jeep in your pocket?"

"Yes."

"Right. If Ike doesn't have those keys then getting back to the Jeep isn't going to do him a damn bit of good. Give him the GPS."

Reluctantly, Tom handed over the device and Ike immediately took the point position, threading his way quickly along the top of the cliff until the incline became less steep and more navigable. Meryl surmised that they had roughly walked in a wide half-circle from the point where they had found Big Girl's and A Quart Short's bodies. It had proven a phenomenal waste of time, but at least their mutual fear had kept them from talking more than was necessary. The tree-knocking had receded into the distance and had become less rapid. Meryl wasn't sure if that was a good sign or not.

They squatted down in a stand of fir trees and Ike quickly reconfigured their position relative to the Jeep. *"Calculating new route... Please stand by..."* the device chirped. Ike immediately slapped his hand over it to muffle the voice.

"Jesus, can't you put that thing on vibrate or something?" Meryl whispered. "The quieter we are the better."

Ike fiddled with it quickly and silenced the artificial voice. They sat still and listened to the wilderness. Two taps. Quite distant. Probably to the north of them, back in the direction of the ravine where they had found the bodies.

"Maw-mee, can we goat now?" Alexander whined.

"Yes. We'll go... But as quietly as we can."

They pushed on, proceeding as much in a south-by-southeasterly direction as the landscape would allow. Every impassable ravine, every unscalable cliff, every impenetrable hedgerow was an exercise in both patience and endurance. But as the morning drew on, it became clear that the wilderness, separate from the actions of the hairy beasts that hunted them, was conspiring to keep them trapped. To the west, storm clouds were building mountaintops. From their current position, Ike estimated the storm would be on them within an hour.

"Can you imagine trying to climb though all this when it's muddy and wet?" Meryl asked no one in particular. She looked at Tom and frowned. "Can you pick up the pace?"

His face was red and he was sweating profusely, much more than he should even for their level of exertion. Clearly, his fever was spiking and she worried that pushing him harder might led to his total collapse. But not trying meant never escaping at all. Tom, perhaps typically of him, insisted that he would keep up no matter what pace they set.

Ike extended him one of the canteens from the backpack and said, "You drink my portion of the water."

"You'll need it," Tom responded hoarsely.

"You'll need it more and in a little while we'll have more water than we know what to do with. If worse comes to worse, I'll drink out of a rain puddle."

Tom reluctantly accepted the gift and guzzled down several huge mouthfuls.

"I'll carry Alexander for a while if you carry the pack," Ike suggested to Meryl.

She smiled a little. "He's hot and heavy."

"Not as heavy as this freaking gold, I bet you."

They exchanged burdens with the child climbing onto Ike's back without hesitation. They started moving again, sometimes at a fast walk, sometimes at a slow run where the terrain would allow it. Every five minutes or so Ike would check the GPS and then the darkening sky. He knew the storm would reach them first, but at least there was the chance to close some of the distance between them and the Jeep.

They finally broke out of the thick trees and found themselves standing at the top of what appeared to be the last sloping foothill until they reached the valley floor. Far to the south, barely perceptible among the dark green swath of wilderness, was an undulating line that cut through the trees. Meryl's heart leapt. It was the highway, still miles away through thick forest but finally visible to the naked eye. Even more thrilling was the thin ribbon of dark brown that ran perpendicular to the base of the slope.

"Is that a road?" Tom panted, teetering slightly.

Ike was madly fiddling with the GPS unit. "Dude, I think that's *our* road," he said excitedly.

"So my Jeep's down there?"

"Naw. We're still too far north, but I'm pretty sure it's the same road we drove in on. If we just follow it south, I bet we'd come right to the Jeep."

Meryl replied, "You're pretty sure that's our road, but you're not *completely* sure?"

Ike bit his lip and squinted harder at the device. "When I downloaded the maps for this forest, it showed the major highways and forest roads. But the lumber companies or the Forest Service may have cut additional roads that don't show up on the software. But this sure looks like the same road."

"But even if it's the same road it's not necessarily the best route right? It could twist through these hills for miles before we reached the Jeep. Maybe we should just stick to a straight line?"

"The road will be easier to travel," Ike countered. "Easier for Tom especially."

"Mmmm."

"If we start going too far off course I can just adjust when needed."

Meryl nodded. "Okay. Lead on."

Ike took Alexander's hand and they began their decent over the loose shale and barbed vegetation of the hillside. Despite their best intentions, fear and collective exhaustion resulted in missteps which sent piles of loose rock clattering down the hill and clouds of dust rising up in their wake. Meryl winced but she refused to let it slow her down. They were so close now... and then the Jeep, the highway and escape. When her feet touched the surface of the primitive road, she allowed herself a sigh of relief. But almost simultaneously a flicker of movement from above caught her eye.

The road skirted the base of the foothills, and all along its northern edge was a series of rocky outcrops and heaps of rounded boulders. Directly in front of them, standing upon a lip of dark granite high above the road was Thunderman. He made no attempt to hide, but instead had anchored himself to the trunk of a tree with one massive hand and was leaning forward over the drop onto the road below.

It was Alexander who reacted first, producing a short squeal of happiness and stepping forward. "Look, Mah-mee!" he said. "It's dat guy."

Ike tightened his grip on Alexander's hand and pulled him back to where Meryl could wrap her arms around him.

"What's the problem?" Tom panted. He was now drenched with sweat. "Big ugly is on our team, right?"

Meryl didn't respond. Her eyes were skipping across the hillside, looking for additional signs of movement, flashes of a shaggy hide, a boulder that wasn't a boulder. She strained to filter the sounds of the wilderness, but there wasn't anything unusual. The wood-knocking had stopped.

"Meryl?" Tom prodded. He ached to move. Standing still was agony.

"Something's wrong," she whispered.

"Thunderman and Big Girl were buddies," Tom insisted.

"Then why isn't he dead?" Meryl asked quickly, her body tensing.

The hairy giant moved, extending himself even further into the void above the road. He was watching them intensely. He parted his lips slightly, inhaled deeply and grunted.

"Ike, if we make a run for the Jeep through the woods, how far?"

"About a mile, maybe a little more," he whispered back. "Shouldn't we stick to the road?"

"The road's a trap," Meryl said. "Thunderman's setting us up. We need to run. Ike, fastest route to the Jeep."

Ike didn't debate how Meryl had reached these conclusions. In the short time he had known her, he had grown to trust her intuition. He bundled up Alexander and took off for the cover of the trees at the road's southern edge. Meryl turned to locate Thunderman through gaps in the canopy, but he had vanished the moment they had started to move. They passed through a narrow grove of trees and found themselves briefly back on the road. To their right, dark, shaggy shapes were skipping along the tops of the stone ledges, moving with greater agility and coordination than Meryl had yet witnessed from the creatures. As Big Girl had done when she led Meryl down into the gold mine, the beasts used their overly-long arms to swing, pivot and anchor themselves to the terrain. Despite their girth, they moved with tremendous speed as they attempted to outflank the comparatively slow and clumsy humans. Ike led them for several hundred yards down the road and then veered again to his left and back into the refuge of the forest.

"If we stay in the trees I don't think they'll be able to spot us," Ike whispered between gasps for air.

"They're not tracking us by sight," Meryl said. "Tracking by sight doesn't work out here. Thunderman just took a big whiff of us back there."

"They're tracking us by scent," Tom said.

"And by sound. I think that's what all the knocking is about. They're reporting into each other by banging on the trees."

"If they can smell us, then we need to mask our scent."

Meryl shook her head. "I don't know how to do that, do you?"

Ike quickly recalculated the route to the Jeep and murmured, "We're about a half of a mile…"

"You know which way to go?" Meryl asked urgently.

He nodded.

"Good. Then reset that thing to find the walking route between here and like, Washington D.C., or something... Someplace far away..."

Ike looked horrified.

"Please," Meryl insisted, "just do it and turn Miss Margaret's stupid voice back on. Full volume."

"What the hell are you up to?" asked Tom.

"Hopefully, I'm slowing them down a little."

Ike handed her the device as it began to make the complex calculations for the absurdly complicated cross-country hike she had requested. *"Calculating new route... Please stand by..."* the device broadcasted loudly in its feminine voice. *"Calculating new route... Please stand by..."*

Meryl quickly tossed the device to the base of a tree and kicked a clump of dried pine needles over it. They started running again, or as much as the terrain would allow. They had been moving for less than a minute when a series of tremors shook the trees ahead and reverberated through the soles of their feet. They all slid to a stop and fell onto the ground behind a large crumbling log strewn with moss and mushrooms. Meryl immediately tucked Alexander under her body and clapped a hand over his mouth. He shuddered but stayed quiet. Several hundred feet away, three creatures shambled out of the tree-line, each of them carrying a spear similar to those which had killed Big Girl and A Quart Short. They made no pretense at stealth and Meryl presumed that they had no reason to do so. She could not imagine a situation in which these giants might feel physically threatened by any of them. Whatever taboo Meryl and the others had silently, unknowingly broken, it had been enough to bring an otherwise reclusive species out into the open to hunt them down. The trio of animals lumbered forward and then paused, each of them raising their flattened faces toward the sky and sniffing loudly.

In the distance, faintly, the tracker continued its monotonous updates: *"Calculating new route... Please stand by..."*

One of the creatures tilted his head slightly to the left, as a dog might do when someone had called his name. The beast made a sound in the back of his throat, a dull clacking noise, and his companions immediately fell still and quiet. Even though her gaze never left them, Meryl was amazed by how, when motionless, the animals melted into the environment. She had to blink quickly and readjust her eyes so as not to lose their outlines among the trees.

They waited.

One of the creatures huffed softly and the trio quickly broke apart and headed back into the trees, toward the artificial voice. Within a few seconds, they were no longer visible.

Meryl waited a few more minutes to make sure that they did not reappear and signaled the others to continue on. Ike led the way, following his nose through the brush with Alexander riding on his back. After another fifteen minutes of hard marching through waist-high greenery, they slipped out of the wood and into a clearing filled with old tree stumps and young saplings.

"This is it!" Tom panted. He was too exhausted to feel any excitement, but his voice trembled with relief. "We made camp that first night on the edge of this field right? The old logging site?"

Ike pointed. On the opposite side of the enclave sat the Jeep Cherokee and the crumpled shells of the nylon tents. The wilderness didn't ignore anything within its confines, and whether it had been the hulking creatures or raccoons or porcupines or bears, their campsite had been thoroughly scavenged during their absence. Their belongings were strewn all over the area. A bright green wool sock, one of Rose's, hung limply in a blackberry bush nearby. A deep sense of grief welled up in Meryl. She shook it off and hoisted the knapsack higher on her back. The gold-filled bag dug painfully into her spine.

There was a distant roll of thunder and the sky faded to a smoky grey. The field began to resonate with the pattering of rain against the tree stumps. The drops plinked against the hood of the Jeep, almost as though the vehicle were calling to them.

CHAPTER TWENTY-SEVEN

Even as they quickly threaded their way through the field of broken trees, Meryl knew they wouldn't make it to the Jeep in time. There were no ominous shadows moving through the woods around them as there had been on that first day by the stream. There were no knocks echoing through the thicket or the foul musk of the creatures wafting on the cold breeze blowing in with the rain. But still she knew they were there. She understood they were as intuitive as she or Ike or Tom; and even her ruse using the GPS tracker's electronic voice to lure them in the wrong direction wouldn't have fooled them for long. With the Jeep now in sight, it was suddenly clear to her why the animals hadn't bothered to chase them through the forest, although surely they must've been there. Thunderman knew where they were heading. Perhaps it had even been him who'd stood in the break of trees that very first afternoon, watching as she played with Alexander on the tops of the stumps. It didn't really matter. She knew the field was a trap and the Jeep was the bait.

Her mind reeled, struggling to tie together the threads of information she'd gathered about these animals. Suddenly she stopped, dropping the heavy backpack to the ground and squatting down in a pocket of thick forbs. The others immediately did likewise.

"Meryl, no time to rest," Ike whispered urgently. "Get your ass in gear!"

"Get Alexander and Tom to the Jeep," she commanded, unzipping the backpack and dumping the contents onto the ground. "That's your only job, Ike."

He began to protest but she cut him short with a glare. Alexander began to cry and Tom immediately removed him from Ike's back and hoisted him onto his hip with his one good arm as he attempted to both comfort and restrain the child. Meryl could tell from the look on his face that the exertion hurt him. A tear trickled from Tom's eye, but she couldn't tell if it was due to pain or something else. "You need to come with us," he croaked.

Meryl felt her heart ripping in two as Alexander tucked his face against his father's neck and convulsed with mute grief. She replied firmly, "I'm not sacrificing myself to these things, guys. But we're walking into a trap."

Ike looked restively over her shoulder. The boy's cries would be like a beacon to the animals, but so far there was no movement in the trees behind them. "We lost them, Meryl. They're not around." he insisted.

"Trust me, they are. Thunderman appears to have switched teams, remember? He has to know about this campsite." She untied the bright orange coat from around her waist and slipped it onto her shoulders and zipped it up to her neck. Then, holding the canvas bag with both hands, began to rub it across the front, arms and shoulders of the jacket.

"What the hell?" Tom asked.

"Tommy, these things don't run from fire and we can't match them physically. The one thing which stopped them, the *only* thing which made them retreat last night was my stink."

"You think it's because you smell like old dead bodies and that's scaring them?"

"Most animals are attracted by the smell of death, but not humans. We're repulsed by it. If these creatures are something closer to human, than maybe they have the same reaction to the smell of death? I think that's why Big Girl ran from me when I came out of the mine and why they didn't attack last night. There's something on me that smells so offensive that it's scaring the shit out of them, and I bet you it's because when I found those skeletons of the miners and tripped and fell right into them."

"You may be hoping for a lot if you think Thunderman's going to back off 'cause of how you smell," Ike breathed.

She jerked her head in the direction of the vehicle and replied ominously, "He's waiting for us over there. All I need to do is distract him long enough for you guys to get to the car, start it and pick me up."

Then, tucking the canvas bag under her arm like she was carrying a football, she looked Tom squarely in the eyes and said, "I'm going out first, you guys follow. Whatever you do, get your son to safety."

She didn't wait for any further protests or debate, but instead burst out of the saplings and began running toward the Cherokee. The others followed and almost simultaneously the woods behind them broke with motion. A wall of fur crashed through the underbrush and vaulted over the broken tree trunks and fallen timbers, the creatures materializing almost magically from the concealment of the trees. Meryl resisted the urge to turn and face the animals which now pursued them across the open field. She understood that the real threat was still lying hidden and silent somewhere between her and the vehicle.

By the time she was within a few hundred yards of the Jeep, she was trampling over many of their scattered belongings. The sleeping bag she'd shared with Alexander was caught on a tree trunk nearby. A broken tent pole and a discarded skillet lay in the grass. When she reached the camp site, she dodged her way through the crumpled tents without stopping, trying to put as much space between herself and the young men following her. Only a few yards now separated her from

328

the Jeep. Her chest tightened as she closed the gap. The heavy feet of the animals charging after them began to shake the earth, but still she didn't stop, leaping over the slumped back of the last crumpled tent, the one Ike and Tom had shared.

The storm winds gusted, sweeping her hair forward and billowing out the sleeves on her jacket. Almost immediately something shifted in the grass. Thunderman had flattened his body almost like a large cat stalking prey with his fur standing erect in an almost perfect simulation of the texture of the surrounding vegetation. As he rose into a crouch, brandishing a roughhewn spear before him, his dark gold eyes locked with Meryl's and she saw the deep red which stained his hands, arms and chest. But it wasn't his blood, just the remnant of whatever kills he'd made the night before. Whether he had personally butchered or just betrayed Big Girl and the other creatures he'd lived with no longer mattered to Meryl. She suddenly felt more hatred for this being than she'd ever felt before, more than she ever imagined she could feel. Thunderman's nostrils flared as the wind reached him, bringing with it the ancient but undeniable smell of decay, and for a second he hesitated. Meryl hurdled herself forward, charging straight for him as she dropped the gold-filled canvas bag to her right hand and swung it like a club. The creature dodged to his right just as Meryl smashed the bag into the side of his blunted head. Deteriorated by age and rot, the canvas broke open on impact and scattered the rocky pellets across his shaggy hide. The stench dripped from his fur in flecks of gold as his face contorted with terror. He leapt away and began to shake violently, trying to dislodge the smell from his body. He wasn't incapacitated, but Meryl's feint had given them a small window through which to pass. She didn't even notice the others rushing by until Ike grabbed her by the elbow and pulled her toward the Jeep.

Tom got there first, unlocked the front door and tossed Alexander inside.

"Dude, I'm driving!" Ike barked, snatching the keys out of his fingers and sliding in behind the steering wheel. Tom didn't bother to argue as his arm was so swollen that it would've been impossible for him to operate the stick shift in any case. He bellowed at Meryl to get in as he clambered into the back seat and the engine roared to life.

Meryl pivoted to her right, around the Jeep's hood and had almost reached the passenger side door when Thunderman's lance shot passed her head and stuck solidly into a tree just beyond the vehicle. The immense animal had looped around and was vaulting over brush and tree stumps directly toward her. She could still see gold glinting on his shoulders. Behind him, the army of creatures had slowed, forming a wide semi-circle around the vehicle. At the front of the pack was the same silvery male she'd encountered by the fire the night before. He pulled himself up onto a broken log, raised his head upward and gave a long howl.

Meryl couldn't tell if the creatures were aiming for Thunderman, now contaminated by the smell of decomposition, or all of them when they unleashed the barrage of spears which arched elegantly across the meadow. There was only enough time for her to yell "Get down!" and duck behind the Jeep before the weapons began to impact around her. One slammed through the rear window of the Jeep, sending a shower of broken glass across the passengers inside. Another rebounded off the hood, leaving a deep crater in the metal and cracking the windshield as two more crashed into the vehicle's side but didn't penetrate through the doors. Meryl didn't see the projectile which struck Thunderman. She didn't even realize he'd been struck until the inertia of the impact combined with his immense weight sent him smashing headlong through the toppled remains of an old fir tree and then flipped him into the air. As she moved to swing her body inside the Jeep, the entire vehicle slipped away from her, skidding sideways in the mud as Thunderman's body impacted against the front fender. The shaggy hulk slid into a bellowing heap just a few feet from her and

330

immediately Meryl was back on her feet. She screamed at Ike to drive away and he immediately threw the Jeep into reverse and accelerated away from Thunderman's flailing limbs.

The end of a projectile jutted from the muscle and soft tissues just above Thunderman's left hip bone. With one great hand, he pulled the spear from his side and a great spume of blood drenched his legs and feet. With the Jeep now rapidly receding into the rain, the animal refocused his attention on Meryl as she ran after it. Even though the spear had pulverized the bone and shredded the muscle of his leg, Thunderman was still able to move quickly and effectively over the rough terrain on his three remaining limbs. He cut diagonally across the clearing to intercept her, but as he closed in, Ike wheeled the Jeep around and smashed the rear of the vehicle against the animal. The impact knocked the remaining glass shards from the rear windows and crumpled in the tailgate as Thunderman again went sprawling through the mud. Ike leaned on the horn.

She waved frantically at him and yelled, "Drive! Go! Go!" Through the broken rear window, she could see Alexander calling for her from his father's arms.

Ike hit the gas again, sending up a plume of muddy water as the Jeep's four-wheel drive kicked in and they accelerated down the rutted road.

Meryl forced herself to look away, glancing back over her shoulder as Thunderman again fell into a close pursuit, this time moving in an awkward, sideways gait. Out of the thick rain, the entire mountainside seemed to be rolling toward them as the creatures rushed inward from all sides. They reached Thunderman first, and almost effortlessly wrenched him into a dozen pieces. Whatever frenzied thought compelled them, whether it was an issue of territory or taboos, it seemed as though the animals which descended upon him were intent on doing more than just killing him. They were obliterating him. They ripped him into smaller and smaller pieces, flinging the scraps into the air where they — along with the gold nuggets still clinging to his hide — were lost among the brush and trees.

More than anything, the sound of the savagery behind her pushed Meryl down the road. She couldn't differentiate Thunderman's screams for those of the other creatures. Nor did she look back again to watch as the animals finished dismembering him and then turned back toward her. She just ran on, though it felt like the muscles in her legs would snap and her lungs were filled with fire, following the fresh tire tracks on the road although she could no longer see nor hear the Jeep. If she had one consolation before the creatures overwhelmed and ripped her apart as well, it was that Alexander had escaped.

Then she heard a car horn and saw the headlights of the Jeep emerge from the downpour. It bounced recklessly over the furrowed ground, sending up great plumes of muddy water and billowing exhaust. Ike braked just a few feet from her, turning the vehicle onto the grassy verge so it was headed back away from her. Through the busted back window she could see Tom screaming and reaching out to her. Her lungs felt like they were going to burst as she gulped down her breaths, but her actions were instinctual and instantaneous. Flinging herself toward the vehicle, she landed hard against the crumpled tailgate and immediately felt Tom's one good hand grab the folds of her jacket as he half-lifted, half-dragged her through the window. As soon as her feet left the muddy earth, Ike slammed his foot onto the gas pedal and the Jeep lurched forward. For a moment Meryl felt weightless. Then, as though gravity suddenly reengaged, she tumbled forward. There was a sharp pain as she slid into the Jeep's plastic paneling, graceless, bloodied, soaked to the bone but still intact. Splinters of broken glass protruded from the palms of her hands and the front of her thighs had been shredded from the serrated lip of the window. But she ignored all of it, lifting her head just in time to see the wall of howling fur disappear into the rain and mist behind them.

She collapsed back onto the floor of the Jeep, laying awkwardly between Tom, the spare tire and the ice chest full of food they'd locked up in the vehicle before leaving for their campsite for the last time. Alexander appeared over the top of the back seat, tears still rolling off his long lashes but at least this time it was from relief.

"You okay, baby?" she asked softly. The child just wept, reaching out for her but blocked by a seat too tall for him to scale. Tom lifted him over and tucked him in under the crook of his mother's arm. She stroked his hair, inadvertently smearing it red.

"Now before you say anything," Tom said weakly, barely able to hold himself upright. "I didn't put him in his car seat. There wasn't time."

Meryl nodded. "I know," she answered with a thin smile. "We won't worry about it this one time."

"Everyone in one piece back there?" Ike bellowed from the front seat.

"Yes," she called back. "We need a hospital, Ike."

"No worries," he replied. "I'm on it."

CHAPTER TWENTY-EIGHT

The cable weather channel called it the "coldest, wettest winter in thirty years." Nothing in the foreseeable future but dark skies and precipitation for the Oregon coast and the valleys and mountains beyond, the TV weathermen promised. It would make for an excellent ski season, and even Cameron, whose last act of true physical exertion had been to float down the Willamette River on an inner-tube, was talking about learning how to snowboard. He'd winked at Meryl when saying this, and asked if she was interested in taking lessons too. But she declined with thanks. One day she'd return to the mountains, she told him. But for now, she was quite content to keep her wanderings among the familiar sights and sounds of Corvallis.

She sealed another cardboard box with a long strip of tape just as the rain began to softly ping against the windows again. The bedroom had been half-empty for weeks after the sheriff's department had carted away Rose's laptop and voluminous notes. Whatever the investigators hoped to glean from these materials — whether it was the former school teacher's state of mind or the veracity of the strange story the other eyewitnesses told them — it'd done nothing to help locate the missing woman. The search parties had found their destroyed campsite and apparently a number of "unusual things" they refused to describe to Meryl. But when it came to actually locating Rose — everyone had come up empty. And now that the winter storms were fully upon them, it was unlikely that anything more could be learned until the spring. So the search and rescue teams withdrew. Tess stopped texting constantly, wanting endless reiterations of the story even though she'd been thoroughly briefed when Meryl spoke to her from the hospital. Ike returned to San Diego, but she couldn't tell if it was because he was traumatized or, like her, just wanted to be surrounded by familiar people and places. Even the news crews had lost interest, except for the one nature network who'd purchased the photos Tom had snapped of the creatures that first morning in the glade. He'd been disappointed that he hadn't received an offer from *National Geographic*, but the money he got would at least help pay for all the physical therapy he would require to make his arm useable again. After all of this, Meryl began to think of the experience not as the most terrifying event of her life, but as the most tedious. It was with this realization that she decided to pack up what remained of Rose's belongings and squirrel them away in David's attic where they'd surely sit untouched for years to come. It was an unfortunate end to Rose's story, but after so many weeks with no sign of her, it also seemed like the only end possible. The forest still conspired to keep its secrets.

"Maw-mee?" Alexander tugged on her blouse and held up one of the decorative pillows which had once festooned Rose's bed. "Where goes this?" he asked.

"Would you like to keep that?" she suggested. "I know you liked Rose's pillows, huh?"

The boy nodded, gently set the pillow next to the door and returned to sorting his friend's huge collection of nicknacks. Meryl hoped that packing up the room would help Alexander accept Rose's disappearance. He still didn't fully understand what had happened to them, and there were times when it didn't feel like Meryl did either.

She walked to the far side of the room and examined the cluttered shelves. A plastic vase containing the artificial flowers stood before her and she sniffed at them, but all she smelled was dust. The vase and flowers went into one box, along with Rose's framed photographs and assortment of student artwork. In another she arranged her books and a third was reserved for more fragile mementos including the oversized champagne glass. The last thing she came to was the small wooden treasure chest, now empty. This she wrapped carefully in newspaper and tucked it down next to the photographs. Once everything had been cleared away and the boxes sealed up, she lifted the end of the bookcase and prepared to dissemble it. Something fell from where it had been wedged between the shelves and the wall and thumped against the floor.

"Mah-mee, what is?" Alexander asked, reaching for the parcel.

Meryl squatted down on the floor next to the child and was able to grab it with her fingertips and pull it loose. She turned the heavy bundle over in her hands. It was a large padded mailing envelope which had her name written neatly across the front of it. "It's from Rose," she replied and it made her shiver.

"What is?" he repeated.

She knew what was inside even before she broke the adhesive seal. Bundles of twenties, fifties and hundreds spilled onto the carpet. Meryl had always suspected that Rose had an additional stash of money besides what she and Ike had found in the treasure chest months earlier. Although that amount had been a small fortune in her eyes, it certainly wasn't enough to bankroll all the furniture and other household items Rose had purchased, nor the new camping gear she'd acquired just days before they left for the mountains. Clearly, this was the rest — the culmination of Rose's life savings and maybe whatever she'd won at those casinos she was so fond of.

Alexander picked up a sheaf and looked confused and delighted. "Mah-mee, you so rich!" he cooed.

She chuckled and shook her head. "Nope, 'fraid not, sweetie. It's Rose's money."

"Rode id rich?" he asked.

She didn't answer, knowing she'd just confused him again. After all, how could Rose be rich if Rose was gone forever? Well, Meryl silently corrected herself, maybe 'rich' wasn't the correct word. She ran her fingers over the parcels of cash. Not rich, but certainly not hurting. There was something still stuck at the bottom of the padded envelope so she shook it again and a small lavender envelope fluttered out of the parcel and landed on top of the money. Meryl opened it carefully. The card inside was dated to the night before they had left for the mountains and written in Rose's precise, almost decorative cursive. It read:

Dearest Meryl: After nearly of decade of planning, I am about to embark on my great adventure. If we find the mine then you won't need this money, for we'll all be rich!! But if we have no more luck than poor Elijah, I ask you to use this to provide for Alexander & to begin your new life as a university student. There should be plenty here to help with both. Be happy. With great affection, Rose.

Meryl sat silently for a long time, long enough for Alexander to stack the bundles of money into a neat pyramid, grow bored and wander off. She flipped the card over and over between her fingers and struggled to make sense of all the emotions which washed over her. Just like Elijah, Rose was now speaking to her from a different time and place through words scrawled on paper but whose meaning was just as obscure as doodles in the margin of a very old book. Monsters aside, was it Rose's intention never to return if they didn't find the mine? Or was there something more ominous there, perhaps the smallest indication that her roommate knew something else awaited them, something she could never bring herself to acknowledge until the very end?

Meryl looked around at the remaining clutter but couldn't bear to pack any more. She left the money sitting on the floor, turned out the lights and shut the bedroom door behind her.

At the end of the hall, she found Alexander standing in a pool of sunshine staring up at the small window which lit their bedroom. She almost expected to see Rose's smiling face there, pressed against the glass on the other side, asking in her befuddled but pushy way where the front door was.

"What're you looking at, baby?" she asked him.

Alexander turned and smiled broadly. "Sun's out, Maw-mee," he replied. "Can we goat to the park?"

She nodded and replied: "I can't think of anything I'd rather do more."

THE END

ABOUT THE AUTHOR

Marsh Myers is an author, artist, filmmaker and photographer. Over the years, he's worked in fields related to the protection of children, animals and the natural world, and these themes can often be found in his works of fiction. Marsh is also an unabashed nerd, toy collector and fanboy.

His first young adult novel, His Life Abiding, was published in 2013. The paranormal story was set largely around a foster home and based in part on the early life experiences of his adopted sons. His third book, My Summer with Robots, will be out in late 2015. (See the next page for additional information on this upcoming release.) Marsh is also the author of numerous online articles, reviews and short stories, many of which can be accessed through his website at **marshmyers.com.**

Marsh currently resides in Oregon. When not writing, he can be found exploring the wilds of the Pacific Northwest or the cluttered aisles of local bookstores and comic book shops.

UPCOMING RELEASE
MY SUMMER WITH ROBOTS

A mysterious house in the desert, a best friend turned back-stabber, the return of an old admirer and a beat-up robot rabbit. Welcome to Quinton's last summer before high school!

The summer before starting your freshman year in high school should be nothing but wall-to-wall fun.

That is unless your best friend has stopped speaking to you and your fiendish older sister has filled your head with tales about a sadistic high school ritual called "The Freshman Stomp." If all that wasn't bad enough, you discover that your father, still fresh from divorcing your mother, has started a relationship with the city's most notorious barfly and your neighborhood is being menaced by a 29-year-old stoner who fancies himself a warrior-prophet.

It's the Summer of 1977 — where the only things bringing Quinton Wyatt any relief from his daily angst are repeated viewings of *Star Wars* and an imagination which often gets the best of him.

Maybe a reclusive heiress, a robotic rabbit and an admirer from his past can salvage Quinton's summer and launch him into the difficult, unwanted, but often hilarious world of young adulthood?

<u>My Summer with Robots</u> is the third novel by Marsh Myers and the first installment in the *Quinton's Curious Mind* series. It will be available in late 2015.